Why Should You Doubt Me Now?

Why Should You Doubt Me Now?

MARY BREASTED

FARRAR STRAUS GIROUX
NEW YORK

LIBRARY OF CONGRESS CATALOGING-IN-PUBLICATION DATA
Breasted, Mary.
Why should you doubt me now? / Mary Breasted. — 1st ed.
p.   cm.
Ireland—Dublin—Fiction. I. Title.
PS3552.R3575W48 1993   813'.54—dc20   93-3561 CIP

*For Ted, Nicholas, Sally, and Jennifer, and
in memory of Gladys and Charlie Smyth*

Profoundest thanks to my friends Susan Dooley, Dan Wolf, and James Downey, and to my husband, Ted Smyth, for all their patient help along the way. Huge thanks also to my agent, Dan Green, and my editor, Jonathan Galassi, for their very astute advice and criticism. Heartfelt thanks to all the babysitters who watched my three children while I was working. I am indebted to the critic Peter Brooks for the term *Deus Absconditus*. Finally, a hundred thousand thanks to my Irish friends Nell McCafferty and Nuala O'Faolain and all their guests at a certain Easter Sunday luncheon in Dublin where the idea for this book was conceived.

Why Should You Doubt Me Now?

1

$\mathcal{I}$f there is a fate that can befall a man worse than having the Virgin Mary appear in his bedroom just as he is about to seduce the most beautiful apprentice horoscope writer in Dublin, Rupert Penrose did not know of one. When the apparition came he suddenly knew nothing at all except that he dared not move a muscle. His heart, which had been pounding wildly ever since Attracta Dorris had climbed naked under his duvet, now threatened to break out of his rib cage and catapult itself onto the floor. He was not a young man. The violent shock he got the moment he turned to look in the direction toward which Attracta was dementedly squinting might have killed him if he had not blessedly taken a bit of wine just before the Virgin descended. He might never have turned to look if he had thought he could smother Attracta's distraction with kisses. But Attracta was a nervous girl who had required three preliminary glasses of wine to stop clutching her elbows and hunching over her wonderful upspringing breasts. She had required a subsequent three full glasses to tell him the sorry tale of her first and only love affair, a shameful business carried on in the unclaimed parcels room of the Glenageary Postal Sorting Office. She then revealed that her lover had promised to marry her as soon as he acquired enough money to move out of the family bungalow. Instead, he went off to Canada to seek his fortune in the dishwashing trade. He sent Attracta one postcard, which said, "Wish you were here," without a return address. She never heard from him again.

"I hope you are not going to tell me you are still in love with that scoundrel," Penrose said to her, pouring one last dollop of wine into her glass. "He doesn't deserve to touch the ground you walk on. Besides, you could have hundreds of others."

"But no one will want to marry me!" Attracta protested, bursting into heartfelt tears.

"Don't be silly!" Penrose said scoldingly and took her into his arms to stroke her head in decent fatherly fashion. She was undressed and under the duvet five minutes later.

He climbed into bed beside her and commenced to make amends for the six long years that Attracta had waited for her dastardly dishwasher to return. She had been responding with what seemed like six years' worth of unspent passion, so that when she suddenly broke off and whispered, "Rupert, stop! It's a visitation!" he thought she was having a hysterical attack brought on by the intensity of her attraction to him.

"Don't be silly," he said, more tenderly than before, while kissing her flushed cheek and attempting to steer her chin toward his. Ardently he added, "We're all alone here."

But Attracta was gripping the duvet and squinting her eyes in a most convincingly insane manner. Penrose turned around to be able to tell her authoritatively that there was nothing in that corner of the room except a small pile of laundry. What he saw terrified him so much that he forgot to cross himself.

In the circumstances, he was to reflect later, the gesture might have seemed a bit hypocritical. He was a married man, and Attracta had come to his flat in the sincere belief that he would offer her only his best professional advice. She badly needed tips for dealing with Madame Bukowski. Attracta had been working for her for nearly a year, and in all that time Madame Bukowski had not told her one thing about the art of horoscope writing. She had merely used Attracta to fetch cups of tea, sort her mail, answer the telephone, dust off her desk, and shop for secondhand paperbacks by Barbara Cartland. Penrose had an idea that Madame Bukowski never intended to teach her the horoscope-writing trade, but he did not say this to Attracta. His intuition told him that Attracta, though not aware of this herself, would be only too glad to move on to another topic. Much experience with troubled young women had given Penrose the coiled patience of a panther. After the poor girl had drunk her first three glasses of wine and confessed that she sometimes mislaid pieces of Madame Bukowski's mail, Penrose needed only to say, "I don't understand what a beautiful girl like you is doing in the horoscope-writing business at all. Surely you have a fiancé," and she was holding out her glass for more.

Pitiable creature, she did not deserve to have the Virgin interrupt her first passionate embrace in the space of six years. Penrose listened to the wild thumps of his heart. What would Attracta do if he were to die of a heart attack here and now? Would she have the good grace to dress him? Would she be able to?

"Isn't she beautiful!" Attracta whispered. She seemed to be crossing herself under the duvet. "Do you think it's really her?"

"Her?" said Penrose, still too stunned to have asked himself as much. Nervously he ran his finger down Attracta's warm, silky arm.

"Rupert!" she whispered crossly. "Stop!"

"Attracta, I didn't mean—I wasn't—perhaps it's best you got dressed, my dear," he said.

"Not when she's looking at me, when I can *see* her looking at me!"

Poor child. Did she think the Virgin Mother had appeared only to reproach her? She could scarcely have amassed enough sins, waiting in her bed-sit for endless postcards that never arrived.

"The Virgin Mary sees you getting dressed every morning, or if not the Virgin, certainly God," said Penrose rather pompously. Bishop Meany was expected to come by in less than an hour.

"You can't see God," said Attracta, adding sourly, "whoever He is. Anyway, I don't see you jumping up to get your clothes. It's you she's coming to visit, seemingly."

"Oh, don't be silly," he protested, although he knew himself to be the greater sinner.

"Yes, Rupert, I'm absolutely certain it's you she came to see. Because she likes your column."

"You don't think—" he started to say, and then he went crimsonly silent with gratified authorship. The Virgin liked his column! Had such a thing happened to a columnist before?

Rupert Penrose was, despite his English name and his inability to uphold his marriage vows, a good Catholic. He respected the Pope. He strongly disapproved of divorce, abortion, and secular education. He thought that the women's liberation movement was the worst thing to have happened in the world since the invention of the automobile, which last he also considered an offense against the natural order of things. On the subject of artificial birth control, he was not quite to be pinned down. He usually dealt with it only by implication, when praising the practice of celibacy in marriage.

That he was also a good Irishman, everyone in Ireland knew. His weekly column appeared in the popular Dublin *Sentinel*, a newspaper not too respectable to print the daily horoscope of Madame Bukowski but hardly gritty enough to publish the photos of topless beauties that appeared daily in the British tabloids. Penrose bemoaned the influence of all things English. He sometimes went so far as to urge that jamming devices be erected throughout Ireland to block out all radio and television signals from Britain. He was very proud of the fact that he had turned down the London publisher who once made him an offer for the rights to *Ourselves Alone*, and he always mentioned the incident in the column he wrote to young university graduates at the end of May, exorting them to go forth and do likewise in the face of all British blandishments. He dispensed much free advice to the young, seeing himself as the lone voice of moral sanity in a world growing ever more senseless with moral decay. He thought that the only hope for Ireland was to return to a simpler lifestyle back on the land, a life without modern machinery to deprive her strapping young men of honest labor and without television or cinemas to give her young women false ideas about the uses to which beauty ought to be put. He was so opposed to the automobile that he refused to own one, getting himself about Dublin on a sturdy English Raleigh of indefinite age. When it was pointed out to him that a bicycle is also a machine and that his was doubly damning because of being English, he would snort impatiently and say that he never pretended to be anything other than a poor sinner trying to make his way through the wilderness of this world. He was, he said, as much in need of protection from temptation as the next fellow.

He sometimes wrote that he looked forward to the coming catastrophe of worldwide economic and moral collapse, for then Ireland would be cut off from pagan America and Satanic London, and within one hundred years no one on the island would have heard of Candice Bergen or bulimia or Wimbledon.

When he said he was as much in need of protection from temptation as the next fellow, Penrose was being modest. He had quite a bit more than the average fellow's share of opportunities to sin. He was not particularly handsome, but he was certainly noticeable. A man of medium height, slender build, and rosy, healthy complexion, he had only one distinctive physical characteristic. His eyes protruded too much. He looked continually surprised or even alarmed by what he saw in the world, and this made him immediately appealing to women, most of whom wanted to quell his anxiety. But there was a certain kind of woman, the sort who read his column and admired it, who seemed to want to share his anxiety. These were invariably women, like Attracta Dorris, who had been mistreated by men, and they had vague but large fears about what the world was coming to. They were never happier than when lying in Rupert Penrose's arms listening to him denounce their favorite television programs.

Such women sought him out. They wrote him letters. They came to his lectures at the Toyota Night School where he reluctantly obliged himself to earn extra cash teaching Irish history to Japanese microchip company managers and the wives of foreign diplomats. Unhappy women had pursued him ever since the days he wrote a column in the Ballybunion *Blotter*, when the ideas of the women's movement were seeping out into the Irish countryside. All of Penrose's female admirers had in common a dread of the women's liberation movement and agreed with him that women were universally better off in the days when the female orgasm was a mystery that men were meant to solve.

If it had not been for the complication of a Mrs. Penrose, he might have been the happiest of men. But, alas, his wife was one of the prime examples of a woman being gradually ruined by the trendy articles in the Sunday magazines telling about husbands who did the family ironing and wives who worked on oil rigs. Further complications, in the form of little Penroses, developed along the way, which meant that the laundry pile which no one in the Penrose household would violate his or her principles to touch grew by leaps and bounds, while outside his home Penrose found himself more and more frequently called upon to relieve the psychic pains of women whose whole raison d'être was being torn from them, now that their husbands had started doing the washing up. Penrose was all too willing to dirty these women's dishes and lift not a finger toward the sink, and ere long, illicit passions flared up over the soiled teacups. There ensued a couple of rather scary encounters when inflamed and whiskey-besotted husbands with dishpan hands came around to deal with him at three o'clock in the morning. Mrs. Penrose did not like being awakened at three o'clock in the morning, nor did she like having to defend the household against another woman's irate husband, Penrose having directed her in each case to please inform the gentleman that he was abroad on assignment, a patently absurd assertion, considering the size of the Ballybunion *Blotter*. Nevertheless, the first intruder swallowed it and exited blustering, "I'll be waiting for him!" But after the second cuckold sneered, "In a pig's arse he's in Moscow!" then chased Mrs. Penrose around the piano with a pistol and locked her out of her own home, leaving her no recourse but to run to the Garda station in her dressing gown, where the Guards required her to fill in seven forms in triplicate before they would go forth to arrest the armed aggrieved husband, who by then had fallen asleep atop the unspent pistol, Mrs. Penrose took the six little Penroses off to her mother's house in Mullingar and refused to speak to Rupert again.

In defiance of his beliefs, she obtained a legal separation, and he began receiving very chilly letters from her solicitor demanding her weekly check. He did not see the logic of this. If she hated being an appendage of his, then she ought to support herself. As for the children, they were getting child allowance from the state.

Penrose swiftly moved to Dublin to an undisclosed address and, for the sake of his unshakable convictions, spent five years groveling on the bottom rung of the Dublin *Sentinel*'s career ladder, covering funerals of the lesser-known residents of fashionable Dublin 6. Never in all that time did he ask for or receive a byline.

The day came, however, when he could not resist the summons of fame. The *Sentinel*'s chief funerals correspondent had gone to Saudi Arabia on a brief holiday visit to see his daughter, who was a nurse there. He was caught smuggling twenty bottles of Jameson's inside a leaking golf case. He was thrown in jail forever. The Arabian concept of the infinite was altered in a twinkling when two boatloads of healthy Irish bullocks arrived in Dhahran Harbor courtesy of the Irish government. The *Sentinel's* chief necrophiliac, as he was lovingly known back home, was released to the Irish ambassador.

By then Penrose's reputation had been made, for he had outdone the chief correspondent in slavish veneration of the famous newly dead. The editors decided to try giving him his own column. It was a success, but two weeks after he started it, his wife's solicitor sent him a court order stipulating that four-fifths of his weekly paycheck should go to her. At this point, he relented and began sending her the money.

He lived close to penury in the bed-sit in Rathgar, not because he liked the neighborhood's trendy shops and bistros but rather because he thought it afforded him as much anonymity as a newspaper columnist could achieve anywhere in Dublin. In truth, every merchant and landlady up and down the street knew who he was and took note of his comings and goings as well as the ages of the ladies who often came and went with him, and they did not fail to record mentally which ones emerged flushed and sparkle-eyed and which ones did not. But being merchants and landladies of urbane sophistication, they never let slip in front of one of his lady friends a reference to another.

He knew that his private life did not match the elevated moral tone of his column, but he had long since reconciled himself to contradictions inherent in a nature like his own. He was helped in his complacency by the knowledge that many men of genius seemed to have had, like himself, an unusual ability to empathize with unfulfilled women. He was soothed also in his conscience by the awareness that his columns were often read from the pulpits on Sunday mornings, and he had discovered a very tolerant confessor in the little church of St. Barnabas around the corner from his flat. On duty every Friday evening, this man had helped him achieve a sort of moral equilibrium that allowed him to sin and be sorry as often as he liked.

•   •   •

Aside from the weekly annoyance of having to write a check for three hundred pounds to a woman who would not talk to him, there was only one other real sorrow in Penrose's life. His last book, his magnum opus, *Where We Went Wrong,* had been cruelly panned by Dublin's chief man of letters, Dennis Davitt McDermott. A self-confessed patriotism hater who never should have been allowed near a book built upon the premise that both Egyptian and Greek civilizations were founded by Celts and were once Gaelic-speaking, McDermott had written Penrose the world's worst review.

Dennis McDermott was, unfortunately, brilliant. He had great intellectual stature in Dublin notwithstanding his scandalous past. He was a spoiled priest who had left his first parish in Tanzania without permission, taking with him the sixteen-year-old daughter of the British consul. He had married her and brought her to Ireland to live, but somehow people still thought of them as living in sin. McDermott's critics liked to advert to his marriage when attacking his ideas, but they were divided as to whether the source of the wrongheadedness was the English wife or the desertion of the priesthood, although he also came under suspicion for having taught at Brandeis University and for giving the odd lecture at Oxford. He wrote as though he expected to be read beyond Ireland, with a tinge of disloyalty to his race. He was keenly respected by Dublin literati and popular also with Dublin's better hostesses, for McDermott could be counted upon to create a stimulating evening.

Penrose well knew that a stimulating evening was more valued than all the gold of the Indies in his tiny island nation, and he prided himself on his own social talents, which, if not schooled in foreign universities, nicely made up for that deficiency with his fund of accumulated newspaper gossip. But for weeks after McDermott's review appeared, Penrose had received no dinner invitations at all, the worst sort of disgrace a famous man could suffer in Dublin.

When he did get invited again, his friends treated him as though he had just recovered from a terrible illness. They were sickeningly solicitous. They studied his face for signs of unusual strain.

But only his enemies mentioned the book. They would wait until the inevitable visiting foreigner began gushing about Irish history.

"Rupert's just written a book on the subject," one of them would slyly announce.

"Oh, really? What's it called?" would come the thrilled response.

"*Where We Went Wrong,*" some unfeeling fellow guest would reveal. "What an intriguing name for a history book," the foreigner would remark, seeming to sense odd undercurrents. "How's it doing?"

No Irishman expected Penrose to answer this question. It was how he didn't answer it that interested his enemies. He would always forge ahead with a capsule history of Ireland, keeping his eyes on the table-cloth so as not to see how alertly his fellow Dubliners were poised to hear the quaver of defeat in his voice. It was a horrible ordeal. He knew now beyond a shadow of a doubt that all of Dublin, when they saw him coming, recalled the title of McDermott's review, "Godhead Meets Dunderhead."

Briefly he considered leaving Dublin, but in his heart of hearts he knew there was no escape. The Irish kept track of their celebrities, just as though they were family. And wasn't he the first to say that was the charm of the place? Hadn't he written that Irish people put no distance between themselves and the great ones, that politics in Ireland was a very intimate affair? Hadn't he also written that the beauty of Irish society was its small size, that Ireland could still be looked at and grasped as a whole by one human brain? Dunderhead he would be from now on over every inch of his beloved Emerald Isle.

Any normal man would have wanted to murder Dennis Davitt McDermott, but Penrose was a man of letters. He wanted a revenge more humiliating than murder. He knew that Dennis McDermott's fondest wish was to be appointed to the Kerrygold Chair of Irish Literature at the City University of Dublin. Penrose was passionately determined that Dennis McDermott should not get his wish.

But thwarting the cruel critic would be no easy matter. The word was that McDermott stood a very good chance of getting the appointment. The university trustees were eager to show that CUD was no longer an exclusively Catholic university, and McDermott was now sufficiently irreligious to bolster the new image of the university as a place where great minds of any sort were welcome. McDermott was also highly regarded as a literary scholar in the United States. He had written the seminal textbook on Irish literature, the abridged version of which was already required reading for all first-year CUD students.

As a sort of holding action against McDermott, Penrose had put his own name forward for the Kerrygold Chair. He had succeeded in getting onto the short list of candidates, although he had no real hope of being chosen. His strategy was to scare the trustees into thinking that he had a major constituency, however, in order to make it appear that the appointment of McDermott would cause offense among them. He hoped thus also to create the impression that McDermott commanded his own constituency, the small but influential group whose members had run the last government but one. They might loosely be described as liberals, although they were not liberal on every issue. Penrose himself described them in his column not very accurately as "the godless" and much more accurately as "the ultra self-regarders." This last label was of course a sour echo of the ones which critics were always sticking on Penrose and his fans, "the ultra-Catholics," and "the ultra-Irish."

The CUD trustees were nervous of constituencies altogether, and Penrose had been writing them letters from phantom supporters of both McDermott and himself to further the illusion that they each represented a "side" rather than a middle. The appointment had generated woefully little real public excitement to date, but Penrose was not discouraged. It would take so little controversy to overwhelm the trustees with political dread, he did think he might succeed in blocking McDermott in the end, for, given the slightest bit more show of pressure from each side, the trustees should be persuaded to at least consider a bland compromise candidate who commanded no constituency whatsoever.

But who was bland enough to fit the bill?

Penrose had been pondering this question when Attracta arrived, and now, truth to tell, as they lay paralyzed together under the duvet with the sorrowful figure of Mary gazing down at them, Penrose could not help turning his mind again to the quest for an ideally inoffensive candidate to fill the Kerrygold Chair. It was difficult to find a qualified man in Dublin academic life who was well and truly bland. The brilliant men always seemed to veer off into dangerous political extremes or they were drunkards or were not on speaking terms with the other experts in their field, or else they were simply adulterous to a degree that would put them outside blandness forever.

Thus far, Penrose had only come up with two names, and he feared even these might not be inoffensive enough. The first, Ulick Brown, whose vast published work, *An Irish Post-Structuralist's Reading of the Oxford English Dictionary*, no one had read, at least sounded promisingly dull. But if his name were put into play, the trustees would be forced to read his book, and so would Penrose. He did not know whether he could bear it. The fact that Brown had focused on an English dictionary might scare the trustees right at the outset. And no one Penrose knew had ever met Brown. He was said to be a photographer and a chess champion, both of which suggested difficult opinions.

Penrose thought his second choice, Michael Groarke, was a safer bet. Groarke was actually a historian, but he wrote a quite passable column on Irish letters in *The Countrywoman* magazine, and his Ph.D. thesis from Galway City University was rather famous. Groarke seemed physically excellent for Penrose's plan. He had the kind of face you know you've seen somewhere before, perhaps behind a post-office window, perhaps just before you underwent anesthesia, a reassuring, forgettable face. He was a sweet man. Penrose knew him slightly. Groarke never disagreed with anyone. But of course the title of his thesis, "Irish Milking Through the Ages," would not be regarded in some circles as suitable for a professor of literature. Penrose wondered whether Groarke might be persuaded to change it.

Pleased with this idea, Penrose took a deep breath and stretched his limbs in anticipation of victory. He smelled perfume.

"What's that smell?" he said to Attracta. "Do you smell something?"

"White Shoulders," said Attracta. "It's my favorite scent."

"How odd," he said. "You didn't seem to be wearing it before."

"I'm not," said Attracta. "It's her."

Penrose shivered involuntarily. What if the presence were to speak? He was beginning to feel a distinct urge to get out of there. He groped behind Attracta's back for his watch.

"Get away with you, Rupert!" Attracta whispered sharply.

"I wonder, love, whether you might fetch my watch," he said quietly.

"Wherever from? I'm not moving while she's looking. That's for certain."

"It's just right next to you there on the floor."

Attracta reached out for it without a word.

"Oh, my God! I hadn't realized it, Attracta. You must dress yourself right away. I've a bishop coming here in five minutes' time."

She did not respond.

"Attracta, did you hear me?"

"Rupert, there's never been any perfumes in any holy visions, has there?"

"Attracta, I'm telling you, you must get dressed! Bishop Augustine Meany, who is top assistant to the Papal Nuncio, will be here in five minutes, no, four minutes!"

"You never said anything before about him coming. What if I'd decided to spend the night with you?"

"You told me you had to leave early to meet a friend, don't you remember?"

"I did. But it wasn't true."

"Please get dressed, Attracta, this instant!"

"Why don't you, if you're so close to the Papal Nuncio. I don't see you moving."

He reluctantly heaved his naked form out from under the duvet. Keeping his back to the Virgin, he swiftly dressed himself. He thought he detected a flash of critical appraisal in Attracta's eyes. She was nearly thirty years younger.

"It's just that I can't figure how she would have got White Shoulders back there in Palestine. Unless they had that scent, I mean, Rupert."

Should he try locking Attracta into the cupboard? She might protest rather too forcefully. The cupboard latch was none too strong. How to explain a naked girl tumbling forth from his meager wardrobe. How to explain her in the bed. Bishop Meany would never buy a story about a young cousin stricken with the flu, not a cousin as strikingly beautiful as Attracta with her color up. Bishop Meany had already seen two or three of Penrose's lovelier students fully clad. He was not a pious idiot.

Oh, Virgin Mother, Penrose silently addressed the apparition, why did you not think of coming to my office?

Bishop Meany could have him ousted from the paper. He was indeed a very powerful cleric. Penrose had invited him to tea because the good bishop had lines in to various organizations that were known to influence the trustees of CUD. The bishop had accepted the invitation with pleasure, saying he had been interested to hear Penrose's name in connection with a possible university post recently.

"Attracta, you simply must get up!" he commanded.

"I couldn't!"

"Well, get dressed under the duvet, then," he said, and he gathered up her clothes and handed them to her.

She squinted at the apparition again, wasting precious seconds.

Three loud knocks sounded on the door. Attracta looked at Penrose with large frightened eyes.

"Bishop Meany," he whispered, making a sign of a slit throat.

Now he saw pure terror. Up she got, naked as the day she was born. Scooping her clothes from the floor, she tiptoed toward the wardrobe and, utterly of her own volition, stepped inside it and pulled the door shut on herself.

2

"We'll say nothing about this for the moment, I'm thinking," had been Bishop Meany's circumspect response.

Penrose was just as glad. He did not relish the thought of his cozy flat being invaded by pilgrims. Unless of course it might give him more influence over the selection of a candidate for the Kerrygold Chair. Naturally it would give him more influence. Why should the bishop be hesitating? Had he heard Attracta's voice? Certainly he did not look happy.

"I could truthfully use a pint," said Bishop Meany, pulling on his collar with a sort of glum restlessness that suggested his Meath farming ancestors tugging at their ties after too long a funeral service in an overheated church. He looked all wrong in his scholarly rimless glasses tonight.

"Yes, it's terribly close in here," said Penrose. It was true, the flat seemed to have grown warmer since the vision appeared. Penrose knew, though, that he had turned up his convection heaters to encourage Attracta to be rid of her clothing. Oh, God, Attracta!

"Perhaps we should retire to Queary's Hotel," he said.

"Good man," said the bishop, clapping him on the shoulder. He stood up heavily and Penrose saw little gleams of sweat on his wide forehead. The cleric had turned his back to the Virgin, which in itself seemed odd and was additionally most inconvenient for poor Penrose, whose overcoat was hanging in the wardrobe.

"Shall we go, then?" Bishop Meany said to Penrose, who was still seated in his only other easy chair, pondering how strange it might seem if he were to go out into the chill November air in his thin sweater.

"How long has she been here?" asked the bishop, still facing the wardrobe wherein Attracta was hidden, and Penrose's heart gave another life-threatening leap. But just as he was about to mumble, "Who do you mean? My cousin?" Bishop Meany swung around and contemplated the glowing figure of the apparition full frontally. The movement had clearly cost him much effort. On the instant Penrose opened the wardrobe. He reached for his overcoat. It wouldn't come off the hanger.

"Penrose, did you hear me?" said Bishop Meany, now turning to look at the columnist, who was engaged in a tug-of-war with the unseen Attracta.

"How long has—ah, let me see. About an hour. No. No. About fifteen minutes," said Penrose peculiarly. He darted his head around to see which way the bishop was looking now. At the vision again, thanks be. Penrose seized his chance and yanked at his overcoat with all his might. To her eternal credit, Attracta did not scream when her naked body was revealed in all its white completeness beneath the jangling hangers.

Penrose slammed the wardrobe shut and spun around to find Bishop Meany again looking in his direction. The cleric's face gave no hint of what he might have just seen.

"Yes, I suppose the sense of time would go," said the bishop, not unsympathetically. And as they proceeded toward the door of the flat, he continued in this patronizing tone. "Rupert, is there something you haven't told me about yourself?"

To which Penrose lightly replied: "Naturally, Bishop. Shouldn't I be saving something for my deathbed?"

"Aren't you the guilty one," said Meany, seeming to brighten as they emerged into the streetlights. "But I wasn't asking for a confession. All the same, we'll go slow on this one. Say nothing for the moment."

"Well, you might want to bring the cardinal around," said Penrose. "And of course the Nuncio and whichever bishops—I would leave it up to you who you bring 'round. You're very welcome, Gus, at any time."

"You're a good man, Rupert. Yes, we'll handle it that way. We'll not tell the world. Not yet."

They really did see eye to eye, those two, when it came to the affairs of men. They spent a very agreeable two hours together and hardly bothered to flinch at the icy rain that whipped into their faces when they emerged at last from Queary's, full of lamb chops and strong porter.

Some hardy souls were waiting outside Penrose's building, one of them a little photographer from the *Daily Mail* who knew him on sight.

"Rupe!" said this fellow, giving him a thump on the chest. "One journalist to another, right? You going to let me in?"

"Is it true? Is the Blessed Virgin really in your flat, Mr. Penrose?" asked one of the drenched strangers.

Penrose shot an anguished look at Bishop Meany. Attracta would have let the cat out of the bag, but how could the bishop know that?

Through the rain came running the *Sentinel's* photographer, Nick Slattery. Now he was for it. They'd all have to come in. He hoped fervently that Attracta had had the wisdom to go home.

"This is incredible," he said to Bishop Meany.

"I'd best be going," said the bishop, and he backed off into the storm before anyone should recognize him.

3

⌒he news reached His Excellency the very ascetic-looking Archbishop Paolo Giuseppe Destino, the new Dublin Papal Nuncio, just
after he had flung the Vatican pamphlet on "Abstinence and Christ's
Example" across his bedroom. He had always been a gentle man, not
given to violent gestures, and so when his telephone rang some three
seconds after the pamphlet hit the far wall under the gloomy reproduction of Glendalough Monastery in winter, his first thought was that
the Vatican thought patrol were on to him. But this was his private
intercom line, into which Papal infallibility could not penetrate.

"Hello, Bishop," he said, because of course it could only be his
tireless assistant.

"Excellency, it's yourself, is it? I'm afraid I woke you."

"Bishop, what can be so important at this hour?"

"I thought you ought to know there's an apparition of the Blessed
Virgin has appeared in Dublin tonight."

"What do you mean, apparition?"

"A vision, a figure. It glows. I have seen it with my own eyes."

"Where is this figure?"

"In the home of a journalist who has been a very loyal parishioner.
You've met him. Rupert Penrose. He attended your first afternoon reception."

"This man, your friend Primrose, he is the one you are thinking of
for the university position?"

"Aye, he is."

"I have never heard of the Virgin anointing a literature professor
before, but I suppose it could happen. This is nice for your friend."

"I'm not certain of that, Excellency. We've not had anything this, this vivid in Ireland before."

"These apparitions usually manifest themselves to children in communities where there is no television—or to women of a certain mentality," said the Nuncio.

"If I hadn't seen it with my own eyes, I wouldn't have placed much credence—and it may be that she's too clear, you know—but the thing is, Nuncio, the press is on to this, and they'll be ringing up first thing in the morning to ask what the Vatican has to say. We've got to have something to say to them."

"It's very simple," said the Nuncio. "Tell them the matter is under investigation."

"Under investigation. Right. Have we got someone to investigate?"

"Tomorrow you ring the Vatican. Ask for the Permanent Tribunal on Miracles and Visitations. They will be able to help you. Good night, Bishop. We must get our sleep."

"Yes, Excellency, I know. But I'm worried now about what some people could make of a thing like this, some unscrupulous people. When there's talk of another divorce referendum, and of course the other thing."

"You will not perhaps find it so alarming after a night of sleep, Bishop."

"Good night, Excellency. God bless."

"Bless you, my son," said the Nuncio, and Meany let him go.

• • •

But naturally he could not sleep. He fetched a woolen cardigan out of a drawer, switched on the electric kettle in the small pantry, and pulled out from its hiding place under the bed his copy of Freud's *Moses and Monotheism*. He had been rereading all of Freud since coming to Ireland. He found the country was driving him ever deeper into doubt, which in itself wouldn't have been so troubling, since doubt had been with him in various forms all his life. In the past, though, the absence of God had seemed somehow containable, a tragic void that he could keep confined within the secrets of his heart, all of them dwarfed by the importance of what he was doing in the world. Here suddenly doubt surrounded him, and doubt of his doubt, and doubt of that, too, engulfing him in a foreign, cold ubiquitous grayness which was like what he looked out upon every morning from his window.

It would serve him right if the Virgin Mary really were to appear in Dublin.

The kettle boiled. He poured himself a soothing cup of camomile tea. He realized he was tired of Freud. On good nights Vatican pamphlets had been most effective soporifics. He fetched "Abstinence and Christ's Example" from the floor and opened it at random.

"It follows from the inherent sinfulness of contraceptive methods," he read. Yes, precisely, inherent sinfulness, Your Holiness, I like your choice of language. They are naturally unnatural. And isn't that why our Church is thriving, Your Holiness, why millions upon millions of young men and women are forgoing the pleasures of the flesh the world over. And millions more are taking vows to join us. No one believes the insidious lies about priests quitting over the celibacy rule. They are the devil's own propaganda.

Abstinence and Christ's example, indeed! Tell that to the Italian cardinals. Even here in holy Ireland they don't take it all literally. Holy Ireland, holy Ireland. God, the God that wasn't, had sent him here in punishment for his arrogance. The Vatican had certainly meant it as punishment. Ireland was the perfect retribution for an archbishop who had no faith. Not that the Vatican would ever admit to having known his state of belief.

Padre Destino, as he insisted on being addressed in his own style of following Christ's example, had been sent to Ireland rather abruptly. He admired Christ the man and enjoyed annoying those in the Church who treasured their titles. For many years his attitude had been overlooked in favor of his skills. A Pontiff could bear to have a few doctrinal inconsistencies pointed out to him by a highly intelligent political analyst who spoke seven languages, among them Russian, Polish, and Serbo-Croat. Several Popes had found Paolo Destino indispensable. But with the Communist regimes now in tatters and the Pontiff now feeling he controlled the world's spiritual future, Padre Destino's abilities had become less attractive. The rebel priests who had been his secret networks in Poland and Russia were not taking easily to sterner Vatican control. Some of them were married, a transgression which had been tolerated while they were undermining Communism's grip. Now Rome wanted them to give up their wives.

Paolo had started to make cheeky remarks about deserted wives and had asked how the Church intended to feed all its returning faithful. He would toast the victory of the Church in all the former captive nations and solemnly opine that it was better to starve to death in a state of grace as a Catholic than as a godless Communist. In idle moments, he had long been in the habit of asking certain cardinals why, if artificial birth control was inherently sinful, shouldn't it also be wrong to tamper with God's plan among microorganisms? Why not condemn the smallpox and polio vaccines? Why not condemn all of science?

He had actually said as much to the Pontiff the last time, and not a week later he was informed he was being sent to Ireland, the previous Dublin Papal Nuncio having suddenly retired to Monaco. That was three months ago in August. Three months of rain. And the company of Augustine Meany.

The irony was, many ambitious clerics envied him. The Pope loved Ireland. Where else in the world had one third of the country's population turned out to see him? The Irish could make a Papal Nuncio look very effective. Not even a man as disenchanted as Paolo Destino could lead them astray, his friends in the Curia had said in toasting his appointment.

"You know they are threatening to legalize divorce," one of his savvier friends told him on the eve of his departure. "If you can stop that, there'll be a cardinal's hat in it for you."

After three months in Ireland, he no longer wanted a cardinal's hat. He wanted to go back to Rome. He was homesick and lonely among the Irish bishops who were all so impenetrably agreeable. He missed the centrality of the Vatican. All those years of subduing his nature to his ambition, he had rationalized his hollow conformity by saying to himself that the Church was as good a vehicle as any for the salvation of mankind. He did not mean salvation as the Church meant it, of course. He meant that the Church could soften the horror of death.

He was discovering how spoiled he had been in the Curia, for he was learning there are other horrors that loom larger than death to a man in full health. The horror of an unending series of days spent with company not of one's choosing. The horror of constant chill. Of ceaseless rain.

He still did not understand the simplest things about the Irish. He could not tell whether the bishops approved or disapproved of his asking them to use his priestly title when addressing him. He could not tell whether they approved or disapproved of the Italian cuisine he had introduced at the residence. He could not, if it came down to it, tell whether they believed or did not believe in the institution they were upholding.

They had sent him as his chief assistant Bishop Augustine Meany.

One night in the first month, he had escaped Meany's clutches, stumbling alone upon a thicket of collarless theologians at Milltown College who made a show of getting drunk in front of him and singing all the verses of "McBreen's Heifer," raising his hopes for the possibility of an interesting conversation. He was not disappointed, but he was up until four o'clock in the morning.

When the little party was in full swing, he had taken the plunge and asked them whether churchmen in Ireland read Sigmund Freud.

"But of course, Padre!" a learned Augustinian had said. "And isn't it so, lads, that on the long winter evenings in Kerry there is talk of little else?"

"Aye, truly," said a grinning Dominican. "Here on the Emerald Oyle, good Father, Sigmund Freud is your only man."

He did not actually remember how they had got from there to questioning the Church's rules on celibacy and freedom of thought, but he awoke the next morning with a hangover and a wonderfully youthful feeling of being on the brink of a great spiritual discovery.

He made the mistake of asking Bishop Meany later that day whether he knew the words to a song about someone offering to give a heifer to the man who married his ugly daughter.

"You mean 'McBreen's Heifer,' I think, Nuncio, Your Excellency. Don't tell me you were speaking with Father Liam O'Mahoney over in Milltown last night. You wouldn't want to be unburdening yourself to Father O'Mahoney. The man'll be quoting you all over town."

After that, Bishop Meany would not let him go out alone, a distressingly easy restriction to insure for a man so important that there were always servants or other staff watching his moves. Bishop Meany also made a point of telling the Nuncio each time another report of the scandalous Milltown evening reached his ears. The bishop said he always denied it had ever happened.

"I tell them you don't drink," he said to Padre Destino. "Which is quite true by Irish standards. No one would call you a drinker. Not at all."

The bishop followed him everywhere, from the time he appeared at the Nuncio's breakfast table in the morning uninvited to the moment when he left him with a respectful "Good night, Excellency" at his bedroom door. He was driving Padre Destino to the most childish level of deceit, making him sneak down to the residence kitchen in his stocking feet when he was ostensibly taking a nap so the homesick Nuncio could hear his native language, even forcing him to feign headaches and disabling illnesses that could put him to bed in his room alone with a good book. Padre Destino was taking to his bed ever more frequently now and doing it earlier and earlier in the day. He simply must have Bishop Meany replaced.

But he did not know how to get around his principal advisor to find out who should replace him. He needed a man he could trust. Someone who would not report his every impolitic utterance back to Rome. Otherwise, he would never come to grips with Ireland, and they might leave him here until he died.

The Vatican would yank him home in a flash, of course, if they thought the Virgin really had appeared in Dublin. What did Meany think he had seen? Conveniently, on the wall of the most Catholic journalist in all of Dublin. The bishop was not overjoyed. Afraid of how some people might use her. Would Meany give her a bodyguard, too?

If only he had someone to talk to! Padre Destino had never felt so friendless in all his life. He might as well be stuck among hallucinating goatherds in Yugoslavia.

He switched off the light and saw a momentary after-image. It was nothing, but he switched the light on once again, then off again once more.

If God had read Freud, He might have been more forgiving about the abuses of free will, Destino thought disconnectedly, sleepy at last. It was beginning to worry him that his companion Freud might have been something of a believer.

4

$\mathscr{T}$he pilgrims started ringing the bell downstairs in Rupert Penrose's building at half past seven that morning. They had heard about the Virgin on the radio. He did allow the first ten or so to come up and have a viewing. After that, he ignored all comers.

But the landlord had his own key. He used it after Penrose failed to respond to all his knocking.

Penrose had been attempting to write a column, but it was not an easy thing to do with the most spotless woman who ever lived looking over his shoulder.

"Mr. McGuire," he said, relieved at least to see that it wasn't a stranger breaking in. "What brings you around here this morning?"

McGuire was the sort who did not take off his overcoat when it was quick business he was doing.

"It's about your rent," he said to Penrose.

"I'm paid up," said the columnist. "I paid three weeks ago."

"I'm after having to raise it, you see," said McGuire, tilting his head in the direction of the Virgin.

"Raise it? But I thought I was paying an exorbitant rate as it was. Surely you're not trying to cash in on the Virgin Mary!"

"Not on her. I wouldn't do that. I couldn't. But her coming here changes the value of this place, you see, quite substantially."

"Mr. McGuire, I can scarcely believe my ears! You wish to extort money from me because the Virgin Mary has appeared in my home?"

"Not to be getting technical with you, Mr. Penrose, but the premises are actually mine. I'm after raising your rent to a thousand a week."

"But you can't do that! You simply cannot! I'll be on to my solicitors!"

"There's people lined up half a mile down the street, just about. We can't keep them out of here, Mr. Penrose. It wouldn't be right."

"But this is my home!" said Penrose. "You can't do this!"

In answer McGuire opened the door and invited in the pilgrims lined up on the stairs, asking each for a contribution as he or she passed through the door.

5

"The man's a shameless whoor," Dennis Davitt McDermott said early that same morning to his lovely wife, Caroline, she of the famous African episode. They were eating a hurried breakfast of hot porridge, toast, rashers, and tea before Dennis was to be vetted by the City University of Dublin's academic assessors. They had lost time during a humiliating half hour when Dennis's best trousers were let out and resewn to fit under his bulge. His unruly white hair had also been subdued with something that came out of the children's cupboard and looked and smelled like an after-dinner treat.

"You don't think anyone will be fooled, really, do you?" she said. "The children were all sneering at the photo."

They meant the front-page picture of Rupert Penrose peering out with his look of alarmed piety beneath the glowing figure of the Virgin

Mary. On this of all mornings to have it appear. But Caroline did not share his gloom. She had been up two hours already, packing their six children off to school and university. Having slept through all that, he was at a moral disadvantage, which increased his gloom.

"They're all hopeless unbelievers, our lot," he said. "I do wish I'd given them more of a sense of their heritage."

"Then take them to the House of Lords to see their grandfather dozing."

"They do boast about him, you know, in rather off-putting ways."

"You think if you'd taken them to Mass every Sunday they'd have renounced their English blood?"

"I didn't mean, Caroline—I meant the heritage of belief, not nationality."

"But you've said yourself a million times that Catholicism is a matter of political identity in this country. It has nothing to do with belief," said Caroline in her snootiest Bayswater accent.

"I've said a lot of things in my time," he said bleakly. "Just because it's political doesn't mean it isn't the other thing, too. Look, don't think Irish souls wouldn't snap right back into place if given half a chance. Stop laboring to reassure me, Caroline," he said, trying to keep himself from thinking how much the university trustees' wives must resent her when she talked that way. "He's outmaneuvered me this time, and that's that. I'm done for. I can't make holy visions hang from the ceiling."

"If CUD picks a professor of literature who stages a visitation from heaven in his bedroom, then they don't deserve you. Why don't we go to Brandeis?"

"Have you hidden my Nikes again, Caroline?"

Dennis had taken to wearing running shoes constantly, though no one had actually ever seen him break into a run.

"I wish you wouldn't wear them this once, darling," she said prettily, which meant she had hidden them.

"Why don't you want to go to Cambridge?" he came back, knowing the suggestion irked her. "We could go to Cambridge."

"And live like paupers."

"We live like paupers here."

This was an old argument. It was the sister in Cambridge she dreaded.

"I thought you liked Brandeis, Dennis. You said the students were so open, so alive."

"They are. They simply don't know anything."

"But you said you liked having students whose minds hadn't been filled with wrong theories. Don't you remember how excited you were with those impressionable young brains?"

"For six months it can be exciting. Caroline, where have you put my trainers?"

"Dennis, trust me. I know they are your trademark. But you mustn't give the trustees a chance to rule you out over such an irrelevant detail."

"If it's so irrelevant, then why are you *making such an issue out of it?*" he yelled.

She sighed her most powerfully in-the-right sigh and went off upstairs. Then he felt ashamed. He watched her faded old denim skirt swinging with her gait and those awful, sensible Marks & Spencer shoes she wore every winter because she refused to spend money on herself. No matter how shabbily she dressed, she could not hide her blond sleek upper-class British beauty. She did deserve to have a husband in the Kerrygold Chair.

Dennis took the dishes over to the sink to make it up to her. When she came back down with the Nikes, he was doing the washing up, which was ordinarily a signal that he wanted to make love. But this morning she would surely understand that there wasn't time, that it was merely meant to show he *wished* there were time because he still adored her if he could mentally squint the image of matron away.

"Here they are," she said gently.

"They think Belfast and Dublin are in the same country," said Dennis without turning around. "Americans do."

"Oh, Dennis!" she said, putting her arms around his chest from behind. "Leave that. There isn't time."

He turned toward her with soapy hands and a silly caught-out expression meant to convey his embarrassment over giving her the wrong signal, but a woman like Caroline couldn't reject her husband when he was about to be judged by the world.

"Oh, Dennis!" she said again, kissing his chin. "There really isn't time."

"I know there isn't," he said, but the thought of being late for the academic assessors suddenly filled him with a wild ardor.

6

*B*ishop Meany took it upon himself to ring the new head of the Special Branch, Chief Superintendent Fionn Bloom, to ask could he get his men to make a discreet judgment about the Blessed Virgin.

"What do you mean 'judgment'?" the Chief Superintendent said rather curtly.

"Well, your opinion as to the, concerning the authenticity—if it could be done with absolute discretion, between ourselves, you understand," Bishop Meany implored.

"You mean you want us to find out if it's the real Virgin Mary? I would have thought that was your department, Bishop."

"We are not equipped for an investigation of this sort, Superintendent."

"But surely you're closer to heaven than we are over here in the Special Branch, wouldn't you say?"

"We like to think so, Superintendent, but if you'll forgive me for observing that you are perhaps a bit closer to the criminal element than we are over here in the Nuncio's office, and it's because of the possibility of, of fraud, that I, we were hoping you might be able to investigate."

"I am not aware that it is against the laws of Ireland to cause a figure of the Virgin to appear. You'd be looking at freedom of expression, you know, which is the right of every Irishman except—"

"Don't we have laws forbidding the desecration of religious symbols?"

"I can't see any desecration here," said Chief Superintendent Bloom.

"Well, fraud, then."

"You might be able to go for a civil prosecution under the fraud statutes. Have you consulted your solicitors, Bishop?"

"Oh, we wouldn't be looking for a prosecution, Superintendent, not at all. We would simply like to get to the bottom of this thing, discreetly."

"There are one or two very good private detection agencies in Dublin, Bishop."

"Oh, I wouldn't trust any of those chancers, Superintendent, and think how it would look if it ever came out that the Nuncio's office had hired the fellows who gather evidence for divorce cases."

"Sure there's no divorce in Ireland," said the Chief Superintendent.

Bishop Meany thought it best not to respond.

"Between ourselves, Bishop," said Bloom after the awkward pause, "I can't do anything official where there's no criminal complaint or evidence of a crime. But as a courtesy to your office, I'll pass along any pertinent information that should come my way. That's the best I can do for you, I'm afraid."

"That's wonderful, Superintendent. Just a discreet indication as to the nature or possibly the identity of the individual responsible, should it prove to be, that is, not a bona-fide miracle."

"I understand, Bishop. You won't hear it on the nine o'clock news."

"You're a good man, Superintendent. You'll go far."

7

*D*ennis told her to stay in bed. She looked so beautiful lying there with flushed cheeks and eyes gone suddenly deeper violet.

Of course she would have been right about the trainers in England. But in Ireland a pair of expensive brown wing tips could cause a subtle undercurrent of begrudgery. Even her beauty put him at a disadvantage with certain of his colleagues in certain of their moods.

"You're forgetting your shoes," she said, bestirring herself onto one elbow.

"The trainers are downstairs," he said.

"You don't think they give the impression you're not entirely sane?"

"This is an Irish university, Caroline. Besides, I rather think they convey an image of good health. Couldn't hurt me after all those columns I did about the doctor telling me to give up smoking. I can't have them thinking I'd drop dead after two weeks in the Kerrygold Chair."

"Why ever not?" she said cheerily. "They would love it. Then they could give the chair to Rupert Penrose. And if they were really lucky, he, too, would die within two weeks, to be replaced by the next fellow who wants it, what's-his-name, Brown, who might also be of conveniently frail health and die obligingly soon, and so on, until every deserving scholar in Ireland has had a go at the Kerrygold Chair. Call it an Irish solution to an Irish problem."

"Since when is Penrose a deserving scholar?" Dennis asked.

"Well, for the purposes of his obituary," she said fetchingly.

"Where are my specs?" he asked.

"In the loo."

"How is it you always know where things are?" he said from in there.

"Dennis," she said, shifting her tone to the one reserved for proposing major expenditures, "I'm thinking of going to university."

"You don't need to go, Caroline! You've as fine a library under this roof as you'll find anywhere in Dublin. Besides, you're quite well educated. You've typed all my books, haven't you?"

"That's just it. Now I would like to hear someone else's ideas. I think it's time."

"That's a great send-off for your husband this morning."

He leaned down to kiss her, feeling far better than he had at breakfast, nevertheless.

"Dennis, do try to control yourself," she said, returning his kiss rather brusquely. "You are so brilliant on Beckett and Joyce. Isn't that my scent?"

"No time to shower," he said. "Everyone's brilliant on Beckett and Joyce."

"Remember our house in Tuscany."

"Gentlemen, my wife would like me to plead with you in behalf of a little house in Tuscany which sits right up on the crest of a magenta-colored hill—"

"Dennis, if you're taking the DART—"

"You know we Irish all secretly believe we should have been Italians but for the cruel God who placed us here in the Hibernian climate. It was because our mothers were all guilty of a greater degree of Original Sin. Randier than thou. There's no end to the secret vanity of the Irishman."

"I know you hate it," she said, "but once you have tenure, you can stop kowtowing to them."

"Kowtowing at CUD," he said dreamily. "God, why am I putting myself through all this to work at a cow's pacifier of a university?"

"Dennis, you must never utter that phrase outside this house!"

"Long-suffering Jesus," he said to the ceiling, "my wife thinks I'm a complete eejit."

The wrong thing to have said. Now she'd probably follow him downstairs and try to lock his mood into the right position for the rest of the day. But, no, she seemed to be heading for the loo.

He trotted down the stairs, swiftly put on the Nikes, and then rushed to don the bulletproof vest. He quickly covered it with the mac. Caroline hadn't yet noticed. She thought he was gaining more weight.

" 'Bye, love!" he called up to her. He heard a muffled "Good luck."

He scooped up his briefcase and sped out the door.

•   •   •

"Morning, Dennis McDermott," said the widow Crookshanks, appearing out of the mist with her gigantic dog, Horace. "I see we startled you. Sorry."

"Not at all," said Dennis, who had jumped half a mile.

"It's terrible cold this morning, God save us all," she said, blocking his way with the dog and her two-wheeled shopping cart.

"Well, I'm all in a lather from running to my appointments, Gertrude," he said, trying to induce her to move aside. "You're looking well yourself."

"I don't know how. This cold makes my bones ache. Poor Polly O'Byrne is down with the pneumonia, God love her, and three of them from the bridge club are down with the flu."

Then she tilted her pretty white head to one side and pursed her lips knowingly before lowering her voice to a confidential tone: "I don't suppose we can believe the strange things we see in the paper this morning, can we, Dennis McDermott?"

"Oh?" said Dennis, knowing full well.

"The picture of himself underneath the Blessed Virgin. Surely you've not failed to see it?"

"Oh, that piece of nonsense! Someone's little joke, I'm sure."

"Well, there's them that would say she wouldn't like what she saw in that man's bedroom if it was the Virgin, I don't mind telling you. And what's he got against you? He's always having at you, seemingly."

"I expect he envies me my powerful gonads," said Dennis. "Not to worry, Mrs. Crookshanks. I'm wearing a bulletproof vest."

"Go on wit' you, then," she said with a chortle, finally stepping aside to let him pass. "God bless."

"Bless yourself!" he called back over his shoulder, thinking it sounded like an insult. But he was in a terrible hurry.

He was in a complete sweat by the time he boarded his train. It was bloody awful wearing that vest, but he simply could not bring himself to venture forth upon the streets of Dublin without it.

For months now, Dublin's chief man of letters had been receiving death threats. They were written in varying styles, typed on different machines or pasted together from magazines, but something commonly demented in all of them made Dennis think they were all coming from one person. He had formed an image of the man in his mind—he was sure it was a man—a figure in a trench coat with the collar turned up, hiding in a dark alley, a tortured, brilliant soul who had a gun and who would one day step out of the alley and shoot Dennis through the heart.

Dennis did not consider it proper for a grown man, especially an Irishman, to be going to the police about his professional enemies. That would be informing, a family betrayal. And it was also possible that the death threats were a joke. Worse than dying at the hand of an assassin would be the shame of treating a bizarre joke like a serious threat. Dennis was determined to discover the culprit himself.

There were endless possibilities, for there could scarcely be a person of conviction living in the twenty-six counties whose ox had not been gored by Dennis at one time or another. But Dennis did not suspect the common run of Irishman, who he knew would not kill anyone for his ideas unless he was in the North. Dennis was sure the suspect could be found in that elite group of people in the literary trade.

This was because he and two other men, whose names he had taken a blood oath never to reveal (not even to his wife), had for the past three years served as judges for the Fionn Mac Cumhaill Literary Prize, than which there was no higher prize in contemporary Ireland. Indeed, some critics considered it the highest prize to be awarded in all the lettered world. Little money went with it, but the prestige of the Fionn Mac Cumhaill gave the winner instant command of visiting lectureships on campuses in some of the sunniest parts of the United States, Australia, and New Zealand and compounded book advances to the tenth power. It was a highly coveted prize. The judges' standards were so severe that in some years there was no winner at all.

In point of fact, there had been no winner for the last three years, coincidentally the span of time that Dennis had served on the panel. He had fearlessly been the first to reject many of the most famous names in Ireland for the award, and his fellow judges had followed suit, both of them being considerably more timid of conviction than he. Behind his back and later, his co-judges had sometimes regretted having fallen under the sway of his arguments, and recently a few of these regrets had found their way to the ears of rejected authors. The rumor was going around Dublin that Dennis McDermott was out to ruin the chances of any Irish writer more talented than himself. Nothing could have been further from the truth, but unfortunately paranoids were abundant in the literary field, many of them equipped with fiercely jealous Celtic temperaments. There might well be more than one of them plotting to murder him, Dennis thought, although he could only envision that one figure in the raincoat stepping out from the dark alley.

To steady his nerves, while he went about trying to discover his would-be assassin's identity, Dennis had quietly approached someone with rumored IRA connections to obtain a bulletproof vest. It had arrived one week ago, a little sullied with fresh dirt, the source of which he did not ask about. He was tremendously relieved. His only remaining anxiety was over how to hide the vest from his wife—and from the crowd at friends' book parties. Already he was afraid to go out without it. Anywhere in Dublin it was possible to encounter an aggrieved author.

8

*T*hat first week after the apparition Rupert Penrose took up residence in the tiny Dublin *Sentinel* office shared by the gardening correspondent, the sports editor, and the arts editor. As the latter two titles were held by one man, it wasn't quite as bad as it sounded, but it was bad enough. The tiny room contained a sagging couch, two ancient filing cabinets, a desk, a table, and a chair before Penrose arrived, and he brought another chair with him. There was scarcely space to set it down. The gardening correspondent worked all day from the couch that was Penrose's uncomfortable bed at night. The sports and arts editor spread his papers over the entire surface of the desk and table, frequently spilling them onto the floor as well. To make matters worse, the gardening correspondent wasn't speaking to the sports and arts editor because, several weeks back, the Offaly–Galway hurling match write-up had appeared under the heading, "To Prune or Not to Prune? Now Is the Time."

They did not even address one another directly when the sports and arts editor went mad on deadline and threw his papers all over the office in search of that night's copy. The gardening correspondent, an enormous bearded man named Miles, regularly helped in the search, never breaking his disgusted silence. Each night the couch seemed to have suffered deeper incursions from Miles's occupation, and Penrose's back was developing cricks that worried him.

Attracta, who had told not another soul about her having been the first to see the Virgin, worked in the office two doors down from his new home. She seemed to be avoiding him. Once, when she actually bumped into him in the hallway, she said nothing and simply walked on. Penrose wasn't sure how to interpret this. His instincts told him she was holding something in reserve, and when he thought about her, which wasn't often, he felt uneasy.

Penrose was generally assumed to have been the Virgin's chosen one, and a yearning world sought him out. His correct moral views, people seemed to think, had drawn the Blessed Virgin as a lightning rod draws the lightning. Of course, there were thousands flocking to see the Virgin herself. But there were many who, having taken her appearance as proof that there was indeed a God, wished to reassure themselves that He knew what He was doing. There were still others who, fearing death, illness, or intangible demons of the spirit, wanted Penrose to intercede for them with the heavens. He could not go out without being approached for an autograph or a blessing. He was mobbed on his way to appear on the "Late Late Show" and had the shirt torn from his back and lost one expensive black shoe. The producers quickly found him a spare shirt, but a shoe wasn't so easy. In the end he was given a heavy black sock to wear, still warm from its owner. He felt out of balance all through his interview and had trouble concentrating. A young man in the audience stood up to ask: "How do we know this really is the Virgin? Why has the Church said nothing about her?"

Penrose, who had been asking himself the same questions, answered haughtily: "I suppose we have to take it on faith."

By now thousands of people who had seen the Virgin were convinced of her authenticity from the sight of her alone, and Penrose was in danger of being idolized to an extent that even he considered excessive. He could not find a reasonably priced apartment. Every landlord in Rathgar seemed to think the man who had first seen the Virgin must have endless funds.

9

$\mathcal{C}$hief Superintendent Bloom went to examine the Virgin himself. She looked exactly as a vision of the Virgin Mother ought to look, vivid yet translucent, smiling yet sorrowful, beautiful and spotlessly serene.

She had to be a fake. She was still as a statue.

But he could find nothing in the bed-sit that might be causing her to appear, no strange wiring, no hidden projector, nothing at all. She looked like a hologram, but he couldn't bring himself to stick his hand right up through her and see if she really was. The landlord had only given him ten minutes in the room alone with her. He said the pilgrims couldn't be made to wait any longer.

"How would you feel, Superintendent, if one of those oul' wans died out here before making peace with the BVM and you sitting in there with her all to yourself?"

This compassionate soul had installed a turnstile downstairs and was charging all comers five pounds each.

Bloom duly paid his five pounds and assigned three men to search the surrounding area the following morning. They were told to go quietly through the back gardens looking for odd electrical devices or anything that struck them as strange about the wiring around Penrose's building. The youngest among them seized what he thought were three marijuana plants, and the other two cut down a laundry line. An old woman rang up the Special Branch in a state of tremulous outrage, complaining that their men had seized her rare African ferns. The housewife with the severed laundry line turned out to be a new city councilor in the Green Party with strong ideas about individual rights and the size of the criminal justice budget.

Chief Superintendent Bloom called off the search.

He then decided to treat the case like an ordinary criminal investigation. Thus the first witness to discover the apparition became the prime suspect, and if that didn't make sense, one would go for motives. Rupert Penrose and his landlord, Mike McGuire, were right at the top of the list.

McGuire had already impressed him as being too heavy-witted a man to be able to invent a device that could project a three-dimensional image through a solid wall. He thought he would start with Penrose.

"As you can see, I've a column to do this evening, Superintendent," said the prime suspect, who sat at his typewriter squinting at the phrase "defeminization of Irish women." He turned in his chair to wave Bloom toward a collapsed couch in the windowless cramped little room at the *Sentinel*.

"Can I offer you a cup of tea? A glass of spirits?"

"No, nothing, please. I won't be keeping you long."

"Well, what is it I can do for you? Has my solicitor told you how I was illegally evicted from my flat? Are you going to arrest McGuire?"

"Crude sort of a fellow, isn't he. But I'm afraid we have no grounds," said the Chief Superintendent. "It is a pity to see him exploiting people's piety like that, but there you are."

"What brings you here, Superintendent? Oh, just a minute," said Penrose, holding up a finger. He spun around and rapidly crossed out "defeminization," typing in its place "unwomanizing." Then he spun back, giving his visitor a pleasant smile.

"Between ourselves, Mr. Penrose, this is a kind of courtesy call," said Bloom. "Unofficially, I am investigating the circumstances of the apparition that has appeared in your bed-sit."

"Investigating? How so?"

"It's as a courtesy to the Church, in case there's a secular explanation here which might prove embarrassing to them and indeed to yourself."

"I see," said Penrose guardedly.

"What do you think? What were the circumstances when you first saw the figure? It was evening, wasn't it? Did you come home and find her there?"

"No. No, she appeared when I was there. I was napping."

"You awoke and found her there after a nap?"

"Yes."

"Did something awaken you? Was there a noise?"

"No. There was no noise."

"Forgive me for asking this, but were you alone at the time?"

"Of course, I was alone! How else would I be napping?" Penrose snapped.

"And you heard no noise?"

"I said that. There was no noise."

"What do you suppose awakened you?"

"I wasn't asleep for long, Superintendent. I was only dozing over a book."

"Do you happen to remember which book?"

"No, in point of fact I don't, Superintendent. But what earthly difference could it make which book I was reading?"

"I've never had to inquire about anything like this before, Mr. Penrose. I don't know what I'm looking for. I was hoping to jar your memory. Tell me this, did the apparition flicker? Did it waver in intensity?"

"No," said Penrose unexpansively.

"Did it make any sound?"

"You asked me that twice already. Why haven't you asked me about the scent?"

"What scent? There was a scent?"

"Yes. I told the newspapers. It smelled like an inexpensive women's perfume. Not unpleasant, but rather unnerving."

"It did not speak?"

"I have told you it made no sound whatsoever, Superintendent. I do have work to do here. I would suggest to you that, instead of badgering me, you should be out badgering my landlord. The vile man had all my books dumped into the basement of this building."

"Cheeky bugger," said Bloom. "Where are you staying now?"

"Right here."

"Here? Where do you sleep?"

"Where you are sitting. I can't go out without being mobbed."

"You poor fellow. It must be most unsettling."

"It is extremely unsettling."

"Being turned out of your home. If someone was trying to upset you, he did a good job," said Bloom. "Is there anyone you can think of who might be capable of pulling off a hoax like this?"

"I have plenty of enemies, Superintendent, as does the Catholic Church, but none who would be capable of calling Mary down from the heavens."

"And you noticed nothing odd about your electrical appliances that day? You saw no strange people lurking about your building?"

"No, Superintendent. I've gone over it all in my own mind a thousand times already. I can find no physical explanation."

"When did you move out?"

"The very next day. That vile man started letting the public in for viewings. It's what galls me the most, Mr. Bloom, Superintendent, the thought that that horrible little man is charging admission to my flat and here I sit, homeless and under siege. When it was myself the Blessed Mother chose to descend to. It galls me so! That despicable man!"

"Yes, he is a crass commercial spirit," said Bloom. "I'm sorry for your trouble, Mr. Penrose." He rose to go.

"Thank you, Superintendent," said Penrose solemnly.

"I suppose there's nothing to stop her following you here," said Bloom.

"What, here?" said Penrose, looking around him in alarm.

• • •

Anyone on earth would have remembered what book he was reading when the Virgin Mary came glowing through the wall of his bedroom, Bloom surmised. Penrose clearly lied about having been alone when the apparition appeared. So, who was the other person with him? Might she (or he) be the key?

Someone on that street would have seen them going in, if they went in together.

Bloom arranged to meet the landlord McGuire at the building the following evening, but it was a Friday and a snowy gale was predicted. All the secretaries wanted to get home early. The Chief Superintendent kindly left his office at three. He went around to Rathgar straightaway, thinking he would have to walk a good distance to the building. Happily enough, everyone else seemed to have headed home in anticipation of the storm, too. He found a parking space right in front of Penrose's building.

The landlord was sitting on the stoop in his overcoat, looking as though the strain of the last few days might have been too much for him.

"What happened, McGuire?" said the Chief Superintendent. "Where are your customers?"

"My solicitors will be on to you, Superintendent," said the dispirited little man. "This is not a neighborhood where you can get away with police-state carry-ons, tramping through people's gardens tearing out clotheslines and ripping up plants. Your men were brutal, feckin' brutal."

"She's gone, is she?"

"You know she's gone. Your people took her."

10

*A*round five o'clock that afternoon, all the lights went out at once in Donal McGaffney's hacienda-plan six-bedroom house in the posh Dublin suburb of Foxrock. Ordinarily his wife, Aileen, would have telephoned him as soon as disaster struck. But this time it was really a double disaster, the second part of which she was loath to divulge to her husband, whose patience had already been stretched to its limit by her telephone calls the previous day. She had rung him something like eighteen times, laboring to work out a way of inviting the present Prime Minister and the former Prime Minister to the McGaffney Christmas Eve cocktail party without having them bump into each other.

Donal was not going to be in any mood to hear that when the electrical system blew she was stuck in her wedding dress. He had been paying out five hundred pounds a year to the Foxrock Ladies Health Spa, an establishment that promised its members they would all fit into their wedding dresses after six months of attendance. Aileen had been a member for nearly two years. A reasonable person might ask whether she was getting value for money.

Aileen knew the circuit breakers were in the barn, down at the back somewhere near the diesel pump. But how to get there without breaking her neck, she had not the first idea. In the pitch dark, in a wedding dress with a long train, trying to tiptoe among Donal's crates and tires and cans of paint would be suicidal. If only she could find a match. If only she hadn't thrown them all out to encourage Donal to give up smoking.

"Oh, God, please don't make me have to go asking Sheila Wainwright for help!" she said to the surrounding gloom. Sheila was her closest neighbor.

Already the house was getting cold. I can put a coat on, Aileen thought, lifting up the train of the wedding dress with one hand and holding out the other to walk into the hall like a blind person. She promptly fell over the laundry basket. But she was not hurt. With hacienda plan there weren't any stairs. That was why she had chosen it, to save herself running up and down stairs with the last two babies, and consequently she grew fat and flabby and disgusted with herself, and Donal no longer bothered to even look at her when they dressed to go out. Which was in turn why she had joined the Foxrock Ladies Health Spa and signed up for the aerobics classes. Donal said they should have known better than to pick a plan with a Spanish name, but the architect had convinced them that even in Ireland plate glass could generate lots of heat. Of course, the house was about as warm as a bus shelter.

She groped her way to the cloakroom and found her warmest coat. Now it was even more difficult to manage the train of the wedding dress. The coat was long and held it down. Feeling ever more foolish, she shuffled on, inching her way to the kitchen in hopes that the girls had hidden a match there.

She knew they smoked and they probably knew she knew, but as long as she couldn't be absolutely certain they knew she knew, she wasn't going to say anything about it. Anyway, all the girls smoked. Aileen saw them cupping their butts in their hands on the way from the bus stop. She had done the same thing herself walking home from Loreto. Thank goodness Roisin and Fiona had not gone to Loreto. They had a much better class of nun at Holy Child, as the incomparable Sheila Wainwright liked to say.

Aileen sighed to herself as her fingers searched the kitchen shelves. The inevitable moment was coming when she must crush her pride and tramp across the street in her extraordinary getup. If only one of the girls would decide to come home early. But Fiona was working at McDonald's until midnight, and Roisin could be copying geometry proofs until all hours. Of course, Aileen could ring her and ask her to come home. But she wasn't exactly sure whose house Roisin had gone to, and she couldn't look up the phone numbers without a light.

Donal might be back soon or he might be back in three hours. He was that way, and he didn't like her asking for a precise time of arrival. He said it made him feel henpecked if he reported to her all the time. She was glad that in all the phone calls she'd made to him the day before, she had never once hinted that she'd like to know what time he would be coming home for supper.

Hallo. What luck! Her fingers found a book of matches. But what was this next to them? A packet of, a packet of—she lit a match and saw a box of Players Number Six gleaming from the cupboard corner. Yesterday they hadn't been there.

Now she had three secret smokers living in her house. I suppose I should be honored they all want to hide it from me, she thought. Or is that what Donal intended? It wasn't much of a hiding place.

This new development so interested her that, as she went out the back toward the barn, lighting her way with the matches, she forgot to hold up the train of her wedding dress. Thus the train got wedged in under the barn door and she wasted five matches trying to pull it loose with one hand. Finally she stopped lighting matches and tugged at the train with both hands. It came free with a tiny ripping sound, and she tumbled forward into the dark barn, dropping the matchbook somewhere as she fell.

"Oh, Donal! Damn!" she said, blaming him for the killer tools on which she was about to impale herself and simultaneously wishing him there to rescue her. Where was he, anyway?

She landed softly against a bag of powdered cement. As her eyes adjusted to the absence of flame, she realized she could actually see things dimly, and she had a rush of feeling for Donal. How clever he was to have put in emergency lighting for times like this! She turned her head toward the source of the light and saw the Blessed Mother glowing down at her from the far corner of the barn. She quickly knelt, crossed herself, and felt her cheeks grow hot with embarrassment. To be caught like this, trying on the wedding dress! She must look a complete fool. This had to be a mistake. The Virgin wouldn't be wanting Foxrock. Aileen glanced up from under her bowed brow. The BVM was still there. Undoubtedly. What on earth should she do now? Inexplicably, she asked herself what her aerobics teacher would advise.

11

*P*adre Destino had as yet managed to avoid going to see the Virgin. This kept him in a state of suspended official judgment, which suited Bishop Meany and a fair number of the other Irish bishops, who were pleased to make up their own minds about her. To date she had not uttered a word. That was probably for the best, Padre Destino reflected. For what could she find it in her heart to say about Ireland after the climate of Palestine?

The Nuncio was more depressed than ever this evening. The wind was actually whistling in his windows. The night seemed to have fallen about three o'clock in the afternoon, around the hour when the Nuncio had failed at his first concerted attempt to exercise his power in Ireland. It was a small matter he had lost out over, but the symbolic indignity was huge.

An all-island parents group had invited him to attend its conference on integrated education, and Destino had casually asked the bishop to pencil the date of the conference into his calendar. Meany had hesitated, then asked, in a tone rather ominously humble, where the conference was to be held.

"In Belfast, I believe they said it was," the Nuncio had recalled.

Bishop Meany had uttered a peculiar sound, something between a gasp and an "Ah," and then he had mumbled something about needing to consult various diplomatic channels, the Nuncio's accreditation being to Dublin, of course, and things being what they were between Dublin and London. But he had dutifully penciled in the date and gone on to ask what the Nuncio's thinking might be about the continued publication of horoscopes in Irish newspapers—in view of the new catechism? No more was said about the conference, and as Padre Destino knew that horoscopes had found their way into the new catechism only because of one of his own impertinent questions back in Rome about doctrinal inconsistencies, he had been happy enough to take up the subject.

That conversation had taken place early in the day, when he and Bishop Meany usually went over his calendar. The bishop would then ordinarily spend the rest of the morning going over his mail with the Nuncio. They would usually break for lunch around noon and resume business at two, when Bishop Meany took up his favorite topic, the disciplining of Church miscreants. But that morning the bishop had excused himself at ten o'clock, "to deal with the backlog in paperwork," and Padre Destino hadn't seen him again until just before three, when he had come into the Nuncio's study to tell him that Cardinal Sotti was on the line.

"You are stirring up trouble over there, Paolo," the cardinal greeted him. "I have heard from twenty Irish bishops this afternoon. They think you are going to dismantle the Catholic schools in Belfast."

"They are fools," Destino had lightly responded and, before he could stop himself, had inquired, "How is the lovely Ursula? I do miss her conversation."

"But you have agreed to be the keynote speaker at a conference on ecumenical education in Belfast?" the cardinal had come back, ignoring the reference to his mistress entirely, a very bad sign. "Is this true?"

"They call it integrated education. I believe I am only one of several speakers. I thought it would be a gesture of goodwill if I attended. I would like to show that all of us can mingle without harm."

"Your impulses are always noble, Paolo, but you are naïve. They are using you. It is the Green Party."

"I wish to hear what they have to say. I am curious about people who kill each other in the name of the Christian faith. I should like to find out why."

"It is over land and jobs, worldly power, Paolo, you know that. The schools have nothing to do with it. Stay out of Belfast, Paolo. You have plenty to do where you are."

"You advised me not to do anything for six months, until I had a feel for the place."

"I meant not on your own initiative, Paolo. I meant you should rely on the advice of the Irish bishops. This talk of divorce is serious, I understand. And that measure about abortion and suicide was a mistake. How did you let that get on to the ballot?"

"The bishops thought it was a good idea."

"It was too extreme. You mustn't let them make that same mistake again. A certain moderation of tone is required now. I understand there are family-planning clinics opening up in Dublin."

"Yes. You know my opinion—"

"I know your opinion. What is the story with the apparition? Have you found any explanation?"

"No. Except that, as you like to say, this is the most Catholic country in all of Europe—perhaps the world."

"Be careful, Paolo. One day your mockery will get to the wrong ears."

"Does it not strike you as a terrible irony that it is hatred which preserves our faith here?"

"Paolo, you must not speak this way! You are beginning to make me think you are seriously depressed."

"I will not stay away from the conference unless you order me."

"Very well. Consider it done. But only because you forced me, Paolo."

12

$\mathcal{U}$nbeknownst to his wife, who had already run out of the garage and summoned all the neighbors to come see the Virgin, Donal was driving up through the blizzard from Rosslare at the wheel of a massive articulated lorry loaded with packages for the IRA. He did not know what was in them because he had stupidly told Angus he didn't want to know. Angus had merely informed him that the cartons were under no circumstances to be bumped or dropped. So Donal had been driving that whole way with a cargo of undefined menace. He had not dared light up a cigarette. He had not even dared turn on the radio in case it were to beam in accidentally on a transistorized device.

"You're the perfect man for the job," Angus had said to him without irony. Probably no one outside the IRA knew about Angus except Donal. True, their fathers had fought together in the last campaign of the fifties, but Angus was an exemplary schoolteacher now and looked the part, clear-eyed and cleanly shorn. Donal was the one who looked the thug, with his broken nose and weathered wide face. When the Guards did their periodic sweeps of the files for new suspects, it was Donal they had picked to investigate, because the construction trade was so notorious for IRA connections. Angus had never aroused any suspicion. Donal had been investigated about twenty times. Of course, each time the Guards had come up with nothing because all those years he was clean as a whistle. That was why Angus called him the perfect man for the job.

Or maybe he was perfect because he was dispensable. Maybe they didn't want to risk one of their regulars on this job because word had leaked out somewhere, Donal thought, his fear springing new scenarios with every bend in the road. He began imagining that every other vehicle he passed belonged to the Special Branch or MI5, that a sudden flock of sheep was in fact a clever police roadblock, and the convoy of six learner drivers all seemingly being taught how to overtake in the teeth of a winter gale were really undercover RUC men operating way outside their jurisdiction in a take-no-prisoners mood. The gale meanwhile had become a fierce black biting thing with curlicue winds that could rip up a tree by the roots and then sheets of driven rain that soon turned half snow and froze on the roadway surface or looked the same when it wasn't frozen, so he never knew when the steering would go. The lorry skidded and began to jackknife around an awful turn that no one had banked right, and he saw the three black spot signs where three previous drivers had died, and it was only by the minutest fraction of an inch that he missed an oncoming car being driven by, wouldn't you know it, a tiny old nun. He actually closed his eyes when he passed her and he could see in his mind's eye the blast that would have killed them both if he had hit her and the cavity it would leave in the road and the bodies of sheep raining down upon them mixed with fragments of the plate glass that was his legitimate load. Somehow the sheep had got into his head, although he had passed them long since, and he thought how horrible it would be to smother under a pile of dead sheep. Stupid fool, there won't be anything left of you to smother if this thing goes up! Why did you ever agree to do this?

But of course he knew why he was doing this. He was bankrupt. He had no choice.

A year ago he had looked like the most successful Dublin developer who ever lived, with his special tax deals from the Dublin Corporation and his incredible planning permission for the Liffey project combined with what should have been a bond issue for the full financial package. A year ago, every major bank in London had wanted to lend him money.

That was when Liam O'Driscoll was still Taoiseach and had visions of himself cutting the ribbon at the entrance to the spectacular glass-encased bridge and aerial shopping complex which for purposes of discussion had been named on all the plans the O'Driscoll Mall. O'Driscoll was a reliable man. The only bribe he needed was to have the project named after him, and he stayed bought.

Not like that slippery sleeveen Fergal Foyle, who by parliamentary sleight of hand had managed to get O'Driscoll dumped and himself installed as leader of the so-called New Coalition in mid-September. Foyle was for the project in the morning when the Industrial Development boys came calling and against it in the afternoon when the nice ladies from the Dublin Historical Preservation Society came by for a photo opportunity and a little chat about honoring Dublin's architectural heritage. After the Anna Livia protesters rode up the Liffey on barges dressed like Viking maidens, Foyle affected to have never heard of Donal's plan. Meanwhile, worldwide recession had hit the banking industry yet again and construction work had come to a crunching halt in all but two of Donal's developments. He was having to take out new loans to pay the interest on his old loans, and his finances were beginning to look like the national budget of the United States. Foyle, getting touchy about the rumors that he had stolen his way into office, suddenly called for an election, and his people told Donal they had come around to seeing the beauty of the Liffey mall. They demanded cold cash to induce them to advise the candidate of their view. At that point everyone thought Foyle's coalition would win, or Donal would never have coughed up a farthing.

To everyone's astonishment, the other thing happened. Aloysius Kavanagh, the grand old man of the Croi na hEireann (Heart of Ireland) Party, cobbled together his own coalition with the Republican Democratic Party, the Greens and Fergus O'Sullivan, the single Dublin Free Socialist who won a seat in the Dail. With hindsight, of course, it made sense. The Irish people didn't like the way Foyle had dumped on his old mentor.

With hindsight Donal knew he should have given Kavanagh's people cold cash, too, but he hadn't actually had any cash to spare in the first place. What he gave to Foyle's Croi Nu na hEireann (New Heart of

Ireland) Party was not, strictly speaking, his own money. It was an overdue payment that ought to have gone to the Blackrock Building Society. They were old friends of his in Blackrock looking the other way until after the election.

Three weeks after the vote, Seamus Luftus, Donal's brother-in-law, offered to buy out McGaffney Enterprises, Ltd. Seamus shouldn't have known what sort of a state Donal's business was in, except that Seamus was with Lloyd's Merchant Banking and this was Ireland, and he knew. Not only did he know, he told Donal, but he had been asked to convey a message from Donal's bankers: Either go in with the brother-in-law or we'll pull the plug on you.

Donal went to see Angus.

The cartons, marked FRAGILE—GLASS, had come off a Danish freighter that sailed from Liverpool. Donal had expected Costa Rica or Libya or even Brooklyn, N.Y. But Liverpool as a port of origin made him nervous. He didn't like to think that a half ton of explosives, or whatever they were, could be bought in Britain by the IRA. Because then the Libyans or Iraqis could buy them, too, and decent people wouldn't be safe anymore.

What was he thinking, decent people, Jesus, who was he? He shivered and sweated all at once. It was drafty in the cab. He had a pain in his stomach and he wanted a smoke. He tried not to think of all he would lose if this job were to go wrong. Aileen had two hundred people coming to the house on Christmas Eve. There would be as many men without jobs if the glass mall was not built. Didn't that make him a kind of hero out there, driving God knew what up the icy road?

•   •   •

Suddenly on the outskirts of Dublin he lost heart. Of course he couldn't be an IRA courier. He *was* one of the decent people. He could not take their blood money. Not even to thwart Seamus. He just couldn't do it. Tomorrow morning, he would tell Angus to come get the load and keep his money. Fuck them all. He, Donal McGaffney, was going to save his honor and go bankrupt.

It was so simple he couldn't understand why he hadn't seen it before. By declaring bankruptcy, he would thwart Seamus most thoroughly. He would have to give the banks, the original banks, all his lorries and diggers. He would have to go back to square one with a trowel and a shovel and a work crew of seventeen-year-olds not half trained.

The girls would have to drop out of Holy Child. And Aileen would have to drop the Foxrock Ladies Health Spa. But she wouldn't mind so much, not when she realized how it would help them get around Seamus. Anyway, he didn't think she liked Foxrock with its snooty neighbors. He had been the one who had wanted to live there because he had had to prove to himself how far he had come from the Coombe. So what if they didn't have their Christmas Eve drinks party with the two Taoiseachs? They would have the satisfaction of knowing they could have.

Such was the power of a clear conscience that the minute Donal reached this decision he thought it would be all right to light a cigarette. His cargo had miraculously stopped exuding highly explosive gases. He felt amazingly free, giddily free, for he realized he was letting go of an obsession. Twenty-five years he had been trying to show Seamus he was good enough for his sister Aileen. The cigarette tasted incredibly good. LaRouge Crescent wouldn't approve. Yuppies didn't smoke. Aileen would doubtless smell it on his breath when he kissed her, but he didn't care. Wait till she heard she couldn't have her Christmas Eve drinks party.

He turned into LaRouge Crescent and saw that it was absolutely chockablock with parked cars and people on foot. He thought it was rather a large crowd for a Foxrock Friday night party, and a twinge of rue went through him for Aileen's plans. He hoped this group didn't include two Taoiseachs. He was too tired to notice that the pedestrians were not in festive attire.

He lit up another cigarette, but he still didn't turn on the radio, for fear, clean conscience or not, that the incoming signal might somehow trigger a device in the back.

Just his luck, a police car with flashing light blocked the road three hundred yards from his house. But they would have to let him up to his own garage, Donal reasoned. He pulled out into the opposite lane and drove on up to the car. A young Guard with a familiar face got out and gave him the palm-up signal. Dennis stubbed out his cigarette in a sudden panic. The Guard was walking toward him.

"Can I help you?" Dennis asked idiotically, as the young man stepped up onto the running board.

"It's ourselves who should be helping you, sir," said the Guard. "Were you hoping to put this thing in your garage, Mr. McGaffney? I suppose you were."

Christ! The boy knew his name! Of course he did. It was all over the side of the lorry.

"Of course I was!" he said swiftly. "Where else did you think I'd be parking a thing like this around here?"

"It's only that I thought you might have heard it on the radio. You've got a problem tonight, Mr. McGaffney. Well, maybe I shouldn't call it a problem. But your garage is full of pilgrims."

"Oh? Why?" said Donal, not comprehending.

"Well, it's like this. Seemingly, the Blessed Virgin has appeared in your garage."

"You're not serious."

The young Guard looked sympathetic.

"But this can't be! Not tonight," Donal said. He suddenly felt completely exhausted.

"Mr. McGaffney, there is a place in Dun Laoghaire," the Guard said kindly, "for when they seize things off the boats, drugs and arms, like. I don't know, but maybe they'd let you put the truck down there just for the night. You wouldn't want to be leaving it out on the street, sure you wouldn't, for thieves to help themselves. Shall I give them a call and see can I get the space for you?"

It was the only thing to do. The Guard disappeared into his car. Donal put his head down on the wheel for a moment. The next thing he knew, someone was shaking his arm.

"Are you all right, Mr. McGaffney? Have you come a long way?" It was the young Guard again.

"I'm fine," said Donal. "Just catching my forty winks."

"Well, I've solved your problem. You can park your truck in the compound. Actually, one of the drug-squad men will drive it down for you. You look done in, and only Guards are authorized to go down there. Come on out of there and give me the keys. I'll look after it for you until he comes."

"Are you sure he can drive one of these fellas?"

"He does it all the time."

"Well, then, tell him not to jolt the cargo around," said Donal, stepping down from the cab. "I've got valuable glass back there."

"He's the best," said the Guard, folding his fingers over the keys. "He has to drive the Semtex—when we find it."

13

The Nuncio lay awake reading the newspapers and drinking his camomile tea. He found the news consoling when it wasn't about the Church. Great errors committed by secular powers were not his responsibility. The Americans and the Europeans were arguing endlessly over how much free food each had promised to the Russians for the coming winter. A Swedish biochemist in Zurich had been arrested for selling skin cream made from human embryos. An Italian motorcar company was being criticized by consumer groups for boasting that a member of the British royal family had been stopped on the M-40 for driving its new sports car at 120 miles per hour. The American Vice President had told CNN her solution to the tensions in the Middle East would be to move the entire population of Israel to Florida.

His private line rang around eleven. It would be Bishop Meany, of course. Had the cardinal told him to apply greater diligence? He had to have been very annoyed at the reference to Ursula.

But Meany was again calling about the Virgin. "I suppose you've heard she's moved to Foxrock," he said gloomily.

"Sorry, who is this who has moved?" Padre Destino was inattentive.

"The Blessed Virgin, Nuncio. This afternoon about half two she disappeared from the flat in Rathgar. She turned up two or three hours later in a developer's garage in Foxrock. The same image exactly, they say. There doesn't seem to be any rhyme or reason."

Meany's voice was full of heavy portent. A man like that would enjoy announcing the end of the world, Padre Destino unkindly reflected. It was a pity he had not been born in the plague years.

"No, I had not heard, Bishop," he said. "Thank you for informing me. You will go to see her, I suppose?"

"The roads are fierce tonight. It's an ice storm."

"Oh," said the Nuncio. "Tomorrow will be soon enough."

He realized he wanted to go out himself, anywhere away from here. Out of the bishop's reach.

How he longed for someone to talk to!

Suddenly he sprang from his bed and sped to his study, where he looked up the number for Milltown College.

Father O'Mahoney had been in bed reading also. "It is late for you perhaps to be going out for a drink?" said Padre Destino, reaching him on the college phone after a ten-minute wait.

"It's never too late for a good drink," said the priest, "but I'm afraid the pubs are closed now. I'd invite you around here, Nuncio, but I've nothing in my rooms, either. In the Christmas season I find the hospitality so overwhelming about the place that I take the precaution of living a dry life at home. Isn't there a gale raging?"

"I must talk to you not using the telephone."

"By all means come around, Nuncio. I can at least offer you a fine cup of tea. I'd offer to drive your way, but I am temporarily without an automobile. I was hit by a drunken signpost the other afternoon. My car is in the shop."

"It is truly not too late for you? I do not sleep."

"I have no morning classes tomorrow."

"Then I will have my driver pick you up."

"Splendid!" said Father O'Mahoney.

But Patrick, the chauffeur, was still out at his daughter's birthday party, the cook informed him. Never mind. He would drive himself. But when he looked in the garage he discovered Patrick had borrowed the Daimler.

He was about to give up when he spotted the keys to Patrick's little red Citroën dangling over its mirror. He took a bottle of whiskey along.

14

"We've got your lorry with the glass, mate, ha, ha, ha!" said an unfamiliar voice. Sort of a raspy voice. A heavy smoker.

"Who is this?" said Donal, trying to keep the cold receiver away from his ear. He had his chin on the pillow.

"It's a big fooking lorry. Must be worth a lot."

"Who is this?" Donal asked more sharply.

"You'll be hearing from us." The person rang off.

"Jesus Christ!" said Donal, sitting up in bed.

"Who was that?" said Aileen sleepily.

"I don't know," said Donal.

"A wrong number, was it? Didn't we always get them ringing with the wrong number twenty minutes after we got Una to sleep?"

"I don't know," said Donal absently.

"What are you doing sitting up there? You'll catch your death. Get back under the covers."

But he still sat up.

"Donal, are you all right?"

"What time is it, Aileen?"

"It's five o'clock in the morning. Donal, you're not getting up already!"

"Um," he said, rooting around in the wardrobe.

"Who was that on the telephone?"

"I don't know," he said.

15

"What are you believing?" the Nuncio asked his companion some-
where on the Vico Road at seven o'clock in the morning. Father
O'Mahoney had told him you could see the Swiss Alps across the Irish
Sea from there at sunrise. Then he corrected himself. They were the
Welsh Mountains. But the pale streak of gray along the horizon was
perfectly straight, not a mountain in it.

"*A heifer's a heifer when all's said and done./ A girl she might lose
her good looks anyhow/ And a heifer might grow to an elegant cow,*"
sang the Milltown incorrigible.

"Perhaps it is time we are going," said Padre Destino gently.

"We're staying to see the sunrise, man! We're going to say the Mass
in Latin. Wasn't that the plan? We've been cleansed. We've heard each
other's confessions. It will be a beautiful moment!"

"I have been what you call a fraud all my life," said Padre Destino.

"Oh, here we go again!" said his companion.

"Since the age of seventeen when I lost my faith."

"Precocious bugger, weren't you, Paolo. Padre Paolo. You've got to
drop that Padre business. They'll never take to it here. Father would
be better, except I think you need every ounce of authority you can
squeeze out of your position. You don't know where you've landed,
my friend."

"You are not disgusted?"

"As to my own spiritual locutions, I can't say when they lost the
run of themselves exactly, was it a Tuesday or a Wednesday, or precisely what my age was at that particular point in time. It wasn't a sober
year."

"What are you believing now?" the Nuncio asked again.

"In the great Deus Absconditus, don't you know. Here today, gone tomorrow. Mr. Flash in the Pan. So you'd better take as much whiskey as you can in this life, Paolo, my man. The next one's an empty cupboard."

The priest took another large swig from the Jameson's quart bottle that the Nuncio had spirited away from the residency stores. Over three-quarters of it was already downed.

"Everyone was starving in Italy after the war," said Padre Destino, although Liam, as he was calling the priest by then, had not asked for the history. "My own family were respectable enough, but they had no money, no connections, either. I was a good student. The Fathers wanted me in the Curia. They told me I would have a brilliant career."

"And haven't you just?" said the Irishman. "Aren't you the Papal Nuncio to the most Catholic country in the world?"

"God is punishing me."

"The God who doesn't exist in most parts of the world today is punishing you by sending you to a place where He does. It makes sense. That is, it would if He did."

"You do not know how I long to be in Rome!"

"Don't be so hard on us, Paolo. We're only just coming out from under eight hundred years of oppression. You wait a couple of centuries more and we'll produce our own soda-based pastas. That's right, carbonated pastas, good for indigestion and guaranteed to fill you up in half the eating time. Meanwhile, we can offer you the sweetest solace known to man: a drop of Irish whiskey."

He proferred the bottle toward Padre Destino, who, against his better judgment, took another sip.

"I cannot stay here, Liam," he said. "Your Bishop Meany will extinguish me."

"You can't go, Paolo! We're only after getting acquainted. You haven't told me how you lost your faith."

"Who can say how? It goes. Or perhaps for some of us it is never there. I remember on the retreat when I was seventeen they kept saying to us, pray for peace. They would try to make us think it is a trick of the mind, like looking at the same spot forever. I prayed. I fasted. I went without sleep for a week. Nothing happened. It is holy hell to be seventeen and celibate."

"Yes, I dimly remember the feeling. I think I discovered at about that age how well I could blot out the demons of lust with whiskey," said Father O'Mahoney.

"You have not asked me why I stayed in the Church if I lost my faith at seventeen."

"You told me why. Your family was poor. The Church promised you a good job."

"This does not shock you?"

"You keep asking me that. There's plenty like you in Ireland."

"I think there are very few. It is all true believers here."

"There's belief and there's belief and there's truth and there's truth, and at the center of your average Irish soul is the square root of poverty. Jesus, Paolo, my friend, the whole feckin' landscape of metaphysics has changed in my lifetime. What's a poor body to believe at all? Why don't the Protestants burn in hell anymore? Can you tell me that? And what's this the Pope says about no sex in heaven? And they've gone and put drunken driving into the catechism. Do they want to lose Ireland altogether?"

"Do you think they will?"

"Not unless England sinks beneath the briny sea. Keep an eye out there, see if you notice any unusual oceanic disturbances."

"What do you really believe, Father Liam?"

"I believe you need to travel around the country incognito, like, taking in the general craic."

"Crack? You are liking this drug crack?"

"It's an Irish version. Perfectly harmless," said Father Liam, pulling another swig from the bottle. "Wake me when you see the sun peekin' up over there."

He put his head back against the seat and instantly began to snore.

"It disturbs me that I cannot prove the nonexistence of God," said Padre Destino disconnectedly. He knew he must be very drunk to try redeeming himself in conversation with a sleeping man.

He fell silent and felt more lonely than ever. He could see that there would be no view of the sun. The gray streak was wider. Perhaps the sun was peeking up already behind it. He might as well get his drunken friend home. He thought he dimly remembered the way back to Milltown.

He turned the car around and started very slowly back down the Vico Road. In Rome it would be an hour later now, of course, and the sun would be up gilding the city. He must not think of Rome. But he would think of Rome. He loved the yeasty bakery smells of fresh bread in the early morning there and the gritty smells of the waking streets. He loved also the thousand and one scents of coffee and the sounds of his loud impatient people going to work. How he missed the place! He even missed the stink of the river.

" 'Tis all right," Father O'Mahoney suddenly uttered out of a sound sleep. The priest kept a tender grip on the bottle neck.

Padre Destino wished his friend had not fallen asleep just as he had been about to confess the full force of his unhappiness. He knew he should not have allowed the poor man to drink so much. Clearly he was a serious alcoholic. At least this time Father O'Mahoney would not be able to remember their conversation.

"God bless us," said the priest, suddenly wide awake and cheerful as a cleansed soul. He held up the bottle in toast to his companion, then drank from it a big swallow. "Sure, retribution's just around the corner, Paolo, my man, where are you takin' us?"

"I am not exactly certain, Liam."

"But the sunrise Mass, the Vico Road! That's our Bay of Naples, don't you know!"

"As you see, there is no sun. All cloud."

"Jesus Mary and Joseph, Paolo, you've got us heading out to Bray!"

"Which is Bray?"

"Which is Bray? Which is Bray? Why it's the Saint-Tropez of Hibernia, Paolo, a scene of such succulently sinful sin as never crossed before my eyes. I wouldn't dare go there on a Saturday morning. Turn around on the instant."

Padre Destino did not think that advisable, as they were driving along a divided highway. He turned off the road at the next available exit.

"I'll drive us home," said Father O'Mahoney.

"But, Liam, you are not—"

"I'm fine. I'm right as rain. I've had a very refreshing sleep."

He got out of the car and walked around to the driver's side. Padre Destino reluctantly walked around to the passenger seat. At least the priest would know the way back to Milltown.

They were soon going at a good clip toward Dublin.

"It's a grand wee car," said the Irishman. He appeared to be in control of his faculties. "What we need now is a sip of the Jameson's to wake us up properly," he said.

"Oh, but not perhaps when driving," said Padre Destino.

"Perhaps not," said Father O'Mahoney.

He went very quiet and gripped the wheel tightly.

"Why do your Irish bishops not wish to discuss integrated education?" Padre Destino asked, thinking to take his friend's mind off the bottle.

"Why is the sky blue, Paolo? Why is the sun yellow? Where's that bottle?"

The Nuncio handed it to him, praying that Liam could stay on the road.

"The sky is gray over Ireland," he told the priest.

"You're a cute fellow. Listen, it's one of the eternal verities of the universe. We can't have integrated education here. It would dilute our Irishness, turn us into little Englishmen."

"I don't understand. This is why you cannot discuss it?"

"Why talk about it if your position is you're never going to do it? Listen, if we talked about having our precious little Catholic children with their clean baptized Catholic souls go mingling with the awful pagan Protestants up North, their ancestors' ghosts would be tearing their hair on both sides. For what did we commit murder? they'd be saying. It wouldn't do at all."

"You believe this?"

"Paolo, you're too fuckin' serious. You've been at me about what I believe in all night long. The only thing I believe in right now is that bloody Guard flashing his light in my mirror. Or am I hallucinating? Is it only another manifestation of the Blessed Virgin Mary, long-suffering Mother of Our Lord Jesus the Crucified Christ?"

[59]

The Guard turned on his siren. Father O'Mahoney put his foot to the floor and took off like a shot. Please God, prayed the Nuncio, do not let me die in Ireland!

16

The Chief Superintendent would have gone over to Foxrock first thing Saturday morning but for the fact that he was effectively the man in charge of Dublin law enforcement for the weekend. His boss had gone to Marseilles with the Minister for Justice to attend a convention on policing an integrated Europe. As the government had just announced a new cost-cutting scheme, they weren't eager to publicize their little junket. Bloom was under strictest orders not to reveal where they were.

It hardly seemed to him that Marseilles in early December could be much of a lark, but he did resent having his Saturday morning interrupted with calls from nervous officers. Saturday was the one day in the week when his family sat together and tried to be civilized with one another. But today most of them had scattered to the four winds, leaving him alone at the kitchen table with his telephone, his newspapers, and the wide gray morning gaping at him from the huge window overlooking Dublin Bay. Only his son Dick was hovering about, cleaning off counter tops and emitting needy sighs, looking like a teenage Uriah Heep with an empty wallet.

Bloom did want to have a word with the boy, but the calls were coming in thick and fast. He had only been head of the Special Branch for three weeks. He did not want to screw up. He was dressed in his good navy suit to be ready for any public appearances.

"You've always looked like a Chief Superintendent, love," his wife had said, inspecting him before she went off shopping. "Now your title matches you."

He didn't tell her that two other men had turned down the job. No one wanted it under such a shaky coalition government, the most sensitive job on the force. Naturally the computers were down again today, which meant all the stolen-car recoveries would come to a grinding halt and no criminal records could be produced for a bail hearing. Naturally, too, the Brits wanted them to question a couple of IRA suspects whose last known addresses were as safe as the secrets of Fatima until the computer should come back on again.

He considered the Dublin *Sentinel* photo of the Virgin in her new niche. She looked exactly the same as she had done in Rupert Penrose's flat. Also there was the fact of the time lapse between her disappearance in Rathgar and her reappearance in Foxrock. Why should a creature of the spirit require two hours to fly between two Dublin southside neighborhoods?

Although there might have been no one in that Foxrock garage when she got there. He made a mental note to have one of his men question that woman Aileen McGaffney. There was a file on her husband because of the father. Looked like a gombeen-man. But they said he was clean.

He made another mental note to have one of his men check the whereabouts of Rupert Penrose between the hours of half two and half four yesterday afternoon.

"What's this I hear about you failing Latin, Dick?" Bloom started in on his son. The boy was going to ask for money.

"Did Mum say that? I only failed the one exam," Dick said. He leaned against the far counter, keeping his distance.

"I understood it was the-end-of-term exam."

One of the phone lines lit up.

"That's in January, Dad. You'll see—"

"Hello, Chief Superintendent Bloom here," he responded, holding up a finger to his son.

"Oh, what's the point?!" said Dick. He left the room.

"I'll be done in a minute, son," Bloom shouted.

But he was not. The first caller, Superintendent Quilty from Tallaght, was interrupted by a Sergeant Wiley on Moore Street, who was in turn cut off by Superintendent Flaherty in Blackrock, who sounded very impressed with his own importance. Might as well deal with him first.

"What can I do for you this morning, Superintendent?"

"We've a sticky case in Blackrock this morning."

"Well, out with it. I've got two others waiting on the line."

"One of our bright young men has arrested the Papal Nuncio."

"He can't. The man's got diplomatic immunity. What was the charge?"

"Driving while intoxicated, which, as you know, is now condemned by the Vatican."

Two new calls were coming in. He seemed to have lost the others.

"I'll call you back, Flaherty. You'll have to let him go," Bloom said.

The two new callers were the old ones ringing him again.

"Sorry to keep you waiting, Quilty. What's your problem?"

"Just to say that you may have heard about a little altercation we had here, but we've dealt with it and the young fella will be getting a severe reprimand."

"You're talking in riddles, Quilty. Just a minute."

He switched to Sergeant Wiley from Moore Street.

"It's about the body they found in front of Arnott's this morning, Superintendent Bloom, sir. They want to know can they give it a Christian funeral?"

"What is this body?"

"This is the t'ing, Superintendent. We don't know."

"What do you mean, you don't know? I suppose a space alien fell onto Moore Street early this morning?"

"Oh, no, sir! This is your ordinary Homo sapiens in a lifeless state. He was a derelict. He died of exposure and possibly alcoholic poisoning. The Moore Street ladies had made him their pet and their gofer. He used to sleep over the grates by Arnott's, where they found him early this morning. They want to give him a Christian burial."

"They can't bury him yet. There'll have to be an inquest. But a funeral won't hurt him."

"But the man's probably a Hindu or a Moslem, Superintendent. He's dark-complected. They called him Mohammed."

"He was hardly a Hindu with a name like Mohammed."

"That wasn't his real name. The women picked it. He couldn't remember his name or how he came to be on Moore Street."

"Is there anyone who's against this funeral other than yourself, Sergeant?"

"It's not right, when you don't know the man's religion."

"If there's a priest willing to accommodate the ladies, let them have their funeral for him. But they'll have to let you take him to the morgue afterwards. You know the procedure."

"What if he's not a Catholic, Superintendent?"

"Do you think he minds, Wiley?"

Someone might mind if the press were to find out, Bloom chided himself, and his irritation carried over into his conversation with Quilty in Tallaght. The officer was a sly one, trying to cover himself for having been soft on a young Guard who was drunk on duty and fell into the general melee, fists flying, after a hot local hurling match.

"How many times has the Guard forgotten himself?" Bloom asked.

"I believe this is the second occurrence, Superintendent Bloom, but the first time he was only singing songs and didn't fight anybody."

"What relation is he to you, Superintendent Quilty?"

"His mother died last summer, Chief Superintendent, and he's only a boy of twenty-three, so you see, when he has to stand by and watch his own people getting pummeled—"

"It's his own people he's policing?"

"It is."

"We shouldn't have a boy that young trying to police his own friends."

"My way of thinking exactly, Chief Superintendent."

"All right, it's the reprimand. Put him in for a transfer. He's your cousin, is he?"

"Nephew."

"You've been keeping an eye on him there, no doubt. You'll have to transfer him now and tell him he'll not get off again, no matter how deeply dead his mother is."

"You're a good man, Chief Superintendent. God bless."

No more calls for the moment, but Dick was gone.

"Dick!" he yelled. "I'm off the phone."

[63]

As soon as the boy arrived back in the kitchen, the line lit up at once. Flaherty was calling again from Blackrock. Bloom put him on hold.

"We'll have to be quick, I'm afraid. This is a bad weekend for father-son chats," said Bloom with a smile.

"It's always a bad weekend," said Dick. "I don't know how you can stand your job."

"Anyway, you maintain you're not failing the Latin, then. I'm glad to hear that," said Bloom.

"I only failed the one exam because I was so jacked."

"Which means you'll be dropping the band appearances."

"It's working in Quinnsworth every weekend that's wearing me out, Dad. I'm the only one in the group works weekends."

"Sometimes I think it was a mistake to send you to Belvedere, exposing you to all those rich boys. I don't know."

"Come on, Dad. You survived it."

"Everyone in Ireland was poor when I went to school."

"I know. I missed the good old days before you had electricity or sex."

"Don't be cheeky, Dick. I'm not raising you to be a rock musician. There's thousands of kids like you eating their hearts out to be the next Bono. What do you think keeps the Dublin marijuana business going?"

"We don't do drugs, Dad. I've told you that a million times."

"I know you don't," Bloom said, holding Dick's gaze with his own. No guilt or innocence in those eyes, only sullen hormones. "The minute you do it, I'll know it."

You won't know it.

"Look, Dick," he said, now averting his own eyes. "I'm sincerely concerned that you're under too much pressure right now. You've got too much on your plate."

"Will you let me drop the job, then? Can't you give me an allowance for the next six months? Until I pass my leaving? It's a crucial time."

With the promotion, there was more money.

"I'd have to discuss it with your mother," he said.

A new line lit up. Bloom answered the call. It was Flaherty again.

"Tell me about the Papal Nuncio," Bloom said.

[64]

"Dad, can I interrupt? Does that mean yes?"

"It means I'll discuss it with your mother."

"Thanks, Dad." No more slouch to him. He was away.

"Was the Nuncio very bad?" Bloom asked.

"I don't know what you'd call bad," said Superintendent Flaherty. "He was in the chauffeur's car, driving like the clappers down the dual carriageway, and he put the pedal to the floor when he heard the police siren. Actually, the other one was driving. Father O'Mahoney, you know, that we've had in on other occasions. They'd be dead if they hadn't run out of petrol."

"They were out on a piss-up together?"

"It would appear so."

"That's a curious business. You'd wonder what kind of a Papal Nuncio would want to be spending time with a one like your man."

"You would wonder."

"What have you done with them?"

"I had them brought in here, Chief Superintendent, into my back office, so as to make them more comfortable. You see, the difficulty is our officer booked the Nuncio before he knew he was the Nuncio, because the man didn't identify himself as such, only said he was a padre. It was Father O'Mahoney told them he was the Nuncio. So you see, they've already been processed, Chief."

"It's an honest mistake. You can simply write 'Void due to diplomatic immunity' across the documents."

"I've kept it off the general roster so as to avoid embarrassment."

"They could have killed someone else, too, of course, which would have proved more than embarrassing."

"I suppose the Lord was with them."

"Your man O'Mahoney must have his license revoked and be made to sign up for the alcoholics classes."

"It's already been revoked, seemingly."

"I suppose the Nuncio's in no state to drive home, is he?"

"It's hard to say. He's been scarfing the coffee. He doesn't have the turgid complexion of your one."

"Well, I leave it up to you to judge. If you think he's able for it, let the Nuncio go home by himself. But keep the O'Mahoney there for a couple of hours wondering is he going to spend the week in jail. This man's a bugger for the self-loathing."

"All right, Chief."

"And, Flaherty."

"Yes, Chief?"

"You did rightly to keep the sharks off them."

"Thanks, boss."

17

$\mathscr{T}$hat noon in Government Buildings the full cabinet, minus the Minister for Justice, was meeting in emergency session at the request of the Taoiseach, who soon wished he had not been so brainless as to summon Dail deputies from their constituencies on a Saturday morning. Aloysius Kavanagh was known for nothing if not his political savvy, and all politics being local, he was ordinarily a genius at making the boys look good back home. He should have considered how many weddings, funerals, and constituent coffee mornings would be missing their most important guests due to his summons. Most important, he should have figured out in advance how the deputies' mileage allowances could be supplemented, in a black recession, to cover two trips down to the country from Dublin and back on the one weekend.

"Give us the bad news, Al," said Russell Doyle, his Minister for Transport. "We know you would never have called us here today unless it was to declare war or bankruptcy, and since no Taoiseach in his right mind would declare war against England three weeks before Christmas when half his constituents are looking for bargains up in Belfast, it's got to be the other thing. How bad is it?"

"You can relax yourselves, the country's still solvent," said Kavanagh.

"By the hair of our teeth," said Paddy Finnegan, Finance Minister, who privately had been telling Kavanagh he thought the country had been bankrupt for the past three months.

"What's the big emergency, then, Taoiseach?"

"While we're on finances, I think we should ask Nigel who's been leaking dribs and drabs of our budget. *That's* not a sporting thing to do to us before Christmas," said Donncha O'Breen, who was himself Minister for Sport. He glared accusingly at Nigel Ricketts, the Taoiseach's press secretary.

"I agree with you that there have been leaks," said the accused, airily. "We were under the impression that the leaks were strategic, that certain ministers might be hoping to arouse public sympathy and so to influence the Taoiseach's thinking on the cuts. It's understandable, but you'd be cutting off your nose to spite your face. I'm sure you all remember when a government fell over one item in the budget. In point of fact, we received quite a few queries about cuts in the sports ministry."

"I resent your suggestion, Nigel! I resent it very deeply!" said O'Breen, turning scarlet. "It was only when I opened up my copy of the Dublin *Sentinel* on Thursday last that I learned my department was to be cut by fifty percent."

"Gentlemen, gentlemen, please!" said Kavanagh. "We've important business to consider here this morning. Could I have your attention now?"

The deputies turned their unhappy faces toward him.

"I received a call this morning from President Henry Pond. He sends all of you and myself congratulations on our election victory."

"That's very kind of him, even if he is four weeks behind himself," said Paddy Finnegan.

"Well, the Vice President had rung us as soon as the vote count was definitive if you remember," Nigel Ricketts interjected.

"If I may continue," the Taoiseach said coldly, and everyone understood that to be a rebuke for his press secretary. "President Pond also had a piece of news. He said he would be sending Vice President Houlihan here in two weeks' time."

The ministers were overcome by a curious quietude.

"Two weeks. That's a bit sudden," volunteered Paddy Finnegan.

[67]

"She's coming to see the Virgin, then, is it? That'll be super," said Finnbarr Heaney, the Minister for Tourism.

"You didn't call us in here on a Saturday morning just to tell us the American Vice President is coming," said the Minister for Transport.

"You're an astute man, Russell," said the Taoiseach.

"It's worrying, all right," said Paddy Finnegan. "She's a bit of a loose cannon, is your woman. I'd say he wants her out of there for his Middle East business."

"Did you read how she wants to move Israel to Florida?" said Peter Flanagan, Minister for Agriculture. "What's to stop her saying she'd move all the Irish Protestants back to Scotland?"

"That might not be such a bad idea," said Finnbarr Heaney, hastening to add, "I mean, coming from an American. I don't understand all this Nervous Nellyism about her. Listen, this could be a bonanza for Ireland. Do you know our Dublin hotel bookings have quadrupled for the Christmas holidays? It's the reason I've been urging you to go pay your respects to the Virgin, Taoiseach. There's a whole untapped mass of semi-believers out there just waiting for a sign. We need you to legitimize this thing, Taoiseach. If you go there and say—well, you don't even have to say she's the real thing if you don't say she isn't. But, Taoiseach, this is our chance!"

"We couldn't be certain the Vice President would want to go near the Virgin," said Kavanagh. "Honoria Houlihan is married to one of the most successful divorce lawyers in America, don't forget."

"More to the point," said his press secretary, "she has served on the board of Planned Parenthood, which, as I'm sure you're all aware, is in the abortion business. She has said many times that although she has never been in a position to require an abortion, she would not hesitate to avail herself of the procedure should she find herself pregnant now, with her current responsibilities."

"Oh, dear God," said Russell Doyle. "We can't have her coming here."

"It might be instructive for us if you were able to tell us just what exactly are her beliefs," came the chilly voice of Deirdre Fanning, Minister for Women's Affairs. "Is she a practicing Catholic?"

"Better for us if she isn't," said Paddy Finnegan. "Nothing worse than a Catholic feminist for raising the hackles of the bishops."

"I wasn't aware that the bishops were a part of this government," said the Minister for Women's Affairs more icily than before.

"What are her beliefs?" Donncha O'Breen asked again. "Does anybody know?"

"Does it matter," said Russell Doyle, "when we know she's willing to kill her unborn child?"

"I'm glad you see it my way, Russell," said the Taoiseach, "and I assume the rest of you concur with our opinion that although we are very proud to have a person of Irish ancestry as the first woman Vice President of the United States, we do feel that this is not the time for Honoria Houlihan to come searching after her roots. If she were the first American woman President, now, like our own Bridget Lambert, that would be a different story. But she isn't. She's only the Vice President, and not one who seems to enjoy the President's confidence on the gravest matters, and as she is given to making unpredictable remarks that often upset people, we feel, I think we all feel, that this just isn't the time for us to welcome her—coming up on Christmas with a difficult budget to announce after the New Year."

"Wait a minute, Taoiseach, you've invoked the name of our own President, Bridget Lambert," said Deirdre Fanning. "What does she think of your turning away America's first woman Vice President?"

"Well, as she's leaving on her world tour in a week, it suits her quite nicely," said Kavanagh.

"Have you actually asked her?" Deirdre Fanning persisted.

"Nigel?" said the Taoiseach.

"We've been in touch through her staff, yes," said the press secretary.

"With respect, Taoiseach," the Minister for Tourism spoke up again, "I feel this is just the time to be focusing world attention on us. You know, whatever you believe about this figure of the Blessed Virgin, people are coming from all over Ireland to see her. We've got buses of schoolboys coming in from Skibbereen and Ardara. We had a charter in from Nashville, Tennessee. I tell you, they're coming from all over the world to see her, Taoiseach. This is our chance! Communism's dead. And capitalism isn't spiritually satisfying. Ireland's the answer."

"What's the question, Finnbarr?" said the Taoiseach grouchily. "You're talkin' Tourist Office tripe. Have you seen our unemployment figures for the month of November?"

"Sure, there's piles more unemployment in the old Communist bloc, and it's all murders in America, murders or diets. What kind of a civilization is that?"

"I think you had better be very careful how you handle the image of Ireland on this, Finnbarr," said Kavanagh. "I don't have time to be debating the bona fides of holy apparitions that happen to be situated in the dead center of my opponent's parliamentary district. But you could make us the laughingstock of the world, when she's revealed to be a hoax, as I firmly believe she will be."

"I don't know, Taoiseach," said Heaney. "There's people who've seen her whose tumors are receding. And the Church hasn't ruled it out."

"All right, all right," said Kavanagh. "Who's in favor of this visit? Can I have a reading on it?"

"Well, obviously I am," said Finnbarr Heaney, cheerfully enough. "And, Taoiseach, if it's the location of the Virgin that worries you, well, what's to stop her moving again?"

"Deirdre, have you changed your mind?"

"No, Taoiseach," she said coolly. "I did not have a position in the first place. I would like more information. It seems to me that if it were to leak out that we rebuffed the Vice President of the United States on the basis of very slender information concerning her stand on abortion—"

"It's very well known, Deirdre," Nigel cut in. "It was in *Time* magazine three weeks ago."

"What would you do if she came into your district, Deirdre, and she was to start in on abortion?" asked Russell Doyle.

"Well, I'd probably advise her not to, privately, you know, ahead of time."

"We are given to understand that she does not take advice," said Nigel.

"I would still like to know more about her."

"Speed is of the essence on this one, Deirdre," said the Taoiseach. "We don't have time to vet her further. The White House is planning to announce her Irish trip in the next day or so. I take it the rest of you are in agreement with me on this?" he said, looking around the table warily.

"I can't help feeling it would be a boost to the economy," said Heaney.

"Do you know how much a visit like this would cost us in security alone? A half a million pounds," said Kavanagh. "That's half a million we haven't got."

"It would be terrible if the papers were to write you turned away the first woman Vice President of the United States, Taoiseach, because you were afraid she might say something silly," said Deirdre Fanning menacingly.

"For God's sake, Deirdre!" Kavanagh exploded. "Will you trust me on this one? Will you believe me when I tell you this woman will embarrass you if you let her set foot in your constituency? She's got a screw loose. She honestly does, the poor unfortunate thing."

"Dan Quayle was worse. He was witless," she came back.

"I'm sure you're right, and we didn't go rushing to embrace him, any of us, did we? Do we have to love every bloody Irish American who comes over here to kiss the effing Blarney stone? I'm sorry to be so blunt about it, Deirdre, but think to yourself a minute how you'd handle a woman who attaches herself to your feminist causes and then throws in abortion, I mean—"

"Some quite respectable people, Taoiseach, feel that abortion is a feminist cause."

"But not in Ireland, Deirdre! Use your head, woman!"

"I don't have to take this abuse, Aloysius Kavanagh!" said the Minister for Women's Affairs. She stood up and walked out of the room.

Everyone examined his thumbs.

"Well, I'm sorry she took it that way," said Kavanagh. "But she's a sensible woman. She'll get over it. And you see right there what a mess we'd get into if we let Vice President Houlihan come to Ireland. I mean, Finnbarr, if you think Deirdre felt backed into a corner defending her, how do you think we would feel if she was our guest?"

"All the same, Taoiseach, I think it's too bad," said Heaney.

"Ach, of course it's too bad, but you can save your breath to cool your porridge with those lamentations. I need a plan. How are we going to turn her away from the ould sod without mortally insulting her?"

18

$\mathcal{M}$en in pin-striped suits and good shoes did not walk up Killiney Hill in lashing rain. But Donal had a meeting with his bankers scheduled after this, and anyway, he wanted to get it over with. Even Angus looked too well-dressed for the outing in his smart corduroy trousers and tweed jacket. They had one umbrella between them. If there had been a Guard about, he'd have thought these were two men in desperate need of privacy.

"This is most unforeseen," Angus was saying. "The Guards out looking for your lorry. This could be tricky."

"But wait till I tell you, Angus. They're not out looking for it. You see, after that call from the one with the raspy voice, I went straight down to the Dun Laoghaire Garda station to check on the lorry, and nobody there knew anything about it. Apparently the fellows on the previous shift had forgotten to fill in the forms. Then one of the fellows said he thought he'd heard something about a lorry, but there wouldn't have been any forms if it hadn't been a criminal seizure, which he assumed it wasn't, and weren't those the men from my shop who picked it up around half four? I had to think then, do I say no and report the truck stolen, or do I say yes and get the hell out of there?"

"And?" said Angus.

They were climbing the steps near the top. Donal was puffed from the climb or the fear. He didn't say anything more until they reached the Victorian obelisk, the silly spire at the summit. The rain was blowing uphill from the Dublin side of the little mountain. Donal sat down on one of the benches out of the wind.

"I asked if any of them knew what the men looked like, the ones who had picked up the lorry. Then they were fucking embarrassed. Because to have a thing like that stolen out from under their noses. Nobody knew what the men looked like. These were the new shift. Anyway, I said to them that before I filed a complaint, I wanted to check and see was the truck now up at my place on the North Side."

"You don't think they were becoming suspicious?"

"Suspicious of what? It was my own lorry that had disappeared."

"I was thinking more in line with a possible insurance scam."

"Well, they seemed so bloody glad to hear the lorry might be where it was supposed to be, I don't think they were at all suspicious of me. I called them back about twenty minutes later and told them the lorry was on the North Side right enough and everything was okay."

"Do you think they buy that?"

"Angus, they were so relieved you could have knocked them over with a feather."

"Good, Donal. Well done."

"Yeah, but I never should.have let that Guard drive off with the lorry. I know it. I was too exhausted to think. I've made a royal cock-up of this thing. I can't take the money."

"Donal, you must be joking! You've been brilliant."

"No, Angus, even before I lost the lorry, I was thinking. I had a lot of time to think driving that stuff up here, and I decided I'm not cut out for this. It's not me. I went through the tortures of hell yesterday worrying would the girls ever find out about it. I was planning to tell you to come get the stuff this morning and keep your money. It's fucking ironic."

"We all go through the tortures of hell," said Angus.

"Well, I don't want you to pay me."

"I'm afraid it's a done thing, Donal. If you check your accounts."

"Oh," said Donal flatly.

"Now, here's what I want you to do," Angus said gently, very slightly tightening his grip on Donal's elbow. By now they were walking down the hill again, sharing the one umbrella. "When those boys call again,

I want you to tell them they've got the wrong number. Tell them to ring the phone box of your local. They'll probably refuse and give you another phone box number. Go along with them on this, and when they ring you at the specified time, tell them they're holding a half a ton of Semtex belonging to the Provisional wing of the Irish Republican Army."

"Angus, I am honestly not cut out for this," said Donal.

"It's where you are now, Donal. What else can you do? Go to the Guards?"

"What do you think, Angus? How long have you known me? Would I do a thing like that?"

"All you have to do is arrange for the one phone call. The way I told you. And tell them about the Semtex. It'll do the trick."

"But what if they tell the Guards?"

"These are hijackers who stole a lorry right out from under the Guards' noses in Dun Laoghaire. Correct?"

"Yes."

"They will not go to the Guards now."

"But what if they keep on ringing me? After the conversation in the pub."

"If they ring you at home after that conversation, rip the phone out of the wall or snip the wire. Immediately."

"You think I'm going to be tapped, Angus. Oh, Jesus."

"Not right away. Not today or tomorrow. But in a week's time maybe. Ten days. If they were to keep ringing you. And depending on their discretion. Our organization could leak as well. This is a large loss. People can't resist remarking on the remarkable. So you must keep your normal routine. Business as usual."

"Well, that's a cute one. I was about to go bankrupt. That's why I called you."

"Yes, I know. You have now received a generous loan from the Jordanian National Bank. But a condition of the loan is that you take Seamus Luftus on your board."

"Angus, no!"

"Otherwise, you would appear to have become financially independent at a mysteriously rapid rate."

"But Seamus will want to run the show. I can't do it, Angus! This is the reason I asked you for money, to keep from having to take Seamus on board."

"Bear with me, Donal. If our partnership is fruitful, you will become free of him in time."

"The fucking bastard's going to outlive me. He doesn't have any bad habits. I can't believe you're doing this to me, Angus. Take your money back! I don't want the goddamn money!"

"I told you, it's a done thing."

"What if I just don't cooperate?"

"You are your own man, Donal. You make your own choices."

He won't say I'll get a bullet through the head. This is no mere kneecapping proposition. Who would be assigned to do it?

They went up to the top of the hill again, though nothing was visible up there except white cloud and the base of the obelisk. When they were boys Donal had protected Angus from the bullies.

"As you say, Angus, it's a done thing," Donal brought out.

19

*D*ennis McDermott had been on pins and needles all afternoon. He was trying to write an article for the TLS on post-minimalism in world literature in which he meant for the first time to introduce his complicated new theory about the interconnections between the end of the Cold War and the dissolution of absurdist thinking. But he was not getting on very well. He kept being stuck in Samuel Beckett's circularities and forgetting he had decided they were outdated, rooted in the pointless certainty of nuclear annihilation, which had now been subsumed into the balmier uncertainties of political fragmentation and ideological dissolution, at the center of which a man sitting in a dust bin doing nothing now appeared to have lost his poignancy, not to speak of the ecological consequences. Dared one say that the world made sense again? In the TLS?

His friend Professor Padraic Gilfiggis, the renowned philosopher and astrophysicist, had promised to report back to him after the faculty-appointments committee luncheon, which should have ended at three o'clock. It was now approaching five, the awful hour when the McDermott children were apt to begin making solitary trips to his study in hopes of securing the family mini-van for the evening. Dennis usually went out well before five on a Saturday afternoon and stayed away until after seven, by which time the entire brood would have despaired of the van and found other means of transportation.

He left his door unlocked, lest the children think he was angry at Caroline or suffering from writer's block such as had afflicted him the previous December when the London *Times* asked him to do an essay on the ten best living Irish writers. He was feeling terribly exposed in his own house. He could only blame himself. He never should have told Caroline that Padraic had promised to ring this afternoon. She had immediately told the children, of course. As it became five o'clock and then five-fifteen and still no children slunk upstairs to ask for the van, he could feel the whole house tensed with dreadful waiting.

The children would naturally tell all their friends, so that if the City University rejected him, it would be all over Dublin by tomorrow morning. He could imagine the pleasure his colleagues would be taking in the news. There was only one consolation in the prospect of such a public humiliation: it might sate the killer urge of his would-be assassin.

Three days ago, his prospects had looked very good. The academic assessors had seemed astonished by his erudition, pleased by his pedantic wit, and rather avidly interested in how one obtained a visiting professorship at Brandeis University. But on Thursday afternoon he had been subjected to a different group, the faculty-appointments committee itself, on which sat a half dozen of the Fionn Mac Cumhaill's rejected authors. None of them uttered a word during his grilling. They left the task to a new young comparative-literature professor from Galway who kept referring to books as "texts" and to every other form of communication, written or otherwise, as "discourse."

Dennis got crotchety with the fellow and began to parry back at him with terms like "literary Nazism" and "academic groupthink." The young man appeared to be holding up quite well, however, seemed even buoyed by the challenge, his young unmarked face growing happier the more insultingly Dennis came back at him. The young man's grip on his trendy terms seemed to tighten, too, the harder Dennis came at him. This irritated Dennis all the more and the irritation goaded him into complaining mockingly about "the level of discourse in Ireland today."

"That leads to my last question," said the young man. "One of the duties of the person in the Kerrygold Chair of Irish Literature would be to deliver an annual lecture on Irish writing and at the same time to give out an award for the best work of fiction produced by a CUD student that year. Would you feel comfortable doing that, Mr. McDermott? How do you see the qualities of the Irish text today, if indeed we may speak of qualities, if that would not be conducting an elitist discourse?"

"*Do you not have any language of your own?*" Dennis had finally yelled at the fellow, who promptly burst into tears and fled the room.

After an awkward interval, it became apparent that the young man was not coming back. Dennis apologized. He hadn't realized how sensitive the fellow was. And of course he would feel comfortable delivering an annual lecture on the state of Irish letters.

"Thank you very much, Dennis," the chairman of the arts faculty had cordially dismissed him. "This has been a most helpful session."

Helpful.

"Are you coming down to tea, darling?" Caroline called up to him in her sweetest tone.

"In just a minute, Caroline!" he called back.

He could stand it no longer. He rang Padraic himself.

"Figgs!" he said when Padraic answered at once. Dennis immediately regretted having used the affectionate nickname. It made him sound desperate. "I've been out all afternoon. I thought you might have been trying to find me," he lied. "Any news? Have they picked their man?"

"No, Dennis, they have not," said Padraic. "What exactly did you do to your examiner? Did you call him a Nazi?"

"Only by implication."

"The committee thought you were harsh, Dennis."

"He seemed to like it. He was grinning away at me and spouting his jargon like a smug parrot."

"It was unfortunate, Dennis. It only adds credence to the rumors that you are the man who's been sitting on the Fionn Mac Cumhaill Prize these three years. O'Dualaing, you know, on the appointments committee, just had his book of poems, *The Walls Despise Us*, turned down again. He's awfully sour on you."

"He had the gall to submit those poems? Well, I ask you, Figgs, would you have awarded them Ireland's highest accolade?"

"Thankfully, I'm not burdened with the task of deciding that," said his friend. "I don't envy those Fionn Mac Cumhaill judges."

"No," said Dennis. "It's—it would be a hopeless business. Ah, well. So you think I'm finished, then? God bless the four green fields! Back to Brandeis with us."

"No, not finished. Not at all, Dennis, not as long as I'm on the governing board. They've just called Ulick in for a second interview is all."

"He'll do very well with the little parrot from Galway. They speak the same language."

"Between ourselves, the students have named him the Man Who Isn't There, he's such a disaster as a lecturer."

Dennis did not volunteer the name the students had given him: He Who Runs in Place. There seemed to be something Padraic was holding back.

"What about Penrose? Is he still in the running?"

"I suppose he is," said Padraic. "They're all being thoroughly vetted. You're still the best, Dennis, in my view. I think it would be a crying disgrace if we lost you to Brandeis. By the way, I wouldn't mention that option quite so much, Dennis. Some of your detractors are beginning to question your commitment to Ireland."

"So am I."

"Now, Dennis, we must do everything in our power to win this seat for you. It means so much to Caroline."

There was definitely something Figgs was holding back. He had never been so peculiarly ill-informed before. Dennis concluded that his friend was too embarrassed to tell him Rupert Penrose was in fact the leading contender. But he had hinted at it in a veiled way, that bit about his commitment to Ireland.

Dennis managed to slip out the front door without attracting the attention of anyone in the family. He went on down to the pub and rang McGaffney's house from there. The phone was engaged. He had a second drink. Caroline did not know he had been cultivating McGaffney, who knew fuck all about Irish literature. But he was a major contributor to CUD.

Dennis was not above politicking for the job that way. But he would not compromise the Fionn Mac Cumhaill Prize for it. He considered his responsibility for that to be a sacred trust. Let him lose the job, then, if O'Dualaing could not forgive him. The state of Irish letters would remain pure.

But if he was not going to win the Kerrygold Chair, he was damned if he would let Rupert Penrose get it. He would expose the man's spurious piety, show him up for the fraud that he was. To that end, Dennis walked back up Nerano Road and, without telling Caroline, took off for Foxrock in the van.

When he saw the tired, damp faces of the people who had been waiting in the queue for hours, he knew he must wait, too, and not use his acquaintance with McGaffney to get a leap ahead through the back garden. He stood in the queue until one-thirty in the morning. Caroline was going to murder him when he got home.

The apparition was quite distinct, actually, quite impressive. He recognized her immediately.

20

$\mathcal{M}$eanwhile, in Donnybrook, about when Dennis headed over toward Foxrock in the mini-van, a hastily assembled gathering of women waited excitedly for the Minister of Women's Affairs to stop by. They were wedged in among Moira McNamara's fourth-hand easy chairs and Oxfam cushions, sipping red wine and tea and Diet Coke and chatting together in the happy, chirpy voices of Irish women in any sitting room of a Saturday evening. Quite a few of them were dressed up for later social engagements, and the well-stocked fire in the open grate was causing their cheeks to turn bright red. They looked distressingly winning, Moira thought. You'd have never known to look at them that their cause had just been set back twenty years. Then again, you might, she reconsidered. Give them a really clear-cut case of outrageous male behavior and Irish women came to life.

"Moira, did the Taoiseach actually say what we all think he said?" asked Una Fenwick, who was a gynecologist from the Well Woman Clinic.

"Let Deirdre tell you," said Moira, looking around the room to see whose glass needed replenishing. She had spent her last pound on the evening's refreshments. They had better do.

"Yes, where is the minister?" Una came back. "Wasn't she supposed to be here at half six? Tom and I have tickets to the Abbey."

"I maintain it's a healthy impulse that makes a woman late," said Claire Norris, the gentle entertainment columnist from *Oneself* magazine. "It's a form of passive resistance against the dictatorship of masculine-controlled time."

"We have to stop codding ourselves about our old neuroses," said Una. "When you're late, you immediately put yourself at a disadvan-

[80]

tage. You're saying: Don't expect anything from me. I can't cope."

"Oh, come on, Una! Irish men are far tardier than Irish women," said Maev Dowling, who was in favor of the Republican violence in the North. "It's because they're still unconsciously resisting British domination."

"They do get a perverse pleasure out of being late for women," said Moira.

"Yes, it's a reversal of the resistance thing, though," said Maev. "Because it's a reversal of the context. With us, they're in control."

"How's Mr. Suffering Masses Adore Me, Moira? Speaking of Dublin dictators," piped up Bridey Nolan. She was referring to Fergus O'Sullivan, the new Dublin Free Socialists deputy for whom Moira did some freelance publicity. Fergus was probably not more of a misogynist than your average Dublin drinking man, but Moira's friends considered him to be her particular misogynist, entirely her fault.

"I'd say he's confused," she answered.

"Confused? Not our Fergus! Why's that?" asked Bridey, whose brief love affair with Fergus had ceased when he banned her from wearing her jacket full of "A Woman's Body Is Her Own" buttons in his Dail campaign.

"Because he finds himself an ideological irrelevancy at the very same moment that he has the power to bring down the government," said Moira.

"That's right," said Maev. "His one vote could do it! Moira, think of the power you can wield through him!"

"It's more likely Deirdre's vote will bring down the government," said Moira.

"Would she do it when she's part of the cabinet?" asked Maev.

Before anyone could venture a response, Deirdre Fanning herself arrived, full of apologies. She gave a quick, accurate account of what had transpired in the cabinet meeting that noon. There were audible gasps at the Taoiseach's "Use your head, woman!" The women were ready to lynch him on the spot.

"Shall we throttle him now, or should we wait till tomorrow morning?" asked Bridey Nolan.

"Not tonight! My sitter's going out in twenty minutes!" protested a scarlet-cheeked woman by the fire. The others laughed. Most of them had left spouses, lovers, or babysitters on short notice.

"We'll hold off for the moment, if you don't mind," said Deirdre Fanning. "The Taoiseach is a practical politician. There are sixteen female deputies in his coalition. I don't think we ought to destroy him just for the sake of it. I want more than an expressive victory, if you know what I mean. I think we can use this amazing outrage that we all feel to demand some real substantive gains for women."

"Like abortion?" said Bridey, cheekily.

"We're not all for abortion, Bridey," said Una.

"Would you shut up and let the minister be heard, sisters!" said Maev. "Could you tell us what you'd like us to do, Deirdre? We're mad as hell, you know."

"Don't think I'm not angry myself," said Deirdre. "I want you all to get in touch with your deputies, to send faxes to the government, and to stand by at the ready for a possible action."

"That's all?" said Maev.

"For the moment, yes," said the minister. "You see, I think we're even more powerful as a threat than we are as an actual force. It's a one-time thing, a negative vote, but it's forever in the coming."

"You're brilliant, Deirdre! We're behind you all the way," said Una Fenwick, leading the applause.

• • •

"Why would she be wanting to come over to Ireland at this godforsaken time of year? Can you tell me that?" Maev asked Moira. She and Claire had stayed behind to help tidy up. Maev was helping by smoking a cigarette. One of Moira's last three Marlboros it was.

"He's having those peace talks, Maev," said Claire. "Sure, he doesn't want her anywhere near them."

"The Minister for Tourism thinks she wants to see the Virgin, seemingly."

"Houlihan wants to see the Virgin?" said Maev. "You're having me on. This is the woman who told *Time* magazine she was prepared to undergo an abortion to keep herself able for the duties of high office."

"That's some careerist," said Claire. "I wonder, would any of us do that?"

"Would we admit it if we did?" asked Maev. "You know, between ourselves and the four walls I'm a little wary of making this woman our cause célèbre."

[82]

"I think Deirdre is, too," said Moira.

"Well, that's the worst of it for you, Moira," said Maev, surveying the room which Claire had been cleaning. "We'd better be off if we're to keep our table, Claire. She's finally agreed to let me take her to dinner," said Maev, possessively.

"Would you like to join us?" Claire asked Moira. She looked flushed and shy.

"I'd love to," said Moira, "only I've got about five hundred speeches to write." She had no money for a restaurant. "Another night I'd love to."

She saw them to the door. They looked a proper couple. Maev had her hand on Claire's shoulder. I'm the only twenty-nine-year-old left in Dublin who has no partner, she thought wistfully. I'll never get one now, either, with those Oxfam pillows. But she knew the tiny supply of cigarettes was what had her depressed. She made a search of all her jacket pockets and found a fiver and two pence. On the way to the news agents she put her soul to the test: If Brian came back tonight and said it was him or the cigarettes, which would you choose? Too easy. What about your life or the fags? Still too easy. What about your mother's life? What if it was a choice between the survival of the human race and your Marlboros?

She bought two packs.

21

At precisely seven o'clock that evening, in the Eagle Tavern in Glasthule, the phone rang inside the call box.

"Hello," said Donal McGaffney.

"Hello," said the gravelly-voiced one. "Are you ready to do business?"

"You've made a terrible mistake," said Donal.

"No mistake, McGaffney. It's your lorry, all right."

"You're holding half a ton of Semtex belonging to the Provisional IRA."

"Don't be stupid. We looked. It's glass."

"You don't know what you're looking at. How many crates did you open?"

"Do you want to do business or not? There's quite a few skites could use a lorry like that, with new plates and a paint job."

"Cop yourself on, Mick. You're holding half a ton of plastic explosive belonging to the Provos."

"Prove it, mister."

"You don't want proof. You and your neighborhood would look like Hiroshima."

"Fook me. You're not serious. You drove a load like that into Dublin?"

"I'm deadly serious, Mick. I don't think you actually opened the cartons. You wouldn't be calling me if you had. And you'd better not drop any of them."

The insulting "Mick" seemed to help persuade him.

"Fook me," he said again. "They're killers. We thought you were a respectable businessman, Mr. McGaffney."

Donal hung up then, as Angus had instructed. Let the hijackers puzzle out the next step. Angus would not believe that his Semtex was in the hands of criminals who had not known what Semtex was. For the rest of the evening Donal kept his home telephone off the hook.

22

At around seven o'clock on that same Saturday evening, the Nuncio awoke with a pounding head and a sense of impending doom. He could not think where in the world he was. Then he heard the rain hitting the windows again, and he remembered all too readily.

It seemed to be pitch-black out. He wondered what hour it was and what day. Had he slept until evening? He picked up the little clock from his side table and regretted every swallow of the whiskey. Or could it possibly be seven o'clock in the morning a full day later?

A quick call down to Marco the cook set him to rights. He asked Marco to send up bicarbonate of soda and aspirin as well as a morning newspaper.

"No trouble at all, Nuncio. It is good to have you among us again. The bishop has been fussing over the dinner."

"Which dinner is that, Marco?"

"The dinner you are giving tonight for the Dublin diplomats."

"Oh, yes, of course!"

He had completely forgotten about it. He forced himself into a vertical position and saw that he was still wearing yesterday's clothes. He hadn't the slightest memory of how he came to be in his bed, but the shocked, grim white face of Bishop Meany greeting him at the back entrance returned to him clear as mortality itself. It was the face to match the voice from the plague years.

"You gave us the divil of a scare," he said. "No note or nothin' to say where you were. An important man like you would be worth a lot of money, Excellency, for those with mercenary tendencies."

He remembered that. Then nothing. He apparently had come home by means of the Deus ex Machina. He remembered earlier patches. Father Liam's songs. An old woman in Dalkey walking an enormous dog. The police-car lights. His many confessions to Father Liam. But what had he confessed? Poor Liam, could he really be addicted to crack cocaine? The Nuncio had never known anyone who was a drug addict.

Compassion for his friend surged through his breast. On an impulse, he rang him up.

"I'm afraid he's out at the moment," said a woman with a voice neither old nor young. "Could I take a message?"

"Tell him his friend Paolo rang, please."

"You're the one gave him the whiskey. You didn't do him any favors."

"Is he ill, madam?"

"He's fit as a fiddle, I'd say. He's gone up there to Ballyfermot to say the Saturday night Mass and hear confessions so they can all get drunk, the eejits."

"I am pleased to hear he is well. You are his housekeeper?"

"Considered existentially, he's in a state of happy equilibrium between the here and the hereafter. He did enjoy seeing the Virgin with you, Nuncio, and your little chat. But you'll kill him if you ever do that to him again. The man's liver is only a metaphysical concept by now. Probably the only Christian thing about him. It operates on faith."

"I am sorry—"

"That's all right, Nuncio. I'll tell him you rang. He was worried about you himself, actually. Said you were having some kind of crisis of conscience. And why wouldn't you? Sitting up there in all your finery."

"He's a good man."

"He's a right heretic. Nice talkin' to you, Nuncio."

"The pleasure was all mine," he said.

Father Liam had not mentioned her in his confessions. Or had he forgotten that, too? How could he have forgotten seeing the Virgin?

Ten minutes past seven. He hastened to the shower. In the frigid air of the bathroom it was necessary to turn the water to a scalding temperature. Even full blast, it emerged in such a disappointing fizzle that his lower body froze while the back of his neck was scalded. If this was the best plumbing in Dublin, what must the average Irishman's be like? No wonder they drank so much. It was the only way to get warm.

"Nuncio, Excellency!" Marco's voice came to him from the doorway.

"Ciao, Marco!" he called, scalding his shoulders.

"Your hangover medicines!" Marco called in Italian. "Be sure to drink the olive oil!"

"God bless you, Marco!"

"Next time you want to get drunk, let me drive you!" Marco shouted, again in Italian.

"No next time!" called the Nuncio. "But I appreciate your offer!"

"Pardon?"

"*I said I appreciate your offer!*"

"*Here comes Bishop Meany! I go!*" shouted Marco.

Padre Destino thought he could hear the bishop saying something to Marco, but he could not make out the words. He hurriedly dried himself and wrapped his body in a lovely silk robe he had brought from Rome. It was far too thin for the temperature of the residence.

"Hello, Bishop," he said as he stepped out into his dressing room. But the bishop was gone.

He dressed, took his bicarbonate of soda, glanced at the Irish *Times's* depressing news about Bosnia, the two fresh bombings in Belfast. Then he saw that Marco had also brought him his mail under the newspaper. Usually Bishop Meany went through it first. Today he must have been preoccupied.

The Nuncio had been wondering whether the bishop kept anything from him, little luxuries no one else knew Meany fancied, ordered in the name of the Papal Nuncio. Even little indulgences for a friend. As the Nuncio dressed, he read the letters.

Many of them were Christmas cards from people or organizations unfamiliar to him. It seemed that either his predecessor or Bishop Meany was a supporter of some political party called the GAA. At least a dozen cards had come from party members. He must remember this. The Vatican frowned on overt political activity for any priest and especially for a bishop.

A letter from a wine merchant protested that the wines Marco had ordered simply were not available. A bishop in Gorey wrote to recommend a bright young student for the Gregorian College in Rome, with the proviso that "he wants watching." Doubtless, what his teachers had once said about the young Paolo Destino. A priest in Limerick wrote suggesting a special fund be established to provide transport for the needy and infirm to and from "this miraculous Visitation of the Blessed Virgin Mary."

This miraculous Visitation. Why had he no memory of it? God, what else could he not remember?

At the bottom of the pile was a letter marked "Personal to the Papal Nuncio." Padre Destino knew from long experience at reading the Pontiff's mail that such letters were invariably from people wanting to share with the Pope the messages which Jesus had sent them through their tooth fillings or their bathroom radiators.

He started to throw the "Personal" letter away when an irrational spasm of fear caught him. Suppose someone had recognized him out drinking last night and already had managed to mail him a blackmail note. It wouldn't be possible, of course. Nevertheless, he read:

Dear Nuncio to Dublin Archbishop Destino,
The secret of the Virgin can be yours for a modest price. You have only to deposit fifty thousand Irish pounds in the account of Redmond Dunne Danforth, 515-43-666, at the Bank of Ireland on O'Connell Street, by the tenth of December.

Yours very sincerely,
RED

It was typed on an ordinary typewriter, suggesting the culprit was not a professional. The deferential signature, too, suggested the amateur. And this very naïve quality convinced him the writer's proposition was authentic. Rather ludicrous, of course, but quite authentic.

"Excellency, did that man bring you all this mail? They are not to bother you with this!" Bishop Meany, irate and puffing from the stairs, appeared in his bathroom doorway without a knock. He walked forward and reached for the tray on which the Nuncio had left the letters. Padre Destino folded the one from Red and slipped it into his pocket, drawing a searching dart of a glance from the bishop.

"A note from a friend," said Destino, smiling like a serpent.

"Which friend is that?" Meany asked. Apparently now he felt free to police everything.

"Oh, you would not have heard of him." Destino smiled again. Perhaps Meany could not see his face. The bishop's glasses had steamed up.

A magazine fell off the tray. Padre Destino leaned down to pick it up.

"GAA's Man of the Year," it said on the cover above the face of a very young, athletic-looking man.

"What is this GAA? They have sent us many Christmas cards," said the Nuncio.

"The Gaelic Athletic Association, Excellency. They've always been great friends of ours."

"A sports group?" Padre Destino asked. How terribly much he wished to find a weakness in his assistant that the Church would not approve.

"That's right," said Bishop Meany.

"What is your question, Bishop? You always have a question."

"It's not a question, per se. I was only wondering what our position will be on the Virgin tonight, as there's bound to be talk about her."

"Our position," said the Nuncio. Did Meany know he had been to see her? Oh, what folly it was to have put himself at the mercy of his assistant! "We have said the matter is under study," he said. "That is enough."

"Sooner or later we will be called upon to issue a definitive opinion."

"That will be when we have formed a definitive opinion, do you not agree?"

"Yes, yes, I guess I do, Nuncio, yes," said the bishop. But he did not move. "Unless we were to make a communication to the bishops to the effect that we would not object if our priests were to use her as an occasion for a reaffirmation of faith. We could encourage those who are married, for instance, to go before her and reaffirm their vows. So as to say how we feel about this proposed divorce referendum."

"It is better that we state our positions without reference to the apparition, Bishop Meany."

"What's to stop a poor demented person coming along and saying they hear her voice? What do we do then?" asked the bishop, now wiping his lenses with a tissue.

"Let us not create difficulties before they arrive," said the Nuncio. "Is that all?"

"There was one more thing I was wanting to mention, Nuncio. I don't think we should be allowing the cook to come upstairs. I've told him he's not to go upstairs again. You never know what kind of talk might be starting, seeing as how you brought him over from Italy with you."

"Talk? Why should we care about talk, Bishop? What could be the talk about my chef Marco, who is so kind as to bring me my mail and newspapers and fruit juice?"

"Well, it would be just some silly nonsense. I'm sorry if I've annoyed you, Excellency, but the Irish are a very imaginative people, and you're an important man here now, Nuncio. You have to be thinking about appearances. You've never been a public figure before. You don't know, with respect, how your every move is noted here. It's a small country, Ireland, smaller than you might think."

"But what kind of gossip could there be about Marco bringing me a tray? Gossip in my own home? Who would be so ridiculous as to think there was a scandal between me and my cook?"

"You will find that the Irish like their bit of gossip, I'm afraid," said Bishop Meany. "And they are very sensitive to appearances. If you could tell him not to bring the thing all the way in to you in the shower."

"Bishop Meany, you are the only person who knows he brought the tray into my bathroom. And of course you are not going to gossip about such an innocent act of kindness. So no one else is the wiser."

"All the same, if Marco should mention it to anyone."

"Why should he mention it? It is of no importance."

"Nuncio, Excellency, I am only trying to make you aware of the high regard in which the Irish people hold you. And it is about your Irish servants I am particularly concerned, lest their native anticlericalism should creep into the running of this house. And it does worry me when they have all seen you coming home in a state of—not at your best—that they might begin to try to take advantage and spread malicious gossip. We can't have the help thinking they can approach you now and worm their way in to an unseemly familiarity simply because they've seen you once when you've a drop too much taken. That's why I've had to tell that fellow I'd send him back to Rome if he comes upstairs bothering you again. We can't have the cook coming in on your bath, Excellency. We really can't."

"You have made your point, Bishop Meany," Destino said icily. "I am certain your services are required downstairs. I shall be down as soon as I have said a few prayers. I'm afraid I slept through the Angelus."

The Nuncio's principal advisor had no choice but to retreat.

One Week Later

23

$\mathcal{R}$ock O'Leary arrived on the Aer Lingus flight out of Kennedy at 7 a.m. on Monday, looking neat, solid, and reliable. He hadn't slept, but he felt all right. For a jilted husband at the wrong end of thirty-nine, he felt normal.

It was a soft, gray, rainless dawn with a little nip of coal smoke in the air. Rock had expected to see green, but everything in sight was gray. He couldn't tell where he was, really. On the tarmac somewhere in winter. Until the skittery fiddle music came on, when there was no mistake, this was Dublin.

They gave him a hundred thousand welcomes and practically bowed to him after he showed his Secret Serviceman's ID. The customs man put a hand on his arm.

"My daughter mailed in four hundred visa applications and never heard a word. It hardly seems fair when the Mexicans can just walk in," he said. But he let Rock through ahead of everyone else, so that he fell into step behind two nuns from another flight.

"We saw the snake in the loo in Nairobi," said the one, "because remember it was after we saw the man without eyes. That's where it was, in the loo in Nairobi. I'm sure of it."

"No, Agatha, it was in Lagos," said the other. "Because remember we saw them selling the African Ninja Turtles."

"Sure, they'll never believe us anyway, Sister, that it was in the loo the whole time."

"They'll never believe us."

The point settled, they quickened their pace. Rock stayed behind them. He took swift note of the posters along the way. Guinness Stout. Silk Cut Cigarettes. A beach in the Canaries. And a beautiful picture of Connemara, steep hills around a shimmering body of water, with a message that read:

IRELAND: THE FASTEST GROWING ECONOMY IN WESTERN EUROPE.

"You must be jokin'," Sister Agatha said to the poster.

• • •

There appeared to have been some confusion about who was to meet him. Eventually a trim, gorgeous brunette with striking blue eyes stood before him, said her name was Bernadette, please follow me. She led him to the Aer Lingus first-class lounge. It looked like a piece of a "Miami Vice" hotel lobby that got misplaced. All mirrors, hard edges, and plush plastic. Rock had a queer feeling of dislocation himself. He was not going to connect with his ancestors here. Unaccountably, he wondered whether he had forgotten a dentist appointment back home.

Bernadette handed him an Irish coffee and an Irish *Times*. He saw:

BUDGET CRISIS THREATENS PUBLIC PAYROLL, and,

VIRGIN SHIFTS TO SEAT OF POWER: BUSWELL'S PUB

Bernadette was calling people in high places. She seemed to have the patience of Job. Her voice was beautifully modulated and she cut every word's consonants with perfect enunciation.

"You wouldn't be free for dinner tonight, would you?" he asked her.

"Oh, I'm sure they have plans for you, Mr. O'Leary," she said, giving him a bright, chilly smile.

"Who's they?" he said, but she didn't hear him.

• • •

He nearly fell asleep in the cab, despite the Irish coffee. He was disappointed there were no thatched cottages. In the part of Ireland his family came from, his mother said, there had been thatched cottages. But he didn't even know which part of Ireland it was. He had forgotten to ask her.

"Visiting family, are youse?" said the cabdriver.

"No. This is a working visit."

"You've come at a quare time."

"Oh?"

"The country's bankrupt."

"I know the feeling," said Rock.

• • •

"Welcome to Ireland, man!" said Dermot Muldoon, the man assigned temporarily to look after him at the Department of Foreign Affairs. "A thousand pardons it's only myself looking after you, but our protocol chief Peter Fogarty's tied up looking after the Saudis today. Terrible job, that. There won't be a drop taken." Muldoon led Rock up and down stairs, around corridors, and into the back beyond. He was a small, red-cheeked man with a shock of black hair that fell down over his eyes. Rock was a full head taller.

"Why anyone in his right mind would want to come here in this miserable season," he said, giving Rock's elbow a companionable tug. "Tell me what you think of us."

"I don't know," said Rock. "I just got here."

"Is Houlihan one of those awful shamrock-covered Americans who pull the paddy-whackery at every turn? Or is your man just mad keen to get rid of her? We're beside ourselves with anticipation, of course. It's a vast honor to be receiving a visit from the woman who's a heartbeat away from it all," said Muldoon, not pausing for answers. "Would you like a cup of tea?"

"Sure," said Rock. "But you don't have to bother, you know, Dermot. I'm only going to crash in a minute. Where's the hotel? Is it near here?"

His host had summoned a sulky male secretary to fetch them tea. He waited for the young man to set it down and exit out of earshot.

"The walls have ears around here," said Muldoon, shutting his office door and taking on the hunched posture of secrecy. "He's not in a loyal state of mind, since I dragged him in here away from the Anglo-Irish division."

"My hotel is a state secret? You guys are more paranoid than we are," Rock said.

"This is the t'ing," said Muldoon. "We're in kind of a quandary here. Fogarty's meeting about it right now with our minister and your ambassador."

"I thought you said he was looking after the Saudis," said Rock.

"That, too," said Muldoon. "That, too."

This country was beginning to annoy him.

"How's your tea?" said Muldoon.

"It's very good, thank you. But, look, I came here to do a job, and I can't do it if I don't get a couple hours of sleep. Would you mind dropping me off at my hotel?" Rock practically pleaded with him.

Muldoon took a deep breath. "I think you might not be needing a room. Didn't they tell you the visit is not a sure thing yet?"

"No," said Rock. "Nobody said that."

"Well, they've been back and forth about it all week, and at this very moment in time our minister is trying to persuade your ambassador to reschedule the visit for sometime after Christmas. The government's in a very tenuous position here, and then there's the Semtex."

"What Semtex?"

"Didn't they tell you about the half ton of Provo Semtex that's gone missing in Dublin?"

"No," said Rock. "They didn't."

"Of course you wouldn't have heard! What am I thinking? You were on a plane. Fogarty tells me nothing. He's the original black hole. Overworked to the breaking point, too, because he can't bring himself to delegate anything. I'm supposed to be his assistant. I assist the molecules in this office to redistribute themselves by a highly secret method known only to myself and the four walls. That is to say, I work with the empty air."

"We've got plenty of guys like him in the White House," said Rock. "All guarding their marbles. Whose Semtex is it? You say Provo?"

"Yes. The Brits tell us it's an IRA shipment. Some grass they've got in Belfast."

"Grass?" said Rock. He felt that it was five-thirty in the morning back home.

"Informer. Sorry. I forget sometimes, even in this job, that we speak a different English. The Brits seem to have informers all through the

IRA. Someday the whole organization will be made up of informers, seemingly."

"How do you know the British aren't lying? To keep Houlihan at home."

"Oh, they wouldn't lie to us about a thing like this. Not now. We're all friends now and it's down on paper. They're a grand progressive lot, these Tories, right up our alley. Every man for himself. It's what the Irish believe in their heart of hearts. Okay, we'll throw money in the coffer for the starving Africans because the priests asked us to and because the Africans are not what we think of as men, not fully formed and ready for capitalism. Whereas we ourselves would all be millionaires now if they'd take the taxes off us. That's what your average Irishman believes. He sits at the pinnacle of human development waiting for the economic situation to catch up with him, does your average individual Irishman.

"You look worried," Muldoon interrupted himself. "Can I get you another cup of tea?"

"When did the British tell you about the Semtex?"

"This morning, actually, at about 6 a.m. Our Special Branch got a call."

"We get thousands of rumors about bombs every week. How reliable is your British source?"

"What? MI5? How reliable? They are when they want to be, just like any other intelligence organization. The Special Branch is checking on it right now. So you see it rather changes the picture for your Vice President's homecoming. Did she truly say they should move Israel to Florida?"

"I only know what I read in the papers," said Rock. "I'd better call the embassy."

"Be my guest," said Muldoon. "You had better know, though, that the Brits listen in on us from time to time."

"I would expect that," said Rock.

Muldoon dialed for him. Indeed, there had been a sudden meeting called. Dixon, chief of security for the embassy, was in it along with the ambassador, Peter Fogarty, and the Irish Foreign Minister.

"I guess I'll have to hang on until they finish meeting," said Rock. "I'd kill for a bed, but there's no point in checking into the hotel if I'm flying straight back. Is there an office I can use here?"

"I suggest we retire to Dwyer's to do some lateral thinking."

"What?"

"An expression used by our former Taoiseach once removed. It means to lie down and wait till the trouble blows over."

24

It was quite true that the Virgin had shifted to Buswell's pub. She appeared right in the middle of Fergal Foyle's birthday celebrations, which were taking place in the small hours of Sunday morning after the bar was legally closed and only the hotel itself selling drinks. She manifested herself at the top of the northeast corner of the bar, much to the consternation of the bartender, who felt constrained from lighting up his fags beneath her purply-eyed benevolent gaze. Fergal Foyle had the wit to extinguish his cigar as soon as he was made aware of that thing on the other side of the haze. He did not encourage the flatterers who rushed to say this was an incontrovertible sign that he ought to be Taoiseach and for life, but he seemed to be taking on an air of almost preternatural self-importance amazing even for a politician.

The birthday celebrations ended with a prayer, and everyone except the bartender dispersed to the defenseless streets of Dublin. He valiantly stayed out the night dispensing small beer to frozen pilgrims and letting the desperate miracle seekers use the hotel loos. By dawn there were hundreds lined up in the street, and hundreds more approaching. The faithful seekers paralyzed the traffic of innermost Dublin, delighting only the Tourist Board, whose bookings were continuing to multiply all over the world.

Buswell's being then the epicenter of the political universe, there were quite a few Dublin Dail deputies and Croi na hEireann functionaries who were wishing the Virgin would leave the pub before lunchtime Monday. But leave it she did not, and what were they to do? Where was the new lunch spot, the place of places? Like loose bees, they were sent grouchily off looking for a new site to swarm.

No one was more grouchy that the center would not hold that Dublin noon than Aloysius Kavanagh, who had been planning to occupy his customary corner table from which he would, as he did every other Monday, take the pulse of the nation. And he had wanted to be seen there, most especially today. The bankers had told him his smile could keep the country's bond rating up. Nigel Ricketts said it would quash all the rumors that there was a hot battle going on behind the scenes between himself and his Minister for Women's Affairs.

Dublin talk could be so poisonous. It wasn't a battle. It was more like a sort of a standoff. He had quietly let her people know he would welcome her back into the fold when she cooled off and learned to take direction from her leader. He was not going to demand an apology, nor would he ever tell the world she had thrown a hissy fit in a cabinet meeting. She in turn had quietly let his people know she would not even consider coming back without: (a) a public apology, and (b) promises for a whole lot of other things she had been wanting anyway, like a four-hundred-fold increase in the child allowance and a new divorce referendum before summer and a promise for the other business before the end of his term.

Neither of them had mentioned Vice President Houlihan, who was incidental to their dispute and not actually a factor that either of them could control. Kavanagh had been trying to send a message to Washington that the woman would be more welcome after Christmas, but the Americans were not taking the hint.

All problems looked less problematical if you could defer them. And Aloysius Kavanagh had not survived as long as he had without becoming an expert at the sublime art of deferral. Today he had sent his private secretary out roaming the streets north of Stephen's Green to search for another suitable lunch spot. Meanwhile, he sat in his office attempting to look through important papers as he listened with ever-increasing irritation to the Gay Byrne special on the radio. Gay was asking for listener opinion about the meaning of this new turn in the twisted skein of miracles.

"If this isn't a sign that the Virgin wants Foyle back in again, I don't know what is," said the first caller, a man who identified himself only as a Dubliner.

"I think it's a warning against drink, you know, Gay," said a matronly-sounding woman from Leopardstown. "Lord knows we need it."

"I completely disagree with your previous caller, Gay," said a cheerful young man living in Foyle's district. "I think it's a sign that the Virgin loves Ireland and all things Irish, including pubs. On top of that, she likes Fergal Foyle."

"That's two," said Kavanagh aloud to his radio.

"Well, now, Gay," said the next caller, winner of last year's House-wife of the Year Award in Limerick, "you have to wonder how people come up with the nonsense they come up with. The Blessed Virgin would never give her bona fides to drunken carry-ons."

"I would like to talk about a woman's right to have control over her own destiny, Gay," said another woman, who clearly was a Dubliner.

"I'm afraid that's not our subject this morning, madam," Gay put in quickly. "We're talking about the Virgin. What do you think it means that she's moved to Buswell's pub?"

"Oh, I know that, Gay, and did you realize that the Virgin was the only woman in history who was able to conceive without the help of a man?"

"Em, yes, well, what is your point, then?" he asked.

"Cut her off, Gay!" said Kavanagh. "She's a nut case."

"My point is, she was the first feminist, Gay, the Virgin was," said the woman. "And I think she came to Fergal Foyle's birthday party in Buswell's to show her displeasure with the Taoiseach that he's trying to stop the Vice President of the United States coming here because he doesn't like her views on abortion, not that—"

"We'll take a little break here," said Gay, cutting her off.

Kavanagh dialed his press secretary, in high dudgeon. Gay Byrne was playing "Heard It Through the Grapevine," as if trying to send him a pointed message. Nigel was just coming in the door, his secretary said. He had been playing squash with the head of the Toyota Night School.

"Ricketts, I want you to get on to the board of RTE straightaway," Kavanagh told him. "There was a heavy preponderance of Foyle electioneering workers sounding off on the Gay Byrne special this morning."

"I'm not certain that would produce the results we would like, Taoiseach," said Nigel. "If you remember what I said to you about how sensitive people in the public media can be about criticism. And they always get the last word in. It would be more effective simply to replace the board."

"What? Because a couple of chancers rang up Gay Byrne and said Foyle should be Taoiseach for life? I couldn't do that. Then they really would scream that I was trying to control the air waves."

"Which we both know you would never dream of doing," said Nigel.

"I've a good mind to give you the boot, Nigel."

"That's grand. Myself and the wife'll be off to Tokyo in the morning."

"You'd never go to Tokyo, Nigel. You couldn't stand to be that far from your old mother. Listen, she's broken her word. She's gone and talked about the Houlihan situation."

"My mother?"

"Don't be cute, Nigel. You know I'm talking about Deirdre. She's broken her word. It was on the radio just now. We'll have to sack her."

"What? Sack her for looking after women's affairs? Are you out of your mind? She's doing what you appointed her to do."

"She has disclosed a very high-level diplomatic secret, Nigel, a secret of the very highest level. It's tantamount to leaking from Privy Council."

"Don't sack her five weeks into the game, Taoiseach. It would make you appear flighty."

"Flighty? Flighty! Deirdre Fanning walked out of a fucking cabinet meeting! I want her silenced!"

"Could you run that by me again, Taoiseach?"

Kavanagh's private secretary appeared in the doorway, a study in watercolor.

"Well?" said the Taoiseach.

"Well, it's hard to say," said the saturated fellow. "Some of them have gone to Doheny and Nesbit's, some to the Unicorn Minor, some to the Shelbourne Horseshoe—"

"Nigel, are you still there?" Kavanagh spoke into the phone.

"Yes, Taoiseach. It's too late to book a flight to Tokyo today."

"Nigel, get off your arse and go on over to Doheny and Nesbit's and save us a table upstairs."

"Should I bring the muzzle with me?"

"What muzzle?"

"For Deirdre Fanning."

"Fuck off, Nigel. There's a good fellow."

25

When Moira's telephone rang shortly after noon she was still dead asleep. Her reasons were that her bed was warm and her cottage was freezing, she had no one to get up for, and she had been awake until three o'clock in the morning with Mr. Suffering Masses Adore Me, discussing the theoretical underpinnings of *Thelma & Louise*.

"Hello. Have I reached Moira McNamara with the Unemployed Feminists?" A very brisk, cheerful sort of a person, cruelly dangling his health and sanity in her ear.

"You might have. Who are you?"

"Jack Higgins with the Irish *Press*. Good evening to you."

"Evening? What time is it, anyway?"

"Half twelve. Sure, the day's waning already."

"Weren't you in Moscow last week?"

"I was, but here I am now back in the center of the world's stage."

"What do you want, Jack? I'm not up for much at the moment."

"Feeling poorly, are we?"

"When last I examined myself, I was not an aggregate."

"Not a what?"

"Never mind. Well?"

"Moira, what can you tell me about the Taoiseach's efforts to stop the American Vice President from coming here?"

"Why don't you call the Taoiseach's office?"

"Would I be bothering you if I'd had any luck with the Taoiseach's office?"

"Well, I don't know anything."

"I understand Deirdre Fanning is the one to talk to on this and that you're the one who can get me in touch with her."

"I don't know," said Moira.

"I'm surprised you're not out demonstrating with them in front of Government Buildings."

"Demonstrating? Who's demonstrating?"

"There's a bunch of your sisters out there."

He rang off and she tried to go back to sleep. But if women were out demonstrating and she had not been told, it could only mean trouble. As far as she knew, Deirdre Fanning did not want a demonstration. She only wanted to use the possibility as a threat. Unless Deirdre had given the go-ahead signal without telling her. Which would mean something even worse: Moira's complete lack of significance.

Could word have got around already that she hadn't liked that supposedly feminist film?

"It's a man's idea of women's liberation," she had protested to Fergus, who said he loved it. Moira had actually called it "Bonnie and Clyde with boobs."

Fergus had then felt compelled to read her passages of Frantz Fanon on the virtues of violence as a tool for liberation of the psyche. He had hoped to liberate his loins into her at the end of it all. His wife was conveniently home with the baby. This wasn't the first time he'd tried with Moira. He said her speech-writing style filled him with desire and that he could tell by the way she smoked she desperately wanted him. When she rejected him again, he turned sour.

"You know, Moira, you're not really a feminist," he said. "You're an intellectual on the rebound from a bad relationship."

Remembering, she pulled the bedclothes over her head. She might be able to fall asleep again if she stayed there long enough.

The telephone rang again.

"Hello," she said to whomever. "Tell me a reason to go on."

"Moira, are you all right?" It was Deirdre Fanning.

"Of course I'm all right. I'm just a bloody fool who stayed up half the night talking with Fergus O'Sullivan."

"Yes, he was telling me you took him to see *Thelma & Louise*. Super film, wasn't it!" said the minister. "Although I thought the double suicide rather sentimental."

"I liked Geena Davis's denims," said Moira. "American women do look better in denims."

"Sometimes I think you're not a serious person, Moira."

"That's what the nuns used to say to me—but I didn't mean to be saying you were like them, Deirdre, only that I've had my bad habits a long time."

"The girls are out there demonstrating, Moira," Deirdre said stiffly. "I thought we'd agreed to hold off on that until I'd exhausted all other avenues."

"I thought so, too."

"Well, go on out there, then, and stop them before they get into the papers."

"It may be too late for that. I had a call from the *Press* just now. The papers know they're out there. You might as well go public about it, Deirdre."

"I don't want to be doing that, Moira, not unless it's absolutely the last resort. I *am* part of the government, after all. And between ourselves, I'm not sure I'd mind if he stopped Houlihan from coming. I was on to her staff a little while ago, sort of to let them know that the women of Ireland are behind her. I was feeling them out a bit on how she might deal with the inevitable questions. Apparently, she takes no handling from anyone."

"Yes, she's famous for her independence."

"We may regret ourselves."

"All right, Deirdre. Because you asked me yourself, I'll go out there and see what I can do to get the cat back into the bag."

"There's a good girl," said the Minister for Women's Affairs.

26

"Hello. What have we here? A wee bit of excitement for you," Dermot Muldoon announced to Rock O'Leary, who was wearily accompanying him along a wide street leading he knew not where. The last thing he wanted was excitement.

It was already after lunch, and a very late lunch at that. Muldoon had taken him to three pubs before settling on the one for their meal. This was the least elegant of them all, serving a congealed kind of onion soup and some sandwiches that looked as though they had been sat on by the cook. But Rock had understood that the palate wasn't what guided a Dubliner among his pubs, nor was it even the quality of the Guinness. It was the configuration of the crowd at the bar and then, after one or two drinks, the quality of their conversation that decided the issue. Although what constituted quality to a Dublin sophisticate of Muldoon's level, Rock could not for the life of him have explained. He had thought the jokes in the second pub, "the craic," as Muldoon called them, were far better and more numerous than the thin fissure of good humor in the third. In the second pub they had encountered a jolly party of half a dozen First Secretaries celebrating someone's posting to Lisbon. When their wandering bark tied up to the railing of establishment number three, it was beside only a twosome from the Taoiseach's department, who did not smile much and spoke in coded phrases that none took the trouble to translate for Rock. They'd say, "Your man's banjaxed this morning," or, "Your woman's got her knickers in a knot," or, "I suppose the Blow-Dried Blatherer'll be born again now," and each time Muldoon would smirk sagely, squint at the floor, and then deliver himself of an apparent bon mot in response. The Taoiseach's men told Muldoon that someone they referred to as "the asshole prince" had been "looking very full of himself this morning." When Dermot replied, "Yes, we're waiting to hear the outcome," Rock had a dim understanding that they were referring to someone who was attending the meeting with the American ambassador. That was about all he understood of the entire luncheon exchange.

He fell asleep atop the bar.

"We've been boring you with our small-town gossip," said Dermot. "Come away now and we'll see what the reigning sphincter has to report."

They walked, it seemed, for miles. They went past what Muldoon said was the campus of Protestant University College and then turned up a wide road leading to the unknown destination. The gray overcast sky had broken open, and the sun was shining in their eyes as they walked straight toward it. Thus, Rock did not even clearly see what it was Dermot meant by excitement until they were right on top of it. A bunch of women with signs. He read one:

FOR SHAME, TAOISEACH!

He heard shouts, felt himself shoved into Dermot, saw police pulling a woman by the elbows, saw more police move in to force a path for some men in civilian clothes who seemed to be heading toward the steps of the imposing building all this was near.

"There's the Taoiseach now," said Dermot. "He won't like this."

"What's going on?" asked Rock.

"The feminists. They think he's trying to stop Houlihan coming here because of her views."

Rock saw a woman kick a policeman in the shins. He promptly cuffed her and hauled her toward a police van. Rock saw another woman run toward the van, trying to aid her friend, apparently. She had unkempt curly red-gold hair and a forgotten shirttail hanging out under her jacket. He could see from her hand gestures that she was pleading for the arrested one, but to no avail. The van drove off.

"You'd think this was fucking England!" she yelled to the others, and he caught a full view of her wonderful face.

"Who is she?" he said to Dermot.

"Just some lunatic Irish feminist. Welcome to Dublin, man."

27

*A*rchbishop Destino, as he was now reluctantly allowing himself to be called, had required the heat to be turned up in the residence, and now when Bishop Meany came near him with a paper to be signed, he smelled faintly of perspiration, that and mothballs, which last came from the thick winter overcoat he must have just taken out of storage. Consequently, Archbishop Destino now found himself physically dreading the dutiful man's approach quite as keenly as he dreaded it spiritually. He was beginning to feel peculiarly degraded.

Long ago Destino had made a pact with himself to atone for the inadequacy of his belief. He had vowed to keep his conduct at least as holy as possible and his heart filled with charity toward all. The idea had been that he should live the Christian life completely, since he could not subdue his mind to its doctrines. But now, feeling his heart blacken against the bishop, he was discovering that what he had thought of as his talent for charity was only the fragile form of an untested ideal, once easy enough to keep pristine in his remote and privileged position in the Vatican.

He had not thrown away the letter offering the secret of the Virgin for sale, his morale was sinking so low. He had been carrying it around in a jacket pocket, not for any action, but rather for the comfort he felt in the secret knowledge of it.

He and Meany had entertained three groups of diplomats in the past week, and the bishop had done a remarkably good job with them. Destino found himself resentful rather than relieved about Meany's good manners (insincere as they were—the man disapproved of all foreigners except the Pope), and then ashamed of feeling resentful, with the shame adding another layer to the resentment.

On the previous Saturday evening, he had found himself crowing inwardly over the French ambassador's surprise at finding the food so much improved. Bishop Meany had not appeared to notice, however, and had soon instigated a discussion about the integrated European currency, which bored the Nuncio silly, but his guests were launched for the night, circling cautiously around the question that was beginning to haunt them all: Will we have to smite the mighty Hun again? No one said it outright, though there happened to be no Germans present. They said, as if hoping it was evidence of a general racial decline, that Volkswagens weren't what they used to be. And were way overpriced.

The Nuncio, who had never actually owned his own car, lost interest in his guests. Keeping a brightly listening face, he considered where, if he were to buy the secret of the Virgin, he might put her to best use. He noticed Bishop Meany struggling with his slippery spaghetti all'aglio e olio and suppressed an urge to bring all eyes to the spectacle by offering advice to him at the most awkward moment. Bishop Meany probably thought olive oil was responsible for the moral laxity of the Italians. He had actually told the Nuncio the Irish diet promoted piety. How smoothly he hid his narrowness in front of the French ambassador!

But the Nuncio disliked his thoughts. He looked around the table, taking stock of his guests' glasses. When he looked down at his own, the waiter slipped a note from Marco into his hand.

"Excellency," it said in Italian, "I am no longer permitted to speak to you so I must resort to this method. Please forgive me, but the bishop has fired my young helper because she is pregnant and unmarried. She was living here. Her mother does not want her. She is in my quarters at this very moment, sobbing in my wife's arms. We fear she may try to harm herself. Please can you help her. Your humble servant, Marco."

So this is hatred, the Nuncio thought, feeling a queer joy in the discovery that Bishop Meany was even worse than he had realized.

Meanwhile, the willing bishop was doing such a fine job of expounding on the British economy that he had seen nothing of what the Nuncio was doing.

"Thank you for informing me, Marco," he wrote on the back of the cook's note. "The girl is not fired. Kindly tell her on my authority. Bless you, Archbishop Destino, Nuncio."

·   ·   ·

By Monday lunchtime, Destino was so pleased with his small defiance that he was able to order Bishop Meany to take the afternoon off. The intractable bishop turned out to be obedient to definite instruction. Padre Destino could not believe it had taken him three months to discover this.

The day was gorgeous, for once. The Nuncio took a stroll around the residence grounds and discovered it to be so warm he did not need his coat. Alas, the warm lambent air gave him a sharp pang of homesickness. He felt terribly lonely walking by himself in his own little park. He ducked back into the residence and rang up Father Liam.

Forty minutes later, they were headed for the Dublin Mountains in the black Daimler with Patrick at the wheel.

"This is high style," said Father Liam. "Do you ordinarily go about like this? Where was your driver when we needed him?"

"He was occupied with his family," said Padre Destino, who thought Patrick was watching them in his rearview mirror rather assiduously. He told the driver to stop and let them out for a walk as soon as they had reached open land.

"Where's this? This is the middle of nowhere," Father Liam protested. But he climbed out of the car after Destino and fell to beside him springily enough.

"I do not trust this Patrick," said the Nuncio when they were out of earshot. They had found a muddy path up the hill.

"What can he do to you? You're the Nuncio."

"Ah, but my authority is only good as long as I am obeyed."

"That's what we here in the ould sod refer to as a tautology."

"Patrick knows you are not an approved companion for me."

"But sure you approve. Patrick can do nothing."

"Bishop Meany most probably receives reports from him. The good bishop is my keeper. He could, I think, have me recalled to Rome."

"I don't doubt it. But you'd be happy with that, wouldn't you?"

"They do not want me in Rome at present. For my sins, I have been able to learn the languages of several countries I would like less than Ireland."

"Meany's trying to have me transferred down to Cavan. You'd shoot yourself if he had you sent down there, Paolo."

"Will you go?"

"I'd sooner leave the Church."

"But how would you live, my friend?"

"Who knows? Playing the tin whistle on Grafton Street. Finding parking spots for Abbey patrons. How does a man live who loses his home and his profession in the one go?"

"But we must not allow this!"

"The college is working to keep me. We'll see what happens. Care for a nip?" The priest pulled a little bottle out of his overcoat pocket.

"No, thank you," said Padre Destino. "Liam, do not kill yourself on this whiskey."

"I'm going on the dry tomorrow, or Agnes will divorce me."

"Divorce? You?"

"A figure of speech. Agnes is my housekeeper."

"You are—?"

"We were, but not for many years now. The drink is a friend to celibacy. Why do you think it's so widely accepted here?"

"Yes, I do not understand your country. No one is shocked that you and I were stopped by the police for intoxicated driving, but my assistant Bishop Meany casts out into the streets a poor pregnant unmarried girl from my kitchen. He fired her when she had nowhere to go. How could he do this?"

"To protect your image, Nuncio, my friend. You must above all things in Ireland appear respectable. It is our curse. But send this girl to me. I will find her a home."

"I cannot allow her to be sent away. I have rehired her."

"Good for you, man! What does Meany say to this?"

"He is not yet aware."

"Be careful, then. He's a sly one."

They stopped again for one of Liam's little sips from the bottle. They could see Dublin stretched out beneath them, looking far smaller than it ought.

"You'll see, if the Church releases her stranglehold on us in her lifetime, Bishop Meany'll go right along with her."

"You do not think he is a genuine conservative?"

"Not like your Super-Slav. Meany goes with the prevailing wind."

"Perhaps you underrate him."

"I think not. Agnes did some work for him years ago. She says he was all for Vatican II until it went out of fashion here."

"Your Agnes is an intelligent woman."

"She likes you, too. You'll have to come by and meet her one day."

"I have never had such an arrangement with a housekeeper. It was recommended in secret when we were young. Have you found it pulls you from your pastoral concerns?"

"I'd have gone bonkers without Agnes," said Father Liam. "Started grabbing at altar boys or sheep. You never made love to a woman?"

"Only once."

"Must have been a disappointment if you only partook once. You don't half know—"

"It was, a little," said the Nuncio. "I had waited too many years. It was no longer actually so important. Celibacy is not that difficult once you are used to it."

"So I've always heard. I never got the hang of it, sober."

"Bishop Meany thinks I am having an affair with Marco my cook. Is it his own wish, do you suppose? What Freud calls projection?"

"Do you load too many compliments on his cooking?"

"He happens to be an excellent chef. I brought him from Rome. No, it was the way he came into my bathroom to talk with me while I was taking a shower."

"Oh, that's very incriminating!"

"Are you Irish all so sex-obsessed?"

"No, some of us prefer hatred."

"Liam, you are very bitter today."

"I'm damned if I'll go to Cavan. It would kill Agnes."

"She could not go with you?"

"No. There's her mother in the nursing home here. All the nieces and nephews. She could never leave Dublin."

He was virtually a married man, like Cardinal Sotti.

"How long do you think it will be before such arrangements become officially acceptable, Father Liam, my friend?"

"You and I'll be dead and buried," said the Irishman. "For the love and honor of Jesus, Paolo, you're going to give me the heart attack before Agnes can do it."

He was breathing heavily. The muddy trail had gone up steeply. They stopped to let him rest.

"Liam," said Padre Destino, "did we go to see the Virgin that night with the whiskey?"

"Agnes says we did. I don't remember."

"Liam, there's something I want you to see," said the Nuncio. "This came in my mail a week ago."

He brought from his pocket the letter from Redmond Dunne Danforth. Father Liam held it at arm's length and turned his face odd angles, attempting to get it in focus. In the end he had to ask Padre Destino to read it to him.

"Ha!" he said. "I knew it! A hoax! Now, there's a bugger who should be arrested. That's extortion. And at the expense of the poor suffering pious Irish people. Redmond Dunne Danforth. What kind of a name is that? It's a code for something. Red Dunne Dan. Cute, you see. He's redundant."

Padre Destino looked quizzical.

"Not working. Unemployed," said Father Liam. "He's taking it out on Irish piety. I wonder how the bugger did it. Have you seen the pictures of her? She's very clear."

"Yes," said Destino. "Too clear."

"It's a puzzle he didn't do a visitation of Karl Marx, you know, God of the workers. Or Eamon De Valera, who thought up the amazing Irish economy, which is itself a sort of heavenly hallucination, you know, the glow worm of the EEC. But he's a cute clever whoor trying to get fifty thousand pounds out of you."

"I confess to you I have been thinking of paying it."

"Paying it? To a con artist?"

"Well, if he gave us the device. For use in very special circumstances."

"You would *use* it? You're that cynical?"

"Our Holy Pontiff, for example, has always had a special place in his heart for the Virgin."

"Paolo, you do astonish me. But this image doesn't talk, sure. What's to stop him lookin' at her and thinking the same way as always?"

"I will have to consider all the, what do you say, angles?"

"Angles is the word. But, Paolo, you don't think it would be a bit shoddy playing around with a toy that people actually believe to be a manifestation of God's Holy Mother?"

"How is this any different from what we allow to go on right now as it is in the Church? You and I and God knows how many more like us who do not truly believe. Yet we do nothing to destroy the illusion for others. Why would we not be in a position to do more good if we were able to control the illusion itself, the symbol of their faith?"

"It would be playing God, man! It wouldn't be right."

"Something there is in you of a belief, Father Liam," said the Nuncio. "You are hedging your bets about your Deus Absconditus."

"It's not me I'm worried about. It's my people in Ballyfermot. They deserve better than a fake Virgin."

They went on walking farther than they had intended to. But at last they both noticed it was growing quickly dark. They turned around and scurried down the hill, sliding on the mud and laughing like schoolboys.

They arrived at the car in a mood of high hilarity, skidding together hand in hand. Patrick emerged unsmiling from his seat and opened the door for them with an air of greatly wounded dignity. The two clerics realized too late the impression they were making, and they moved miles apart from each other in the back seat. Father Liam promptly fell asleep. The Nuncio attempted some polite conversation about the European Community. Patrick answered in sullen monosyllables.

When the priest awakened in front of the Milltown gates, Padre Destino recklessly invited him to come to dinner.

"I'm tired after all my drinking," he responded. "I need to go home and prepare for tomorrow's agonies. Thanks, but I'll accept your kindness another day. Let me think awhile on your other proposal, yes?"

They dropped Liam at his door.

"You'd want to be careful what you propose to that one," said Patrick as they drove off. "The way he might be talking."

28

Rupert Penrose was rescued from his homeless state by his great friend Samantha Doyle, whose elegant Palmerston Road home had more than ample room for a lodger. Penrose had nurtured a soft spot in his heart for Samantha ever since that awful period following the dunderhead review when she proved to be the first Dublin hostess to invite him to dinner again. Samantha was a large florid woman possessed of what the chillier Dublin matrons referred to disapprovingly as boundless energy. She was tireless in her efforts to raise money for the Opera Society, the Abbey Theatre, and several hospital funds. But her reputation for vigorous entertainment of visiting English actors was what the Dublin matrons meant when they referred to her boundless energy. Penrose was aware that by moving into her house he would be incurring certain risks to his own reputation.

Nevertheless, it had been twelve years since his wife had deserted him, and he anticipated many small but consoling creature comforts in the Doyle household. Samantha had already told him that the housekeeper took care of the laundry and she had asked him to provide a comprehensive list of his favorite foods. He did put leek and potato soup at the top of it. Samantha said her husband, Clarence, loved leek and potato soup himself, so they should all be very cozy together.

Penrose's quarters were to be a massive suite on the third floor, much larger than anything he had lived in since he left Ballybunion. He had insisted the Doyles draw up a proper lease. They had insisted on charging him a tiny amount of rent. Even so, with Clarence spending a good deal of his time in London, Penrose thought it most important that he keep himself on a business footing with the household.

Samantha might very well try to take over the life of anyone living under her roof. She had certainly always exhibited an extreme fondness for Rupert. She loved celebrities of all kinds, and she adored his writing. She had been an enthusiastic if not exactly brilliant student of his at the Toyota Night School some years back when Penrose had been involved with the wife of a Belgian cultural attaché. She had seemed to accept the situation in good grace but ever afterwards to regard him as rather owing her a debt of deep attention. She had seemed to hang on his every word during the classes, but she had apparently failed to quite grasp the full breadth of his concept of the Hiberno–Celtic ethos, which certainly did not encourage liaisons between wealthy Irish matrons and Englishmen of any profession. But Penrose made allowances for her defects because she had been forced by wifely obligations to spend so much time in London.

When he moved into his new lodgings, he discovered that his suite did not actually have a door, although his bedroom had—one without a lock. Against his better judgment, he found himself hoping that the rumors he had often heard about Samantha were true. He had always wanted to know how well he compared with sophisticated Englishmen.

Of course he knew he ought not to entertain such thoughts while living under Samantha's roof, and especially not at this time. To his own surprise, the university was giving Penrose's candidacy for the Kerrygold Chair quite serious consideration. Bishop Meany had told him the academic assessors were impressed by his knowledge of Irish writing. Penrose was overjoyed.

He imagined there were some begrudgers who would assume on the face of it that he was having an affair with Samantha. But that did not mean le tout Dublin would believe them. And a man could still be admired in Dublin for his conquests of women. Especially a man who beat out several handsome English celebrities. But if it were to appear that the Doyles were consequently using their influence to put pressure on the CUD trustees for Penrose, that might not be so good. If he were to submit to her charms, then, Penrose must be at pains to persuade her to persuade her husband to stay well away from the men deciding the Kerrygold appointment.

All in all, it would be wiser for him to resist her overtures. But this tack might result in a very powerful lady's hurt feelings, not such a fine prospect, either. There were times, Penrose reflected philosophically, when even he found it a burden being regarded as a sex object.

Little did he know how much more of a burden it could be, for all his experience with women.

"Rupert! How could you humiliate me so, Rupert!"

Attracta came breathing hard into his office early Tuesday morning when he still had the place to himself. It was the first time since the incident with the Virgin that she had spoken a complete sentence to him.

"Attracta, darling!" Penrose greeted her with open arms. "How good it is to see you! Where have you been keeping yourself? Come over here on the chaise lounge and tell me how you've been. You're very early to work this morning. You must be an early riser like myself."

He beckoned her toward Miles's sinking couch. But she shook her head violently and clutched her elbows in the old awkward way.

"Rupert, how could you tell Madame Bukowski to give me my chance as a favor to *you*, wink, wink, nod, nod? How could you do such an unsubtle thing? Now she thinks I'm one of those awful little sluts who sleep their way up the career ladder."

"She thinks no such thing, Attracta. She and I had rather a long chat about you, because I did tell her I was interested in your future. You wanted me to, didn't you? I thought that was what we talked about the day that we—"

"But, Rupert, I *never* told her I was in your flat, never, never! You told her I was in your flat!"

"What's so terrible about having a visit in a man's flat? When you're seeking professional advice?"

"Rupert, I never told anyone I was there with you when the Virgin came, not anyone! And now she's wormed it out of me!"

"Oh, dear, Attracta."

"Yes, and she must be jealous, Rupert. Did you have a go at her, too? She's saying I'm overqualified for the horoscope, anyway, that I don't seem happy at all. I'm afraid she'll ask Gormley to let me go. You have no idea how many jobs I applied for before she hired me."

"I wouldn't stress that aspect with her, dear."

"I don't want you interfering anymore, Rupert. You told her I got honors in the leaving cert."

"Oh, Attracta, my pet, I was only trying to help. I've made you unhappy. I'm so sorry," said Penrose, reaching out to stroke her hair.

The gesture touched off a storm of tears. He wrapped his arms around her and waited until the worst had passed.

"You mustn't be so sensitive, Attracta. We always look after our young protégés here at the paper. Everyone does it. The older journalists bring along the young ones. Sophie wouldn't think anything untoward of you. She's always looked after her protégés herself. It's just that she can be a bit slow about teaching others her particular line of work—"

Worst luck, he was interrupted right then by the telephone. Bishop Meany. The man had a sixth sense for the presence of Attracta.

"You're at your desk early this morning, Bishop."

"Rupert, I wanted to catch you when you were alone. Is it true what they're saying, that you've moved in with Samantha Doyle?"

"Well, not with her, Bishop. I'm renting rooms in the house."

"Ohhhhhhh!" Attracta let out an audible sob. Penrose cupped his hand over the phone.

"What was that?" said Bishop Meany.

"I don't know. We've been having trouble with these phones."

"You say you are renting rooms in the Doyle house?"

"Yes, but it's only a temporary arrangement until I can find something more suitable, Bishop. As you know, my former landlord is a scoundrel who has turned my flat into a tourist attraction."

"But Clarence Doyle is always in London, Rupert. It doesn't look right."

"Oh, I won't be there long, Bishop. Perhaps only through the holidays. I had been living in my office here, which is not—"

"I understand that, Rupert, but it's the appearance of the thing, when you're being vetted—well, I'm sure you take my point."

"Well, I'm always interested in your concerns, Bishop. We should have lunch this week. How're you fixed for Wednesday?"

"Next week I might be free."

"Bring the Nuncio if you like."

"There is one other matter I've been asked to raise with you, Rupert. Or perhaps I should be speaking with your editors. Why is it that a good Catholic newspaper like the *Sentinel* goes on printing the horoscopes? When they've been cited specifically in the new catechism."

"Hmmm," said Penrose. "I hadn't thought about it. That's a good point. I'll raise it with them, Bishop. Until next week, then. God bless."

He always felt strange blessing a bishop, as though it went against nature, like water flowing upstream. But Attracta left him no time to reflect. She commenced her loud sobbing the second he rang off with Meany.

"It is true!" she wailed. "It's true what she told me! You've moved in with a woman on Palmerston Road! Oh, Rupert! Oh, how could you?!"

"Attracta, Attracta, calm down! Calm down!" he said soothingly. "Attracta, I am only a lodger in the Doyle household, and the lady of the house is quite happily married. You mustn't listen to silly talk, Attracta. This changes nothing between us."

The girl grew markedly quieter.

"Have you had many of these, em, protégés?" she asked him, without looking up.

"Many? No. Not many."

"Madame Bukowski told the most awful lie about you, Rupert. She said you were married—"

"It's not exactly—"

"—and that you had two children living in the West, Rupert, which I knew couldn't possibly be true, seeing what you write about marriage and families and all. Rupert, why have you never married?"

This time she looked him full in the face.

"Actually, Attracta, I was going to explain. I have been married. But it's twelve years since I've seen my wife. We're legally separated. She left me, deserted me and took the children, to my great sorrow. I am a man, Attracta. I've not been able to live without the solace of a woman's love these twelve years— And it's worse when you're cut off from the children, too, wrenched away from those little arms."

"Oh, Rupert! She was cruel! What ages are the two of them now?"

"Em, let's see. Michael would be, em, sixteen—no—seventeen, and Padraic would be thirteen."

"Two boys. Rupert, how hard for you!"

"And the twins, now, let me see, what ages would they be? Cliona, Cliona and—Moya! The little dotes! They'd be fifteen."

"Four children?"

"And Rosemary and Eithne, they'd be fourteen now."

"Two sets of twins?"

"And not forgetting Thomas, the baby I've never seen. I knew there was another boy!"

"Rupert, you've got seven children! And I had to go falling in love with you! How could you, Rupert? You black-enameled bastard, how could you never say?"

"You never asked, Attracta, dear."

29

"I'd like to speak to Donal McGaffney, please." It was a lovely low young voice. A woman's voice.

"He's not at home now," said Aileen, who was addressing the party invitations on her kitchen table this Tuesday morning. "You'd have to try him at his office. McGaffney Enterprises, Ltd. Who am I speaking with? Do you have the number?"

"Are you Mrs. McGaffney?"

"Yes. Who are you?"

"Who I am is not important." She rang off. Straightaway Aileen dialed Donal at his office. Orla, his secretary, answered.

"He's not here right now, Aileen, but I think I could reach him for you if it's urgent. He's out at the site with Mr. Luftus. Is it urgent? I could beep him for you."

"No, no, Orla. It's nothing. Someone rang here just now looking for him, a woman. Did she ring you?"

"Well, he's had several calls. Which company was it?"

"I don't know. She didn't say."

"Oh."

"Did you tell me he was with a Mr. Luftus?"

"Yes."

"Not Seamus, my brother?"

"The very same."

"Orla, what's going on? Donal's not spoken to him in twenty years."

"I know."

"Not at Christmas, not at funerals, never a word. Is it that bad, Orla? Has it come to this?"

"Not at all, Aileen. Business is really picking up. I was thinking it was the influence of the BVM. Aren't you sorry she's left you?"

"You must be joking."

"It would make you try to be a better person, having her staring down at you all the time, well, staring down at your car. I know it would me. I would die if she suddenly showed up in my garage. There's awful things in there, things I should have thrown out years ago. Yes, I guess you must be relieved she's gone, Aileen."

Relief wasn't the word for it. She felt she had escaped from hell. No, worse than hell, because in hell she was sure no one had to put on a show of courtesy. What it was like was a kind of purgatory for people whom God had mistakenly assumed to be interested in trying out for sainthood.

The girls had been awestruck at first, quite frightened, from the look of them. But soon enough they had started dressing up for the cameras and swanning around the place, so that she wanted to shake them and shout, "You're only yourselves, you eejits!"

Donal went into a sulk and stayed away at his work till all hours, and Aileen got exhausted trying to take care of everybody outside and she started to notice how ignorant and low-born many of the pilgrims were and then hated herself for being like that. If she was being tested, she knew she had failed.

Her carpet between the door and the loo was black with mud. The garden was worse than Leopardstown Racetrack after a week of races in the spring rains. She must have spent over a hundred pounds on loo paper alone, and then there were the plumber's bills for fixing the loo countless times over and the money she spent on tea and biscuits and sausage rolls and little juice cartons for the children and nappies and plasters and the odd glass of hot whiskey she gave to the old ones standing outside in the queue. Sometimes she let the worst cases come in and warm themselves by the fire, but that was not a good idea, because how did you choose when they were all frozen through? Father Garvey hadn't helped the garden any with his collection boxes that he pounded in on thick stakes. He put them all around the house and the garage, but he never offered to give her any help with the loo paper or tea. And of course all Donal's and her cousins rang up from all over the universe and wanted to come stay the night.

Donal had hated it. He really took it hard. In fact, he started talking as though he thought someone had done this to them, as though it was some kind of a plot. Aileen thought he was going quite paranoid. She put it down to lack of sleep. People had knocked on their doors relentlessly all night every night. She finally had had to ask friends and neighbors to take turns manning the door, even the dread Sheila Wainwright. They had had no peace and no privacy.

Words could not express the joy she felt when Donal told her the Virgin had left the barn. When she got up that next morning, yesterday morning, she looked at the street outside her house, wet and gray with rain, and she clapped her hands at the wonderful bleak emptiness of it. The carpet seemed a mere trifle. The house was her own again.

But today the carpet was still ruined, and that strange woman had called, and then the news that Donal was with Seamus. Aileen began to think again how oddly Donal had been acting. The old Donal would rather have declared bankruptcy and taken his whole family to live in the gutter before he would have turned to Seamus for help.

Was it really the influence of the Virgin, the way Orla was thinking? But Donal did not seem serene or beatific. He seemed worried, preoccupied, sullenly uncommunicative, like Rose McBride's faithful Fenton just before he ran off with their Swedish au pair.

How could a woman ring up their house like that, bold as brass, and ask are you the wife? Aileen wouldn't dream of doing a thing like that, but then she had never been anybody's mistress. Young women were meant to be so bold today. She could picture the face that went with that voice, smooth and clear-eyed, a little tanned even in December. Probably an expert on the sailboard. Not eighteen, either. More like twenty-eight. At the age when other women don't matter. How would she have met Donal? She sounded educated, cool, beautiful. A solicitor or an architect.

She could imagine the woman, but she had difficulty imagining Donal with her. He was such a workaholic, he didn't seem to notice women at all. Sex did not really interest him. He wanted it every once in a while, the way he wanted a good apple once in a while, or a glass of milk, and he was affectionate with her when he remembered to be, like three or four times a year. But she had not doubted that he loved her. She had just always thought he was a normal Irish husband who would rather be with the boys in the pub when a warm mood came on him.

Now she didn't know.

30

By one o'clock Tuesday afternoon, Rock was ready to lie down on the floor of Dermot Muldoon's office and die. The man was a torturer. They seemed to have spent the last twenty-four hours in pubs, although the edges of time were now so blurred in Rock's brain it might have been a week.

There wasn't anything else to do, Dermot had assured him. The negotiations had got deadlocked and now the Taoiseach was in an utter quandary, since it had leaked out that he was trying to stop Houlihan from coming and that the U.S. was not taking the hint. His office, of course, was denying this, but the rumor had such a ring of truth to it, Dermot said everyone in Dublin believed it.

"He's fucked either way, don't you see, if she comes or if she doesn't," said the Irishman. "He can choose to look as though he's bullying a woman or acting the wimp."

"You wouldn't have a Coke, by any chance?" Rock asked, without much real hope. In any case, he would be leaving on the four o'clock flight back to New York if Houlihan's trip was nixed. He hadn't set foot in Bloom's Hotel.

"If you drink any more of that stuff, you'll rot your insides. You've been drinking it all day. It's not good to have that much sugar, you know. Gives you internal eczema."

"All right, a plain coffee."

Muldoon had his own ideas about what should go into a plain coffee.

"Jesus Christ, this is half whiskey, Dermot. What are you trying to do to me?"

"You know, *Private Eye* says your man was bonking her all through the campaign. Having Ugandan discussions, they call it. A reference to someone's affair with a Ugandan diplomat years ago. Pond is supposed to have his eye on some spook's wife now, what's her name, Julia Haifitz. Any truth to that?"

"Bonking who all through the campaign? And what's *Private Eye*?"

"Houlihan. *Private Eye* is a British satirical magazine that keeps track of famous fornicators. They've got good personals, too. You know, 'Psychic researcher close to finding the theory of everything needs help. Please send money to Box XYZ Croydon.' "

"Look, I'm just one of the palace guards. We patrol outside the bedrooms, not inside."

"But surely you see who comes and goes?"

"Yes, we do. But we don't know who hops into bed. Your guy Kavanagh, does he?"

"He's not a fornicator, if that's what you mean. His heart's in the greater glory of getting revenge on the former Taoiseach, who was his protégé and betrayed him."

Muldoon's phone rang.

"Peter! It's yourself, is it? Have you news for us? Yes. Yes. Yes. That'll give us a bit of excitement before Christmas. And won't she make us sit up and listen with her talk about a woman's right to choose. Sure, we'll all be on our toes now, Peter, helping her dodge the fugitive Semtex. Or is it still floating around free, it is? . . . Right. Yes. Chief Superintendent Bloom's our man. Are you back to the towel heads now, Peter? Oh, you're a great man for doing everything yourself, Peter. Throw us a bit of work now and again. Next Sunday morning, then so. 'Bye for now, Peter."

He set the receiver back in its cradle.

"There you are. She's coming on Sunday morning. You're to talk to a Chief Superintendent Bloom, runs the Special Branch. He's in charge of the Semtex. Finding it, that is. Shall we go over there and meet him?"

"What? After three thousand whiskies? You're out of your fucking gourd. Take me to the hotel."

31

*T*uesday evening Moira arrived forty minutes late for the Dublin Free Socialists meeting. She could hardly explain the reason to the assembled membership. She had in fact been detained at a secret strategy session of the Irish Unemployed Feminists. That would be all Fergus O'Sullivan needed to know to seal tight his conviction that there wasn't a feminist alive anywhere in the world who was truly punctual.

The IUF were meant to have met promptly at seven, as they were meant to every second Tuesday, when they planned her secret agenda for the Dublin Free Socialists meeting. They knew the Socialists met at nine and they knew Moira hated to be late because the public policy committee was always passing things in her absence which required her to face down Finglas dope dealers all alone or single-handedly convince eighty-year-old dowager chemists that she would, yes, herself personally use all five thousand condoms which the party had assigned her to buy for its needy-youths program.

Moira was the co-chairperson of the Dublin Free Socialists, which was a splinter group of a splinter group of the Socialist Labor Party, which in turn was a faction of former Labor Party members. The Irish Unemployed Feminists were themselves a splinter group of the Dublin Free Socialists, formed the night eight weeks ago that Fergus O'Sullivan banned Bridey Nolan's "A Woman's Body Is Her Own" buttons from his Dail campaign.

Moira herself had been slow to anger over the body buttons, thinking the ban was merely a tactical concession to Dublin's level of consciousness. She had not walked out with the other women. But after Fergus won his Dail seat and began coming around to her cottage to talk boring political theory until three o'clock in the morning, seemingly convinced that she would want to sleep with him now, although she never had before, she told her friends she was quitting the Dublin Free Socialists.

They wouldn't let her quit. They welcomed her into their own group, but it turned out they were all eating their hearts out to wield a bit of parliamentary power themselves. They conspired to use Moira as their secret one-woman cadre working undercover for Dublin's smallest political party inside the heart of Dublin's second-smallest political party.

Her task was not an easy one. The Irish Unemployed Feminists— who were not all unemployed but had picked the name to convey their identification with Ireland's underclass (which, for the pejorative sound of it, they could not call the underclass) and because they were none of them employed where they wanted to be, at the top of the heap, so why not call themselves unemployed?—were extremely democratic among themselves. It often happened that she was given ten or twenty alternative strategies for the Free Socialists meeting, because every woman was encouraged to speak on every point.

Tonight, for instance, after Bridey forgot the keys to the Protestant University College classroom where they were to meet and had to go back to fetch them, causing the meeting to start forty-five minutes late, probably another twenty minutes were spent in reassuring her that she was a perfectly competent person. This made Bridey all the more abjectly apologetic, compelling her to confess, as she had done before, that she had had a low self-image ever since her convent-school days, when the nuns had made her bathe under a shift. Other convent-school memories of odd bathing rules poured forth then from the rest of the women, and somehow the evening's agenda was taken up an hour and ten minutes late.

What Bridey really should have been apologizing about was the demonstration outside the Taoiseach's department which forced Kavanagh's hand and gave him the excuse to go back on all his promises to Deirdre Fanning. But nobody wanted to tell her that. You didn't hit people in their weak spots in the IUF. It was one of their guiding principles. Women had been put down so long and so badly in Ireland, they should never put each other down within the group.

Not in a million years would one of them go accusing Bridey Nolan of sabotaging all the things she herself had worked for in behalf of the feminist cause just to get revenge on her ex-boyfriend. But they all knew that Bridey knew if Aloysius Kavanagh fell from power, so would Fergus. He was part of the New Coalition.

"So Houlihan is definitely coming? It's official, is it, Moira?" asked Claire, when the bathing shifts had been finally abandoned.

"Jesus, aren't we marvelous!" said Bridey, a little too cheekily.

"Well, I think it's quite an achievement," said Moira, "but Kavanagh is hopping mad. He told Deirdre we forced his hand and it's back to square one with our wish list."

"The bastard," said Maev.

"Deirdre says he might have been right about the timing," Moira added, trying not to cast her eyes in Bridey's direction.

"What do you mean, the timing? We've more women in the Dail now than ever," said Bridey.

"Well, it's the way Houlihan might be talking," said Moira. "Just when we're working on divorce. And they won't even look at abortion for at least another year."

"Irish women don't want abortion on demand, anyway," said Maev.

"No, only on request," said Bridey, looking arch.

"The Irish people will not vote for flat-out abortion," said Claire. "She's right. They think it's murder."

"And so it is," said Maev.

"So's spilling of the male seed murder," said Bridey, "anywhere outside an unobstructed vagina. We ought to put that in the constitution, too."

"Will you talk sense, Bridey!" said Maev.

"Well, she is right, you know, in the absolute sense," said Claire. "Oh, dear! Look at the time! We must let Moira go."

"What's my plan?" Moira asked.

"Get our wish list back into play," said Claire.

"Houlihan should visit the North," said Maev.

"What's the point?" said Bridey. "Aloysius Kavanagh's been voting the wrong way on women's issues since before we were born. I think we should dump him."

"I can identify with your feelings, Bridey," said Claire, "but where would we be then?"

"Forget Kavanagh. Concentrate on Houlihan. She's our ace," said Maev.

"Oh, Moira, you must go!" said Claire. "Good luck."

So she left for the Free Socialists meeting clueless, late, and ready to bring down any government for a nice bit of the supper they all forgot to factor in for her.

32

That same evening, a small, elegant dinner party was under way in the home of the British ambassador, Sir Trevor Drinkwater-Cummings, a Tory of the old school who took great pride in the fact that the Rolls-Royce which had driven him to Eton was still the functioning family car. He possessed vast estates in Scotland, but these could hardly sustain their gamekeepers' salaries, as all the family monies were tied up in

Johannesburg. Present along with the ambassador was his charming second wife, the former Rosella Buckingham, who had distinguished herself in London society during the two weeks of unpleasant publicity about her first husband's indiscretions with a certain pair of twins in the Italian aristocracy. The injured Rosella had faced the cameras each morning with quiet dignity as she took her youngest child off to nursery school, never appearing in the same outfit twice. Still quite a beauty, if gone a bit long in the jaw, she was said to have been absolutely wild about Ireland ever since what she referred to as "some silly women's magazine" put her on its Ten Best-Dressed Diplomatic Wives list.

Present also at this intimate gathering was the ambassador's private secretary, Alan Dreadfield, a young Tory definitely of the new school, whose father had made millions in the greeting-card line, as well as Archbishop Destino and his assistant, Bishop Meany.

It was a dinner that the Nuncio had looked forward to with some happiness. The British ambassador was known to possess a fabulous wine collection. He reportedly never bought anything less than a Grand Cru, and certainly no one had ever complained of the wines after one of his parties. Tonight the red wine was a velvety Pommard that passed over the tongue as sweetly as the old cat used to pass under his fingers when he was reading in the library of his Roman apartment, reminding him of the forbidden delectability of female flesh. Indeed, it was to the old cat he attributed his one transgression from the rule of celibacy, the softness of the old fellow becoming one day so excruciating as to lead then Bishop Destino into a half hour of frenzied carnality with a plump, silky-skinned maid who smelled deliciously of almonds. Already past the age of fifty when he succumbed, he was not crushed by guilt. He had seen too many cardinals dining with their mistresses to be shocked at himself. But it seemed ridiculous to have sullied his own unblemished record at such a late age. He knew he had done it out of curiosity really, so that he would know what he had been forgoing all those years. He had to admit to himself it had seemed better in his imagination. The real thing was too quick and too real. The hardest moment afterwards came, not in confession, but the next week, when the poor maid returned with love in her eyes and he had to send her away. She said she had not pleased him, causing him nearly to submit again, more out of pity than of lust. He hastily arranged for her to be transferred to a distant wing of the Vatican, and he thought of her almost daily for months afterwards and sometimes suffered fresh attacks of tender pity for her when the smell of almonds came wafting up from the street below. But that turned out to have been the last great flare-up of desire in his system, and he thanked the heavens for the mercies of age. Only on the rarest of occasions, such as now when drinking the exceptional wine, would there stir in him the recollection of the hope of a physical pleasure so dangerously absolute as to annihilate temporarily the fear of death, which was to say the fear of—

"Don't you think so, Nuncio?" asked the ambassador.

"I am sorry," he had to answer. "I have been, how you say, transporting myself on your most excellent wine. What is it you have asked?"

"Whether you didn't think it an awful pity the old thatched roofs are disappearing from the Irish countryside."

"I was not aware—I am afraid to say I have not been out of Dublin since I arrive here."

"Eow! That is a pity!" said Lady Rosella. "Sir Trevor and I have had the most delightful hols in County Kerry. You really must make an effort to get out of Dublin. You haven't seen Ireland until you've seen Kerry! The way they speak there is just too marvelous!"

"But we were regretting, weren't we, darling, that the thatched roofs are nearly extinct," said Sir Trevor. "Being replaced by those awful tin things. Most infelicitous. I do wish the Irish Georgian Society would concern themselves over matters like this."

"Oh, they'd only be looking after the tumble-down mansions," said Bishop Meany. "The Georgian Society's not for looking after pokey little cottages, sure it's not."

"Well, they ought to," said Sir Trevor. "We must get H.R.H. the Prince of Wales to give them a talking to. Ireland is losing its Irish look, and that's a great, great pity. But you've not been out of Dublin, Your Excellency? Rosella and I are going to visit Donegal in May."

"You'd be well advised not to go telling people in Donegal the place isn't Irish-looking enough for you," said Bishop Meany.

"Oh, dear, no! Of course, I would never say it to them!" said Sir Trevor hurriedly.

"It's a sore subject up there, they've sold off so many cottages to the Dutch and the Germans," said Bishop Meany. "There's the pity. But then the Irish have always been too poor to live in Ireland."

"Eow, I know!" said Lady Rosella. "And your young people are still flocking to London for jobs that just aren't there. It's still the highest birthrate in Western Europe, isn't it?"

"But, Rosella, what would we do without the Irish?" Sir Trevor hastened to put in. "Aren't they the most amusing people on earth? Don't we agree?"

"Oh, I adore the Irish!" said Rosella. "*I* don't mind their high birthrate. I want more and more of them. I simply feel sorry for the poor children who can't find any jobs."

"Well, we're all hoping the European Community will change that," said Alan Dreadfield.

"Yes, you have a few unemployed peoples in Britain yourselves," said the Nuncio.

"Oh, more than a few!" said Sir Trevor. "More than a few!"

"Is your government not worried about somebody popping over the border to take a shot at you?" Bishop Meany asked the ambassador, whose eyes registered a momentary fright, as if he were thinking this could be a veiled threat from the great Catholic conspiracy. "When you consider what they did to Mountbatten in a place like Sligo. We wouldn't like to see any harm come to you, Sir Trevor."

"Oh, my dear chap," he said breezily, quickly recovering, "Rosella and I are surrounded by the most bloody awful *cordon sanitaire* of security precautions, I can tell you. It's most unpleasant. They virtually send a fleet of minesweepers ahead of us wherever we go."

"I have not such security problems," said the Nuncio.

"No, I don't expect you would, not in Ireland!" said his host.

Destino wouldn't have minded a trip into the countryside beyond the Dublin Mountains. It was the plane ride to Knock Airport that Bishop Meany kept suggesting which held him in holy terror. He had read about the fogbound mountaintop runway.

"The Nuncio's health hasn't been so good," said Bishop Meany. "He's not used to the damp."

"Eow!" said Lady Rosella. "We English aren't afraid of a little damp, are we, darling?" She laughed happily.

"Nor we Scots," said Sir Trevor, causing a subtle shift in Lady Rosella's coloring.

"Sir Trevor is inexplicably proud of his Scottish background," said Alan Dreadfield, looking at Bishop Meany. "His ancestry goes back to McTaggert the Coward, who was quite a brilliant man on the battlefield, contrary to what the name suggests."

"I've heard of McTaggert the Coward," said the bishop. "He was afraid to sleep alone."

"That's right," said Sir Trevor. "How clever of you to know that! You see, Alan! Educated men know the facts. McTaggert was a brilliant soldier. It was at night when the fighting stopped that he was afraid."

"My own family have made many compromises with the Calabrian Mafia," said Archbishop Destino. "Ireland is not the only bloody country in the world, certainly. But I am thinking it has the most poets per hectare."

"Ah, yes!" said the ambassador. "Marvelous poets. Seamus Heaney and, and—"

"I am neither internee nor informer; an inner émigré," said Dreadfield. Everyone looked alarmed.

"Oh, sorry! Just quoting a bit of Heaney," he said.

"Of course!" said Lady Rosella. "I should have known. An inner émigré."

"I have a question for you, Archbishop Destino," said young Dreadfield, growing bold after his poetic flight. "How does the Irish Catholic Church compare to the Italian?"

"I am not qualified to answer such a question, Mr. Dreadfield—"

"Surely you are, Nuncio—"

"I am not qualified because I have been all my life until now in the Curia. That is Vatican administration, as I'm sure you know. Before Vatican II, I would have said there was no difference, all in Latin, uniformly the same. Now I am not completely sure of the differences. The Irish bishops seem more concerned about sins of the flesh perhaps than do bishops in Italy. Do you think I am right, Bishop Meany?"

The bishop had as yet said nothing to him about the pregnant cook's helper, but he seemed to have taken on a new air of wounded deference in the last day or so.

"Well, we've not had legalized divorce or abortion here," the bishop said a bit woodenly.

"Well, all signs are you will soon have, Bishop," said Sir Trevor. "Don't you think, Nuncio, or perhaps you might know the answer to my question also, Bishop Meany," he continued, now looking down at his name card, which Rosella had done so lovingly in her awful girlish lettering. "I mean, abortion is one thing, distasteful business— but don't you think it will bring the North and South ever so much closer together, divorce?"

"That sounds so strange, the way you put it," said Archbishop Destino.

"The problem in the North is injustice," said Bishop Meany.

"Oh, I quite agree with you," said Sir Trevor, "and it has been the view of the Crown for some time that if we could only convince those appalling Protestants to play fair and be good chaps we'd have half the battle won right there—"

"Sir Trevor is of course speaking very much off-the-record, Your Eminences," interjected young Dreadfield.

"But of course they understand that, Alan!" said the ambassador with swift condescension. "Where was I?"

"Divorce, dear," said Lady Rosella sweetly.

"Yes, don't you think the referendum will create a giant step toward peace?"

"I don't know what you call peace," said Bishop Meany. "Or what you think divorce has to do with it. What is your English divorce doing for your unemployment situation?"

"What about your soccer hooligans? What is your legal divorce doing for them?" the Nuncio asked. He hated coming to Meany's aid, but Sir Trevor's tone was peculiarly irksome. It sounded colonialistic.

"You Irish do throw the soccer hooligans in our faces at every opportunity," said Sir Trevor.

"The Nuncio is Italian," said Bishop Meany in a velvety voice. "But, as pertaining to the subject of divorce: the Irish people have always voted their highest beliefs on the subject in the past. They would not see that they should sell out their principles for the sake of a so-called peace, Ambassador. That would not be a peace. That would be more of a capitulation."

A nervous silence ensued.

"Well, we're all in for a jolly time now with the American Vice President coming amongst us, I'm sure!" said Sir Trevor in the heartiest of good-host voices.

"It's confirmed that she's coming, then, is it?" asked Bishop Meany.

"Yes, just yesterday. It's altogether an extraordinary time of year for her to be coming. Absolutely the bleakest in terms of weather," said Sir Trevor.

"We've had a terrible spell of it this year altogether," said Bishop Meany.

"I find it amazing the way the Irish never cease to be surprised by their own climate," said Alan Dreadfield.

"I adore the Irish climate!" said Lady Rosella. "So good for the complexion. Shall we, then?" And with that she pushed back her chair.

The others rose also. Lady Rosella excused herself to let the gentlemen pass around the cigars and brandy. The Nuncio asked for the powder room. The ambassador did not even blink at his error and quickly directed him to a downstairs loo. He was about to steer Bishop Meany to another loo when the bishop said, " 'Tis all right, Your Excellency. I know the way."

•   •   •

"One forgets how long that fellow has been around," Sir Trevor said to his private secretary, with whom he was now alone in the smoking room, each of them lighting a Cuban cigar. "It's so unfortunate for the Nuncio. Nice man. Bit testy on divorce. I thought you told me our file said he was a liberal."

"You won't find out what Destino's going to do as long as Meany's hanging around," said Dreadfield. "I'll have to divert him. I still say a phone tap would be easier."

"The Foreign Office isn't keen on that sort of thing anymore, Alan. We're supposed to be working hand-in-hand these days. The Irish are extremely sensitive about their former masters, you must remember."

"But this would be the Vatican, not the Irish."

"The Irish might not see it that way."

"They needn't find out."

"Have a go at diverting the bishop for me. There's a good chap."

The Nuncio returned first. Dreadfield went off in search of the bishop.

Destino declined cigars and brandy but asked for more of the "most excellent wine." The ambassador lit his own cigar again and the two men walked over to the fireplace.

"We're a little concerned," said Sir Trevor. "That is, there is *some* speculation in the FO that this Virgin Mary figure might be a hoax, and we are just quite worried that whoever is behind it might want to —well, you can imagine how inflammatory the Protestants would find it if the figure were to appear in Belfast."

"Inflammatory?" said the Nuncio, taking a ruminative swallow.

"Yes, you see, Irish Protestants, well, some Irish Protestants venerate the Virgin like yourselves, but the majority of Irish Protestants feel quite strongly that the Virgin has got out of hand as a symbol, that she's sort of taken over for God in the Catholic Church. I'm not defending them, heavens, no! I'm merely trying to explain to you how they would see it if she were to appear in their—"

"It would be tending to say to them that Henry VIII was a blasphemer after all, yes?"

"Well—but if they thought someone, a human hand, was behind this and was causing the Virgin to appear in order to taunt them—"

"Whose human hand?" said Padre Destino. "Do you know this person?"

"Oh, my goodness gracious, no! And I do not even mean to be suggesting that we know finally whether there *is* a human hand behind her—Nuncio, what has the Church been saying about this, this vision?"

"Most often we say nothing about such matters."

"Is there any concern, is the Church trying to find the source—if there is a source—?"

"Rome is considering all questions relevant."

"Ah. Well, I hope you wouldn't have any objection to others, and indeed, if you would like us to lend you investigators, we would be happy to. Perhaps the British Museum, which helped to prove that the Shroud of Turin was a fake, a very old fake, mind you—but you must understand, the PM is really quite worried that whoever's behind this will take it up North. The Northern Ireland Office are beside themselves. Nothing like this has ever happened before, you see. I mean, they had the Pope here, but he gave a really tremendous speech about the violence, and he didn't go to Belfast, splendid chap that he is. You've got a winner there. What a man with the crowds! The trouble with this Virgin business is we don't know who to talk to about it, which is why, well, we've had to turn to you. I mean, how could we ask the Irish government to deal with a thing like this?"

"You are telling me you think the Virgin inflames this war in the North?"

"Has the potential to, Nuncio. Oh, yes. Oh, very much so."

"This is a strange country."

"It is unique," said the ambassador.

"What if she is not a hoax?" Destino could not resist asking him.

"Then I suppose we shall have to rely upon your prayers to guide her," said Sir Trevor, and he laughed heartily at the joke of it.

Archbishop Destino gave him a polite smile. He was actually relieved to see the wary face of Bishop Meany, who returned just then with Alan Dreadfield. Lady Rosella, too, reappeared, looking bright-faced and freshly kempt.

"Now, Archbishop Destino," she said, sipping gracefully from a glass of mineral water, "you simply must tell me what the Pope thought of Princess Diana."

33

"*Y*ou've got strange women calling my house, Angus. Aileen's beginning to suspect something."

"Donal, the difficulty seems to be, the Guards have no record of holding your truck in the Dun Laoghaire yard."

"I explained that to you, Angus. They were embarrassed. The bloody thing disappeared out from under their noses."

The two friends were sitting in a construction caravan beside the half-finished McGaffney Estates on the outskirts of Leopardstown. Donal's crew had long since gone home. The little office was freezing. Donal had offered Angus tea or whiskey, but his friend took nothing. They sat in their overcoats. Angus kept his gloves on.

"You did something you had never done before, you were that desperate for money."

"I'll not deny that."

"They think you might be lying."

"What would be the point of that, Angus? You know I'm a man of my word. Look, I even offered to do without the money. I know I fucked up."

"The best liars are people who've never lied before."

"Angus, what the hell am I meant to have done with that bloody half a ton of Semtex?"

"Sold it to an organization with a bigger bank account."

"Like who? The fucking Sultan of Brunei?"

"There are several possibilities in the Middle East."

"Angus, I don't know any organizations in the Middle East. You are the only terrorist I know. Jesus, Angus, if I had sold off your Semtex, do you think I'd be hanging around here? I'd have to be totally fucking daft!"

"This is probably the last time we can meet on this matter, Donal."

"Angus, you're not going to desert me now."

"We have reason to believe the Guards might be aware of something."

"Now, that's great news!" said Donal. "I'm facing either assassination or jail. That's bloody fucking wonderful news. The Guards know. Can't you Provos keep any secrets anymore?"

"Calm down, Donal. I said they knew something. They don't know anything about you. It's just best that you and I not be seen together right now."

"Well, you can tell your friends not to call my home, then."

"I agree it's unwise. But they have to satisfy themselves that you have told the truth."

"Angus, for the love and honor of Jesus, our fathers fought together. How could you even think I would do such a stupid thing?"

"It is not what I think at this point, Donal."

"Why do you sound so strange, Angus? Holy Christ, you're not going to shoot me out here, are you, Angus?"

"We are not fascists, Donal. We do not kill people for making mistakes."

"But you said yourself they don't believe me."

"They don't disbelieve you, either. They want the goods in the truck."

"I followed your instructions to the letter."

"Then why hasn't the truck shown up?"

"You think they're bloody just going to hand it back? They're common thieves, Angus, criminals."

"They won't want to stand in the way of a United Ireland."

"I'll tell them you said that, Angus Keenan, if I ever hear from them again."

"If you do, use the same method as before, but tell them to choose a different pub. Tell them they're under orders to return the truck. Send me a postcard of Dalkey Island, unsigned, of course, if you hear from them. If we get no results, someone else may contact you. You'll receive a postcard of Dalkey Island and you'll know to look for someone with a white umbrella on top of Killiney Hill the following morning at half nine. Understood?"

"Yes, I understand. What does your wife think when you get unsigned postcards, Angus?"

"Let's hope you're the one to send the postcard. Do you always work this late?"

"What's going to happen if the truck never turns up, Angus? What if these are the people who took Shergar?"

"I believe you, Donal. 'Bye for now," said Angus, and he stepped out into the darkness and was gone.

34

When Moira finally arrived at the Dublin Free Socialists meeting, she found to her astonishment that the group actually was considering a motion to bring down the Kavanagh government. But bringing down the government was only incidental to their purpose. They were angry with Fergus for the way he had stopped listening to their advice, and they wanted him to resign from the Dail and submit to extensive criticism sessions to make him a good socialist again. They had got sidetracked onto an exchange about what precisely constituted a good socialist anymore at all when Moira entered their shabby meeting hall above the Dawson Street Yoga Studio.

"Now, that's a debate and a half that you're into there," said one of the older members. "Someone'll be citing Cuba to us in a minute."

"*What's he talking about?*" Moira whispered to her seat mate.

"*They're mad at Fergus for getting above himself,*" came the answer. "*He's gone and hired a secretary without authorization from the party.*"

"*Sounds like Fergus,*" she whispered back. "*Are they going to make him fire her?*"

"*No, they're going to make him resign.*"

"You can't do this when Houlihan's coming to visit!" Moira jumped up to protest. "You'll put her off! Can't we rise above our differences here? We've got a divorce referendum to pass. Listen, we can all become pure bloody socialists when we control the Dail. We've got one vote! The people are sick of elections, besides! They don't want another election. They've had three in the last three years."

"I see our co-chairperson has finally arrived," said Paul Feeny, who seemed to be leading the attack on Fergus. "It is the people who are demanding the overthrow of the government, you would have learned if you had been present for the first hour of our discussion. Or if you had at least been listening to your radio. Have you gone off timekeepers altogether, Moira?"

In point of fact, she had not been listening to her radio, as it was broken and the fellow down the road who usually fixed it for a few quid and nothing said to the tax man was away in Portugal, presumably fixing radios tax-free there.

Moira sat down to whisper to her seat mate again. *"What's he talking about?"*

"Rumors of a new cigarette tax. The country's up in arms. But Feeny doesn't care. He wants to get Fergus."

That really was a hard choice, divorce or affordable cigarettes. She was never going to get married herself. But she mustn't just think of herself. She raised her hand to speak.

"I think it would be a very elitist, selfish move for us to take Fergus out of the Dail just to please ourselves," she said.

"Fergus is the fuckin' elitist!" shouted someone near the front.

"How's that, Moira?" asked another helpfully.

"Well, for us to be worrying about the finer points of our purity when there's social legislation to be passed and the divorce referendum. I think we'd be very selfish to let all that go by the boards only so we could teach Fergus O'Sullivan a lesson in humility, as much as he might need it."

"Thanks a lot, Moira," said Fergus sardonically.

"Could we adjourn before the pubs close, please!" someone yelled from the back.

"Is that a motion?" asked Fergus.

"There's a motion already on the floor!" yelled Feeny in fury.

"Yes, it is, and I'll second it, too!" said the one in the back.

"He can't do that!" yelled a friend of Feeny's.

But Fergus quickly called for ayes and nays and the ayes overwhelmingly had it. He adjourned the meeting.

• • •

They usually went to Buswell's after their meetings because one of the bartenders there was a Dublin Free Socialist and had a talent for fiddling the cash register. That was out of the question tonight, of course, with the pilgrims still lined up for blocks to get in.

They headed instead for the Black Bull down by Protestant University College, going at a fierce clip and sending runners on ahead to put in drinks orders before last call. Moira tagged along. She feared Fergus would be out to get her now for the remark about the lesson in humility. And Bridey would be pissed at her for defending him at all. There just was no way to keep everybody happy. Anyway, that was such a pre-feminist kind of a worry, it made her cringe to think of it. She hated being such a nice person. Everybody ended up distrusting her politics.

"I like the way you handled yourself tonight," said Kathy McGee, a tall, serene young woman who had fallen into step beside her. "It was a relief to hear someone stand up for us. I'm not sure I know what you meant by elitism, though."

"I'm not sure myself," said Moira, "but I'll murder you if you tell anybody I said that."

"Moira, you know me," said Kathy, but in truth Moira only slenderly knew her. Kathy had arrived one evening fresh from the Dawson Street Yoga Studio looking as though she might still be in a daze of deep relaxation. Fergus used to remark unkindly behind her back that she must have confused the Free Socialists with the Free Spiritualists, who met in the same quarters the second Thursday of the month, when the Socialists met on the Tuesday.

"Look what's happened!" Kathy said.

There on the bonnet of Paul Feeny's old banger of a fifth-hand Mercedes stood the glowing figure of the Virgin Mary.

"Who has done this to me?" Feeny cried in a panicky voice. "Somebody's trying to fuck me!"

The others were hanging back. Only Fergus, well aware that he was the leader of this group, had the nerve to come forward and observe the Virgin full frontally. Feeny himself was standing a little off to one side.

"Now's your chance to become the savior of Ireland, Feeny," said Fergus sneeringly. "Just drive her away. Take her out to Sandymount to the all-night car wash, why don't you?"

"Would you ever bugger off! You drive her yourself, you're such a model socialist gobshite," said Feeny, and he threw his keys at Fergus's feet. "I need a drink!" he uttered, stalking off.

Fergus did not immediately pick up the keys.

Suddenly Kathy McGee darted over the road and scooped them up. "Come on, Moira," she said. "Let's go for a ride."

There was nothing for it but Moira must get into the car beside Kathy, while the others hung back watching. Kathy started the motor with ease and off they drove into the Dublin night, the Virgin Mother of Our Lord glowing before them like some kind of holy portrait made of light. But after half a block the Virgin wobbled, then skipped over to a nearby shop window, slid along it, and disappeared.

35

$\mathcal{T}$he following morning dawned bright and crisp. Mrs. Gertrude Crookshanks was out early, walking her huge wolfhound, Horace. She saw no drunken priests this morning, only Dennis McDermott in his study window with a dark face on him, and then she remembered that word he had used the other day which she had forgotten to look up. Gonads.

"And isn't it just like a spoiled priest to be talking riddles to an old widow lady like me, Horace?" she said to her vast dog as she came back into her house, and straightaway she went to the dictionaries her father gave her with high hopes they would accompany her to university, the dear deluded man. The closest she ever got to that was taking a shortcut through Protestant University College to meet Michael on the sly.

Gonads wasn't in Collins Junior or Collins Senior.

She wandered into her kitchen, feeling a bit at loose ends, as if she'd misplaced something important but couldn't think what it was.

"I'll find him out yet, Horace," she said, while the dog eyed her sympathetically. "I'll go look it up at Noleen's house. But first I'll bake her a poppyseed cake. She won't want me coming around before the Gay Byrne Show is over, sure she won't. She dotes on that man, Horace. It's not half healthy."

The dog seemed to agree with her. Horace had such an intelligent look.

Gertrude switched on the radio as she rooted through the cupboards, assembling her ingredients. Gay was entertaining a very dull guest who wanted to talk about raising tuberose begonias and hare coursing. She'd been invited on to discuss homemade Christmas wreaths. Gay resorted to taking calls from the listeners until he got three in a row about hare coursing, after which he put on an old recording of the "Tennessee Waltz."

"Poor Noleen!" said Gertrude as she tucked the cake into the oven. "She'll be bored starkers this morning."

Gertrude went off upstairs to make the bed and tidy up. Whatever it was about the day, she had a fierce amount of energy. And with one thing and another, she would have completely forgotten about the cake if it hadn't been for Horace's barking. He started to growl and bellow as though he had seen the devil and his mother coming up the walk.

"Now, who could that be, I wonder?" said Gertrude, looking at her watch and giving a quick glance around the sitting room for unsightly dust.

"Oh, the cake! Oh, my goodness!" she exclaimed, but first she rushed to the front door and opened it. There was no one there.

Horace was still barking as though his life depended on it, but he seemed to be barking in the kitchen. Children came to the back door. Perhaps it was one of those tinkers begging again.

"I knew I should never have started giving them money, poor things," said Gertrude. "Their parents only spend it on drink. What is it, Horace? Quiet yourself, now. All right, all right, I'm coming!" And she sped into the kitchen to find Horace cowering in the far corner, scrunched down in the stalking-lion position, his eyes fixed on the figure of the Virgin Mary hovering over his chipped white-enamel water dish.

"It's herself!" declared Gertrude, falling into a chair and hardly daring to breathe, unable to move yet seized with a terrible urge to flee.

She was awfully glad when she came to her senses that she had been paralytic with shock in those first few moments. Otherwise, she would have gone off and left the Virgin Mary staring at her vile kitchen floor.

Doesn't she know I'm a Protestant? she wanted to say to Horace, but she did not yet utter a word. She felt light-headed and weak in the limbs, the way she always had when the children were almost killed running over the road in front of cars. Was it to let her know she was about to die? And did the presence of the Virgin mean automatic absolution? Not that she needed it, from all those years of living among Catholics.

She's telling me that I am a Catholic now, Gertrude suddenly thought, sliding her eyes over in the direction of the corner. The Blessed Virgin was still there. Her face seemed to be smiling, yet she seemed faintly sorrowful. She's saying that it's happened from all my years of spending Christmas with Noleen and all my secret times with the holy water and crossing myself. It's happened just the way Claire warned me it would if I didn't keep my distance. Oh, God, I'll never tell Claire about this, never in a million years, not with my dying breath. I'll never tell anyone.

"*Stamp out scour!*" She heard the radio ad, and she snapped to and said, "Oh, Jesus, the cake!" She rushed to take the cake out of the oven and of course burned herself in two places.

"Shut up, Horace!" she said, as if the dog's barking had made her clumsy, "Horace, do be quiet."

Really she was worried someone might be passing the house and think she was in trouble and come bursting in on her with the Virgin right there. He was such a silly dog. The children had insisted she keep a dog. They all lived halfway around the world and probably thought she was more lonely than she was.

But at least the cake hadn't got burnt. So, now what? What does a poor respectable sixty-six-year-old Protestant widow living in Ireland do when the Virgin Mary appears in her kitchen? She couldn't exactly call up Gay Byrne and ask. Even if she didn't give her name, Noleen would recognize her voice.

She decided, while she was pondering what to do, to ice the cake and mop the horrible kitchen floor and get on down to Noleen's as fast as her legs would carry her.

Noleen sat up when she came in.

"Hello, Horace!" she said heartily. "I thought she'd never bring you to see me. She thinks I'm allergic to you."

"I've brought you a poppyseed cake with butterscotch icing," said Gertrude. "Oh, that's right! Your allergies. We'll put Horace in the back garden."

"Mother's not meant to have sweets," said Maureen, the daughter, looking awfully posh and haughty with her way of tossing her gleaming straight hair back over her shoulder. She was married to Prince Charles's scalp therapist and was only over visiting to help her mother since the operation.

"I'm sure a little bit wouldn't hurt, darling," said Noleen. "Why don't you go around to the shops now I've got some company. You need a bit of fresh air."

"It's gorgeous out," said Gertrude. "The Rrrreverrrend Boxley was out taking the air," she said, pursing her lips to mock his social pretension.

Noleen laughed. Her daughter did not.

"You really shouldn't have brought her that cake," she said sternly. "She's not meant to eat sweets."

"Well, she'll give most of it to her friends," said Gertrude. "You know her."

Maureen didn't soften. She put on her beautiful, creaseless English mac and went off unsmiling, flinging her hair back as she faced the street.

The minute the door slammed, Noleen was up on her feet and running to the kitchen to put on the kettle. Gertrude let Horace out into the back garden.

"What are you doing?" she asked her friend. "Are you meant to be up and about?"

"I've been up and about the whole time, you eejit! It's only for her that I'm poorly."

Noleen did suddenly look fully recovered. It was only a few gallstones, after all.

"Perhaps it's time you let her know. Two weeks is a long time for a young woman to be away from her husband. I expect it's rather a fast crowd he moves in."

"There's something wrong there," said Noleen. "That's why I've been holding on to her. I was hoping she'd say something. But, Gertie, she hardly speaks of him."

"They don't have children, amn't I right?"

"They do not, and it's been five years now."

"They're very young, though, when you think of it."

"Gertie, this cake is only gorgeous!" said Noleen, licking a bit of icing off her finger. "I'm starving, absolutely starving! She won't feed me anything. Carrot juice. It gives you the gas."

"Have a go at it, Noleen. I'll pretend I ate the half of it."

Noleen cut herself a hefty piece and gave Gertrude another. She poured out tea, and the two of them sat at Noleen's old stained kitchen table listening to each other's contentment.

"You've always had the fine touch, Gertrude. Culinary genius, you are."

"I don't know about that at all," she said. "What about this talk of changing the government?"

"It's been in the air ever since the rumors about the budget, and imagine telling her she can't come here. I mean, she is a bit different to us, but all the same."

"I suppose it will be Foyle again."

"The awful polished up sleeveen that he is. That wasn't true about his girlfriend, by the way. She didn't have an abortion when she went in for that procedure in London. It was the liposuction."

"Liposuction? Does Peter go in for that sort of thing? Doesn't it sound disgusting, Noleen! Weren't we lucky to be born in Ireland when we were and allowed to grow old as we pleased!"

"Peter's strictly a scalp man, my dear. He has nothing to do with anything below the cranium. Do you suppose that's their problem?" she giggled.

"That reminds me! Could I look at your dictionary? Do you have the one Patrick used at university?"

"Try his room. The shelf around to the left."

The Collins Compact. She found it straightaway, and there was "gonad": "Noun in biology. An organ that produces sex cells."

How had he put it? Envies my powerful gonads. Clutching the dictionary, she ran downstairs to tell Noleen what Dennis McDermott had said to her.

"That man's so full of himself," said Noleen. "Did you know it's because of him there's been no Fionn Mac Cumhaill Prize for the last three years? It was in Rupert Penrose's column this morning."

"There's no love lost between those two."

"Penrose says he's been costing the writers of Ireland thousands and thousands of pounds. He thinks nothing he reads is good enough, seemingly. All the judges have to agree."

"That explains the black look on his face this morning."

"Well, it is awful if it's true. Think of the poor writers, Gertie. Three years without a prize."

"She's coming up the walk, Noleen. Do you want her to see you out of bed?"

"No!" shrieked the invalid, and she ran like a healthy woman of twenty back to her sickbed.

"Mother, you and Gertrude have eaten half the cake!" Maureen shouted from the kitchen.

"We wanted to leave some for you, dear," called Noleen in a sweet invalid's voice.

They heard Maureen stomp into the sitting room and turn on the TV.

"Don't mind her," said Noleen. "She's saving me from myself. That's not easy without Sky Television."

"She loves you," said Gertrude. "But you should send her home."

"I know," said Noleen, sighing. And, after a pause, "She's upset because someone's been telling more lies about Charles."

"Not more tape-recorded ones?"

"People say all sorts of things to their scalp therapist, apparently."

"I heard he was getting the hair transplants," said Gertrude.

"Yes, that's false, you see. But somebody's found out he's seeing Peter, who can do the transplants if you want them."

"But that's nothing," said Gertrude.

"Oh, you and I know that, but try telling Maureen. She's deathly afraid the Prince is going to drop Peter."

"Poor things," said Gertrude. "It's such a small bald spot."

She soon said her goodbyes and took Horace out the long way home. She had kept her silence about the Virgin. She and Noleen were of a generation that could make most of life's problems go away by not talking about them.

36

This morning for the first time since arriving in Dublin, Rock was truly hungry. He had decided he was going to eat an Irish breakfast, quite an ego trip for a man who had lived with a serious vegetarian for ten years. Rock's ex-wife, Brenda, had been such a food purist that she refused to get pregnant for fear that it would make her want to eat the wrong things. She even taught his mother to cook tofu when Mrs. O'Leary came to visit one weekend and never left. It was an emotionally deadening experience, having those two women plot together to make him live to be a hundred on foods with no tooth resistance at all. It took all the spark out of him, so Brenda fell for one of her students. Rock knew his marriage was dead when he spotted her sitting across from the handsome young brute, looking as though she might drown in his gaze, at a small table for two in McDonald's. She had never let Rock take her to McDonald's.

His mother learned Brenda's cooking style so well that after Brenda left there was no change of menu. Consequently, Ireland in the middle of winter hadn't seemed such a bad prospect. To a meat-and-potatoes man, it was a regular Shangri-la.

Rock's mouth was watering with pleasure as his food arrived in the Bloom's Hotel restaurant, steaming and swimming in grease, when along came Dermot Muldoon, with his air of smug, self-satisfied pessimism that marked him as a really top man in the civil service.

"How can you eat that revolting stuff?" he asked, peering disdainfully at Rock's ham, sausage, egg, and potato. "Fills your veins with fat, you know. Highest heart-attack rate in the whole world's right here in Ireland. Eating the Ulster Fry. That's what you've got there."

"You sound like Brenda."

"Who's Brenda?"

"My ex-wife."

"She must be a sensible woman. Would she like to meet a shabby Irish civil servant? I have a wife of my own somewhere, but she won't admit to it."

"Sorry, Brenda's already taken."

"Ah, a reconciliation. How touching."

"She didn't come back to me. She's got someone else."

"Oh, I am sorry. Perhaps she didn't like sharing you with the Vice President."

"My regular job's with the President. This is a special assignment."

"You're to keep Houlihan in line, is that it? We wish you all success, by the way. The slightest glitch could cause our present government to collapse. And whatever about her being blown up, if the government falls when your woman is here, it could be awkward," said Dermot, handing him the Irish *Times*, as if to illustrate his government's nervousness. Rock saw:

VIRGIN QUITS BUSWELL'S
ATOP SOCIALIST MERCEDES
THEN VANISHES.

Down the page was a story about the Kavanagh government being in a shaky position after rumors of a proposed new cigarette tax had circulated. Chances were Houlihan wouldn't come if the government fell before next week. The President could pawn her off on some other country.

"Nobody keeps Houlihan in line," said Rock.

"That's what our Taoiseach seemed to dread," said Dermot. "Many courtesies can be dropped during Dail campaigns. We would hate to see her embarrassed."

[148]

"She's not easily embarrassed," said Rock. "She was Miss Sarasota, don't forget."

Dermot nodded in glum acknowledgment.

"My job is to advance her trip," said Rock. "Nobody wants my advice on the wisdom of it."

• • •

Dermot took him to see Chief Superintendent Fionn Bloom, head of the Special Branch, which was meant to be the receptacle of all knowledge about the IRA. Bloom did look the part, with neatly trimmed white hair and a steady, faintly suffering gaze, the expression of a clean man spending his life considering society's garbage.

"I'm afraid I can't tell you much," he said, predictably enough. No police force in the world liked to share with outsiders. "We don't know much ourselves. We get so many rumors about arms shipments. We'd be searching every boat and lorry that comes into Dublin if we believed them all. But half a ton would give you pause. It looks like *some* sort of a shipment is missing. The Provos are conducting an investigation."

"You guys should join forces," Rock said pleasantly.

"Excuse me, Chief, but your son's French class is here," said an officer who poked his head in the door.

"Thanks, John. Show them in to the conference room."

"We've all the maps in there, Chief. The Semtex maps!"

"It's the Belvedere senior French class. I think we can trust them."

"Of course we can, Chief."

The officer disappeared.

"Half a ton of Semtex could be a bitch to hide," said Rock. "In such a small country."

"Ever hear of a race horse called Shergar?" said the Chief Superintendent.

"No," said Rock. "Why?"

"Doesn't matter," said Bloom. "The horse was hijacked years ago. We never found it."

"He's trying to tell you that the Irish as a race are innately reluctant to come to the aid of a police investigation of any sort whatsoever, except perhaps in cases of sexual deviance or nonpolitical murders that strike them as particularly unjust," said Dermot. "Am I right, Chief Superintendent?"

[149]

"You must have a lot of unsolved crimes," Rock said before Bloom could answer.

"I'm afraid we do," Bloom said. "Do you have the woman's itinerary?"

"Not yet," said Dermot.

"Ah, well—" Bloom started to dismiss them.

"She wants to see the Virgin," said Rock. "The paper says she disappeared last night. What's the story there?"

"I could be cute and tell you to read the Bible," said Bloom.

"Buswell's must have horrified her," said Dermot.

Bloom was searching through papers on his desk. "I was just going over my notes when you came in." He opened a file. "There's nothing, not a common thread. I've had my men inspect the site for one consistency. That's all we need is the one. But there's not even a connection between the people in those places. Your one man was an important Catholic spokesman, and it stood him to his advantage, I would say, so there's a motive there. But why the others? They didn't know him. McGaffney had met Foyle, I guess, but it was only to shake his hand. It's actually quite amazing that we haven't a clue. We know more about the birth of Jesus than we do about this strange image. At this point in time. I've no doubt we'll get to the bottom of it eventually. Someone reports on the strange goings-on around the appearances of the Virgin, he won't feel like he's giving the national honor away, you know, which some would with a load of Semtex. Wrong-headed, but they would. I'm convinced it's in a van," he concluded, tapping his finger on the final page in the file. "You see, it would take a sizable telegenic device to do this. We think it interacts somehow with the normal wiring in a house. It would be a sizable device. But there's no consistency in the cars parked around these places. We've been speculating that it might even be someone in RTE having his little bit of fun."

"Didn't they say it appeared on a car last night?" asked Rock.

"Oh, those were the socialists out drinking," said Bloom. "They might not have been seeing what they thought they were seeing."

•　•　•

The Minister for Women's Affairs was next on their tour. She offered them tea and brewed it herself from an electric kettle she kept on a shelf behind her desk.

"Old habits die hard," she said, smiling sweetly at her visitors. "Anything in it?"

"No sugar," said Rock.

"That's right, you Americans are going to conquer death," she said. "We still die in Ireland. It's expected of us. What do you think of Ireland?"

"Great breakfasts," said Rock.

"I like you," she said. "How ever did you get a name like Rock? Suits your profession. And you look solid. But how was your mother to know that? Did she give you the name? She did? Do you like your job, Rock? Is it thrilling to guard those people? Do you know all their secrets? Is it true what they say about her and him?"

Rock sipped his tea and tried to look implacable. "Nice office you've got here," he said.

"Ach, it'll do," she said, "for something approximating dignity. So, you're discreet enough, are you? I suppose they wouldn't have sent you if you weren't. And you, Dermot Muldoon, if you ever breathe a word of this, I'll have you promoted to counselor in the mission to the Malvinas. The thing is this, gentlemen, we're coming up to some very sensitive negotiations over a whole list of women's issues here, and it is simply not the time to have anyone talking about abortion on demand."

"Nobody controls what Houlihan says," Rock told her. "The President has some sensitive negotiations coming up, too."

"We can keep the press away from her and just let her go for photo opportunities," said Dermot. "But we'd need the manpower. How many agents will you have, do you think?"

"Fifty, sixty," said Rock.

"But that means you have only fifteen to twenty on duty at a given time, am I right?" said Dermot.

"Right," said Rock.

"That won't be enough if we have big crowds," said the minister. "Dermot, you must get Foreign Affairs to put in a request for more agents."

"Yes, we'll do that."

"You can restrict crowds if you never publish her schedule," said Rock.

"Yes, and the airport greeting group will be by invitation only," said Deirdre. "Believe it or not, we're having trouble rounding up enough dignitaries to go out there. Her staff has asked me to put her in touch with our feminists. I think a selective group, you know, might be good for the photo at the airport.

"Now, what worries me," the minister continued, leaning forward toward Rock, "is the fact that your agents don't know what our reporters look like. We'll need somebody working with you who can familiarize you with the ones who might try to get around our system. And I think I have just the person for you. Moira McNamara, my speech writer. Don't mind how she dresses. She's got a good head on her."

3 7

$\mathcal{T}$he dinner with the British ambassador had softened Destino's view of Meany, and in the morning the bishop had kindly let him sleep in, which meant that he awoke after the sun was up and streaming into his bedroom. Ireland was not so dreadful.

He smelled the mothballs again, however, when Bishop Meany came in to him at his breakfast, interrupting him in the pages of *Ulysses*.

"I don't like to bother you over small household details," said the bishop, "but I'm afraid it's the cook again. With respect, Nuncio, he's taken advantage of your kindness with the girl in the kitchen. She's not of good character."

He was holding his head at an angle which made his glasses catch the light, so that the Nuncio could not see his expression.

"I understand she had nowhere to go," he told the bishop.

"There's plenty of places she can go. We've a fine list of homes for girls in her situation. She knows that. She likes it here. The cook's wife is looking after her. It's interfering with the household routine."

"We cannot turn away a girl in her condition, Bishop."

"Nuncio, Excellency, that girl will steal us blind."

"I have made my decision, Bishop."

"Very well," said Meany, obediently enough. Yet Destino had a very shallow feeling of triumph. How could he assert control over territory Meany knew so much better?

"I wanted you to know, Nuncio, I've been making some progress with the horoscopes," he said. "I've been planting the idea in some influential minds about changing them to advice to the lovelorn. That's hardly better, I know, but it's not guessing at God's intentions."

• • •

To the Nuncio's great delight, the morning routine was abandoned. Bishop Meany had an errand in town. The Nuncio took his heavy book into the library.

Marco came sneaking in to him there an hour later.

"Oh, my God, Nuncio, what have I done?" he exclaimed, holding his hands to his head tragically. "This girl is a catastrophe! She is using my Visa card!"

It seemed that Marco's wife had taken pity on the pregnant girl, bulging as she was out of her last pair of sweatpants and without a maternity dress to her name. The two women had gone to Grafton Street together to see what could be done. A great deal, apparently, in three hours' time if you knew what you were after. The women had spent over three thousand pounds, and nothing was returnable. It was all final sale.

"I am finished, Excellency! That's ten weeks' pay! What will I do?"

"Never mind, Marco, I will pay this bill."

"Oh, Excellency, but you must not! You are a saint! Let me kiss your hand!"

Feeling that he had set a dangerous precedent, Padre Destino went deeper into the recesses of his library and resumed his furtive reading.

Bishop Meany came in to him there shortly before lunch. "You've a phone call," he said coldly. "It's Father O'Mahoney. I did warn you about him."

"He gives up his drinking now," said Padre Destino.

"They all say that around Christmas, when the hangovers get to them. Have you only just begun to read *Ulysses*? It's old hat, you know, here in Ireland."

The bishop had the good grace to leave him alone for his conversation with Father Liam.

"How are you, my friend?" Padre Destino asked him.

"Wondering what's so great about life if there's no whiskey in it."

"I am sorry. Perhaps you will feel better soon."

"I was thinking about your proposal."

"My proposal?"

"That we should purchase the secret of the Virgin."

"Oh, that! It is quite wrong of me."

"I think we should do it. If you've got the money there."

"What has made you change your mind?"

"Better ourselves than anyone else, I was thinking. Do you still have the letter?"

"Yes. I have kept it in my bedside table." He had it tucked inside "Abstinence and Christ's Example."

"Could you get the money?"

"Certainly. Yes."

"What do you think? Would you give it a try?"

He said he would, and his heart began to beat faster. The extent of the deceit would be staggering.

"Will you just make the payment and wait and see?" asked Father Liam.

"What else could we do?"

Lunch was disappointing. It looked suspiciously like the fettuccine Alfredo they had been served for lunch the previous day, warmed over in the microwave.

He told the bishop he would go for a walk afterwards and then perhaps for a nap. Despite the bad food, he was feeling marvelous. Criminal deception seemed to stimulate the endocrine glands.

He found the pamphlet right where it had been, on top of the two Simenon novels he kept in the drawer for very lazy nights. The letter was still tucked inside at the chapter headed "Grace and Celibacy."

The bank would not be open until 2:30. It was only 1:30 now. An hour had never seemed so long. He went out into the residence grounds to tread his little circle like a prisoner taking exercise. A soft, misty rain started, but it did not bother him. He was too busy thinking where he would have the Virgin appear. Perhaps the National Library. No, the crowds would be bad for the books. The Phoenix Park might be good. Except that he didn't want to make it appear that she was anointing the spot where His Holiness had preached. That could too readily be taken as an endorsement of his policies. Stephen's Green, then? Unless the gardens would be ruined. Why not the grounds of Milltown College? She could be saying there is room for dissent within our mission. Would there actually be a way to make her talk?

By now it was 2:15, and Destino was more excited than ever. He hurried back inside the residence and fairly loped upstairs to his bedroom to change his wet shoes and fetch the letter.

"Abstinence and Christ's Example" was still on top of the bedside table where he had last set it down. But he did not see the letter sticking out of it. He picked up the pamphlet and opened to the "Grace and Celibacy" chapter. The letter was not there.

He thought perhaps he had moved it and forgotten. He searched *Ulysses*. He searched all his pockets. He searched the pamphlet again. He searched the little bedside-table drawer. He looked under the bed and all through the bedclothes

The letter, quite simply, was gone.

38

$\mathcal{D}$ennis McDermott was annoyed that the Virgin had disappeared. He had been meaning to write about the painting she resembled ever since that night when he had gone to see her in Foxrock, but Italian television had suddenly descended on him for three days to get his views on the Irish imagination. It was a pleasant enough diversion from his gloomy prospects. But when Rupert Penrose got the jump on him this morning with that column about the Fionn Mac Cumhaill Prize, Dennis berated himself for his procrastination at the game of revenge.

He went straightaway to the university library to look for the old catechism prepper. But it wasn't there. He looked in school libraries. He tried Milltown College. No one had that prepper anymore.

Finally he rang a professor of art history who at least remembered the booklet and the reproduction that had been opposite its table of contents.

"It's not a particularly good copy of a mediocre Fra Angelico," he said. "There's even some question about whether he painted it. Why do you want it?" the art historian asked.

"You'll see," said Dennis.

He found it in the CUD library's art section with no trouble then. He checked out the Fra Angelico volume and brought it over to the Dublin *Telegraph*, where he wrote a weekly column. He showed the painting, alongside the photo of the apparition, to Sean Wells, the editor.

"It would be you who discovered this," said Wells. "Not that it matters much anymore. But I'll never stop a columnist from flogging a dead horse. Sure what's column writing all about? Good luck to you, Dennis."

With that dubious encouragement, he became even more determined to talk sense to his readers. "We Irish are too easily manipulated by our favorite myths," he began. "It is time we learned to face facts."

He was finished by six o'clock. He handed in the column. Then he rang Bishop Meany, who happened to be still at his desk, answering the phone with alacrity.

"How are you keeping, Dennis?" he said warmly enough. "It looks poorly for Mr. Kavanagh, doesn't it, now?"

"I'm afraid it does," said Dennis. "Bishop, I was ringing just to warn you. I've been able to identify the Virgin figure, you know, that has been appearing around Dublin. It's the spitting image of a painting called *The Unfinished Virgin* by Fra Angelico. Do you remember it?

We used to have it in the front of our catechism-prepping pamphlets."

"I can't say I do."

"Ah, well, I expect you'll be getting some inquiries. I'm writing a column about it tonight. What would be the Vatican's response, do you think?"

"Well, we wouldn't want to be commenting on that, now, no. Not at this particular point in time."

"I didn't expect you would, Bishop. All the same. Forewarned is forearmed."

"Well, thank you, Dennis. It was good of you to think of us. I'm sorry they didn't give you the Chair. I thought you were the best man for the job."

"No one's told me anything yet. So it's decided, is it? Who's won?"

"I'm not certain they've made a final choice. I was surprised to read about you and the Fionn Mac Cumhaill, I must say, Dennis. I wouldn't have thought you'd advance yourself among the literary crowd that way. Did you really deny them the prize these three years?"

"I certainly couldn't tell you if I had, Bishop. With respect."

"Please yourself, Dennis."

"You know I've been eliminated."

"Well, if no one's said it to you, Dennis, I could be wrong."

"I'm sure you're not in error, Bishop. Thanks for the tip."

"A warning in return, don't you know. Thanks for yours, Dennis. God bless."

"May the road rise with you, Bishop."

•   •   •

He told Caroline he was going out to walk Cordelia, their nervous Irish setter. He took the dog to the Dalkey Island Hotel, where none of his friends would see him. They all went to The Club or Finnegan's. He downed a few and came home after last call.

"Where've you been?" Caroline said crossly. "The paper's rung twice."

"I stopped in the hotel," he said. "It's a cold night."

"Yes, I was worried about you."

"What did they want?"

"They wanted to tell you they were holding your column."

"Holding it? Holding it for what?"

"Maybe until it's more timely."

"It couldn't get more timely. I smell a rat."

He strode angrily to the phone.

"Let it go, Dennis. They've all gone home by now," said Caroline.

"I'll ring the bloody bastards at home."

He fetched his little address book and found Sean Wells's unlisted number.

"Dennis, you're not exactly sober," said Caroline. "Do you think it's wise?"

"Hello!" Sean said heartily.

"Hello, Sean," said Dennis. "I understand you pulled my column tonight."

"Who's this?"

"Dennis."

"Oh, Dennis! We did?"

"That's what my wife told me. I was out walking the dog."

"Why did we do that?" said the editor.

"Did you get a call from the Papal Nuncio's office?"

"What was the column about, Dennis?"

"The BVM hoax and the Irish mind."

"Oh, that's right! We did pull it. And now I remember the reason. We thought it was a bit harsh, Dennis. That's why we pulled it. You know, you're such a brilliant rationalist, you don't actually cotton on to the way you sound. At times you can be, well, almost offensive. I didn't think you meant to be offensive. But there you are. That's what editors are for. Better luck next time, Dennis. A little more tact maybe?"

"You got no phone call about the column?"

"Oh, no! Nothing like that! How would anybody but ourselves know what was in your column before we've printed it, Dennis? You don't go showing it around, do you?"

"No," he said glumly. Two could play this game. "Sorry to bother you at home, Sean."

"That's all right, Dennis. That's what I'm here for."

Caroline had mercifully gone to bed. He took his time about undressing. He wanted her asleep when he crawled under the covers. But she was poised.

"Well, what did Sean say?" she asked as he settled in.

"He says I'm a brilliant rationalist."

"What does that mean?"

"It means he didn't like the column. No, it means Bishop Meany didn't like the column."

"Bishop Meany? How would he know what was in it?"

39

$\mathscr{A}$ileen had been sitting at the kitchen table in her pink tights and purple BURN BURN BURN leotard reading the *Ireland of the Welcomes* magazine which Betty Worsthorne had loaned her because Aileen had said she didn't know anymore where to send tourists in Ireland, and Betty's son Colm had a photo in it of a flock of sheep grazing in front of a TV satellite dish, when Donal suddenly burst in the door and summoned everyone in the family to the sitting room, no questions asked.

Aileen did have questions about the postcard which had arrived that Wednesday morning addressed to Donal, but she took one look at his eyes with the demented socked-in strangeness of them, and she decided just to hand it to him without a word.

"I'll be looking for you in the usual spot," it said on the back of a picture of Dalkey Island. Aileen wondered if they would be so bold as to have it off in the Dalkey Island Hotel. They were as apt to run into people they knew there as they were anywhere on the South Side. But people might have known about Donal and his girlfriend for years and never told her. That was the way in Ireland. The wife was always the last to know. They all conned themselves into thinking they were protecting her from humiliation.

"Where are the girls? Why aren't the girls coming?" he asked her sharply, not saying a blessed thing about the postcard. Was he going to announce it to the whole family?

"Can't you leave them? They're doing their schoolwork, Dennis. They've got their headsets on. They haven't heard you."

"Bring them here," he said.

"You get them!" She lost her temper. Why should she help him do this?

He stared at her as if he had not understood.

She went to fetch them herself, starting to wonder whether something might indeed be drastically wrong with the business. It was all too peculiar, his making up with Seamus after so many years.

Sure enough Roisin and Fiona both had Walkmen plugged to their ears as they studied side by side. Aileen put her hands on their shoulders to get their attention.

"Dad's home. Listen to me. He's in a very bad mood. He wants a family conference right now."

"Why now, Mum? Why's he home so early? Is something wrong? Have we gone bankrupt?" asked Fiona.

"That thing's too tight for you, Mother," said Roisin gravely. "It just digs into you and shows all your rolls."

Donal was pacing by the courtyard windows when they came into the sitting room. He nodded at them wordlessly when they greeted him. This frightened Aileen more than any amount of yelling would have done. She sat down on the big divan and pulled the girls down beside her.

"You know how you girls have always wanted to get away in the Christmas season to somewhere sunny and warm," Donal said.

"Oh, yes, Dad!" gushed Roisin.

Fiona and Aileen said nothing.

"Well, I'm going to take you there this year."

"Dad! You're such a love!" said Roisin, jumping up to kiss him.

"Where are you taking us to, Dad?" asked Fiona quietly.

"We're going to Jersey at the moment," he said. "But then we'll go on to the Canaries as soon as the weather breaks."

"You're not thinking of going in the boat?" asked Aileen.

"As a matter of fact, I am," he said.

"Not the boat, Daddy! Not this time of year!" whined Roisin. "We'll freeze!"

"When were you thinking of sailing, Donal?" asked Aileen, trying to gauge his state of mind.

"Tonight," he said.

"Tonight? But what about the drinks party? Have you forgotten about that?"

"Daddy, we can't leave before the party!" wailed Roisin.

"I've never heard of people sailing on a tiny yacht in the Irish Sea in the dead of winter," said Fiona.

"What you've never heard of would fill volumes, girl. We're going tonight and that's it."

"Donal, you can't be serious!"

That made him furious enough, and then when she suggested he consult her brother—who was a very expert sailor—about the wisdom of sailing off in a 38-foot boat from Dun Laoghaire Harbor in early December, Donal went completely bananas.

"*Don't you go telling me what to do, woman!*" he yelled. "*Don't you go telling me to ask Seamus anything! I've had it with Seamus, the slimy bloodsucker. Don't you tell me to go asking Seamus how to save my own life!*"

"Donal, stop this!" she implored.

But he wouldn't, and pretty soon he had his hands on her neck and he was yelling, "*Pack, you eejit! I said pack! pack! pack!*"

Both the girls had to jump on him to stop him strangling her. That seemed to bring him to his senses, or at least to change his tone. He quieted down.

"Go pack me some food," he said to Aileen, and he went off to put his own things together.

The telephone rang while she was in the kitchen.

"Are you sure you want to leave tonight, Mr. McGaffney," poor old Declan in the boatyard was saying. Donal had picked up the phone in the bedroom.

"Yes, I'm sure," he said. "I'm coming right down."

"She'll be ready," said Declan.

"Oh, dear God!" said Aileen, but no one heard her.

Donal embraced them all at the door.

"Why are you doing this, Donal?" Aileen pleaded. "This is crazy! Tell us what's happened. I'm sure we can work it out."

"Oh, I almost forgot," he said, not seemingly hearing her at all. He went into the kitchen and ripped out the phone.

"Donal, what are you doing?" said Aileen, feeling really frightened then.

He went on into the sitting room and pulled out the phone there. Then into their bedroom. The girls started to weep.

"Goodbye," he said from the doorway. "You may not hear from me for a long time. Remember, it's for your own good."

He blew them all a kiss and stepped out into the night.

• • •

Aileen waited only until his headlights had disappeared. Then she took the girls straight down to the Galloping Green and rang the Guards. They were very understanding and quick when they heard it could be a potential suicide. They said they couldn't actually have him committed without a doctor's authority, probably two doctors' authority. But they would hold him until she could arrange for that if she liked. She rang Dr. Hennessey and told him the whole story.

"Well done, Aileen, you did the right thing," he said.

Well done. How could a thing like this ever be well done? What were they going to do to Donal if he didn't go quietly? Was it like in the films where they held them down and gave them horrible spirit-breaking injections? Or that straitjacket that made them look like tangled monks? What if the doctors decided he needed the electric shock? She hadn't asked Dr. Hennessey about that. Oh, no! What if Donal got really violent and they used it to subdue him? And when she saw him in the morning, he would be one of those zombies with black caves around his eyes . . .

"Hello, Aileen!" Sheila Wainwright caught her standing at the telephone looking lost. "Look at you in your leotard! Did you just come from your classes? Straight to the pub, you naughty girl!"

"Oh, hello, Sheila!" She had forgotten she was still in the leotard, and she had let her mac hang open. Please God, Donal was never to hear about this. "No, I'm just here with the girls. Donal had to work late, so I thought I'd take them out."

"My kids wouldn't be caught dead in here," said Sheila. "They call this the fogies' pub. Ah, well. We're fogies now, Aileen."

Aileen gave her a sympathetic smile and sped over to the girls.

"Christ, Mother, the Wainwrights are here! Do we have to stay?" said Fiona.

"She's afraid Alastair will hear she was in here," said Roisin.

Her sister shot her a withering glance. Was Fiona in love with Alastair Wainwright?

"Let's go," said Aileen. "You girls let me come in here still in my leotard."

"You were beyond hearing, Mother," said Fiona.

They smiled brightly at the Wainwrights.

"I thought I saw Donal's car there earlier," Sheila said to Aileen.

"He's come for his tea and gone again," said Aileen.

"You poor thing!" said Sheila, rubbing her husband's elbow.

Aileen tried to look like a normally irked housewife.

"I wonder what's happened with Dad," said Fiona when they were back in Aileen's car. "I wish we could call the boatyard."

"The Guards will come by and tell us," said Aileen.

"What do the Guards have to do with it?" asked Roisin.

"They had to take him to hospital."

"Hospital? Where? What's happened, Mummy? Did he crash the car?"

"They had to take him to St. Patrick's."

"Mummy, you didn't! I'll never be able to show my face in school tomorrow! Oh, Mummy, how *could* you?" said Roisin.

"Of course you'll show your face at school, dear. You'll go on just the same, just as if it never happened. No one'll be the wiser."

"No one'll be the wiser," Roisin mimicked bitterly. "Well, then, how did Alison McDermott know that the Virgin Mary was in our barn before I did?"

"It was on the radio, silly. You were too busy listening to your tapes."

"How did Nora Wainwright know that you were on the Slurpyslim diet before we did?"

"I haven't the faintest idea," said Aileen as she pulled into the drive. "Perhaps her mother has a hidden listening device placed underneath our kitchen table. In which case, the entire Wainwright family has been listening to our whole drama tonight, and they went down to the pub afterwards to gloat."

"I'm serious, Mum. Nobody has any secrets in Ireland."

"Someone has a secret relationship with Players Number Six right in my own house," she said, looking from girl to girl. They were standing in the hallway outside the kitchen.

"Well, if my friends find out my mother had the Guards put my father in St. Patrick's, I'm going to kill you, Mother," said Roisin, pointedly ignoring the mention of cigarettes, although Fiona was the one who was blushing. "I swear I will."

"That's the second person who has threatened to kill me this evening," said Aileen. "I think it's time we all had our tea."

A telephone rang and they all nearly jumped out of their skins.

"He forgot the one in our old room," said Fiona.

It was Dr. Hennessey ringing back to say the whole thing had gone as smoothly as new milk into, into, he forgot what, but it had gone smoothly, he could assure her.

"Hospitals can be quite reassuring to paranoids, you know. They feel they're in safe hands. Which is the way I'm sure Donal is feeling right now. So you needn't worry yourself, Aileen. You did the right thing. You're a brave woman. He was almost in that boat, you know, when they stopped him.

"Oh, and tomorrow they'll want you to ring up and give them a case history. Perhaps you could tell them what triggered this thing, although you may never know. The mind is such a funny bugger. I had one patient who went blotto over a Christmas card."

[164]

40

What with one thing and another about the security arrangements, looking at Dublin Castle, finding hotel rooms for the agents, and exploring a safe jogging route for the Vice President, Dermot did not actually take Rock to meet the woman Moira McNamara until Thursday morning. They were late getting to her place because it was lashing rain, as Dermot said, and Dublin drivers didn't know what to do in the rain. They were stuck behind a Dublin Gas truck for fifteen minutes before Dermot braved the oncoming traffic and went around it. They got a glimpse of the workers inside the van having their morning tea.

"What a country!" said Dermot. "And now they've taken the Sky Television from us again. Sure, it's hopeless!"

"What's Sky Television?" Rock asked.

"Satellite television. We saw everything. We got Dr. Ruth."

"That woman who gives the sex advice?"

"Yes. She introduced the concept of foreplay to Ireland. My mother thinks she is disgusting beyond words. They say Sky was demanding extortionate rates, and we wouldn't pay them, but it's a pity. Mother was monitoring the filth week by week. Between Dr. Ruth and those vivid BBC documentaries on the eunuchs of India, she got through the winter. I don't know what she'll do now."

Rock was picking up Dermot's comfortable habit of expecting the worst of his working day. It made small pleasures into existential bonuses and being all washed up at thirty-nine feel like humanity's normal frequency. Maybe this was getting in touch with his ancestors, after all, the psychic linkup with their cheerful defeatism.

He remembered thinking that as they stood in the rain outside the dingy little house in Pembroke Gardens, trying to ring the broken bell and keep out of the stream of water coming from a hole in the roof gutter, because it was his last thought as a whole and free man, before she opened that door.

"Holy Mother of God," said Dermot, or something very like.

She was the one they had seen on the street Monday afternoon shouting about fucking England, and she was wearing that same shirt with the tail hanging out. She was, up close and in focus, beautiful beyond telling.

"Well?" she said, because they were staring. "Who are you?"

Dermot was able to explain.

"What are you doing standing out there in the rain? Come in before you catch your deaths, the pair of you," Moira said. "Although it's no warmer in here," she added as they came in.

It wasn't.

"Can I offer you a cup of tea?" she said. "You'll have a cup of tea."

"We'll have a cup of tea," said Dermot, smiling at Rock, who had lost the power of speech.

"I've the names of twenty-eight women for you if you want that many for the airport greeting," she told them as she filled her kettle. "Deirdre said they'd have to be vetted for security, and they've all agreed. But I do hope your men will be careful how they do it. Some of these women don't want their parents to know their domestic arrangements, if you understand my meaning. I know the Irish police think all feminists are secretly lesbians and that lesbianism is an abomination they're absolutely thrilled to investigate. But we assume you Americans are light-years ahead of us."

She smiled at him, and he thought: Save yourself, O'Leary.

"Yes, yes," said Dermot. "They are light-years ahead of us."

"Can't he speak for himself?" she said. "You are the American Secret Service agent, aren't you?"

"He is," said Dermot. "I already told you that. Rock, old man, have you come down with terminal jet lag?"

41

The White House sent Pete Grazos and forty-nine other agents across as soon as word got through that the missing Semtex was no rumor. They arrived on Thursday morning. That afternoon Dermot Muldoon gave them the names of the twenty-eight women who had agreed to appear at the airport to greet Vice President Houlihan.

"This should be fun," said Grazos, taking a quick glance down the birth-dates column. "I'll take charge of this."

Pete Grazos was on a lifetime odyssey through female flesh. Rock ripped the list out of his hands.

"Leave this one to me," he said, and he crossed out Moira's name and passport number.

"Why, my man, help yourself to more than one!" said Pete. "I hear Irish girls are really hot."

"Who the hell told you that?"

"Sullivan. Who else? He says they can't get their men out of the pubs. You know this girl, O'Leary? Don't tell me you've made a hit already. Not you. What is she, let me guess, a feminist vegetarian this time? Do they have vegetarians here in Dublin? I like the Aer Lingus stewardesses myself. They're kind of old-fashioned and tight-assed but you see their rosy cheeks, you know their temperature's raised. I tell you, they are needy women, Rock, ours for the taking."

"These are feminists, Pete. Do me a favor. Try not to sound like Attila the Hun with a hard-on."

"You're the guy with the hard-on. I've never seen you so grim, Rock. What's the matter? Things not progressing?"

"Back off, Grazos."

"Okay, okay. This broad must be something. Maybe I should check her out for you, man. How can you trust yourself to give her the full background thing when you feel like this? Maybe she's the IRA's Mata Hari."

"Leave her for me, Pete."

"Chill out, man. I'm only doing my job."

They were interrupted by a phone call from Chief Superintendent Bloom's office. Rock was summoned to hear some new information about the Semtex.

•   •   •

What Bloom had didn't amount to very much. The Semtex was still missing, and they still didn't know where. They had traced it to Liverpool, but not beyond.

"We've made some progress tracing it backwards," said the Chief Superintendent. "We thought at first that it had come from Argentina, which of course makes sense, given the relations between the British and the Argentinians, but Argentina was only a port of call. It came from Prague. You look worried. The gravity of the situation is, I suppose, coming home to you. Cup of tea?"

Rock did indeed look worried. He was thinking Pete would not be able to resist going to have a look at her.

"Tea? Um. How did it get from Prague to Argentina? Does the IRA have a network like that?"

"Was that a yes or a no?"

"Pardon?"

"Would you like a cup of tea?"

"Oh. Sure. Why not? Thanks."

Like the Minister for Women's Affairs, the Chief Superintendent had an electric kettle in his office.

"To answer your question about the IRA," he said, pouring water from a bottle of Ballygowan into the kettle, "we don't know. We don't think the IRA has such a network, but we honestly don't know."

"How did you trace the stuff back?"

"The Czechs. They've been cooperating with Western law-enforcement agencies since their free elections. We think their sources are Middle Eastern, though, actually."

"Who bought the stuff from the Czechs?"

"An Englishman everyone's been watching who buys most of their material and then sells it all over the world. The Czechs told us he had already sold it by the time it was shipped. He was the broker. They sent the shipment to Haifa. It was going to an Israeli who is based in South Africa."

"I'm getting confused. When was this?"

"Four years ago."

"How can you possibly connect it with this stuff you're looking for now?"

"The Brits again. They've got someone in Argentina who has been there for the last five years. This person knew of a shipment of Semtex that came to Buenos Aires three years and seven months ago."

"Now I'm more confused."

"From Argentina it went to Libya."

"All roads lead to Libya."

"Precisely. But the curious part is, it went back to Argentina again from Libya and *then* it came up to these islands. Sailing under the flag of Panama. We know where she docked in Liverpool. That's all."

"It can't be only IRA," said Rock.

"They don't even enter the picture until Liverpool. They are very upset, by the way. We're quite certain of that."

"Are you talking to them?"

"Indirectly," said Bloom. "They know they've been double-crossed, but they're not sure at what level."

"Wouldn't it be nice if they gave us a few Libyans," said Rock.

"Wouldn't it just," said Bloom.

42

*D*ennis McDermott took Bishop Meany's news far harder than he had expected to. He drank brandy alone in his study for two days. On the third he awoke feeling wretchedly in need of a cigarette. He did not expect to be discovering new flaws in his character at his late age, and now he was hiding constantly from his wife and children. He could not understand why the trustees had not picked him. Everyone knew he was the best literary historian in Ireland.

The awful thing was, he could not even enjoy the satisfaction of pure martyrdom. His martyrdom was ignominiously sullied.

In his own way he had tried to buy the Kerrygold Chair. He had curried favor with that thug Donal McGaffney, and he had accepted the censorship of his Virgin column without a whimper, in the vain hope that Bishop Meany might mistakenly think he was complicit in its being killed. That was truly the reason he had rung Bishop Meany, to give him the chance to have the column killed. Of course, he hadn't admitted as much to himself at the time, but now, with hindsight, he could see what a craven wretch he was. He, Dennis Davitt McDermott, the bravest intellectual in Dublin, had sold out his integrity.

It was the spine of his self-respect, the thing that he had always held fast heretofore no matter what the consequences might have been. Hadn't he held fiercely to his beliefs about the Fionn Mac Cumhaill Literary Prize? Didn't he know he had risked alienating every writer in Dublin? There he was, walking around in a bulletproof vest, his beliefs were so provocatively pure.

Pure for other people's manuscripts, he thought bitterly. You sing a different song for your own employment future.

He did not bother going down to breakfast with Caroline. He wasn't hungry. He remembered there were some cigarettes tucked away in his desk drawer underneath the rejected manuscripts. And somewhere in there was an extra brandy flask.

The cigarette tasted awful. It was probably three years old. He should have known, too, that Caroline would smell the smoke all the way down in the kitchen. She stuck her head in the door as he was lighting the second one. His hand shook badly. And there was the brandy bottle sitting in front of him, opened, the amber liquid down an inch already.

"Are you going to stop this or shall I take you to hospital?" she said crisply, watching him wince at the pain from blinking his eyes.

"When I need you in my study, Caroline, I shall ask for you."

"Dennis, you've eaten nothing for two days. Now you've started in on the cigarettes. What are you trying to prove?"

"Would you like to join me in a drink, Caroline, my pet? How about a fag?"

"Oh, Dennis!" she sobbed, and she ran weeping from the room.

•   •   •

He managed to escape undetected, but it meant leaving behind his macintosh and his bulletproof vest. He took the DART into town and tried to smile at people in his normal way, although his face felt bent and drunken. He walked up from the station without a destination. He went into a pub he didn't know and ordered a Guinness and a shot of whiskey. When he came out into the street, he felt ill. He only just made it back into the pub loo.

That put him off Guinness. He decided whiskey and water would be safer and ordered a glass of each, the whiskey a double.

He went out again and now felt fine, although every crack in the sidewalk seemed obtrusive. He walked up through Protestant University College and tripped on the cobblestones and went sprawling.

"Isn't that Dennis Davitt McDermott?" he heard.

"Look, yes. He's drunk!" another whispered loudly.

Dennis felt the need to move. He started going forward on his hands and knees.

"What's he doing?" the whisperer whispered.

The yard seemed to have lost its bearings. Dennis sat back on his haunches and willed it to stop swaying. He pushed his hands against the ground to bring himself to a standing position.

He smiled crookedly at the students, who were pretending not to look at him. Look at me, boys, the scourge of the Catholic hierarchy. Amn't I magnificent!

He thought he might be ill again. He seemed to be walking. The college was no longer there. Cars were beeping at him. Many people. A tin whistle sounding sharp in the cold. It was piercing without a mac. Stephen's Green not green at all. Young man with a guitar busking for small change. If God so loved the world, why did He invent the Eurovision Song Contest?

Dublin's bravest intellectual steps up onto a bus, a singular act of courage considering the state of his digestive system. We are proceeding vaguely south. Oh, dear, the nausea rising again. The bus driver seemed to be seeking—or is it seems to be seeking? our man is not sure which tense he belongs in—out all the bumps and cracks and potholes he could find. The bus lurched up over the Canal, and Bravery fell sideways onto his own shoulder. His stomach hung in the balance between self-hatred and a small wee knot of civic pride which was pulling for the cleanliness of a public vehicle. A neat elderly lady regarded him with a look of absolute horror. The bus halted.

"Adieu, my fine lady," Dennis said to her. He stepped very correctly off the bus. He knew where he was. He could see the Rathmines tower. Too many friends passed here on a Saturday morning. Could be afternoon. Time flies when you're having a piss-up. Let them not see him vomiting.

He crossed the street and went on in that direction and very soon felt he was lost geographically as well as the other way, which seemed to offer a kind of symmetry to his situation. He saw a little church. He went into the gloom. An old widow came out of the confession box, looking purged and humbled. Dennis knelt down in her place.

"Father, I suppose I should introduce myself. But I am not the person I thought I was, so I wouldn't know how to present the person formerly known as myself. A transitory being. Fresh off of public transport, too, in point of fact. Do you remember that phrase, the 'passionate transitory'? Where was I? Lost. Yes. Probably lost my mind, too, in which case I should probably not be here. I should present myself to the Missing Persons Bureau. Ha! God hates me, Father. I can palpably feel His disgust beaming down upon me. It is a most uncomfortable feeling, rather like the way I felt this morning when Caroline caught me smoking. It's horrible to think I am falling apart only over a rumor that I will not be getting the Kerrygold Chair. You see, I'm in line for it. Only, I lied to you just now. I'm not falling apart over losing the Chair. It's over what I've been doing to get it, which I'm still doing, too, even now, in case of the slightest chance that the Chair is not lost. There! You see? I can't even give you a full confession because this is Ireland, and you might talk to someone who might talk to someone else who knows one or two of the trustees at CUD. Do you see why God despises me, Father? Do you understand? Father, are you there?"

Dennis peered through the grate. It was too dark to see anything.

"Are you there, *Father? Hello-o!*" he yelled. *"Is anyone there?"*

He felt dizzy again. He leaned his head against the cold wood. He heard footsteps. Someone was coming down the stairs.

"Hello," he heard a voice behind him. A young man, an organist sort, clasping his slender white hands together anxiously. "Were you calling?"

"Are you the priest? You're not," said Dennis.

"No, no. I'm the organist. Father Connolly is not here at the moment."

"You mean there's no one in the box."

"No, actually."

"I thought as much," Dennis said agreeably.

"Are you all right?" the young man asked, although his face seemed to say he hoped Dennis would not tell him.

"I'm not, actually," Dennis said, mimicking his accent. Oxford perhaps? "When will there be a priest in the box?"

"They don't use it very often," said the organist. "Only before the big holidays, I believe. I'm not actually a Catholic, you see. I do concerts here. You could try Christmas Eve."

"They gave up the one thing that was ever worth anything."

"You're sure you're all right?" said the young man, already backing away.

"No," said Dennis. "But there's nothing to be done."

The young man sped away.

•　　•　　•

Dennis did not remember the next interval. He awoke the following morning feeling a little foggy.

"How did I get here?" he asked Caroline.

"How do you feel?" She placed a cool hand on his brow.

"Not bad. Considering. A little peckish."

"That woman gave you an injection. You've slept for eighteen hours."

"Which woman?"

[173]

"Dr. Gebortsglück. Don't you remember? The rabbi's wife."

"The rabbi's wife? What rabbi?"

"Darling, you fell asleep in the reform synagogue on Leinster Road yesterday morning during the services. The rabbi and his wife brought you home. They recognized you."

"Oh, God, how awful for you, Caroline! Darling, why did you ever marry me?"

"You couldn't have put yourself at the mercy of nicer people, Dennis. I mean, think of it, you could have been robbed and left in a gutter to freeze to death."

"I hate not remembering. Oh, Caroline, why did I do it?"

"You did tell Rabbi Quinn you want to become a Jew."

"Yes, I seem to dimly remember telling someone that."

"Well, he isn't going to hold you to it, of course. Dennis, it's so good to see you looking cheerful again!"

43

That Saturday morning, the same day Dennis had gone wandering out alone and drunk, the mysterious woman rang the McGaffneys again, she of the velvety voice who said, "Who I am is not important." Fiona spoke with her.

"Mummy, what's going on?" she asked. "Has Daddy taken money from someone he shouldn't have?"

"Your father is a sick man, Fiona. Don't be talking that way about him! What did that woman say to you?"

"She wanted to know where he was."

"You didn't tell her!"

"You think I'm stupid? I said he'd gone to Donegal to see his parents."

Donal's parents had retired to a seaside village and were always freezing. Aileen said that was the one thing would make her leave him, a retirement cottage in Donegal.

"Mother, what's going on?" said Fiona.

Roisin brought in the post. There were forty-eight replies to the drinks-party invitations, all acceptances.

"Mummy, what are we going to do?" asked Roisin. "I mean, do I get the new dress or not?"

It really was serious, and she had no one to turn to. What could a hostess conceivably do in such miserable circumstances? She looked at the pile of acceptances. She straightened her back and looked Roisin in the eye.

"Come along, girls. You'll shop for frocks while I go in and have a wee chat with your father."

Aileen dropped them off at the top of Grafton Street and went back around the Green three times, trying to compose herself for a visit to the depressives ward. She'd never been inside St. Patrick's. Donal had told her it was pleasant enough when she'd spoken with him over the phone, but he hadn't been very loquacious.

The doctors had asked her to stay away for the first few days. They had wanted to know whether she could think of anything Donal might be feeling guilty about, once they heard the Virgin had appeared in their garage. They said religion could be a dangerous thing for a neurotic self-punisher.

"Self-punisher?" she had said. "But that's not my Donal. My Donal goes to Mass twice a year, on Christmas and Easter. And he hasn't got a drop of guilt in him. My Donal is the most guilt-free man on God's green earth!"

It just came right out of her before she remembered about the postcard, and then afterwards she couldn't find a way to bring it up. Anyway, she wanted to ask Donal about it first.

No one challenged her at the door. The place looked and smelled like an ordinary hospital. She took the elevator up to Donal's floor and didn't see any obvious madmen.

Some women in leotards were taking aerobics class in a large airy room she passed on the way to Donal's room.

Donal was lounging back reading an English tabloid. He looked rested and wonderful.

"Hello, Aileen, love!" he said when he saw her, his whole face alight. He stood up to give her a warm embrace. He introduced her to his roommate, a clean-cut medical student who was sitting on his bed doing precise anatomical drawings.

"Ah, you must be Mrs. McGaffney, what a pleasant surprise!" said a tall thin doctor, appearing in the doorway. "I'm Dr. Roscoe Nixon. We've talked on the phone. You'll be amazed at your husband's demeanor this morning. He seems almost too well to be in here. It's hard to believe he tried to kill you three days ago!" said the doctor, crinkling up his eyes at them. "Well, you two have a nice visit," he said, walking off.

Donal took Aileen around to the solarium for a cup of coffee. They found a little niche where they could speak without being overheard.

"You know you're looking splendid these days, Aileen," he said as he watched her pulling over a wicker chair. "I've been meaning to tell you that. You must have lost at least a stone."

"I'm glad you finally noticed, Donal. You stopped looking at me entirely there for a while."

"Yes, I know. I was—worried about—things."

"Donal, what got into you the other night? And why is that strange woman calling us? Who *is* she? Did she send you the postcard? Are you having it off with her? I do have a right to know."

"Aileen! Aileen! What do you think you're saying!" he said. "Having it off? Why, Aileen, I can't believe you would even ask me such a thing!"

"Well, what am I meant to think with her calling and the postcard? What is going on?"

The oddest look came over his face. He was sizing her up in some way.

"And why ever aren't you angry with me for sending you here?" she asked, although she hadn't meant to. His expression made her uneasy. Maybe he was cracked.

"It was a brilliant move, Aileen, a brilliant move! I wish I'd thought of it myself. You're a wonderful woman. But then I always knew that."

Dear God, what was wrong with him?

"What do you mean brilliant move? Donal, I was desperate. You tried to strangle me. Don't you remember that?"

"Oh, yes, and I'm so sorry, Aileen," he said, tenderly kissing her cheek. "Can you forgive me?"

"Of course I can, Donal," she said impatiently, "but I still want to know who that woman is who keeps calling."

He studied her face broodingly.

"I don't know myself," he said. "But don't tell her anything." He pulled her against him and whispered into her ear. "You see, they'll never think of coming after me in here. Even if they find out I'm in here, they probably wouldn't dare do anything. It would look too heartless, even for them. Still, best not to take a chance."

"Who would never think of coming after you, Donal? What are you talking about? Now you're sounding as cracked as you did Tuesday night!"

"You're better off not knowing," he said, gently squeezing her arms.

"Better off not knowing what? There I am sitting in the house without a phone that works for calling out, thanks to you, and the two girls sitting there with me. Donal, if there's someone actually trying to kill you, I have a right to know! What is it, the woman's brother?"

"I'm not absolutely certain they're trying to kill me."

"Who are they, Donal? You must tell me! I can take it if you've been unfaithful, believe me. But I don't want the girls to get shot by someone who's gunning for you. For God's sake, we have a right to know what's going on!"

"It was the only way to save the business. It was wrong, though. And I tried to renege, but just my luck, it was too late. Somebody stole the lorry."

"You're insured, though. You've had lorries stolen before."

"This was different. This one had a special cargo. Well, I'd rather you didn't know everything, Aileen. It's better for you that way. Anyway, they don't believe me, the people who want the cargo. They think I've done something with my own lorry."

"You sound like you're talking about the Provos."

He gave her a pleading look.

"Donal! How could you!"

"How could he what? What's he done now?" Dr. Nixon suddenly materialized again.

"How could he still think his life was in danger?" she said just as coolly as any experienced felon.

"You're not still afraid, are you, Donal?" said Dr. Nixon.

"Not when you and Aileen are here, Doctor," he said meekly.

•   •   •

"He's putting on an act," Dr. Nixon said to her as he walked her to the elevator, "and we don't know why. You'll have to help us, Aileen."

"You're thinking we can't have the party, aren't you, Mum?" said Roisin, because her mother went so moodily silent on the way out of Dublin.

"I'm thinking about your poor father," said Aileen, plunging her daughters into deeper despondency. Neither one had found a dress to her liking.

"Listen, girls," she went on, "if that woman rings again, let me talk to her. Do you understand?"

"Yes, Mum," said Roisin.

"Is that his girlfriend? Did Dad have a girlfriend?" asked Fiona.

"Don't be ridiculous!" said Aileen.

"Then who is she, Mum?" Fiona persisted.

"If you must know," said Aileen, "she represents a dissatisfied customer, and you're not to tell her anything at all, in case of legal ramifications."

The girls both sighed audibly.

They were passing the Galloping Green.

Suddenly Aileen was inspired. "Just a minute, girls," she said, and she pulled over and ran inside to ring up Dr. Nixon.

Come to think of it, there were some things Donal might be feeling guilty about, she said, and she proceeded to rattle off a list of Donal's transgressions as long as your arm, things like forgetting Mother's Day every year and their anniversary, too, and her birthday, and neglecting to tell her every Friday night that he was going to Goggins with the boys and not taking out the garbage and not remembering to have the car serviced or to fold up the newspaper or to pick his wet towel up off the bathroom floor and leaving her with an empty petrol tank at least eight times a year and never telling her the time he used up their entire savings on the boat so that she had to put two thousand pounds' worth of kitchen tiles out in the garage for three years because she couldn't afford to pay the men to put them down, this after she'd told all her friends she was redoing her kitchen, and never once attending a parents' meeting at Holy Child and worst of all leaving her to sit with his mother on Sunday afternoons when his mother came to Dublin while he went to Goggins. What did he marry her for, anyway?

"That's a great start," said Dr. Nixon patronizingly, "but it might not be what *we* think he ought to feel guilty about, Aileen. If you could try to ask yourself what *he* thinks he's done wrong."

44

$\mathcal{M}$oira was nervous about the security check. The other day when the Guards pulled in Maev Dowling for yelling at the Taoiseach, they had held her for five hours in case she wanted to tell them why, the last time she had crossed the border to see her cousins in Crossmaglen, the British Army found thrush medicine in the boot of her car. The Special Branch of course also wanted to know whether Maev could tell them anything about Semtex shipments. But it was the thrush medicine in the boot which they dwelt upon pointlessly. How would Irish police know what the British Army had found in her car six months before? Maev had asked them that, and they laughed. You didn't have to be a rocket scientist to figure it out.

Moira had never told her parents she was dismissed from her teaching job at the Sacred Heart Academy three years past when the nuns discovered she was living with a man to whom she was not married. It might not have mattered, the nuns said, if he hadn't been the Sacred Heart's adored drama teacher, but he was, and so what could you do? She had never told her parents about Brian, either, who jilted her for the London stage three months after causing her to lose her job. They would not have expected her to tell them.

The Donegal McNamaras prided themselves on the things they did not know about each other. They were always in the public eye, being schoolteachers, and they had learned how to live with that. Whatever you say, say nothing, could have been their motto, too, only not for hiding their crimes. They committed no crimes. Moira herself had never been arrested. She considered this a political deficiency which she had hoped might have been made up for the day of the demonstration. She thought she had been just as menacingly in the Taoiseach's face as Maev had been, but she had no cousins in Long Kesh Prison. She had no dangerous cousins at all. As she told her friends, she came from a long line of grammarians.

"It's a great mystery to me how they were able to reproduce themselves," she confided to Claire. "Not a mystery that they wanted to. There's nothing more stimulating to sexual desire than diagramming sentences in the bleakness of the Donegal climate. I mean, it mystifies me that they were able to find anyone else who desired them."

It seemed obvious to her friends why outsiders would desire a McNamara, but to Moira the family looks did not outweigh the family curse of dullness. She had been raised to regard her beauty as a sort of embarrassment which could lead to dangerous extravagances and, worse still, confused thought. That Brian Blades, the most amusing man to wander into her young life, could leave her for a walk-on part in a new play called *In the Moment* did seem to prove out her miserable family's contention that beauty was a thin twig on which to hang one's all.

Moira's family did not approve of smoking or central heating, either. In fact, they approved of nothing that could cause envy or unnecessary expense. This narrowed their range of possibilities considerably. They were left with teaching school and long walks.

Moira had made valiant attempts to break out of the family mold, but she had done so in the McNamara family manner, in secret from them and on a very modest budget.

[180]

Today, as she labored over a speech which Deirdre Fanning was planning to make at the national Housewife of the Year Award dinner, Moira wore her winter anorak, instead of stoking up the coal fire, because she hadn't the money to buy more coal until Tuesday, when her dole check was due. She was saving the last bits for friends' visits. She had also rationed herself to three cigarettes an hour.

Yet, when the telephone rang and she heard her mother's voice, she reflexively crushed the one she had just lit.

"Darling," said her mother, "the Americans were on to us about you yesterday. You're all right, are you?"

"Yes, of course, Mother, I'm fine."

"That's all right, then," she said.

"I suppose it's raining there, Mother," Moira said.

"Yes, it's raining. Why, is it not raining in Dublin?"

"Not at the moment. No. It's just a blank cold."

"You'll be up soon, then, to see the wet rocks."

"Oh, yes, of course, Mother, I will."

Translation: the Secret Service told us you've had no job for three years. God knows who else they told in the village. You'd better come up here for Christmas as usual and hold your head high.

45

*M*oira's parents had been so thoroughly unforthcoming with Pete Grazos that he was ready to rule her out of the airport scene, and the White House and the Special Branch agreed. Why take a risk with anyone doubtful at all? Rock tried to explain that Moira was a politically important person, hand-picked by the Minister for Women's Affairs. But Pete had seen her picture.

"I wouldn't trust myself with a looker like her," he said. "And you don't have my experience, Rock. You know our rule: when in doubt—"

Rock tried to get Dermot to intervene in Moira's behalf, but Dermot was down at Shannon Airport giving Fidel Castro a tour of the duty-free shop during his brief touch-down for refueling.

He decided to go around to her cottage by himself. It wasn't a decision so much as a concession to the inexorable force that had taken over his being.

She took forever to come to the door, and when she did finally open it to him, she said: "I shouldn't be talking to you. But wait, I'm on the telephone."

She ran back to her phone, which was lying on the counter by her little kitchen alcove. "I know, Maev, but you told me you thought they had guessed already, anyway, so what does it matter? What am I saying? I know why it matters. Jesus, Maev, there's one of them here right now. Let me ring you back."

Rock had been looking around the sitting room. She had a fire going in the grate, very feebly. He saw the coal bucket nearby. He stirred the glowing embers and put several pieces of fresh coal over them.

"What are you doing?" she called to him. "Please don't use up my coal! I've only just enough for tonight!"

"Sorry," he said. His first word to her.

"I know, Maev!" she spoke into the phone. "I've been trying to get through to someone to call off the dogs. Jesus, I don't know what all they told my parents, and my phone's been ringing nonstop with the women in a panic."

There was a photograph over the fireplace showing her standing behind a group of girls in Catholic school uniforms. She looked scarcely older than the girls.

"Maev, I have to go. I told you, there's one of them here now. I'll ring you back."

She put the phone in its cradle and lit up a cigarette, drawing deeply before she spoke. A smoker! He could still remember the days when smoking was the innocently wicked way of getting your mouth ready to kiss.

"I could murder you. I could murder all of you," she said.

"Listen, I'll buy you another bag of coal. I didn't know you were running low."

"I could care fuck-all about the coal at this point, Mr. Secret Service. Your people are making a huge mess of their so-called background investigations. They've been trampling all over people's lives like it was nothing to them. Just get out of the way, the Vice President's coming!"

She would look more gorgeous than ever when in a fury.

"Moira, I'm sorry. That's Pete Grazos. He's a little insensitive."

"That's the one. He's got them all so angry with me, they're ready to expel me from the Irish Unemployed Feminists."

"Pete can get a bit macho with people, you know, but he's only worried about the half ton of Semtex that's supposed to be missing somewhere around Dublin."

"I don't care if there's five thousand tons of Semtex missing around Dublin. He has no right to ring up my parents in Donegal and tell them I've been three years redundant from the Sacred Heart Academy. He told them. I just know! Now my parents are worried sick, wondering who else in the village he's told!"

"He won't tell anyone else. He has to find out the basics, Moira. Actually, your parents were not cooperative."

"Good for them! You mean he was asking them things about me? Oh, that's even worse!"

"He just wanted to know how you've been supporting yourself since you got laid off."

"My parents don't know that! How could they know when they didn't know I'd left off teaching?"

"I assume you get unemployment insurance."

"What is this? You're interrogating me now?"

"Somebody has to, Moira. Otherwise, you can't go to the airport."

"I don't care if I go to the fucking airport!"

"I think you're smoking your filter," he said.

"Holy Christ, you Americans are bullies!" she said. "We're complete fools to think that our principal enemy is still England!"

She was trembling. He should not have told her she was smoking her filter.

"May I use your phone, Moira?"

She nodded. He got through to Pete at the hotel. "Listen, Grazos," he said. "I'm pulling you off the background checks."

"Too late. They're all done."

"You're off them, Pete."

"I told you. It's too late. We had a whole team doing them. We're finished. They got a couple of IRA sympathizers on the list, Rock. We've got a tricky situation here. Who turned you on to these women?"

"People's private lives are being trampled on," Rock said.

"Your girlfriend, for instance, has got no visible means of support."

"I'll be the judge of that, Pete."

"You calling from her house? Boy, have you got it bad."

" 'Bye. Pete."

She was wearing the same flannel shirt she'd had on those other times. Maybe she had only one shirt. It was hanging out over her jeans again, and her hair did not seem to have seen a comb since last he'd glimpsed her, but who would put a comb to perfection?

"Moira," he said, taking a step toward her.

She took a step backward and crossed her arms over her chest.

"Yes?" she said warily.

"Where can I buy coal around here?"

"Never mind that," she said. "I'll manage."

But he found a shop nearby where small bags of coal were being sold for four pounds each. He bought two of them.

"One would have been sufficient," she said coldly. "I can't eat coal."

"Let me buy you dinner," he said.

"I haven't time for that," she said. "The sisters are coming around to give me a tongue-lashing in twenty minutes."

She hadn't invited him to sit down. She was standing with her arms folded across her chest again. His throat felt tight.

"You must have a boyfriend," he said.

"He's in London," she said.

"Just my luck," said Rock.

"He's been there for three years," she said.

"How do you support yourself? You work for this Fanning woman?"

"It's unpaid work. I'm on the dole. I write a few articles. I eat coal."

[184]

"I'm sorry, Moira. Um. This boyfriend. He left you after you got laid off?"

"Is this an interrogation or what?"

"Help me out, Moira. I'm not on familiar ground here."

"No, I don't suppose you would be. But if you can pry so deeply into my private life, let's see how you feel when I turn the tables on you." She fetched her packet of cigarettes from the little counter in the kitchen, lit one by the gas from the stove, and took another deep drag.

"What about you and your wife?" she said. "Are you getting on? Are you faithful to her? Does she greet you at the door in those Total Woman costumes? Do you have one point nine children like all other average Americans? Do you cheat on your taxes? Do you employ illegal aliens? Come on. You can tell me. I won't tell the Special Branch. I won't breathe a word to your parents."

"I'm not married," he said.

"Oh. Don't you like women?"

"I was married, and actually, I couldn't cheat on my taxes. My wife was an Internal Revenue agent."

"God! She must have been a live wire. I take that back. That was unkind. It's just I have difficulty picturing a female revenue agent with any feminine graces, not that we need feminine graces anymore. But what happened between you two?"

"We had an eating incompatibility," he said, watching her face take on a distrustful smirk. "That's a very serious thing back in the States. That's why I need to find out what kind of restaurants you like."

"What do you mean, eating incompatibility?"

"It's complicated. What about you? Are you still seeing the guy in London? Is there anybody else in the picture?"

"Not at the moment. How long were you married?"

"Ten years."

"Children?"

"No. Cats. I got custody."

"Who's feeding them while you're in Ireland?"

"My mother. She's staying with me for the time being."

"What really happened to your marriage?"

"What really happened was my mother came for a visit one weekend and forgot to leave. Then Brenda got laid off, and she hated that, and I was out on the campaign trail guarding Presidential candidates. She and Mom thought I was having a wonderful time. I guess they weren't. It looks sort of significant on the evening news when they show one minute out of a long, boring campaign day. Mostly you stand around shopping malls listening to the candidate say how much he loves the country and how happy he is to be there with all the good people of K mart. Anyway, Brenda and Mother started to resent me as a team. When she moved out, Mom almost moved out with her."

Moira laughed. Then she kicked him out of her house. It was a start.

46

Patrick kept his lips tightly closed during the entire journey to Milltown College on Sunday afternoon. Archbishop Destino felt the force of his disapproval. What a fiercely moral people were these Irish! So different from our cynical selves. The driver who used to take him around Rome liked to tell him stories about the Vatican Bank in between light-opera arias he performed from beginning to end, flawlessly as to words. He was always a little drunk, that one. But this Patrick was like a descendant of John Calvin, always taut under the keen eye of God.

Father Liam looked like a different person, as though he'd been reborn, and with a new set of clothes on him. His hair was combed, and his eyes were clear.

He welcomed the Nuncio into his rooms, which were chilly and ancient-feeling with their high ceilings and dark stone floors. But there was a fire going in the sitting room.

"Come sit yourself down here by the fire," said his friend. "You can't be used to our damp, sure you can't. Now, what'll it be? Earl Grey or the good black Irish tea? I'm afraid I've not a drop of alcohol on the premises, for reasons you know too well."

"Irish tea is fine," said the Nuncio.

"Good man! You're developing a refined taste, now," he said, jumping up to attend to the tea. He was back in a flash.

"Agnes wants to know do you take sugar and is it lemon or milk? She's baked you cakes, please to indulge her. I'll be the divil's own companion if they're not sampled."

"Milk, please," said Destino. "You have many books here."

"Yes," said Father Liam. "Far too many, probably. For all the good they've done me or my poor flock."

He disappeared again, returning with a tray carrying the tea things. A woman followed him with a large platter of cakes and cookies. She appeared to be at least fifty, but her hair was still dark, and she had strong coloring and beautiful cheekbones. It was easy to see how striking she must have been twenty years before.

"I'm Agnes Dawkins," she said, nodding her head toward him because her hands were holding the heavy platter. "Pleased to meet you, Nuncio."

"It is my pleasure," he said, rising in his chair.

"I hope you convince him he's mad to think of buying that Virgin creature. Not to speak of the blasphemy involved," she said, looking him steadily in the eye.

Destino glanced at Father Liam, who was smiling indulgently at his woman. The Nuncio tried not to show his alarm.

"She's all right. Agnes won't tell a soul," said Father Liam.

"I'm on my way to the shops," she said. "I only wanted to lay eyes on you, Nuncio, put a face to the voice I've heard on the phone so often. You'll have a few of these cakes, won't you! I'll set this down here on the sideboard right near you so you can take whatever suits you."

He obligingly took two pieces and pronounced them divine. She set down the platter and exited.

"She did want to see your face. She wasn't lying," said Father Liam.

"An ordinary man."

"No, not at all, my friend. You look exactly as a Papal Nuncio should look."

"I am not certain this pleases me. What do you mean by this?"

"You look faintly aristocratic and Italian and possessed of a spiritual melancholy."

"Aristocratic I am not. My family are all bourgeois, doctors, lawyers, some hopelessly impractical artists like my father, and of course priests."

"Have you done it, Paolo? Have you put the money in Mr. Redundant's account?"

"I cannot find the letter. It is most strange. It was in my pamphlet on the bed table before I went out for a little walk after lunch on the day we spoke. Wednesday, was it? And when I returned, it was not there. I have looked everywhere for it. I keep thinking I have forgotten where I put it. My unconscious resisted against our plan. Yes?"

"Your man could have taken it."

"Which man is that?"

"Bishop Meany. Who else?"

"But why would he do such a thing?"

"To buy the device himself."

"But Bishop Meany is a believer, a proper Catholic. He would not approve of creating false visions."

"There's your chance, Paolo. Tell Rome about this, and they'll punish him."

"I would have to prove he is doing it first, Liam, and it would be the height of hypocrisy to cause his punishment for buying the Virgin when we ourselves were thinking of doing the same thing."

"Paolo, you and I would have made better use of her. You know that."

One Week Later

47

All was in readiness, the green carpet on the tarmac still looking as fresh as when it was kissed by the Pope, the Hundred Thousand Welcomes banner over the door, the special VIP steps with their non-slip vinyl covering, the military band, the pipers, the sixteen best-behaved Loreto girls in all of Dublin, the three Irish Unemployed Feminists who had shown up on time, and atop a tray in the Aer Lingus VIP lounge the makings of the finest Irish coffee to be had anywhere in the world at eight o'clock in the morning. Dermot, Rock, and the Chief Superintendent had already had their first cups. Dermot said they deserved it after what he'd been through. There were five hundred Houlihans going to carry eternal grudges against him and all his progeny for refusing to grant them permission to greet their cousin at the foot or the toe or whatever you called it of Air Force Two. The Taoiseach wouldn't thank him for that. But the Taoiseach was the one who said to keep them away. The Secret Service had been nervous enough about the Loreto girls. And the trouble he went to to find them! You try getting ahold of the sixteen best-behaved Loreto girls on a Saturday night in Dublin, he told Rock, who had been waiting for him alone in Dwyer's that night for hours.

The Taoiseach had definite ideas about how things were done. First along the carpet would be himself and his cabinet, then the Nuncio and the top twenty ambassadors, then the head of Aer Lingus and the sixteen Loreto girls, and behind them the feminists, and finally the Cardinal Archbishop of Armagh along with Archbishop Weeks, his Church of Ireland equivalent, and Rabbi Quinn. It was important to keep the Church in the background on these state occasions, "especially when we're looking for an American loan," they said Kavanagh had warned.

"The Irish do not like to think the Church is running their country," said Dermot and punctuated the remark by patting the cream off his upper lip with a shamrock-bedecked paper napkin supplied by Aer Lingus.

"Is everything all right?" the immaculate Bernadette asked them.

"It's perfect," said Dermot. "It's absolutely grand."

"Any news on the Semtex?" Rock asked, after Bernadette had moved out of earshot.

"Just that the Provos are still looking for it," said Bloom. "We've got everyone going through the metal detector. They're being very cooperative."

"We'll have to inspect the roses," Rock said.

"You Americans are really something," said Dermot. "You could do with a little healthy fatalism."

He wanted to eat his words when he saw what was happening outside on the tarmac. Out of nowhere, people were appearing with signs that said HOOLIHANS OF CARLOW, HOULIHANS OF BRAY, HOOLIHANS OF TIPPE-RARY, HOULIHANS OF CULLYBACKEY. They were bunching up behind the ropes where the dignitaries were meant to stand. This was all supposed to be as secure as Fort Knox. He saw a sign saying HOULIHANS OF DUBLIN 14.

"Where the hell is Dublin 14?" he said.

"Who are all these people?" Rock said.

"This calls for a consultation," said Dermot.

He started back to the VIP lounge with Rock in tow. There were more Houlihans with signs in the terminal lobby, scores of them looking amazingly cheerful, considering the chill gray bleakness of the day.

"Dermot," Rock said, "we could always tell her to land at Shannon. There's still time."

"Not to worry," said Dermot. He thought he spotted Padraic Gurney, the Aer Lingus public-relations chief, moving in and out of the crowd.

"Paddy," he said, shoving himself under the PR man's nose. "Just the man I want to see."

"Hello, Dermot, my good man! How are you keeping? Isn't this very exciting for us all! Sure, it's a wonderful tribute to the first woman Vice President of the United States! We're all very proud of her!"

"Paddy," said Dermot, "there are hundreds of unauthorized people out there on the tarmac. We've a security problem, Paddy."

"It's all under control," Paddy said unctuously. "Working like a dream."

"And I suppose you made them all go through the metal detector?" said Dermot.

"They're all right, Dermot. They're dying to see her. They're her cousins!" said Paddy.

"We promised the Secret Service there'd be no crowds on the tarmac. It's meant to be strictly VIPs."

"Well, you've got those ridiculous feminists. Sure, we wouldn't want to be embarrassing her with them, Dermot, you know, she's not that way. She's normal! This way they'll be lost in the crowd. Listen, it's going to be wonderful. It's all been cleared with Washington, too, so don't you worry."

"No, it hasn't, Paddy, not with the Secret Service."

"This has higher approval than that," said Paddy. "The Vice President has expressly requested that her cousins should be allowed to greet her."

"How the fuck do you—they're not all her cousins, for Christ's sake!—and how the fuck do you know what the Vice President requested? The White House told us—"

"Because her PR man's an old friend of mine. It's all fixed, Dermot. It's what she wants. Relax. Go have another Irish coffee. No one's a bomb thrower here. I'll promise you. You look after your dignitaries and I'll look after the crowd."

Dermot and Rock retreated to the VIP lounge, where the Dublin diplomatic corps were now enjoying the Irish coffee.

"This could be a hairy situation," said Rock. "Let me call the White House."

"I knew I should have left the arrival time at 7 a.m.," said Dermot.

Then in walked the Taoiseach with a black face on him. "Where's the man from Foreign Affairs?" he demanded. "Who the hell's bused in all those people with the signs?"

"I'm your man, Taoiseach," Dermot said, putting out his hand. "Dermot Muldoon, protocol section. I think there might have been a misunderstanding. Aer Lingus had been told—"

"Since when is Aer Lingus in charge of Ireland's external affairs?" said the Taoiseach. "This is a colossal cock-up! I gave my assurances to the ambassador that there would only be a small number in the greeting party! You're to get rid of that crowd, Muldoon, or you'll pay for it!"

"Right," said Dermot hopelessly.

"The White House doesn't know anything about any request for crowds," Rock said, appearing by his side, "but that doesn't mean Houlihan didn't make it on her own."

"She's that independent, is she?" asked Dermot.

"Very," said Rock.

"Don't look so worried, gentlemen," said Chief Superintendent Bloom, coming upon them with a fresh glass of Irish coffee in his hand. "I've called up reinforcements. We'll have it all well contained."

• • •

The crowd turned out to be so well contained the Taoiseach couldn't get out of the VIP lounge. When he finally did join the queue for the elevator, it was too much of a squeeze, with all the ambassadors and cabinet members, so he graciously waited for the second run. The cabinet was not in sight when Rock, Dermot, and Chief Bloom emerged with him downstairs. No one knew where to direct them.

Dermot asked an air hostess, who pointed vaguely around the corner. The three of them followed the Taoiseach, the two archbishops, and twenty ambassadors through a maze of hallways. They came to a dead end and had to go back and try another channel of the maze. This happened three times before they arrived at a door being manned by a young Guard who stopped them all on his commander's orders. Dermot was able to persuade him that the man standing next to him who looked like Aloysius Kavanagh, the Taoiseach of Ireland, was in fact he, and the Guard let only the two of them through. With difficulty, they made their way through the crowd to their appointed spot on the green carpet.

Paddy Gurney greeted the Taoiseach with a big, warm handshake.

"Where are the Loreto girls, Muldoon?" Kavanagh asked through clenched teeth. "What happened to all the ambassadors? *Where are the goddamn Loreto Girls? Muldoon, the ambassadors! Do something fast!*"

Dermot desperately turned to the Guards.

"Orders came down a short while ago," he was told. "The Special Branch said no more on the tarmac."

"But they didn't mean the dignitaries or the Loreto girls," said Dermot. "Do you have a radio? Can you call Chief Superintendent Bloom? You've left him stuck inside there, you know."

"Here she comes," said one of the Guards, and in the distance they saw a plane descending.

"*Hurraaay!*" cheered the Houlihans.

"This is of the utmost urgency!" said Dermot. "The cabinet and all the ambassadors are stuck inside!"

The Guards finally acted. Rock, Chief Superintendent Bloom, and the ambassadors, these last looking red-faced and insulted, were led onto the green carpet. From another direction, looking ready to skin their party leader alive, came the cabinet along with Archbishop Weeks, the Cardinal Archbishop, Rabbi Quinn, and the Papal Nuncio, who had been waiting on the wrong side of the airport for twenty minutes.

"The Loreto girls," the Taoiseach taunted Dermot out of the side of his mouth just as Air Force Two taxied to a halt. The door opened and a Secret Serviceman was cheered by the crowd.

"Muldoon, will you tell me where in Christ's name Fergal Foyle thinks he's going out *there?*" Kavanagh sputtered.

Dermot saw the former Taoiseach leap over the rope and trot to the foot of the steps.

"He wasn't invited," Dermot said evenly.

"Then the Guards can take him away, can't they, Muldoon!" said Kavanagh.

"I think, sir, as there are members of the press around, it might not be—"

"And why is the arse-brained Mr. Gurney of Aer Lingus standing out there like the official greeter of Ireland?"

"I think he assigned himself that position, Taoiseach."

Four Secret Servicemen now emerged from the plane, holding compact little machine guns. They came menacingly down the stairs with the guns pointing straight out, looking at the crowd as though every single person in it was an assassin. They glared also at the Irish cabinet and the cream of Dublin's diplomatic corps.

Someone emerged back first in the doorway of the plane. Then he turned around. He appeared to be gripping things in his hands. He went down a few steps and lifted these things onto his shoulders. It was one end of a stretcher. He was carrying someone on a stretcher. Another man emerged from the plane holding the other end.

"They didn't tell us somebody needed medical attention," said the Taoiseach.

An ambulance pulled up almost under the belly of the plane. The stretcher-bearers reached the bottom of the steps, and everyone could see the injured person was a woman. She was waving. But she apparently couldn't lift her head. She raised two fingers in the V sign.

"Jesus, Muldoon, that's her!" said Kavanagh. He took a tentative step forward. The stretcher-bearers seemed to be turning aside. They weren't even going to come down along the carpet.

Kavanagh took another step forward, but something, some innate sense of delicacy, made him hesitate.

Paddy Gurney had no such qualms. He walked straight over to the stretcher and shook the woman's hand. Two seconds later Fergal Foyle appeared at Gurney's side. He, too, shook the woman's hand as Gurney appeared to do the introduction.

"The whoor!" yelled Kavanagh. "The shameless whoor!" And he plunged forward like a fighter bounding into the ring.

It must have been the pugilistic thrust of his body combined with the terrible expression on his face that frightened the Secret Service, for the first four gun-toting agents grabbed him and flung him to the ground. In those few seconds before their mistake could be explained to them, the stretcher-bearers moved into the ambulance. Foyle, who had been clasping the Vice President's hand, jumped up with them. The doors closed. The siren started. They were away.

"Muldoon!" yelled the Taoiseach, too furious to see the cameras flashing at him. *"Muldoon! How did that miserable blow-dried cunt get in there, Muldoon!"*

Out of the plane came tumbling, helter-skelter, the White House press corps.

"Where can I get a taxi?" they started asking the Taoiseach, his cabinet, the ambassadors. "Where's the nearest phone?"

The crowd of Houlihans, not quite sure what they had seen but beginning to suspect they had been cheated of their great moment, surged forward, breaking the rope. The Taoiseach was nearly knocked down again. A couple of Guards took hold of him and escorted him off toward the building. Eight Guards surrounded the British ambassador. Dermot was swept along.

He spotted Rock talking to one of the feminists. Bit of a cock-up there, too. Houlihan had been meant to meet them after the dignitaries. How many fresh enemies can a man make in one day?

Then he spotted at long last the sweet-faced Loreto girls, who were standing in a double row, looking straight out at a film crew from CNN as they silently smiled and held aloft, with the aid of their two nun chaperones, a huge sign that read:

HONOR OUR MAKER

LIFE IS A GIFT

48

"Hello, Aileen, is that you?"

Here was Donal's father now ringing up before closing time on a Sunday night, which he had never done in all the years she'd known him. He must be getting too old for the pub, she thought. She didn't want to hear the worry in his voice.

"Yes, it's me, Dad. It's great to hear your voice! How are you keeping? How's Ma? Are you frozen through?"

"We're snug as a bug up here, girl. They know how to build a hearth in these parts. And yourselves? How are the girls?"

"They're grand, just grand. How's Spike?"

"Spike?" said the old man quizzically. "He's the same."

Stupid of her to go asking about the dog. A dead giveaway to her state of nerves.

"What's Ma been up to?" she said because she couldn't stop herself. "She doing her five hundred Christmas cakes?"

"She's busy as ever, aye. You'll be up for Stephen's Day again? You will!"

"Oh, I expect so," said Aileen. The day after Christmas seemed as far off as the land of Oz.

"Do you know who stopped by to see us this afternoon? Angus Keenan. He's a face from the past. Looks the picture of his Da."

"Angus Keenan?" said Aileen.

"Donal's school chum."

"I don't believe I've met him."

"You've not met him?"

"No. I don't believe so."

"That's a bit odd. Angus said he was talking to the girls this week. He said the girls had told him Donal was up here with us. There's nothing wrong with you two, is there, Aileen?"

"I could murder those girls sometimes. Did they really tell this Angus Donal was with you? I can't trust them with the telephone at all."

"Well, you'd think Angus would have asked you. He drove up here from Dublin. He seemed deeply concerned about something. Is Donal there? Could I have a word with him?"

"He's gone out for his nightcap, Dad. You know him. You could try ringing Goggins."

"Have him call me, Aileen, if I don't reach him myself. I'm a bit worried about Angus. He's a pair of brains is Angus. Speaks four languages, you know. His Da always said he didn't know where it came from. Funny thing for a man to be doing midweek when he's teaching at Belvedere, driving all the way up to Donegal. He didn't say it, but he'd the look of a man on the run."

"Perhaps it's the mid-life crisis, Dad. A chum of Donal's would be the right age."

"I keep asking myself why he would come up here looking for Donal without calling you back or ourselves. Is he afraid of the telephone?"

"I wouldn't know, Dad. As I say, I never met this Angus."

"I told Donal the time for all that has passed."

"All what, Dad? Oh, you mean them—"

"We'll outbreed them in the end, son. That's what I always told him. You tell him to ring me all the same, Aileen."

"Oh, yes, Dad, I will. But I don't know when he'll be in tonight. You know him."

49

$\mathcal{T}$here was no mystery about the circumstances of Houlihan's injury. She was a fitness freak and had insisted on bringing Myron Shakespeare, her personal trainer, along on the trip. Shortly before the plane landed, he had had her doing a new set of yoga twists which were said to work wonders against jet lag. On the third twist, the Vice President got stuck.

Her condition greatly simplified the security situation. She was put in traction at St. Vincent's Hospital and given painkillers that made interviews with the press unthinkable. There were still leaks. A hospital cleaner told reporters the Vice President was disturbed to find so many American programs on Irish TV. The kitchen staff said she had also complained about the lack of whole grains in her diet.

The newspapers found other material to print. A couple of the English tabloids had discovered that on the same Sunday morning she arrived in Dublin, Honoria Houlihan had appeared on American television in a taped interview with a woman named Barbara Walters, who asked the inevitable question: "How do you really feel about abortion?"

"Abortion is as simple as having your tonsils out," Houlihan had told Walters. "It's easier than having your wisdom teeth pulled."

That created an uproar in Dublin for a day or two, and then the same British tabloids sent reporters to cover the current divorce case the Vice President's husband Lloyd Shilling was handling, a bizarre and bitter contest between the movie star Clint Clunk and his estranged third wife, the starlet Barbee Brooks. Barbee was asking for the highest alimony in history and also custody of the frozen Yangtze terrier embryos which were left in the Carmel Canine in Vitro Fertilization Clinic in suspended animation after Ms. Brooks discovered her husband in a clinch with the couple's organic gardener. Shilling found the case intellectually challenging, it was reported, for the contest posed a sticky legal dilemma: how could an odd number of frozen family pets be evenly divided to satisfy the fifty-fifty community property law in a California divorce? The number of frozen embryos involved was three.

The tabloids said Shilling had a great mind and a cool temperament. He was innately unable to connect with the hot blood of a warring couple, but he could relate to big money without any difficulty, and he was America's most successful divorce lawyer. His wife Honoria's political career had been bankrolled by the wages of his dispassionate brilliance. Even the President owed a fair portion of his success to Shilling's gifts, for once it had been determined that Honoria Houlihan was to be his Vice Presidential nominee, Henry Pond's political action committee budgets had quickly doubled. All Shilling's clients contributed. Shilling had been involved in at least three thousand famous divorces. It could be said, and more than one paper said it, that if it had not been for the broken plates and bitter tears in the mansions of the rich and famous, Henry Pond would not have been elected President of the United States.

Rupert Penrose was profoundly disapproving. He wrote that it was all the work of Providence, even the Vice President's slipped disk—or especially the Vice President's slipped disk. It offended God's sense of political propriety to see a politician from the land of abortion and divorce (he called her husband a divorce profiteer) come claiming her Irishness right at this moment in time when Ireland was incontestably the holiest spot on earth. He said it should give the next American politician pause before he or she tried to wrap him- or herself in the mantle of the Virgin through an Irish surname. Certain transgressions might slip His notice in other parts of the world where there was chaos and severe congestion, but in Ireland, not a sinner went unseen, Penrose told his readers. That was the virtue of living in such a small place. God could keep track of it all. For what other explanation could there be for Ireland's steadfast adherence to God's laws?

50

"What's he talking about, 'steadfast adherence to God's laws'? Where's he been living?" Moira said to Deirdre Fanning, who had stopped by her cottage Monday morning to go over the Housewife of the Year Award speech and have a confab about the airport debacle.

"Rupert Penrose is more savvy than you might think, Moira," said Deirdre. "He knows what happened to our great hopes for the divorce referendum last time. He understands that sort of don't-count-me-Lord strain in the Irish people, you know: 'I'm just a poor sinner myself, but I'd never drag the laws of the country down with me.'

"Kavanagh's hanging on by a thread now. He won't come near us women after what she said about abortions and having your tonsils out. What an image, Moira!"

"I know," said Moira. "It's a mercy for us she's in hospital."

Naturally, Dermot Muldoon rang the next instant to ask whether he might expedite feminists' visits to the famous patient's room in St. Vincent's.

"There was rather a thin showing of feminists at the airport," he said. "We were lucky all those Houlihans were there."

"I guess the feminists weren't very enthusiastic," said Moira. "They did resent those awful security investigations."

"You'll be happy to know they all passed."

"They might not all see that as a plus."

"No, they might not. On the other hand, they can all slip right up to her room in hospital. We'd like a few visitors for her, Moira. The woman is a heartbeat away from a significant post."

"Irish women don't think abortion is like a tooth extraction, Mr. Muldoon. Why did she have to go saying that when she was about to visit us?"

"Oh, I know. Isn't it ghastly! It's enough to make you begin to see why the Taoiseach wanted her to come later."

"Did you have a question, Mr. Muldoon?"

"Yes. Why aren't you women out there beating down the doors of St. Vincent's trying to get in to see her?"

"I told you. We're not on the same wavelength."

"Why did you organize that demonstration in front of Government Buildings, then?"

"It's not for the Taoiseach to go criticizing her or barring her from our soil."

"Ah," he said.

"Women can support each other without agreeing with each other. Do you follow me?"

Deirdre was giving her the thumbs-up sign.

"I think I do," he said. "Well, tell me this. How would a State Department cultural-exchange tour strike you?"

"What are you talking about?"

"The U.S. State Department sometimes arranges trips to the States for culturally significant citizens of foreign countries. Might a few of your women friends be interested in coming to St. Vincent's to discuss the program?"

"Let me see if I understand you, Mr. Muldoon. You're willing to buy our hospital visits to Houlihan with trips to the States?"

Deirdre Fanning grabbed the phone from her hand.

"Hello, Dermot," she said. "I couldn't help picking up on what you were saying to Moira. I'm over here going over some strategy with her."

"Minister Fanning, good morning! It's always a pleasure to speak to you. Your office said you would be tied up in meetings all day."

"Quite right they were, too. Dermot, this sounds like a wonderful proposal of yours to give Irish feminists some exposure to the American system. How many would you be thinking of inviting on the trip?"

"How many do you think would want to go, Minister?"

51

*T*he government fell the next morning. Everyone went around saying it was because of the proposed new cigarette tax, but when Fergus O'Sullivan had stood up in the Dail to call for a vote of confidence, he did not mention cigarettes. He simply held up to the members the photo that had been all over the Irish front pages: the Taoiseach's livid face in the foreground, watching the American Vice President's ambulance recede under the belly of her plane.

Rupert Penrose of course said he had seen it coming, that the liberals had overreached themselves and couldn't find the money anywhere but in cigarettes, the poor man's luxury, and it was too bad because the last thing the country needed, coming up to Christmas, was another election.

The deputies actually contrived to delay the start of the campaign until the sixth of January and call the missing time in between the

Christmas recess. They knew the Irish people would never forgive them for interfering with their three weeks of Christmas parties.

Chief Superintendent Bloom was put into an awkward position, rendered a kind of lame-duck commander at the head of the Special Branch. He had been frustrated in all his attempts to trace the Semtex from Liverpool to Dublin, and now his British sources of information were all closing off, leery of sharing top-secret stuff with a man who might be shunted aside by the next Irish government.

The Virgin, at least, had not been seen for a week, and Bloom hoped she would remain out of sight indefinitely. That would mean one less police-deployment nightmare. It should also mean the American Vice President had nothing to keep her in Ireland. Her staff was not for the moment talking about moving her, but he had no doubt she would be taken home in another day or two.

52

"*A* man has to keep things in perspective," Dennis said to Caroline as they shared their eleven o'clock coffee. He had recovered his sanity and was preparing to go meet Rabbi Quinn for lunch at Après Moi. "There will be other governments."

"Yes, but they don't fall every day," said Caroline. "I mean, it is a sort of national convulsion each time, and you take it so much upon you, explaining things and all. I've never seen you finish a column before three o'clock in the morning on a day when the government collapses, Dennis, and you aren't getting any younger. Surely you can postpone your religious conversion until next week."

He knew she was afraid to let him out of her sight. He hadn't left the house since Saturday. Or touched a drop.

"But I've already explained to you, darling. This is not my conversion. It is my pre-conversion study."

"Study with him, then, but come home for lunch. I don't see how you can spare two hours with him in a restaurant, Dennis. Not today. Honestly, I don't."

"I'll only have one glass of wine."

"I wasn't meaning that."

"Well, what are you fretting about, then? Is it my being seen in public with Rabbi Quinn?"

She did her bored upper-class look, which meant he had hit home.

"You're afraid it will turn off the appointments committee, aren't you, Caroline? Admit it. Well, you needn't worry your pretty little head about it anymore. I told you I'd lost the Chair. And I'm glad. It's liberating, do you know? I can plan my life without reference to the trustees of CUD at last."

"Oh, Dennis, you don't *know* that you've lost the Chair. It hasn't been decided. Padraic promises it hasn't been decided."

"Padraic is not in the inner circle, my pet. He's only on the advisory board."

"He's the bloody chairman of the faculty, Dennis!"

"He won't pull for me if the bishops and the conservatives don't want me."

"What makes you think the bishops don't want you? I can understand the conservatives, but—"

"Caroline, you have lived here for thirty years. Try to think like an Irish bishop. Would you really want me in the most coveted literature Chair at CUD?"

"And so it's time for you to go off and become a Jew, is that it? There is a Rome elsewhere sort of thing. If I were Rabbi Quinn, I'd feel used. I'm certain of that."

"Rabbi Quinn understands me."

That sent her off in a huff long enough for Dennis to don his bulletproof vest and the mac.

"I suppose I ought to convert to Mohammedanism to keep up the spirit of this marriage," she said when she came to kiss him goodbye. "The children are saying I should."

"It would save us buying Christmas gifts."

"Dennis, Jews give gifts for a solid week during Hanukkah."

"How did you know that?"

"I grew up in a tolerant society."

"Which despises the Irish."

"Yes, and you brought me home, where they despise not only the English but women as well."

"Caroline! You are full of grievance this morning."

"What happens to me if you become a Jew?"

"What do you mean, what happens to you?"

"Will they expect me to convert? It's so foreign."

"Heavens, no, Caroline! And I may not. I'm simply exploring."

"At what point in your explorations do they circumcise you?"

53

*E*verything seemed to be going splendidly for Rupert Penrose. His strategy with the university trustees had worked better than he ever dreamed it would. Three of them had rung him directly to say they had actually read *Where We Went Wrong* and were looking forward to discussing it with him at his earliest convenience.

The fall of the government would surely mean an end to all the talk about divorce and abortion. The plain people of Ireland did not want to turn themselves into Americans. Rupert was taking Bishop Meany to lunch to celebrate. Their last appointment had had to be postponed.

It was just as well, actually, because Samantha Doyle had meanwhile been able to warn him about the ultra-Catholic problem. Ironically, now that the Kerrygold Chair was almost his, the strategy which had brought him so close to the prize was causing a slight bit of hesitation among some of the more timorous trustees. Samantha said they had been very profoundly impressed by his scholarship and also by his popularity with the students at the Toyota Night School. They could never imagine him yelling at a student. But the more seriously they took him academically, the more comprehensively did they examine his standing in the community. And it was here that the problem lay. For the very supporters who had worked so hard to get him into serious academic consideration were the most Catholic Catholics in Ireland. Samantha, not a subtle woman in the best of times, had wondered aloud whether he had any Protestant friends.

"They're looking at the whole person, Rupert, I must warn you, so if there are any little pockets of naughtiness in your life, I hope you keep them out of sight," Samantha had laughingly warned him.

Naturally, he had thought of Attracta.

And because it was going to be a sticky thing explaining the Catholic problem to Bishop Meany, who had been nagging him anyway about the horoscopes column, Penrose went in to Niall Gormley, the editor of the Dublin *Sentinel*, that Tuesday morning, to see if he might kill two birds with one stone, get rid of Attracta and the horoscopes in the one go.

"You're right. The horoscope is an embarrassment, Rupert," said Niall with amazing swiftness, "and Sophie's, between ourselves, a bit past it."

"Oh, Sophie's all right," said Penrose. "Perhaps you could give her the odd book review."

"What will we put in place of the horoscopes, Rupe? We need a young person's column. What do you think of Sophie's protégée?"

"You mean her present apprentice? Sophie says she's hopeless, about the worst horoscope-writer trainee she's ever had," said Penrose. Sophie had told him this when he was trying to encourage her to give Attracta her chance. But now Penrose thought Attracta too dangerous to keep around.

"I hear she's a few poems being published in *Oneself* magazine," said Gormley.

"She does? *Oneself*? Do they do poetry?" asked Penrose, a bit flummoxed.

[207]

"Sophie told me, actually. She thinks the girl might be able to write something for the lovelorn. Said she had an affinity for that sort of thing. She said you had noticed this, too, Rupe."

"Oh, I can't remember what I said." He shrugged. "I may have been trying to offer some sort of encouragement. But she hasn't quite honestly struck me as a person of great ability. Between ourselves, I think she may be happier back in the Glenageary Postal Sorting Office."

"The Glenageary Postal Sorting Office? You mean, where she was seduced?"

"What?" said Penrose, fearing to say more.

"In one of her poems, she mentions it."

"Ah."

"Curious place for a seduction, I would have thought. But you don't think she's got ability? Have you read anything of hers?"

"Um—"

"Never mind that. What do you have for us tonight? The last word on the government's collapse?"

"No," said Penrose. "I've a rather startling personal column. You'll have it before lunch."

"Good man," said Gormley. "I'm feckin' bored with governments collapsing."

54

$\mathcal{L}$ater that morning the Secret Service agent who seemed sweet on Moira came around again. She found she actually liked him, although that was probably because a relationship was out of the question. They had fragments of their Catholic education in common, but not much else. Being rejected. She did find herself wondering in a distanced abstract sort of a way whether a man that old could be any good in bed. He had an all-American jaw and those pouty James Dean lips they got from drinking Cokes maybe, and nice eyes, although his hairline was going back a bit far by his parting. But she had to admit she found him attractive. There was something touching about his wanting a woman who was so inappropriate for him. He was so different from Irish men!

She was sweeping the floor when he came in, but the telephone soon interrupted her. He took the broom from her hand and got on with it. Then he found the kettle and fixed a pot of tea and brought her a cup. The vulnerable smile he gave her put a stitch in her heart. But that was all right. He'd be gone in a few days.

"Moira," Dermot said to her on the phone, "are you busy tonight?"

"I've two meetings. Why?"

"Ah. Well, we should get together to talk over this State Department cultural-exchange business. They are willing to offer a fair number of tickets."

"I thought Deirdre was handling that."

"Yes. Yes, she is. You can tell her what I'm conveying to you, all right?"

"That seems cumbersome, but go ahead."

"Here's the thing. They are willing to offer a fair number of tickets, But the tour starts on the thirtieth of January in Tulsa, Oklahoma."

"Is that in what they call the sun belt?"

"Well—yes—in a way. And it's only a two-week tour and then you would be free to go around on your own, you see."

Someone knocked on her front door. The agent opened it.

"Moira, where's Feeny's car?" bellowed Fergus O'Sullivan.

She could see the American trying to size up the situation. She rang off with Dermot.

"Here he is, the Samson of the Irish Dail. Has he introduced himself to you, Mr. O'Leary? This is Fergus O'Sullivan, the man who brought the government down this morning. You realize what a cock-up you've made of it, I hope, Fergus," she said. She could sense how he wanted to wreck things here, too, whatever they were.

"Moira, what have you done with Paul's car?"

"What have I done with it? Nothing."

"It's gone again. He thinks the party stole it for use in the Dail campaign."

"Fergus, I've not seen it for a week. But I remember Kathy saying her poor sick aunt might get better from a go-round in it. Perhaps she's borrowed it for the purpose."

Her telephone rang again. This time it was Deirdre wanting to know whether Moira could help out in her constituency office during the campaign. Of course there would be no pay, only tea and sandwiches.

"I'll do it, so," said Moira. "But I thought it wasn't starting until after the holidays. You'll win hands down, of course."

"I don't know," said Deirdre. "Between ourselves, I could wish a certain important American had gone home. You'll come over to my office straightaway, yes?"

"I've a few things to clear up here, Deirdre."

What might Fergus be saying to her American? Her American. Will you listen to her.

"Moira has sworn off men," Fergus announced gleefully.

"Off Irish men."

"Give us a drink, then, to comfort us in our loss."

"I don't have time to be sitting around drinking," she said. "I'm not a member of the Dail."

But her house was freezing. She hadn't lit a fire. The two men were keeping their macs on. She fixed them small whiskies to keep them happy while she shut herself in the bedroom to change into clothes worthy of a constituency office.

"What's the best restaurant in Dublin?" Rock asked Fergus as she emerged.

"Oh, I'd say Après Moi. That'd set you back a couple hundred quid."

"We'll go there for lunch," said Rock.

"Splendid!" said Fergus.

"He's not inviting you," said Moira.

"Don't be shocked by her rudeness," Fergus said to Rock. "Moira and her Sapphic sisters are at odds with Irish society as it is presently constituted, its basic unit being the nuclear family clustered around a heterosexual union. Two thousand years of cultural wisdom crammed

into those pretty little heads and all they want to talk about is clitori-
dectomy on the Indian subcontinent."

"Fuck off, Fergus!" said Moira.

"God bless the women of Ireland!" said O'Sullivan happily. "Not
half a hundred of them believe the feminists make any sense at all. I
don't care who they elect to the Dail, the likes of Moira will not make
a dent in the average Irish woman's impermeable respectability. Women
crave authority, Moira, don't you know that? It's only the few mad
creatures from West Donegal and the lesbians who insist on rebelling.
Listen, when Britain left Ireland, the women of this country covered
the empty seat of the oppressor with spotless table linens and on top of
them placed the spotless posterior of the Cardinal Archbishop of Armagh. Give us a drop more, Moira, and ring up your friend Kathy.
Tell her I need Paul's car."

"Ring her yourself, Fergus O'Sullivan. I am not your secretary."

"I don't know her number."

"You are fucking helpless, aren't you!"

"I don't know why that good Anglo-Saxon word always sounds so
shocking on your succulent lips, Moira, but it does," said Fergus.

"Stop being so bloody condescending!"

"You must find this very boring," he said to Rock. "Did she tell you
she was fired from her job for her shocking behavior?"

"And you're the model husband, aren't you, Fergus?" she said.

"Your quarrel is not with me, my dear Moira, but rather with the
unjust heaven that gave me gifts so far superior to your own."

"And I suppose you drove Feeny's car home the other night, did
you? Because of your superior courage in the face of the supernatural?"

"The supernatural? Did she tell you that one of her sisters actually
tried to assert that the Immaculate Conception was a feminist act? On
the radio. Was that you, Moira? The Virgin Mary is a feminist, and
I'm the Rose of Tralee, Tralee, Tralee!"

"We can continue this over lunch," Rock said.

"I'm afraid I can't join you," said Moira. "I'm going to work."

"Ah, then, Mr. O'Leary, it will be left to me to entertain you with
tales of the wild exotic lives of Irish politicians, in exchange for which
I hope to hear the most intimate secrets of Henry Pond's domestic life."

"Moira, please come with us!" Rock begged so fervently that she agreed to share at least the starter with them. Somehow she ended up staying until coffee. Unpaid workers had to take their meals where they could find them, she told herself. But she hadn't actually eaten all that much.

55

"My wife is worried I'll have to be circumcised," Dennis told the rabbi, who looked as Irish as his name, Quinn, blue-eyed and black-haired and with an enormous head on the short neck. They were seated near the back of the restaurant, in keeping with their rather modest fame.

"That is not required unless you wish to convert to the Orthodox religion," said Rabbi Quinn. "We are a liberal congregation. We only circumcise babies."

"That's what I told her."

"I take it she is not pleased with this idea of yours."

"A bit apprehensive."

"Well, you can reassure her that I'll not allow you to convert unless I'm convinced of your absolute sincerity."

"Ah, sincerity! How do you test a thing like that, Rabbi?"

"We make you walk on burning coals, of course."

"I thought that was the Hindi."

"Rabbi, how good to see you!" It was Bishop Meany, offering a handshake.

"And you, Bishop, you're looking well," said the rabbi warmly, standing up to offer his hand. "And isn't that Rupert Penrose attempting to secrete himself behind you there."

"Oh, hello, Rabbi!" Penrose then brought out heartily, emerging from behind Bishop Meany. "And it's yourself, is it, Davitt McDermott? Where've you been keeping yourself these days? And why didn't we see your column last week? Hiding from the literary crowd, are we? They must all be gunning for you. I hear you're in line for the Kerrygold Chair."

"I hear the same about you," said Dennis, feeling compelled to rise himself. "You're looking well for a man who's been sleeping in his office."

"Sit down, sit down, please, gentlemen!" said Bishop Meany.

"We'd ask you to join us," said the rabbi, "only I'm dispensing religious instruction here." He smiled an unreadable smile.

"Instruction?" said Meany, looking from the one to the other.

"That's right," said Dennis, with a little thrust of his chin.

"I've found accommodation now, thanks be," said Penrose.

"I gather your former residence has been turned into a shrine," said Dennis.

"It's a terrible crass business," said Penrose. "Charging admission."

"A bit like the Shrine of Knock," said Dennis. "I s'pose your tap water's got holy. Well, at least you're off the street."

"Yes, I've a roof over my head for Christmas," said Penrose.

"Oh, God, how I dislike Christmas!" said Dennis. "My children spend the entire time trying to convert me to whole grains, this awful oat-bran stuff and nonalcoholic beer. And then it's the other extreme with the incorrigible aunts in the country, who attempt to poison us in their own houses with force-feedings of beef, turkey, and ham, followed by puddings, cakes, and a couple of really disgustingly sweet mince pies. It's enough to make you long for bread and water, Rabbi. You have no idea how lucky you are to have been able to escape Christmas."

"Who escapes Christmas in Ireland?" Rabbi Quinn said with a shrug. "But we have our own feasts, too. And mothers who get insulted if we don't eat three times too much of everything. I would have thought, Dennis, that at Brandeis you would have been introduced to the concept of the Jewish mother."

"My wife hasn't let the children spend Christmas with me these twelve years," said Penrose. "Not that I'd have known what to do with them in my one little room."

That was a conversation stopper.

"We'll leave you to it now," said Bishop Meany. They went off to a table on the far side of the room.

"There you have the classic example of the Irish poormouth," said Dennis. "Your man deserts his wife and young children, comes to Dublin for the glamorous newspaper job, and wants to make you believe he's the most bereft of creatures."

"I can find it in my heart to pity him," said Rabbi Quinn. "They say the wife did walk out on him. We all have our contradictions. We Jews also have our poormouthing tradition, you know. I have often thought how at home the Irish would feel in Judaism. Catholicism is far too austere and hierarchical for them. It's much better suited to the English. I maintain that if the Celts had been Jews and had come to Ireland before St. Patrick, he'd have given up and gone back to Wales—or wherever he came from."

"Then we'd have fought Hitler and the British would have stayed neutral?"

The rabbi nodded.

"What about the suffering Jesus?" Dennis said.

"Why are you doing this, Dennis?"

"I am sick to death of the great Irish divide."

"So you are not embracing Judaism as much as you are disembracing Christianity."

"Perhaps."

"I suppose that could be a reason to convert. We shall have to see. You are not doing this because you think CUD could use a Jewish professor of Irish literature?"

"I told you I'm out of the running there," said Dennis.

"Penrose is not your intellectual equal. Surely he will not get the Kerrygold Chair."

"There is more than intellect involved. And others are being considered, I understand. But don't be fooled. Rupert is more intelligent than he lets on."

"A characteristic of the Irish," said the rabbi. "They think someone is waiting around the corner to steal the copyright."

"Occupied peoples develop habits of deception."

"Your conversion to Judaism, what would that be? Another disguise?"

"My wife is British, after all. I have to be constantly on my guard."

•   •   •

On the other side of the room, Rupert Penrose and Bishop Meany were drinking a very good Château Lynch Bages.

"You don't think he's serious about the religious instruction?" said Penrose.

"Probably not," said the bishop, "but he's attracted to apostasies wherever he finds them."

"There are those who would say he's got a streak of the Antichrist," said Penrose. "I wouldn't go so far myself. Although he's not one to set an example for the young minds of Ireland. You saw what he wrote in the *Times*, of course."

"You mean about abortion and the changes in canon law?"

"Yes."

"I think I'll have the duck for the day that's in it," said the bishop. "Bad luck for the Taoiseach."

"Someone ought to bring it to the attention of the trustees," said Penrose. "His *Times* piece."

"I expect someone has," said Bishop Meany. "Myself, I'd let sleeping dogs lie."

"How do you mean that?" said Penrose, hit by a sudden blind fear that one of his conquests might have had an abortion somewhere.

"A thing like that could backfire. Between ourselves, the Vatican does not like us to remind people that canon law ever changes."

"Ah, well, then," said Penrose. "You'll be happy to know I've killed our horoscopes column."

"Well done, Rupert! That is good news," said Meany. "Very good news, indeed."

The bishop held his glass up to Penrose, who toasted his friend in return.

"It's a great day for Ireland," said Penrose. "I suppose we'll have Fergal Foyle again."

"In and out like a fiddler's elbow," said Bishop Meany. "A cute whoor of an ambulance hopper, too."

"Yes, there was fast footwork there all right. They say she didn't realize it was the former Taoiseach she'd invited along for the ride."

"I'd say Foyle had a few helpers on the tarmac."

"Nice wine, this."

"Excellent wine, Rupert. To what do I owe the honor? Have you heard a whisper from the trustees? Someone told me they were very close to a decision."

"I heard the same thing. In fact, they may even have decided already and not in my favor."

"But late last week I heard that as many as eight of them were your confirmed supporters."

"That was last week, Gus. This week, this very morning, I heard they were inclined to think I am too visibly Catholic. They like McDermott's lack of religious affiliation, his devotion to, quotes, independent thought. Frankly, I think that puts him outside the Irish context altogether. But I'm not the one to say."

"Quite so, Rupert, quite so. Well, is there anything I can do? Would you like me to call some of my friends?"

"I think actually not at this juncture, Gus, as you might inadvertently point up the, em, Catholic connection. Of course, I know you're not judging me as a Catholic. You're an Irish scholar in your own right. But the trustees are not aware of your versatility."

"You flatter me, Rupert."

"But you are a very impressive Irish scholar, Gus, and I know you would never bring the pressure of the Nuncio's office to bear on this, but it's the *appearance* of not bringing pressure to bear that we—"

"I quite understand, Rupert. Although it isn't as though they've minded in the past. They've been known to come to us to seek our opinion."

"I know that. How well I know that! They are not being consistent. No one is accusing them of being consistent. The thing is, they don't seem to know their own minds. McDermott seems to have intimidated them with his, his pseudo-intellectualizing. Of course, it's all an old rehash, but I won't go into that. He's got the trustees utterly confused. One minute they want a so-called relevant Catholic, the next minute they want an atheist. Do you know, I heard they were even making comparisons of book sales? I don't think that's fair. I don't think it's fair at all. God knows how many copies of *Ourselves Alone* I would have sold if I hadn't turned down all the London publishers! I really don't think they ought to figure in his American textbook, because there again, the Irish context—"

"Absolutely," said Bishop Meany. "McDermott describes himself as a 'questing agnostic,' by the way, but I take your point, Rupert. The trustees sound like a terrible lot of changers and about-facers. Perhaps you're better off not trying to think what they want."

"I agree with you completely, Bishop! It's to the students, the future leaders of Ireland, that I have a responsibility."

"Nobly put, Rupert. You've a fine character, a fine character."

"And it is self-created, Bishop. I don't think you know that I was born a Protestant."

"You weren't!"

"Yes, I'm afraid I was. I converted at the age of twenty-three."

"Does anyone know this?"

"Two old ladies in Greystones and my aunts in Merrion Square. The priest who baptized and confirmed me is long since dead."

"Am I the first to be told?"

"The first. You can see why I wanted to tell you in person, a matter of this magnitude."

"Yes, yes, I do understand. But, Rupert, you're surely not thinking of reverting, not for the sake of the Chair—"

"No, no, Gus, rest assured, I would *not* do that. No, I was merely thinking of writing about my deep, dark secret at last. The moment seems right."

"You'd want to be careful how you put it."

"I thought I might say I was like the country of Ireland herself: ninety-six percent Catholic and four percent Protestant."

"But surely when you're Catholic, you're all Catholic, Rupert. Is it still as high as four percent?"

"Yes, I've checked with central statistics."

"I don't know. I don't think you ought to say that part of you is Protestant, not in the present tense, not in bold print, Rupert."

[217]

"Well, it would simply be a way of stating for the trustees what we both know to be true, that I do have a broad vision. After all, if I win the Chair, Bishop, I shall be able to give Catholic principles a loftier platform."

"Rupert, your enemies could take a thing like this and—"

"Once I'm in the Kerrygold Chair, no one can touch me."

"They could call you a spiritual opportunist."

"A man has to take some risks in life, it seems to me, Gus, in order to reach the pinnacle. At the very least I will have aired a shameful secret that has haunted me all my adult life. Don't you think it makes me an even stronger voice for the Church, knowing I am a convert?"

"You're sounding as though you have already written this, Rupert."

"I have. It's in Wednesday's column."

"To be honest with you, Rupert, I'm not sure the bishops will know what to make of it."

•   •   •

Later that afternoon, when Rupert was back at the *Sentinel*, Bishop Meany rang him up.

"That is apparently true about your man McDermott," he said. "He is actually studying to be a Jew."

"Really!" said Penrose. "You don't say!"

"It does actually place him outside the Irish context altogether," said Bishop Meany. "The man's lost his marbles."

What was more, the university trustees had soured on Ulick Brown, who turned out to be simultaneously seeking a tenured position at Queens College in Belfast, and it now appeared that Michael Groarke never was a serious contender. "Irish Milking Through the Ages" had simply ruled him out from the beginning.

"Oh, dear! That leaves them only myself, the poor unfortunates," said Penrose.

"I do think you have a very real chance now, Rupert, very real," said the bishop. "I would hate to see you ruin it with an indiscretion."

"Indiscretion?"

"I don't think it's such a good thing to start writing about your Protestant beginnings just at this point in time, my friend. It would only confuse the issue. I'm sure it's a fascinating story which ought to be told in the bye-and-bye. Could you pull that column, do you think?"

"Certainly. But, Gus, I wonder if it's as damning as you think."

"I believe it could do you harm, Rupert, serious harm."

"Surely not a conversion this way, Bishop. If it had been the other way, it goes without saying—"

"No, no, no, Rupert, you misunderstand me. Not the actual conversion or indeed the fact that you were born a Protestant. I think people will find that fascinating. No, I mean the fact of your disclosing it right now at this sensitive time."

"Well, it would actually be more timely for me to write about the fall of the government. Why don't I ask Gormley to hold the column until later?"

"Exactly," said Bishop Meany.

56

$\mathcal{P}$enrose rode his bicycle all the way to his old flat before he remembered he was no longer living there. With hindsight, he could see he never should have handed in the column before discussing it with Bishop Meany. He had let himself become rattled by Gormley's remark that Sophie thought he knew something of Attracta's affinity for the lovelorn. He knew Gormley would be pleased with the column. But he had badly misjudged the effect it would have on the bishop. Penrose himself genuinely believed that a convert was a better Catholic than a born one. He likened himself to the Indian husband who tells his wife after many years with her that theirs had not been, after all, an arranged marriage. But his "I *chose* you" had fallen very flat. Indeed, it might have introduced an element of doubt about his suitability for the match, traces of which he thought he had seen occluding the bishop's gaze once or twice during their lunch after his disclosure. It was an expression he had not seen on Augustine Meany's face before. The man had looked at him with eyes that said: So that is your secret, you are not one of us.

A large gilded cross with a little oval portrait of the Virgin at its center stood by the front gate of Penrose's old building. But the turnstile was no longer there. The fickle public had moved on. What an awful kip of a place it was, compared to his grand new lodgings on Palmerston Road! And sweet, generous Samantha had promised to have tea ready for him when he arrived from work. What a comfort to an aging bachelor, he thought, turning his bicycle southward.

"Alone at last!" said his landlady as he came inside her grand abode. She stood unambiguously on the landing in her dressing gown. She seemed to have quite forgotten the promise of tea.

"Are we, then?" he said without ardor. "Is Clarence out for the evening? A nice cozy cup of tea would put us to rights, don't you think?"

"Clarence is in London, Rupert, dear. We are entirely unchaperoned. I suppose it's quite naughty of me to be going about like this in front of you—with your reputation," she said, gripping the banister with a sort of coy intensity.

"Oh, you're quite safe with me, Samantha," he said, turning away to fiddle with the umbrella which had gone askew under his greatcoat. He felt it best not to venture upstairs past her. He had work to do.

"That is not what my friend Sophie Bukowski tells me," she said.

"Oh, you know Sophie, do you? Pet of a woman, old Sophie. She has a fierce power of imagination, does old Soph. I expect it's all the Barbara Cartland novels."

"I wish you would stop calling her *old*, Rupert. She's hardly old!" said Samantha, now coming down the stairs with a brisk step, all coyness fled from her being. "Come along into the kitchen. I shall make your cup of tea. You seem out of sorts, not yourself. Is there anything wrong?"

"I've a packet of work to do this evening," he said, following her at a discreet distance. "I've suddenly got to write a new column."

"Yes, of course you do!" she said cheerily, as if she were his nanny making light of his homework. "I suppose Foyle will get in again?"

"It is not a foregone conclusion. His party may come apart at the seams."

"Oh! That's bad news for Mildred Burns. She's just got him onto her board for the Zoological Society. You like two spoons of sugar, don't you, Rupert?"

"Yes, thank you."

"You see, I don't forget," she said, bestowing upon him a long, tender smile.

"You are very good to me, Samantha. I wish I could take you out to dinner tonight to cheer you up while Clarence is away, but I really must get to work."

"Don't be silly, Rupert! I'm going to take my tea upstairs and crawl into bed with a really delicious novel full of women I'm sure you wouldn't approve of. Go on wit' you. Get to work!"

"Actually, I was wondering whether I might use your phone first," he said.

"Go right ahead. You don't need to ask," she said, her face falling ever so slightly as though she suspected the packet of work might be an invention to cover for his other plans. "I'll leave you to it."

She departed in her pink satin robe, trailing a very expensive-smelling scent.

He rang the city editor first and was greeted with unwanted enthusiasm.

"That's a fascinating column, Rupert! You were brave to write it. We're flagging it on the front page," he said.

"Actually, I've decided to pull it," Penrose told him. "I think the fall of the government's the subject of the day."

"Everybody and his mother will be writing about that, Penrose. I don't think we can pull it at this point, anyway. You see we've already sold ads on the basis of—well, ask Gormley. Don't tell him I mentioned the ads."

It took the usual twenty minutes to get through to Niall Gormley's office, and then he wasn't there. His secretary claimed not to know where he was. She promised to relay the message, however.

Penrose went up to his room to try to compose his thoughts about the government. He found it difficult to focus. He thought he wanted Kavanagh to be Taoiseach again. On the other hand, Kavanagh's guest of honor at his first state dinner after the election had been the British ambassador.

"There's a call for you," said Samantha, speaking through his door. "You can take it up here if you like."

He felt it would have looked like too sharp a rebuff if he were to go downstairs. He followed her into her room.

"What's up, Penrose?" Gormley sounded pressed. "The Virgin following you around again?" He was using his swaggering tone. He must have an audience. "We had a report she was kidnapped the other day, did I ever tell you that? Of course we didn't believe a bit of it. What's up?"

"About my column, the one I gave you for tomorrow—"

"Yes, I've read it. Fucking marvelous, Penrose! It takes courage to write a thing like that. We're flagging it on the front page under your picture. We used the old one, hope you don't mind. Called it 'My Protestant Beginnings.' Gets right to the point. The whole city will be talking about you, you realize."

"Actually, I'm pulling the column, Niall. I think it's too, well, self-absorbed a piece to be running right now when the government's fallen."

"Don't be modest, my dear boy. Elections in Ireland are getting to be an everyday occurrence. But it's not every day our readers find out Ireland's most articulate Catholic spokesman was born a Protestant. They'll be fascinated. I expect it will boost circulation by several thousand."

"Niall, you must let me change it. You absolutely must. I can't—I don't think—I disagree with you—I do not think my own private crisis of belief of thirty years ago is nearly as important as what's happening to the country right now. I want you to pull the column."

"Relax, Rupert! Tomorrow's paper has already gone to bed," he lied, and they both knew he was blatantly lying. It was only half six. "Listen, it's all anyone can talk about here. I've got the mayor here. Grainne and I are having a few friends around to dinner, and I've been telling them about you. They're dying to read the column. Just relax. Write your political piece for Friday. The election's six weeks off, don't forget. You'll run out of political thoughts by the time it's over. I must let you go now, Rupert. Hope I put your mind at ease. It's a great column."

"Bloody hell!" said Penrose, but not to his editor. The phone was back on its cradle.

"What'sa matter?" crooned Samantha, holding her arms out to him from her bed. He pretended to take this as merely a gesture.

"Oh, editors!" he said. "Sometimes I think we could do without the lot of them."

"Come and cuddle with me and I'll make you forget all about them." She smiled a deceptively maternal smile.

"Samantha, darling," he said, taking hold of one of her hands, "there is nothing I would like better than to make mad passionate love to you at this very moment, you are so lovely and sensual."

"Why don't you, then, you wicked man!"

"I don't feel well, actually. I seem to have caught a chill coming home. I think I had rather too much of a fabulous Lynch Bages for lunch at Après Moi. I've got a splitting headache."

"Not to worry, love. There's plenty of time. Clarence is not coming back until Saturday. You poor dear! There's Disprin in your bathroom cabinet."

"That's good news, then!" Penrose said, kissing her hand. But it was not. Clarence Doyle was one of the few CUD trustees who had never wavered in their belief that the only person for the Kerrygold Chair was Rupert Penrose.

57

$\mathcal{R}$ock had gone to bed after lunch. The early winter darkness and the phenomenal amount of money he had just paid for the meal made him sleepy. He had asked the front desk to give him a wake-up call at ten, just in case. He was to go on duty outside Houlihan's hospital room at midnight.

But the hotel staff must have thought he meant ten o'clock in the morning. They never rang him.

He awoke when someone banged on his door at eleven thirty-four.

He couldn't believe his luck. Moira standing there smelling of cigarettes. The girl of his dreams on his doorstep, and he had two minutes for the whole thing.

"Moira! Moira! It's you! How wonderful!" he said, trying to take off her coat and kiss her at the same time. "Oh, Moira! I can't believe you're here! How did I get so lucky?"

"I kept thinking you would only be here for a few days," she said. "I'm not, I don't usually do this sort of thing."

"That's my attraction? I'm leaving? How flattering!" he protested, but he did not feel insulted.

"Oh, Rock, I'm sorry!" she said, pulling away. "I didn't mean—"

"Never mind," he said, trying to tug her close again. "There isn't time to be sorry. I've got about one minute before I have to leave for the hospital."

She lit a cigarette. Her fingers were shaky. "Why are you a Secret Service agent?" she asked.

"I'm just doing it until I figure out what I want to be."

"But—how old are you?"

"Almost forty. And you?"

"You know how old I am. You saw my birth date."

"Moira, I wouldn't care if you were eight years old or eighty. I've been thinking about you from the moment I laid eyes on you. Let's exchange life stories when we have more time. I'll die if you don't put that cigarette out right now."

She crushed it without looking at him and then approached him with her eyes still down, shy, speechless. He felt his whole heart contract and his job go out the window. He kissed her hot, moist, cigaretty mouth. He got her coat off and she stopped tasting like cigarette. He wanted her more than life itself. Every inch of her was covered from the throat down. He never thought corduroy and wool could feel so erotic. He was on her on the bed, cupping her taut corduroy-encased breast in his hand and taking from her hot sweet mouth the reparation for a lifetime of missed chances. The phone rang. He ignored it. He felt the skin of her belly. It was like hot silk.

Grazos pounded on his door. "Answer your phone, Rock! It's the White House!"

His phone rang again.

"Agent O'Leary?" said the White House switchboard operator.

"Yes," he said.

"We're patching you through to the Vice President."

"I don't believe this," Rock said.

"Don't go away, Mr. O'Leary."

"I'll be here," he said.

The phone went dead. He dove back on top of Moira. It rang again. Moira picked it up for him and held it to his ear.

"Hello. Rock O'Leary here."

"Hello, Agent O'Leary. You're late, you know. But I'm glad I caught you. I understand you're coming out here to watch me sleep tonight."

"I take it I'm speaking with the Vice President?"

"Oh, sorry! Forgot to introduce myself. All doped up. But I still can't sleep. O'Leary, I was wondering whether you could do me an eensy-weensy favor. Could you, do you think?"

"I can certainly try, Madam Vice President."

"Call me Honor, please. Everyone does. Madam Vice President is such a lot of syllables. President would be a lot easier, I always say." She guffawed at her own wit.

"Right," said Rock. "What can I do for you, Honor?"

"They've got a VCR set up here in my room, but none of my tapes works in it. I guess it's different wavelengths or something. So I was wondering whether you could go by a video shop on your way out here and pick me up a couple of movies. Could you do that?"

"If I can find one open at this hour."

"Well, the nurses say you can if you're quick. Actually, they were going to call and ask them to stay open until you get there. I had my heart set on watching *The Quiet Man* tonight, and I've never seen *My Left Foot*. Could you get those, O'Leary? I'd be eternally grateful. I've been watching this one called *The Dead*, but it's really boring. Don't tell the nurses! I don't want to hurt their feelings."

"You want *The Quiet Man* and *My Left Foot*."

[225]

"Yes, please."

"Where do I go, then?"

"You're a doll," she said. "Hold on. I'll ring for a nurse."

The nurse took forever giving him directions. Moira was sitting up smoking another cigarette when he finally rang off.

"You'd better go," she said. "That place closes at midnight."

"Why don't you stay here," he said. "I'll be back right after eight."

"I have to be at work by nine," she said.

"That'll give us more time than we had tonight. Stay here. Order up room service. Moira, even my room wants you."

She laughed.

Grazos, who had a nose for these things, came knocking on the door.

"Go away," said Rock.

"You're on duty tonight. Remember?"

"Leave her alone," Rock said, emerging quickly and shutting the door on his trench coat. When he opened it to extricate himself, Grazos took a peek inside.

"You're leaving *her*? Call in sick, man. Don't you know anything? She could be a Provo, Rock. You got gun clips in there?"

"Pete, if you touch her, I'll tell Willard what you did in the Lincoln bedroom."

"I've never seen you like this, Rock. You know you can trust me!"

58

*C*hief Superintendent Bloom was waiting for Rock in the lobby when he arrived back at 8:20 in the morning. The man's pristinely pale blue eyes had a hooded, worried look.

"I came to invite you to breakfast," he said. "Perhaps you've eaten already."

"I wasn't going to eat," Rock said. "I've been on duty all night. What can I do for you?"

"Come have a quick cup of tea. I won't be keeping you long."

"Sure," said Rock. "Just let me make one phone call."

He rang his room on the house phone. Grazos answered.

"What are you doing there?" he asked.

"I've been looking after your girlfriend for you, Rock. They wouldn't take her breakfast order until I intervened. Where are you? I filled her in on your domestic situation. I don't think it appeals to her."

"Let me talk to her."

"Hello, Rock," she said warmly. A screen of friendliness. A morning voice. "You do have a fabulous shower. Where are you? I've got to leave early. I forgot I'm supposed to open up the office."

"I'm downstairs. Listen, the head of your Special Branch was waiting for me in the lobby. I have to find out what he wants. Can't you hang on?"

"I'm sorry, but I really can't. Deirdre wants the constituency office open as early as possible."

"What if you came by in your lunch hour? Take a cab. I'll pay for it."

"Perhaps we could meet in Tulsa, Oklahoma, in January." She giggled.

"Has Pete been harassing you?"

"He's been very helpful, actually. The hotel was being beastly. Wanted to know was I registered and so on. They seem to think you are a very important person. What are you doing with the head of the hateful Special Branch?"

"He hasn't told me yet. Moira, I can't stand this! Meet me for lunch."

She did not commit herself. Even her sort of half refusal was pleasure to his ears. The cadences of her voice excited him. She sounded of hayfields and milk buckets somehow combined with her Marlboro-woman body in jeans from the Gap. He could not remember what he was supposed to be doing. Grazos could seduce a woman between four subway stops. Well, he said he had done it between twelve stops. And

Moira was dying for it when Rock left last night. Ready for the perfect Grazos relationship, hello, in, out, goodbye. No fuss, no muss, and pray to God nobody's got AIDS. What did women see in the son of a bitch? What they did not see in Rock O'Leary. Danger. Risk. The heart's high diving board. Women who went out with Rock came home to an apartment he shared with his mother.

Should he go upstairs? Betray his desperation?

"Oh, there you are," said Bloom, coming around the corner.

"Yes, I was just coming," Rock said. "You look worried." He followed Bloom to a quiet table.

"I'm stumped is what I am," said Bloom. "We've a packet of leads that go nowhere."

"You can't round up the usual suspects and threaten tax audits and stuff like that?"

"We've put everyone we possibly can in jail until your woman goes home. It's not, strictly speaking, legal. We can't hold them forever. When is she meant to be going home, exactly?"

"I'm not sure myself," said Rock. "Her doctors say she shouldn't be moved."

"Her doctors take their cue from the White House, don't they?" asked Bloom.

Rock didn't say anything.

"We are not at this point in time looking at a departure date, is that it?"

"That's the shape of it as far as I understand. She's not too happy about the situation."

"Neither are we, to be honest with you. It's very awkward. We have no government to host her. There's that Semtex at large out there somewhere. Even the IRA is stumped, our intelligence tells us. This visit is costing us an arm and a leg in overtime."

"There's a lot of bad feeling between her and the President at the moment," said Rock.

"Which one do you work for?"

"Both," said Rock. "I take that back. I work for the American people. I safeguard democracy."

"So they both distrust you. He has virtually exiled her to Ireland, then."

"Oh, she did prefer it. There was sort of a toss-up between Denmark and Ireland, but she's a Houlihan and Denmark didn't have the Virgin."

"What a peculiar thing to do. You'd think he would want her close at hand, where he could keep a certain amount of control over her."

"It doesn't work that way," said Rock. "She has this very active PR guy, and she's in demand everywhere, the first woman Vice President, a looker and a flake who will say things that make good, shocking news stories. Pond hates it. He's jealous sort of the way they say Prince Charles was when his wife turned out to be such a hit. Only this isn't a wife who could at least appear on his arm. He can't even fire her, the way he could a cabinet member who didn't play along. He's stuck with her, and she keeps saying things that screw up what he wants to do. The First Lady really hates her. She's a flake but she gives better parties than the Ponds do. Her husband knows all those movie stars, you see."

"The slipped disk begins to look like an awfully convenient accident."

"But Myron Shakespeare's her guy, her yoga instructor."

"The President could have bought his loyalty. Everyone has a price."

"I think the President just got lucky."

59

$\mathcal{M}$arco's Visa bill arrived with amazing swiftness. It was even higher than expected, £4,352 in all. Padre Destino tried to imagine the furnishings of a baby's room that could cost so much money. Marco said, though, that it wasn't all furniture. The women had branched out into clothing for both mother and child. They had bought holistic baby bottles, the latest thing in combating colic, also an electric food masher and a juicer, a pram, a stroller, a small bathtub, a baby backpack, a Snugli, several pairs of German wool maternity tights, a lamp that played lullabies, and for Mama in her outcast state a fake fur coat, a silk dressing gown with matching nightie and slippers, a rather large TV with videocassette attachment, and a portable CD player with seventeen of her favorite disks. Padre Destino, who had never shopped for anything other than his personal linens and his books, was quite amazed at the amount of things the women had been able to purchase in one day.

He was amazed, too, that instead of feeling alarmed or repulsed by this extreme display of bourgeois materialism, with which he was now connected by his promise to pay, he felt an odd pleasure. There was a primal satisfaction in having a young pregnant woman dependent on him. He enjoyed paying the bill, as though he were shouldering, in a dignifiedly remote and innocent spirit, the burdens of a father.

He had been used to dealing in such large sums of money during the days of the secret networks in Poland that he did not even think to mention the check to Bishop Meany, whose job it was to balance the books. Meany would see the stub in the large checkbook, in any case. Padre Destino was not looking forward to the discussion that would inevitably arise. Bishop Meany would certainly have the upper hand. Even a quite charitable person could question the wisdom of extending unlimited generosity to a girl of Christabelle's character.

But Bishop Meany had not yet mentioned the check. He had seemed unusually distracted for the last couple of days. He said he was working on a pastoral letter for Christmas, but he had spent more time pacing around the residence than he had at his desk. For the first time since Paolo Destino had come to Ireland, Bishop Meany ignored him for three days.

If the Nuncio had not been feeling so thoroughly on the defensive for his own rash behavior, he would have thought Meany's conduct quite peculiar. The bishop was clearly in an agitated state today, Thursday, not able to sit at his desk at all. He paced the rooms and rushed to answer the phone every time it rang, as though he was waiting for very important news.

When Meany did focus on Archbishop Destino, he showed him a degree of solicitousness which he had not evinced before. He actually encouraged the Nuncio to go see his friend in Milltown—"the weather would get you down so." He said Patrick had told him "it's the only time he sees you laughing is when you're walking with Father O'Mahoney."

Liam was not at home, however. Bishop Meany seemed quite disappointed to hear this. He pulled on his chin for a minute and then said: "It's cold enough to freeze your bones through. I know you feel it. Won't we have one of the boys make you a nice fire in the little study upstairs where they won't be bothering you with the telephone. Sure, the calls have been fierce today!"

Destino was only too glad to comply with Bishop Meany's wishes. He was tucked under a lap rug, sound asleep under the weight of Joyce's imaginings, beside the cozy fire when Marco shook his shoulder.

"I am sorry, Nuncio. It is your bank manager on the telephone. I have told him you are sleeping. He asks me to wake you."

"The bishop can take care of it," said Destino irritably.

"The bishop has gone out."

"Well, when he comes back."

"The bank manager says he will only talk to you."

"Oh, dear, Marco!" said the Nuncio. He walked stiffly to the telephone in his bedroom. "Better hang it up downstairs. I'll take it up here. But please hold all the other calls. They'll all be for the bishop."

"Ah, Nuncio!" said the bank manager. "I don't believe we've met. My name's Ryan McGrath, and I'm terribly sorry to be disturbing you, but I was wanting to speak to you about some funds transfers that have come to our notice. You know, ever since the Bishop Casey affair, we've had to be on the alert for unusual transfers of Church funds. I wonder, would you be able to come down to the bank without, em, well, on your own?"

Bishop Meany had taken one of the cars himself, leaving Patrick at home. This, too, was highly unusual. Padre Destino asked the chauffeur to get the Daimler ready. He wished he trusted Patrick. He felt certain there was much Patrick could tell him. But the driver presented him always such an implacable courtesy, there was no way of reaching him.

• • •

"So good of you to come down, Nuncio, really so good," said Ryan McGrath, with a face all creases of confidentiality. "It's probably a completely unnecessary trip I've asked you to make, but where's the harm, then, I always say! You see, there's a bit of an overdraft on your household account, and Bishop Meany said we weren't to worry you about it. Now, a couple of years ago, I wouldn't have given it two thoughts. It is only ten thousand pounds that you're overdrawn. And I know there'll be money coming in to cover it in the New Year. But you see, the Vatican has asked us to make everyone aware of unusual funds transfers, and so that's why I called you down here. And it did, to be honest with you, it did raise a little bit of a red flag in my mind when the bishop asked us not to bother you about it at all."

The Nuncio attempted to look shocked and grave, but he felt a rising happiness.

"How much money has Bishop Meany been transferring?" he asked solemnly.

"It's been two payments of twenty-five thousand pounds each."

"And to whom were these payments made?"

"They went into an account at the Bank of Ireland which, strictly *entre nous*, is registered to an individual named Redmond Dunne Danforth."

"Ah!" said the Nuncio.

"I take it you know the fellow?"

"I have heard of him," said the Nuncio.

"Perhaps the bishop hasn't wanted you to meet him? Well, I'm only speculating as to motives. But first I should ask you, were these authorized payments?"

The Nuncio hesitated.

"Ought we to consult you if the bishop attempts to make any more of them?"

"I will speak to the bishop. There will be no more payments. Do you have an address for this Danforth person?"

"We do, but it is a sham. The address is the same as that of the Anne Street School of Irish Cookery, which no longer exists. You see, with bank cards it is possible to withdraw money from machines all over Ireland—all over the world, actually. This man has withdrawn five thousand pounds to date. He never goes to the same machine twice. We did really go beyond ourselves in gleaning this information from the Bank of Ireland, just as a precaution."

"No one has seen Mr. Danforth?"

"We have photographed him, yes, but he wears a balaclava when he withdraws the money."

"Like a criminal."

"Precisely. You see, this is why we were worried. It looks like a case of criminal blackmail. I am so sorry, Nuncio! Bishop Meany is such a highly respected man. We will do all in our power to keep this from going beyond the bank. I am sorry."

60

*R*upert Penrose's "My Protestant Beginnings" column did sell several thousand extra copies of the Dublin *Sentinel*. The response among his friends was gratifying. Once again he had caught the attention of Dublin, and they were proud to say they knew him personally. The reaction of his female friends was more than gratifying. The Friday night confession at St. Barnabas went on for forty minutes on this occasion, and by the time Penrose emerged from the confessional, looking, God forgive him, pink and proud of his sins, an hour had passed since the time he had entered, so long had it taken to calibrate what he owed in penance.

He had not heard from Bishop Meany, but he dared to hope now that the public reaction had proved so positive the good bishop would be pleased. Just in case, however, he had written one or two letters to the *Sentinel* under false names to further his purpose. Interestingly enough, he had not mentioned this little deceit during his confession. Dublin was such a small city, really, and he so famous in it, he could not be absolutely certain that what he said to the priest would not find its way someday to a trustee of CUD or to the bishops' advisory committee. He knew that sexual sins were ones that Irish bishops could always forgive, whereas they might not find it in their hearts to pardon forgery in the service of self-promotion.

"Sirs," began the first of his letters to the editor, "I was most interested to read yesterday's column by Rupert Penrose entitled 'My Protestant Beginnings.' I knew Mr. Penrose as a young man, although I doubt he would remember me. His conversion was a shock to his family and indeed to the entire Protestant community of Dublin. I felt it was the choice of his private conscience, and I tried to intercede for him with my husband, who had been about to hire him. But my efforts were fruitless. Catholics were not to be trusted in a Protestant accountancy firm, and converts to Catholicism were to be actively shunned.

"I believe Mr. Penrose took a job on the Ballybunion *Blotter* because that was the only position he could obtain and because Ballybunion was about as far as he could get from Greystones without drowning himself in the Atlantic. You must understand that in the Irish Protestant community in 1962 a conversion to Catholicism was a traitorous act of very great magnitude. We never saw Rupert Penrose in Greystones again, and no one mentioned his name in front of his parents, who had lost an immeasurable amount of social standing in consequence of their son's defection. At their then advanced age, they felt so disgraced that they emigrated to Canada. Thankfully, those days are past us, and it is now no longer a social disgrace to become a Catholic in Ireland. I congratulate Mr. Penrose on his candor. Name Withheld, in Greystones."

Penrose knew that no one in Greystones would write in to contradict Name Withheld because no one except his parents had ever known the full story, and they were dead. They had not actually emigrated to Canada. They had gone out for a long vacation and had unfortunately locked themselves into their bearproof rented caravan in the middle of the Yukon. They had wanted their son to become an accountant. He had never wanted the profession. He applied instead for jobs with all the great Dublin newspapers and was turned down by all of them. A kindly old editor for the Dublin edition of the *Daily Mirror* told him to go off and work for a small paper in the country. The editor said it would help him to get a job if he was a Catholic.

61

*T*he morning his column appeared, Samantha brought Penrose his breakfast on a silver tray. When she learned his headache was gone, she did not allow him out of bed until noon. She was so thrilled to discover her famous lodger had once been a Protestant, she forgot she had left the bath running in the master bathroom, and a chandelier fell down with the rest of the ceiling onto the priceless Princess Anne coffee table in the front sitting room. They heard the crash of course and thought it was burglars until Samantha's housekeeper, whom Samantha had also forgotten about, came upstairs to see where all the water was coming from. She discovered the overflowing bath and her mistress in bed with the famous lodger. Penrose was finally freed from the adoring embrace, and the housekeeper was told she'd be getting a substantial raise. She recognized Penrose, and, thinking of her friends, she suppressed the shock at finding him in bed with a married woman, in order to ask him calmly for an autograph. He courteously scribbled it on a piece of Samantha's notepaper.

That evening he taught his Toyota Night School class. Afterwards he was absolutely swamped with students wanting to make arrangements to meet him for special sessions. He was able to find time that night for Won Thing, a beautiful Chinese ballet dancer, who told him she had thwarted her career for the sake of her husband Mai, whom she thought disgustingly ambitious in his ruthless rise through the ranks of the People's Republic's trade ministry. She said he never read books anymore but filled his time with Kung Fu movies, and she didn't know what had attracted her to him in the first place.

"Ilerand is vely spilituar countly," she said, as she lay back against the sagging gardening correspondent's couch. They had been forced to retreat to Penrose's office, where neither Samantha nor Mai Thing would be apt to intercept them.

The couch was so shapeless that it took all the skills of a former prima ballerina to keep both the balance and the rhythms required to make this illicit union one that the two of them could take pleasure in. The beautiful Won Thing, upon completing the difficult *pas de deux*, looked at her watch, said Penrose was "rike poetly," and hastily left to resume her wifely duties.

He was waiting a discreet amount of time to allow her to exit the building well before he did, when Attracta came around the corner and threw herself straight into his arms.

"My dear girl, this is most unexpected!" cried Penrose, kissing her warmly on the cheek. "Come sit down," he said, unable as yet to contemplate a carnal encounter again. She sat down next to him, but she was not to be deterred.

"Oh, Rupert! This changes everything!" she said. "Now I understand you." Her eyes were shining with ardor.

"Whatever do you mean, my dear girl?" Penrose asked her.

"You're a Protestant."

"I am not! I became a Catholic at the age of twenty-three. I'm surprised at you, Attracta. I would venture to say that I am more devout than most Catholics."

"All the same, Rupert, you've got the morals of a Protestant."

She was not being fair to him. However, he discovered, much to his surprise, that the exquisite Mrs. Thing had not drained all desire from his body. Attracta was no athlete, though, and so they both rolled naked onto the floor, where Penrose's knees began to hurt like the bejaysus, a detail he actually mentioned late in confession as he thought it might soften the priest's judgment to hear how sexual ecstasy was not always an unmitigated pleasure. Attracta, at last giving vent to all that had been pent up in her supple young body since her final visit to the unclaimed parcels room of the Glenageary Postal Sorting Office, gripped him with all four of her limbs as tightly as a dog might grip a bone when afflicted with the lockjaw, and although Penrose would have dearly loved to excuse himself for a moment to fetch his overcoat and spread it out underneath the panting girl and his own tender knees, he thought she would probably have murdered him if he had tried. There was in the back of their minds the awful fear that something might interrupt them again, but nothing did, and there came a point when Penrose was no longer conscious of the pain in his knees.

"Oh, Rupert! Oh, God forgive me! Oh!" Attracta cried out. Penrose was in awe of his own achievement.

"Look at you. You've gone all raw," said Attracta when she saw what had happened to the skin on his knees. She rummaged around in her handbag, producing iodine and plasters. How was he to explain his telltale wounds to Samantha?

He packed off the serene and glowing Attracta to her bus and quickly pedaled home. Samantha had gone out, leaving him a note telling him not to wait up. The next morning he went out before she was awake.

He had made an appointment with another Toyota Night School student who had said to him after class the previous evening that she needed help understanding the Irish mind. On Thursdays, Penrose had the use of a neat little office in the Toyota Suite overlooking Stephen's Green. He planned to redo his Friday column while waiting for his student to appear. The political piece now seemed beside the point. He wanted to do a little essay on the spirituality of Ireland and how that distinguished the small gem of a nation from the great former super-powers which were both now in serious decline.

"No nation without a coherent belief system that is in fundamental harmony with Christian values has survived for very long," he had written before rosy plump Lara van Gufsten arrived with the notes for her term paper, which became crumpled but not unusable under the couch cushion where she rested her fine Dutch head as she took in all that Penrose had to offer. She was the wife of a Dutch oil magnate who had bought a small castle outside Dublin where he entertained business contacts who bored Lara silly. She was studying for a Ph.D. in Irish history to escape them.

Lara seemed to think Penrose was a prototype for a disappearing breed of Irishman. She made him sound like a rare and special piece of the national heritage, a quasi-tragic being connected with Ireland's greatest warrior-scholars, all dead eight hundred years.

"You really encompass it all," she said to Penrose in flawless English. "I wouldn't be surprised to learn that you had been a member of the IRA, too, and a British spy."

She chewed his earlobe expertly, and he let that last remark pass as a mindless utterance symptomatic of desire. She applied herself skillfully to other parts of his anatomy, and Penrose reflected to himself how infinitely superior in this regard were the Europeans. He would not have said so to anyone, for he did not approve of people who in any way contributed to the insidious Irish inferiority complex. Besides, was it such a bad thing that Irish women were unschooled in the sinful arts?

Yet, as Lara stuffed her crumpled notes into a slim suede briefcase, he gazed wistfully at her knowledgeable hands and wished he could swap her with Samantha. He kissed Lara's large lips and told her she could consult him about the Irish mind whenever she liked.

"I will call you," she said noncommittally.

"There are certain advantages to being an island nation," he continued the column. "One hesitates to use the term 'purity of race' with its sinister echoes, but Nazism aside, there is much to be said for preserving the pure Irish stock."

He watched Lara drive off in her white Volvo. It was lashing rain outside again and the Toyota offices were closing. He would have to finish the column at home.

The rain was unrelenting. He arrived back at Palmerston Road soaked through and there he added to his column the caution that "our greedy-guts leap into the European community could do more to destroy the Irish identity than England ever did."

Samantha heard him typing in his bedroom.

"You've got a letter," she called from the doorway. "Where've you been all day? I came in with your breakfast tray this morning, and you were gone."

"On Thursdays I go to my Toyota office," he said. "I have to hold office hours for my students. You remember. You used to come 'round."

"And you were so standoffish, Rupert. I thought you'd never warm to me."

"How you underestimated your charms!" he said. "What's this letter?"

"It's on the hall table downstairs. Would you like a cup of tea?"

"That would be splendid, Samantha."

He went down with her and found the letter. He recognized the handwriting immediately. It would no doubt be another pleading request for extra Christmas money. He hadn't the heart to read it at the moment. He followed Samantha into the kitchen, stuffing the missive into his pocket.

"That's the first letter you've had here," she said. "Was it good news?"

"It's from my wife," he said. "Send more money."

"Oh, poor Rupert!" she said.

He left it in his pocket unopened.

62

$\mathcal{R}$ock did not see Moira again until Friday afternoon. She asked him to meet her at a place called Finnegan's Sorrento Lounge in Dalkey, where her candidate was dispensing Irish coffee to her constituents. Moira said they could steal an hour maybe, and she took him up the hill to show him the Green Walk, which went by the long white cottage that curved to match the curve of the land. She said there used to be a gate in the wall that had a shelf for milk bottles and you could look through it and see the garden with its view of the sea. But they found the gate had been replaced by a massive wooden door. The milkman had had to leave today's bottles on the ground beside the path. Moira made Rock lean against the cold wall of the long, white-washed cottage to see how it curved with the land. Smoke rose up out of the cottage chimney in a neat coil as in a child's storybook. Moira said it was the way Ireland used to be before the housing estates with two hundred chockablock drab bungalows whose owners got lost trying to find their way home amid the implacable gray sameness.

"I love this place," she said. "If I had the money, I'd buy it."

He turned her toward him and kissed her hard against the wall. She tasted of fresh air and Irish coffee. They had drunk to the success of Deirdre Fanning. The whiskey had gone straight to his cock, which anyway was behaving like a twenty-year-old's at the sight of her, and his heart had raced so as he ran up the hill behind her he thought with his luck he would die chasing her. If she said fucking England again in that beautiful Donegal singsong, he was going to ask her to marry him.

God almighty, he was practically in her up against the wall. Then the door opened and a woman in a very posh olive-drab suede jacket picked up the two milk bottles.

"Chilly day, after all," she said, quite as though the three of them had been talking an hour ago about the predictions of a warm spell.

"Yes, it is chilly, yes," said Rock, trying to assemble himself behind Moira's skirt. She slipped away. He sensed her struggling with tights somewhere behind him.

"Perhaps you are not aware that this is a public right-of-way," said the posh woman.

"I wanted to ask you, ma'am," he said, smiling pleasantly, "how much you would take for this house."

"It is not for sale," she said crisply, turning on her heel to disappear behind the massive wooden door.

Where was Moira? He seemed to be losing track of things. He ran along the path and soon thought he was in the village again. Those were eucalyptus trees, he could swear. Or he was catching the local psychosis, having visions of the Holy Land. Pull yourself together, man. They come from Australia. Palm trees on Sorrento Road could be from Africa. Nobody tells you you're going to see palm trees in Ireland. Not a feature of the St. Paddy's Day parade. They don't mention the video rental stores in the middle of tiny villages, either.

Where was Moira? Maddening girl. Couldn't call her girl to her face.

To him she looked so incredibly young. Twenty-seven. At her age, he had still had plans to become a torrid genius. Regis High School's first Montana ranch hand. But then Brenda entered the picture and she always hated sleeping on the ground. Whereas this girl had almost let him do it on a public right-of-way in the middle of December in fucking Ireland, where they had no divorce, they were so morally sure of themselves. Or unsure. Women used to be like her back home until they all got shoulder pads and went for careers in law.

"Moira!"

No answer. He seemed to be leaving the village again. The path dipped down a bit, then up out of the underbrush, and there he was in the center of the travel posters, looking out upon a wide, silver sea that any minute was expecting the descent of God Almighty down the beauteous rays of light shooting out around a radiant cloud. The wind pressed against him, and even that was erotic. The sun came out. The breeze seemed warmer. He sat down on a bench which a wise soul in the previous century had placed here in anticipation of his wishes. He loved it that Moira was practically starving for her principles. What was she doing with him? She could be just in it for the thrill of their differences, going for a night or two behind enemy lines.

A night or two! He'd take one good quarter hour. Where was she?

The sun went in again, and out in the bay, cloud shadows shifted over the waters like a restless painter's changing vision of beauty. Suddenly cold again. How did she stand that frigid little house? They used to say it wasn't the cold but the damp that killed you. And the nuns could see into your soul. Myths passed down to his mother. How would Moira take to her? Dangerous to think like that. Next thing he'd be pleading with her, please come home with me, please come or I'll die. But we don't die of love. Please, please, come with me, Moira, or I'll develop a potbelly and end up with my dental hygienist.

He leaned back, closed his eyes, and fell asleep on the spot. He dreamed that Brenda was pregnant and wanted to come home.

He awoke with his head in Moira's lap.

"Hello," she said quietly.

"I thought you'd left me forever," he said.

"I considered it," she said, starting to stroke his lips with her finger.

"Don't do that, Moira. I'll have to ravish you on this bench."

"Her daughter was in school with me."

"Who was?" he said, sitting up.

"The woman back there. I know her daughter, Philippa D'Arcy. She read law at Protestant University College. But now she's gone into art auctioneering. Her mother's best friend and my mother are very good friends."

"So? What's she going to do? Tell her friend she saw you having carnal relations in front of her house?"

"Yes. But my mother will not put it that way to me. She'll say, 'What's this I hear about you being engaged to an American?' "

"Will you marry me? You're not a Protestant, are you?"

"Of course I'm not a Protestant! Why would you ever think that?"

"Protestant University College."

"It's just the name. It's not a Protestant school anymore. There aren't enough of them."

"You didn't answer my question."

"Which was that?"

"Will you marry me?"

"Rock! I'd never get married when I didn't have a job. And I'd certainly never agree to marry a man I hadn't slept with."

"You have a job. You're working for Deirdre Fanning."

"She's not paying me. Anyway, it's just for three weeks. I'm one of the long-term unemployed, Rock. I'm on the dole."

"That's exactly when you should get married."

"And have to ask my husband for pocket money? I'd be mortified."

Rock fell forward on his knees and crawled around to face her.

"Marry me, Moira, and I promise I'll find you a job."

"Where? In the White House? You're not serious."

"Why not? The surroundings are pleasant. I've only been mugged outside it once, and that was at four in the morning. The First Lady has done a great job overhauling the cafeteria menu. You can get tofu for lunch there now."

"I hate tofu," said Moira. "Get up off your knees before someone else who knows my mother comes along."

"For a liberated woman, you are awfully scared of your mother's friends."

"You don't understand. This is Ireland."

"I have a warm, clean hotel room where nobody your mother knows can see you."

"I'd have to be back by six o'clock."

"Moira, this is it. You're the love of my life. You don't know what it does to my heart to hear you say you hate tofu. Say it again."

"I do hate tofu," she said, and he kissed her so ardently that she was cast into a swoon and followed him unwaveringly down the hill to his car. Rain started just as they got into the car and darkness fell before they were out of Dalkey, which was not until after five because they were slowed by some road repairs and a bank-robbery bomb scare for which they were made to stand still for twenty minutes. Then the traffic was crawling on the way into the city, which didn't make any sense at all, but there you are, said Moira. Mostly she said nothing and they sat in hot erotic silence watching the windshield wipers, or, as she said, windscreen wipers, go back and forth and the cars go inching forward. Only later did they learn there had been a fresh rumor of a Virgin sighting at Après Moi, which accounted for the traffic jam. But at last they got to Bloom's Hotel and were the only ones in the elevator, so he was nearly able to do the deed again standing up with her, and various zippers had been undone already, various buttons and straps had been loosed before they even reached the floor of his room. In one motion he opened the door and swept her around by the waist into the room and into his arms, and long and long they kissed until at last one of them began to take off the other's shirt.

"Brrrrt," went the telephone. "Brrrrrt."

They were already too far gone to care who was calling. Rock took the phone off the hook but never answered it and the woman on the switch downstairs in Bloom's had the thrill of her life and future historians would, too, because the White House was taping itself again, Henry Pond felt important enough, and the microphones he had installed were the finest in the world. If you knew what to listen for on the tape, other than the foreground noise, you could make out very faintly in the background a sound like someone knocking on a door and then a man's voice, muffled but shouting: "Goddamn it, Rock, I know you're in there! Get your ass in gear! We're taking Houlihan to see the Virgin!"

63

For the past nine days, no one except Gertrude Crookshanks had known the whereabouts of the Virgin, and Gertrude was gone from her house. She had found she couldn't face sleeping alone there with a glowing figure from the world beyond. She might have turned to Noleen, but Noleen would have told everyone in Ireland, and Gertrude couldn't have faced that, either. She was a tolerant woman. She was even boycotting her church because of something Reverend Boxley had said that she thought was wounding to Catholics. But she was still an Irish Protestant to her core and very loath to be seen to have deserted their little band, which is what she would appear to be doing with the Virgin in her kitchen. And even if they were intelligent enough in their response to the news of it to realize that she hadn't crossed over, the Dalkey Protestants would think it wrong and vulgar of her to reveal that the Virgin had come into her kitchen. It wasn't the sort of thing any of them would have been proud of.

Thus, she had chosen to go down to Waterford to visit her sister Claire, pretending to be lonely for the sight of her close to Christmas. She should have known better than to surprise Claire at that time of year. Claire hated being caught out, and this time her house had been in a terrible state of fumigation, carpets rolled up, chairs upside down on top of tables, beds laid bare of their linens, the works. Claire's children and grandchildren were coming in less than a fortnight, and

Claire was a house perfectionist. Worse still, Gertrude had got the jump on her with Christmas presents. Claire hadn't even started dressing up her puddings. She seemed way behind this year. But naturally she didn't complain. She merely seethed with the most considerate-sounding cruelties.

"It must be lonely for you coming up onto Christmas now," she would say over breakfast in her gracious Miss Hall's Academy style interlaced with little steel filaments of false pity. "I wonder if your boys really needed to go as far as New Zealand to sell insurance." Or at teatime, when a mother always misses her children most keenly, Claire would be pouring out the cups and she'd suddenly pick up a spoon and say, "These spoons always remind me of your Jillian, the little dote!" Jillian was forty. "Do you remember the way she used to love to take them into the garden to fix tea for her dolls? It's a pity *she* wouldn't come over for Christmas with you. *She's* only in New York."

Gertrude had offered to help with the housework, but Claire had resisted all her overtures and made a great show of trying to settle Gertrude down with a magazine or a cup of tea or an old family album, as if implying that Gertrude was too old to be of use around the house. That was a ludicrous notion, as Claire was the elder sister. It was really only bullying. Claire's ministrations grew both more vehement and more superior in tone as the days passed, and eventually she began urging Gertrude to rest in her room or go visit the dreadful woman Frances who lived next door. Claire herself despised Frances. The woman did nothing but read magazines, eat bonbons, and complain about young women who breast-fed their children in public.

Gertrude began finally to strike back with honeyed inquiries about Claire's grandson in London who'd been arrested for possession of cocaine. Claire punished her then by inviting her to spend Christmas in Waterford, though she wouldn't have a bed for Gertrude after all the children and grandchildren arrived.

"Perhaps you could stay with Frances," she said grandly. "And then you could have Christmas with us. I'll just pop around to Frances and ask her."

"No, no, no! Please don't, Claire, darling. That's very kind of you," Gertrude swiftly protested. "But I'm afraid Noleen would disown me if

I didn't go to her for Christmas dinner. I'm something of a fixture there now. I'm needed to play the piano."

"How good of her to have you!" said Claire. "But then Noleen always did love the elegance of the Stowe girls. You and she certainly do go back a long way. Do you remember how you scandalized Aunt Henrietta when she saw you coming out of Mass with Noleen's family? All the same, Gertie, you are my little sister. Let me just pop 'round to Frances."

While Claire was gone, Gertrude packed up her little bag of things and rang for a cab. She hated the way Claire always implied that Noleen was social-climbing with her. When Claire came back, she told her a lie about Horace being ill.

"Noleen rang. I knew she'd feed him sweets," she said. "It's been wonderful seeing you in the midst of your happy preparations."

It was too late for Claire to revoke her invitation to Frances for the Christmas dinner. To show how irked she was, she pressed not one but four Christmas presents upon her departing sister and handed her as well a huge sticky pudding which Gertrude was certain she had intended for her own family.

"Noleen will have a lot of mouths to feed," she said when Gertrude tried to hand it back to her.

• • •

After nine days with Claire, she was ready to face the Loch Ness monster over Horace's water dish. Chances were, though, that the apparition was gone. What would be the point in an empty kitchen?

It was raining buckets when the train arrived in Dalkey station. She waited under the shelter for fifteen minutes. There was no letup.

Another train pulled into the station and out stepped Reverend Boxley.

"Gertrude! Where are you going in this monsoon?" he said, coming over to give her a peck on the cheek.

"I'm going nowhere. I'm after coming from my sister's in Waterford. I've been waiting for the rain to let up."

"I've my car around the corner. Let me give you a lift to your door. How's your sister?"

"She's thriving. She likes nothing better than a good spell of housecleaning."

"It's good to have you back, Gertie. We've missed you. We haven't seen you in the church in some weeks."

They had arrived at her house. She ought to invite him in for tea.

"Reverend Boxley, I might as well come right out and tell you, I'm boycotting your church. So if you're scandalized, you needn't feel you must come in for tea."

"Oh, but Gertie, of course I'm not scandalized!" he said, but his eyes showed he was. "You couldn't scandalize me if you put on saffron robes and declared yourself a Buddhist. But you do owe me the courtesy of an explanation. Have you had a change of faith at this late date? Have we done something to offend you? Of course, I'll come in for a cup of tea," he said all in the one breath.

"Very well," she said, bracing herself to turn the key. "But I can't answer for the state of my house. I've been gone since Wednesday week."

She's still here, thought Gertrude as soon as she opened the door. The glow from the kitchen was visible in the dark foyer—though it took her only about two seconds to reach around to the light switch—and a glow like that coming from a kitchen in Ireland in winter made people immediately suspect a fire. Reverend Boxley rushed in ahead of her.

"What's this? What's this? Gertie, have you seen this? Oh, glory be, Gertie! What have you been doing? What is the Virgin doing here?"

She had to go in. And there was the Virgin still hovering with her soulfully sweet expression over Horace's water dish. The Reverend Boxley stood staring at her with his hand over his mouth. He had gone all pale. Gertrude began to be nervous for the state of his heart. She went over to the sink and filled the kettle.

"Oh, dear, oh, dear, oh, dear! Gertrude Crookshanks, what have you been up to?"

"I told you, Reverend, I've been at my sister's house in Waterford."

"It's a good month now we haven't seen you in the church."

"That's right. It's a month since you told us we were to send back the Mass cards when we got them."

"Gertrude, I explained that is because our doctrine holds that the soul of a saved man ascends to heaven immediately upon his demise, whereas they believe the ascent is not necessarily immediate and that the soul can be aided in its journey through the prayers of the living. Of course, we know it's too late by then. We don't want them to be spending their money on useless Mass cards. Are you saying you no longer believe in Church of Ireland doctrine, Gertie, because that could be why—"

"I am not going to hurt my friends' feelings by sending back the Mass cards, Reverend. I think that would be very unfeeling and ungrateful. It's the sort of thing they do in Belfast maybe, but it's not our way in Dalkey."

"Gertrude, tell me honestly now. You know you can trust me. You haven't become—I know your best friend is Noleen Morrissey—Gertrude, you haven't become a Roman?"

"I just got through telling you, Reverend, why I am boycotting St. Andrew's. I am not attending any other church."

"Then what is the Virgin doing in your kitchen?"

"For heaven's sake, Reverend Boxley, you make it sound as though I've done something to make her come here! Maybe it has nothing to do with me. Maybe she made a mistake. Dalkey streets can be quite confusing. Do you think I like having her sit on Horace's water dish? I haven't been able to go near it since she appeared! It's not an easy thing, having the Virgin Mary in your very own kitchen, you know."

"She's been here for a while then, has she?"

"Yes," said Gertrude.

"How long exactly?"

"Since last Wednesday week."

"And you said nothing? Gertie!"

"Well, you yourself said when you saw her you thought I'd gone over to the Romans."

"You're a calm woman," said the Reverend, looking paler than ever. "I think I'll go into the sitting room if you don't mind."

"I'll bring your tea there," she said.

When she brought it to him, he had got on to a new line of suspicion.

"Who owned this house before your husband?" he asked her.

"It's always been in the Crookshank family," she said. "My husband's grandfather built it. And they weren't soupers, if that's what you're thinking. They were Protestants before the Famine."

"This is quite strange. None of the other appearances has been in a Protestant—I just wonder whether your association with that woman mightn't have had something, some connection—you're not trying to spare my feelings with a little white lie, now?"

"What? To hide my conversion, you mean? That's hardly a little white lie in Ireland, Reverend. I'll repeat: no, I have not become a Roman Catholic. But I do resent the way you seem to be implying that my Protestantism has been in some way damaged by my friendship with a Catholic woman."

"Gertrude, I've upset you. I am sorry. It was very silly of me to ever suggest you might leave us. I've had a shock. Oh, dear! I must think what to do. It would be better if no one else were told about this."

"It would keep the crowds from tramping through my kitchen."

"Well, and there's that, too, yes, it would be an awful bother for you. But I meant the political, the sensitivity of it for the community at large. We wouldn't want Catholics thinking we'd stolen their sacred symbol, if you know what I mean. Gertie, I think you'd better not tell anyone, anyone at all."

"Except that if I'm to go about my normal life, someone else is bound to discover her soon enough. I went down to Waterford for a week, but I couldn't stay there forever. What am I expected to do?"

"Oh, dear! I suppose I really ought to tell Archbishop Weeks about her. I mean, he should hear it from us first."

"Oh, Reverend! If you tell him, the world will know! Couldn't you just wait a bit? I keep hoping she'll go away. If only I could think of a way to make her disappear!" said Gertrude feelingly.

"Yes, if there were a way." He frowned thoughtfully. "Something shocking, offensive, Gertie—"

"I couldn't do that, Reverend! And I'm sure you couldn't! Go in there and say something awful just to make her go away! I couldn't live with myself, Reverend. I couldn't do it."

"No, of course you couldn't, Gertie! What was I thinking of?" the Reverend hastened to chide himself. "My mind isn't working right at all this evening. No, now that I've had time to reflect, I can see it is my duty to tell the archbishop," he said, getting up. "I must tell him straightaway. I may have to bring him here, Gertie. But you don't trouble yourself. The man's as easy as myself. That's lovely tea. Thanks, Gertie. I'll be off."

He hurried away. That was done now. No turning back. The pious masses would be coming. She knew that just as surely as she knew it would be raining again in the morning. Reverend Boxley would tell his wife, and she would tell the rest of Dalkey.

So, before Noleen could hear it from anybody else, Gertrude went around to her. She had to fetch Horace, anyway.

64

$\mathcal{D}$own at Finnegan's they had him converted already, Caroline said. What did they know about it in Ireland? He wouldn't be converted for weeks, months maybe, and then only if the rabbi approved. Just the beginning of an inquiry into a new faith made him as good as gone in the pub. They thought you took one step away from the light and you fell into perdition.

"Why didn't they think that when you left the priesthood?" Caroline wanted to know.

"A spoiled priest is a horse of a different color. He's a man who has shown he fears too close a relationship with God. They think the Jews were guilty of ignoring God, before they turned around and killed Him."

"Dennis, you are going out of your way to lose that Chair, aren't you?"

There was a brass placard on the wall outside the front garden at 35

Brighton Road which read, "Dr. Gebortsglück." There was no mention of Rabbi Quinn, but he said everyone who needed him knew where he was. His wife was the wage earner. She ran her psychiatric practice out of their basement flat and in her spare time taught violin. She was a serene little gray-haired woman who wore rimless spectacles and big German sandals with thick socks even in winter. Rabbi Quinn seemed immensely proud of her. She was teaching a lesson when Dennis arrived, some complicated bit of Bach for two violins which she played along with her pupil in a gushing romantic style that the metronomic Kapellmeister to the Duke of Köthen would not have recognized.

"Isn't it beautiful!" Rabbi Quinn kept interjecting into their discussions about the nature of God and man's relation to Him. "It's Leila's music that sustains my faith."

"Mmmmmmmm," Dennis muttered, smiling, although in truth one of the violins was not in tune and he had perfect pitch. The frequency of out-of-tune notes produced by church organs had not been a minor factor in his departure from the priesthood. Yet, curiously enough, he found he did not mind the unplanned dissonances wafting up from the basement of Rabbi Quinn's home. Violins sounded so much more vulnerable than church organs. They had about them an element of the well-meaning, however badly played.

"How do we ever know whether God is pleased with us?" said the rabbi, just as the violin pupil reached an enthusiastic crescendo of wrong notes. "What do we want from Him?"

"Oh, not to die, surely!" said Dennis.

"What about the destruction of evil?"

"Who invented death? And it turns out God is a prude, too. He cuts the life span of the worm each time it ejaculates. He has things to answer for. I find it increasingly difficult to define evil. It is so tied up with everyday living, the ridiculous need for plastic cling film. Sometimes there is a clarity. Hitler. The Famine landlords. But these monsters grew up out of the societies around them. Monsters do. Look at us now. We're all floundering about amid our recycling bins and laughing at Saddam Hussein as a man who doesn't realize his type has come and gone. But it hasn't gone. CNN has revived it. Rabbi Quinn, what is your definition of evil?" Dennis asked.

"Leila says that is my favorite subject," he said. "But before you get me started, what's happening at the university?"

"I am haunted by a feeling of irrelevance," Dennis responded, utterly without reference to the rabbi's question. "I think I have always been, living here in the Republic, the most comfortable part of the Republic, writing things that in no way endanger me or my family."

He had not yet told Rabbi Quinn about the threatening letters. In any case, they were the products of a lunatic mind. They did not connect him with history.

"Talk about irrelevant. How do you think I felt, growing up here as a Jew? My family didn't even suffer in the Holocaust. I still feel guilty about that," said the rabbi.

"You weren't even born," said Dennis, "and I was a child."

"It doesn't matter. I still should have been there, suffering with the others. My parents should have been there."

"My dear fellow, then you never should have been born."

"The idea is my soul would have forgone the privilege of life in order to suffer with the others."

"Sort of an extinction before the fact of living, you mean," Dennis said, munching on one of Dr. Gebortsglück's otherworldly cookies.

"Precisely. Instead, I am born here in Ireland with the name Quinn and taught to imagine my people escaping through the desert. It is a little hard to conjure up a desert in this cold wet sponge of a climate."

"Yes," said Dennis with deep feeling. "I had difficulty understanding why hell was supposed to be such a bad place when I was a small boy, since the seat by the fire in our house was the seat of high privilege."

He was staying too long again. He would have to ring Caroline and tell her to go ahead and feed the children without him. He knew he was waiting for Dr. Gebortsglück to come upstairs and join them, though, and precisely at six she came.

"How are you two wise men getting on?" she asked. "Have you solved all the great mysteries? Why does water have to curl when it goes down the drain?"

"Leila, your five o'clock lesson is improving," said Rabbi Quinn.

"He didn't come," she said. "That was me playing along with Isaac Stern. Tonight I do not cook after sundown," she said, "but for you,

Dennis, I will make an exception. Anyway, it's only the microwave and we are not Orthodox. Sour cream and noodles?"

"I should be going. I must call Caroline."

"Go ahead. Use the phone," she said.

"It has to do with gravity, Leila, *mein Schatz*, and the rotation of the earth," said Rabbi Quinn. "In the Southern Hemisphere, water curls the other way."

"I know the rational explanation, Malachai. But I mean, where did this symmetry come from?" she said. "Any news about your university seat?" she asked Dennis, who had not made a move toward the phone. "What's happening?"

"I have already asked him this, Leila," said her husband.

"And?"

"He doesn't say."

"Maybe he doesn't know."

"I don't think I want the seat," said Dennis. "Anyway, I'm out of the running."

"You don't want it? Why not? You are such a great scholar."

"I have already abased myself too much to get the job," said Dennis. "I have—held back important information from my column to please Bishop Meany."

"So? Who is this Bishop Meany?"

"They say he runs the Church in Ireland, Leila," said Rabbi Bloom. "Although I did not see him there at the airport to greet the Vice President. Meany is meant to be the Nuncio's right-hand man."

"What important information did you hold back?" she asked Dennis. "Can you tell us?"

"Well, you would have surmised it, anyway. This Virgin figure that has been appearing around Dublin is an obvious fake. It's a projection of a Fra Angelico painting. I told Bishop Meany I was writing this, and he was able to bring pressure to have my column killed."

"So? This is not your fault."

"I should never have told him. And I did not fight to save the column. I might well have saved it."

"I think it would be a wonderful thing to have a Jewish professor of Irish literature at CUD," said the tiny woman.

[253]

"Even if he has sold his integrity to get the job?" Dennis asked.

"People are entitled to their beliefs," said Dr. Gebortsglück. "The Virgin Mary isn't hurting anyone. Maybe a few hustlers are making money off her, and quite a few young girls who should be coming to see me are worrying about the impure thoughts they think this perfect woman never had. But mostly the Virgin is their symbol of a mother who forgives them everything. Is that so bad?"

"But a sham—"

"It's not a sham if you believe in it. You know, you intellectuals are so arrogant. You think you did the world a favor with the Enlightenment. Look what followed: two of the bloodiest centuries on earth."

"Leila!" said the rabbi.

"This man loves his metaphysical vacuum so much we found him half dead from alcoholic poisoning," she said.

"Leila!"

"You want my opinion? I think he should shut up about the Virgin, take the job, and feel guilty. Then he'll be happy."

65

He was very late getting home and had forgotten to phone. Caroline said he had never done this to her in all their years of marriage, and she flicked off the TV with hurt, left-alone wife's fingers and went up to bed by herself, leaving him to walk the dog, Cordelia, so named because she was very difficult to love. Cordelia was in a wild mood. She yanked him all over the place and wrapped the leash around his legs five times before he even reached Gertrude Crookshanks's house. Then the dog plunged headlong into a crowd of people that seemed to have materialized out of nowhere, and Dennis asked himself in a panic whether the Dalkey Festival was on and might he have forgotten it was summer? Cordelia yanked him back onto the footpath, and he heard a woman saying, "Don't be talking to me about Christmas! I haven't bought a thing!" and he knew it was December. Why was the crowd here, then? He saw two Guards trying to hold people back to keep the footpath clear. Then he saw a man parading up and down with an open valise displaying lighted candles despite the rain. Good God, the Virgin must have come to Dalkey! And if he was not mistaken, she was inside Gertrude Crookshanks's house. The woman must be mortified.

Cordelia dragged him through the crowd and around the corner onto Nerano Road. Someone had parked an old bicycle in the narrow alleyway. Presumably one of the pilgrims. Cordelia gave it a sniff. No one in Dalkey would be so rash as to leave a thing like that out in the open, ready for thieves. Dennis nearly turned around to warn the people standing outside Gertrude's house. But he might be warning the wrong ones. Anyway, it was a beat-up old serviceable bike that looked like someone's delivery vehicle, with a large tin box over the back fender. The owner must have confidence no thief would ever want it.

The wind was much stronger down by the sea. The rain blew horizontally, chilling his forehead deep into the brain, and even through his double layer of protective clothing, his body felt cold. It was absolutely imperative that he down a hot whiskey before the return trip. He stepped into the bar at the Dalkey Island Hotel, mercifully so crowded that no one saw the dog. He left after two whiskies, ever so much more ready to face the wind again.

He had initially thought of doing the long circuit past Loreto Abbey because Cordelia needed it, and Caroline might soften, seeing his wet head. But it was just too cold. He walked swiftly back up Nerano Road, puffing at the steep climb while congratulating himself that such exertions no longer stirred the cigarette cough.

He saw the bicycle again. Wait a minute. The memories jarred loose in the brain by whiskey. Hadn't he seen that bicycle near Donal McGaffney's house when the Virgin was in his barn?

He went over to it and took hold of the handlebars. He backed it out of the little narrow alleyway. No, this couldn't be the device. There was nothing remotely telegenic about it. He tried to open the lid of the old tin box, but it was closed fast.

"Oh, well," he said aloud.

Cordelia took this as a command to go duck hunting. She went lunging down the hill in a killer dive, but the leash was wound around Dennis's legs, so she was yanked up into the air and nearly beheaded by the jerk of her collar. Dennis at the same time was yanked forward over the bicycle and into a tumbling heap of spokes, dog's legs, and leash. His ankle hurt. His wrist hurt. Cordelia was gasping for air. They both seemed to be pinned under the bicycle, which felt far heavier on its side than it had upright on its wheels.

Cordelia recovered first. She found her breath and began to bark excitedly in the direction of Mrs. Crookshanks's house.

"I suppose the ducks have changed course on us, have they, Cordelia?" he said to the imbecile dog. She was now pointing in the direction of Mrs. Crookshanks's west wall. Dennis looked over and saw the Virgin glowing there.

With difficulty, he eased himself out from under the bicycle. He untangled Cordelia's leash and stood up. His ankle was sprained. He pulled the bicycle upright. The Virgin slid down Gertrude Crookshanks's wall ten feet and settled at an angle. Cordelia barked even more excitedly at this.

"Your namesake was a quiet person, Cordelia," Dennis said.

He pushed the bicycle forward. The Virgin moved again. He hobbled into the back alley, awkwardly managing bicycle and dog, going in the direction of his home. The Virgin floated slimly along the backs of the houses as he went. Twice, when he passed houses with rear extensions, the Virgin seemed to disappear into them, slithering out again on the next back wall.

At his own house, the kitchen extended back into the garden, and the Virgin seemed to disappear into it when he arrived there. He decided to put the bicycle into the garden shed, tipping it up on its end to beam the Virgin into the ground.

The house was very quiet. The children were still out, as the van was not parked outside. Caroline would have made a point of falling asleep, a sign of very bad humor. He was glad, though, because he wouldn't have wanted her to see what he was doing.

He rang Meany's office with little hope that the bishop would be there. Meany picked it up on the first ring.

He arrived in twenty minutes in a black Daimler, alone.

"Where is it?" he said.

"In my garden shed," said Dennis. "Perhaps I'd better let you fetch it. I've done something to my ankle. It's the bicycle turned up on its end. I'll light your way."

Dennis stood outside the shed, shining a torch for the bishop.

"What is this?" said Meany. "So you're trying to make a fool of me, are you, McDermott? You bring me halfway across Dublin to look at an ancient delivery boy's bicycle? Very funny. You've made your point!"

"No, Bishop, it's the real thing. Come, I'll show you." Dennis limped into the shed. "Now, if you'll help me take it off its end, you'll see."

They lifted it down onto its wheels, upending the family trash in the process. The Virgin slithered up the back wall of Dennis's house.

"Where did you find it?" asked Meany.

"Over there near Nerano Road, in the back alley behind Mrs. Crookshanks's house."

"The Protestant woman?"

"Yes."

"How does it work?" asked Meany. "Is there a switch?"

"All I know is, if you hold it roughly upright, the Virgin appears about sixty to seventy feet away from you. Outside or in, I guess."

"Well, I'll be taking it off your hands now."

"I thought you'd have more use for it," said Dennis.

They loaded it into the boot of the Daimler together. They had to tie down the boot lid because it wouldn't close over that cumbersome tin box. The Virgin was on the ground under a blue Volvo fifty feet away.

"There she is, you see?" said Dennis. Meany followed his finger.

"Oh, yes," he said. "That should be all right, then."

"Yes," said Dennis. "It should."

"You were a good man to call me, Dennis. I wish I could help you with the university."

"I don't know," said Dennis.

"You're not going to write about this, are you?"

"I haven't decided."

"You'd only hurt the people who need her."

"I'd like to know what you find in the box, Bishop," said Dennis. "Good night."

"God bless," said Meany.

66

$\mathcal{P}$oor Gertrude was invaded first by Archbishop Weeks and his entourage and then by seventeen Irish journalists who broadcast the news of the Virgin's reappearance from her house. Archbishop Weeks was asked, naturally, what he thought of the whole affair. He said he wanted to think about it, and he went off into the sitting room and drank some of Aileen's best sherry while he consulted with the Reverend Boxley.

Then came the multitudes of pilgrims and the awful din of cars getting stuck in line on the Sorrento Road. The White House press corps came along, trying to elbow everyone out of the way, and then sirens and police lights and a troop of forty Secret Service agents appeared in the crush of it all. The agents showed everyone their badges and did not say why they were there, but it was not difficult to guess, the way they were scanning the crowd with their eyes and openly flashing their guns. Some of them pushed right on into the house, seized Horace, and locked him in an upstairs bathroom, where he chewed up Gertrude's favorite sponge.

The Church of Ireland archbishop emerged from the sitting room after an hour's deliberation. He said he was ready to answer questions.

"What do you think is the significance of her showing up in a Protestant woman's house?" asked a man from the Belfast *Telegraph*. "Do you think she's trying to tell the two sides to bury their differences?"

"Oh, I wouldn't presume to know her intentions," said the archbishop, looking ponderously grave.

"We waited an hour for that?" an RTE radio reporter complained audibly.

"But it is worrying," Weeks said.

"What do you mean, worrying?" asked another reporter.

"Well, that someone should feel the need to go pushing a Catholic symbol in a Protestant widow's face."

"You think someone's behind this?"

"You call the Virgin a Catholic symbol? Why can't she be a Protestant symbol as well?"

"I don't mean to say that we ourselves in the Church of Ireland do not venerate the Virgin Mary, because we do in our own fashion," said Archbishop Weeks, "but it is a fact that she has been appropriated by the Roman Catholics as a symbol of their Church, rightly or wrongly, and I would hope the Cardinal Archbishop of Armagh would join me in asking the authorities to find the miscreant who is trying to drive this wedge between us here in the Republic where we peacefully coexist—"

The rest of his statement was lost in the hubbub over Houlihan's arrival. She was brought in on a stretcher. The pilgrims courteously made way for her. Rock, who was just inside the front hall by then, signaled to the stretcher-bearers to wait until Archbishop Weeks had finished his press conference. But the reporters had already ended it. The archbishop gave a wan smile and fled out Gertrude's kitchen door. As that door shut and as Houlihan was just entering Gertrude's kitchen, the Virgin Mary shot up over the tea towels and disappeared. Houlihan never saw her.

Gertrude gave the Vice President one of the many hundreds of cups of tea she dispensed that night, and she asked had anyone told her about the little man in Bray who was a genius for backs. Houlihan took down the man's name and said Gertrude's tea was wonderful.

The man from the Belfast *Telegraph* poked his head in the room to ask the Vice President whether she thought the Virgin knew her views on abortion and took off when she heard Houlihan was coming.

"You're a rude man!" said Gertrude. "You get out of my kitchen!"

Honoria Houlihan then invited Gertrude to come visit her in Washington. The forty Secret Service agents packed her off to the hospital again.

Chief Superintendent Bloom lingered to ask Gertrude whether she could think of anyone who might be capable of putting the Virgin in her house as a prank.

"You know, someone's clever son."

"You don't think it was a hoax, Superintendent!" she exclaimed. To have spent nine days with Claire over a fake Virgin was too stupid. Bloom did not press the notion. He thanked her for the fine tea and left.

"I'm so glad it's over!" Gertrude said to Noleen. "God forgive me."

"Well, this house will never be the same," said Noleen. "Let's see if you're on the telly."

She was, of course, and she looked a fright with hair that was ruined by the rain. They made it sound as though the Virgin had only got to her house today. Gertrude prayed that Claire would never find out otherwise.

"Stay here tonight," she pleaded with Noleen.

"As long as you promise not to tell anyone if she comes back again."

"Noleen, it was Reverend Boxley let the cat out of the bag."

In the morning Bishop Meany was on the TV saying the way the Virgin left Gertrude Crookshanks's house was a "clear and unmistakable sign from heaven that Ireland must never abandon the unborn."

"Him and his signs from heaven," muttered Noleen. "There's rumors going around about him now that he's another one dipping into the Church funds."

"Reverend Boxley thought her coming here was a sign I'd gone Catholic."

"What, you? The absolute Prod! Wait till he sees you take Horace's water dish to Buckley's Auctioneers!"

"Noleen!" said Gertrude.

But she walked over to pick it up.

"Why? How much do you think it might fetch?"

"You see?" said Noleen, and they both fell about the place laughing.

67

$\mathcal{W}$hen Angus came to the door, she sensed who he was immediately. He had one of those faces without any smile lines.

"You must be Aileen," he said. "I'm an old friend of Donal's. Angus Keenan."

He held out his hand. She shook it. His palm was moist. She stood at the door, not inviting him in. Then she thought, he'll think something's wrong if I stay here. What if he's got a gun? Don't be daft! It's not you he wants.

"Oh, yes! Come in, Angus. Please come in."

But he stayed on the doorsill.

"I was looking for Donal, actually. They're very close-mouthed about him at the office. What's happened to him, Aileen?"

"He's been under an awful strain with the business," she said. "We thought he needed a rest."

"Is he in hospital?"

"You won't breathe a word, Angus?"

"Of course not, Aileen."

"He's had a nervous breakdown. He's in St. Patrick's."

"I'm sorry!"

"Please don't tell his mother and dad. They said you were up there, Angus. What's he involved in? What's going on?"

"Don't worry yourself about it, Aileen."

"What do you mean, don't worry myself about it? He's my husband, and he's convinced his life is in danger."

"Oh, Aileen!"

"The doctor says this could be a psychotic guilt reaction, but I don't know, Angus. Maybe he did get into something he shouldn't have. What do you think? Do you think he's gone in with the Provos?"

"Have you had any strange phone calls?"

"Well, twice a woman has phoned here asking for him. She won't give her name, and she's not much for the chat. I was after thinking she might be his girlfriend, but now I don't know, Angus. I just don't know. I'm worried sick."

"Have you told the Guards?"

"I don't want to do that. Because, what if he is doing something he shouldn't?"

"You're a loyal wife, Aileen."

"Why wouldn't I be?"

"I'll go see him in hospital."

"You're kind, Angus," she said.

But right away after he left, she drove down to the pub to ring Donal and warn him. He said it would not be difficult for him to convince his doctor that anyone outside his family could trigger his paranoia.

68

That same Saturday morning, Attracta Dorris appeared on RTE's "Irish Letters" to talk about her first three published poems just out in *Oneself* magazine, a heady experience for her which caused her to lose the run of herself such that she let it slip out on the air with all her relatives listening down the country that she had been the first to see the Virgin, situated as she had been then, looking over Rupert's shoulder.

Penrose knew he would have some explaining to do. But he imagined the public would accept the idea of his having wanted to protect Attracta's good name. There was gallantry in the lies he had told. Bishop Meany would see this.

"Rupert, you divil you!" called Samantha, who had been listening to the radio in her kitchen. She came bounding up the stairs. "Now I know I can trust you with my life. Come, do your worst! Clarence is coming home this afternoon."

She put him in such good humor that he began devouring her with kisses. In his exuberance he applied too much suction to a kiss at the base of her neck, and she said, "Ow! Rupert!" but she loved it. She was behaving like Lara van Gufsten when the doorbell rang.

"Ignore that," said Samantha. "They'll come back."

Indeed they did, several times over the next quarter hour. The passionate pair were finding it difficult to concentrate on what they were doing. But finally the ringing ceased, and their happy moans took on a more regular rhythm. She was his Celtic queen and she was approaching the throne—"

"Samantha, darling! Wake u-up! Samantha! You've got visitors!" called a voice horribly familiar.

"Oh, my God, it's Clarence. Oh, my God, Rupert!"

"Clarence!" he called downstairs. "Is that you, old man?" He flung on his dressing gown and walked out on the landing.

"I was having a bit of a lie-in. Had such a late night last night. I don't know how your wife can keep up the pace she runs."

"Penrose, what's going on here? Your bloody children are downstairs saying they've come to live with you."

"My children? My children aren't anywhere near Dublin. Someone's having you on. Look out they don't come in and steal the silver."

"Penrose, they're the image of you. They've all got those pop eyes. They were waiting out on the doorstep in the snow. Didn't you hear them ringing?"

"H'lo, Dad," said Michael, his eldest, stepping into the front hall.

"Michael! What a lovely surprise!" said Penrose. "Did the others come with you? All of them?"

"Yes, Dad. Mom wrote you we were coming. Didn't you get the letter?"

"The letter!" said Penrose, looking a little sickly.

"Penrose, dear boy, you're not expecting them to *live* here? With *us*?"

"We'll get that sorted out in a minute. Just tell them I'll be right down."

"All right," said Clarence, squinting as though it was all too much for his eyes to take in. He disappeared into the rear sitting room, where he had apparently settled the children.

"Now's your chance, Samantha! Run for it," said Rupert.

"Can't we just—oh, Rupert, I nearly—"

"Samantha, seconds count in situations like this."

"What are your children doing here, Rupert?"

"We'll sort that out later. Now go!"

"But he knows I wasn't in the bathroom. He went in there. I heard him."

"Go into the bathroom now and turn on the shower, for God's sake. Get going!"

She ran downstairs to the second floor stark naked just as Rupert's daughter Moya was coming up to use the loo. In a flash Samantha darted into the broom closet. If the child had seen her, she didn't let on.

Miraculously, Clarence suspected nothing amiss when he found her showering.

"Darling," he said. "I hate to tell you this, but your protégé's just had his family move in with him."

"What? You mean Rupert?" she said, drying herself behind the shower curtain.

"Yes. All seven children. Rather a mean thing for their mother to do just before Christmas, in my opinion. We can't keep them here, of course."

"I don't see why not. We've the house in London. Why don't we spend Christmas in London."

"Well, I thought you wanted to be here—for Rupert's sake. Samantha! Look at your neck! That's a bit much. Did he give that to you?"

She looked in the glass.

"I suppose he did," she said. "He had a drop too many last night at the Opera Society, and he made a great lunge for me in the car. Forgot himself, silly man. You don't mind, do you?"

"He's hardly a sex object, I should think. But he oughtn't to go bruising you like that. You want to absent yourself from here over Christmas, is that it?"

"Yes. It's the only thing to do with those children here. Of course, we can't let them settle in. We're not a home for traveling people. He'll have to find accommodation. Someone is bound to rent to him. But till after the holidays we'll let them stay."

"Why did I come back from London, then?"

"To see your darling wife, of course!" said Samantha, rubbing up against him in her towel.

"Darling, they're all downstairs!" he said, but he embraced her.

"They can wait," she said.

"Samantha, darling, you are shameless," said her husband, removing her towel.

•　•　•

In his room, Penrose had searched every pocket twice over. He then upended the wastepaper basket and found his wife's letter, still sealed. He ripped it open. It was postmarked last Tuesday.

"Dear Rupert," it said,

Your friend Sophie Bukowski tells me you find Christmas very lonely. I have always thought it served you right. But I am going to send the children to you this year. I need a rest. You're to keep them with you for the time being. They are all healthy and well able for the world. Cliona and Moya are allergic to spirit gum and washing-up liquid. Please do not ask them to do the dishes. Padraic needs his teeth straightened. Michael is quite a good rock musician.

[265]

You will probably want to buy earplugs. The children all have them. Rosemary hates you, but she will get over that. Her sister Eithne hates all men, which I think is the more mature response. I have encouraged her. And not forgetting Thomas, the baby you never wanted to see. He is very sensitive and kindhearted. Do not force him to eat any animal flesh. I will be in touch, but I'm afraid I can't yet supply an address, as I'll be traveling. You needn't send money until you hear from me. I have saved a tidy sum, and the children will be wanting all you can give them, now they are on the threshold of adulthood. They know where to find you. They arrive at noon Saturday. Until further notice, I'm off to follow my bliss.

Merry Christmas,
Bernadette

69

Thursday morning, Christmas Eve, was a golden, balmy day such as could suddenly come upon them in an Irish winter. The sun shone, a warm west wind blew fresh Gulf Stream air from the tip of Dingle Peninsula to the wildest end of Lough Foyle.

Aileen and her daughters were in a state of frantic preparation. They were going to hold the Christmas Eve drinks party after all. The McGaffneys had decided it would be safe enough for Donal to come home in the middle of it. The house would be surrounded by Guards and Secret Servicemen. Vice President Houlihan was coming.

The Irish Department of Foreign Affairs had asked Aileen please to invite her. Somehow the department had learned two former Taoiseachs would be there and the determination had been made that the party would be large enough to swallow up any awkwardnesses over differences of opinion. The Vice President's back had been fixed by a little man from Bray, who walked up and down on it twice and charged twenty pounds. Mobile again, Houlihan had decided to stay on a few days longer to see a bit of Ireland.

Once people heard that she would be coming to Aileen's party, they all began looking for invitations themselves. If the social flow was going with her, who were they to stay away? Aileen had had to issue one hundred extra invitations.

Then this morning the flowers hadn't arrived. The Secret Service had decided to install bulletproof glass on all the windows. There suddenly weren't half enough paper napkins. And Donal's doctor was expressing very mixed feelings about letting him come to his own party.

But these were minor worries after Aileen got the phone call from the man with the gravelly voice, who croaked: "Where's your husband, Mrs. McGaffney?"

"He's in hospital. Who are you?"

"I'm the one with his lorry. I don't want it. You can have it back."

"You're joking."

"Someone'll snitch to the Provos. You can have it back."

"Bring it back, then," she heard herself saying.

"You think I'm fookin' crazy? I wouldn't go fookin' near your house right now. The place is probably crawling with fookin' Provos."

"There's no one here but ourselves."

"Listen, missus, because I'm only goin' to say this once. Your lorry is parked in Blackrock in back of Roches Stores. I'm leavin' the keys under the floor mat. Tell yer husband he better hurry up before someone else cops it."

Click. He was gone.

Aileen sped down to the pub to call Donal.

"Call Angus," he said. "He can pick it up."

Angus's wife answered. Angus wasn't home. Aileen pretended to be wanting to invite them to the party.

She rang Donal back.

"Remember to turn very wide, Aileen, and don't rush yourself. You've all the time in the world. If you swing wide enough around

LaRouge Crescent you can get her into the garage on the first go. Whatever you do, don't hit anything! If you hit that stuff, you're finished."

"What stuff? Donal, can't you come out early?" she pleaded.

"And take one of the girls with you, of course."

"Not them!"

"You need one of them to drive the car home, stupid!"

She told the girls a lie about how Roches Stores were the only ones that sold their particular paper napkins. The lorry was there, all right. It was twice as big as she remembered. Eighteen wheels.

"Isn't that one of our lorries, Mother?" Fiona asked. "What's one of Dad's lorries doing here?"

"I have to drive it home, Fiona. You can drive the car."

"Mother, you don't! What if the Wainwrights see you? They'll just know Dad's in St. Patrick's. I know they will."

Aileen hauled herself up into the cab. Her feet barely touched the pedals.

"Don't do it, Mummy! You'll be killed!" Roisin shouted.

"You girls drive home this instant!" she yelled back. "I don't want you anywhere near this lorry. Do you understand?"

"Why, Mum? What's in it? Oh, no! Oh, Mum! This is what put Dad in St. Patrick's, isn't it! Oh, Mummy, what's in there?! You can't drive it!" yelled Fiona so that the whole of Blackrock could hear.

"Go home this instant, before you're both blown to smithereens!" Aileen yelled back.

At least the girls drove off then.

Aileen said a hundred Hail Marys and then another hundred. She promised the Virgin she would lose another two stone. She put her foot on the gas pedal. Nothing happened. It revved, but nothing happened. Oh, holy Christ, it was the gears. She hadn't driven a car with a gearshift in probably fifteen years.

But won't I lose weight doing this? she suddenly thought, and she giggled and put the monstrous thing into first. Slowly she let out the clutch and the huge lorry moved forward at about .005 mile per hour.

It took her forty minutes to get back to Foxrock. As she inched up into LaRouge Crescent, she thought, dear God, how could I ever have considered bringing this here? Those Secret Servicemen have bomb-smelling dogs! They can smell Semtex a mile away, I feel sure. And there, as if set upon her by the Lord, appeared two agents in front of her, blocking her way.

"What do we have here, Mrs. McGaffney?" One of them approached her window. "Party supplies?"

"I wish!" she said plaintively. "You'll never believe this, but one of Donal's drivers got drunk this afternoon and left this thing parked in the back of Roches Stores. He called me to tell me. It only happens when you're giving a party!"

"You should have let us know. We'd have had somebody drive that baby home for you."

"You know, I should have," she said. "How would you like to put it in the garage for me?"

"No problem," said the agent.

Her legs shook as she stepped down from the cab. He did not seem to notice. What was with these people? They never batted an eyelash when she explained about her husband going crazy with worry from the business and pulling out all the phones in the house. They just nodded sympathetically and said, "No problem. We'll put in new phones."

She went on into the house to find Fiona arguing with the man from Foreign Affairs.

"There are going to be at least forty American reporters here," he was saying. "The Tourist Board says that if even just *one* of them mentions the posters, it'll be worth thousands in free advertising."

"Mummy, this man wants to put tourist posters up in our windows!" Fiona whined. "Please, Mummy, tell him he can't do it!"

"Which posters?" asked Aileen.

He held one open for her. It showed the usual beautiful green fields around a shimmering Connemara lake with sunbeams peeking out of clouds above. Juxtaposed onto this scene at a point halfway up the sky was the figure of the Virgin as she had appeared in her recent visitations.

IRELAND'S THE ANSWER was printed in huge letters at the top.

"What's the question?" said Aileen.

"Well, whether we might put these up in the windows. The Tourist Board says the Virgin is bringing in record numbers."

"I didn't mean—the Virgin's gone," said Aileen.

"For the moment," said Dermot. "Look, I think it's a load of rubbish, but you'd make my life so much easier if you'd let me put up one or two."

"Well, for God's sake, don't put them in my front windows. Ireland's the answer to nothin'. It just is."

70

"We'll only go for a look-in, children," Dennis and Caroline told their brood, who had complained about being left home without the car on Christmas Eve. The esteemed author's ankle was still sore, and he was in a low mood, but Caroline was feeling celebratory. They had just learned that Dennis was the man selected to fill the Kerrygold Chair of Irish Literature. The Dublin *Sentinel* called him, saying they had a tip, and was it also true he would be converting to Judaism?

"What is truth?" Dennis said to the poor reporter.

He quickly rang up his friend Figgs.

"You're not meant to know until tomorrow," he said. "You won hands down. Well, seven to five, your favor. The swing votes were my own and Corriskey's. He said your grandmothers were both born in the village of Street in County Westmeath, aided by the same midwife, in case you think you impressed him. No one mentioned your religious conversion, by the way. That doesn't mean they weren't thinking about it. They voted for you in spite of it, Dennis. Luckily, no one on the board has submitted a manuscript to you lately."

"I will refrain from saying I told you so," said Caroline.

"What? You told me Corriskey's grandmother was born in Street?"

"Oh, Dennis! You are so awful!"

"Must we go to this party?"

"I shall go whether you like it or not," said Caroline, an inauspicious way to begin an outing together.

They were made to park miles away down the road, and Dennis limped all the way up it.

"Posters in the windows, no less," said Dennis. "Someone has taste."

"Shut up, Dennis!" Caroline whispered fiercely.

"Oh, it's Dennis McDermott, the famous writer!" Donal McGaffney greeted them loudly at the door. "And this must be your beautiful English wife! Come in, come in. Happy Christmas! Find yourselves a drink if you can squeeze over there to the drinks table. Or ask one of the girls to get you one. So glad you could come, Dennis. And congratulations on your appointment!"

"How did you know about it?" Dennis asked.

But Donal's attention was diverted, and Caroline hauled Dennis away.

"You didn't even thank him! What's the matter with you, Dennis? You're acting very badly. You know, it's almost as though you don't want to be happy," Caroline told him. And she turned and walked off to find a friend.

Dennis headed straight for the drinks table.

•   •   •

Rock was standing with his back to the wall, scanning the room for assassins, which he knew was a pointless exercise in a situation like this. Even the Special Branch didn't know who was who down to the last person in the room. If it was going to happen, it was going to happen. But the job called for looking as though he never thought that way. He was meant to look like a statue with a trigger-finger set to the speed of light. He had never fired his gun on duty.

Moira was meant to be coming to this thing. He searched the crowd for her and counted the smokers. Twenty-eight out of two hundred. More lighting up by the minute. They didn't like him to talk to people.

It was too distracting. He did silent sociological surveys. How many alcoholics in the room? He could see three with the telltale skin tone. How many priests? Three, no, five. How many happy marriages? Couldn't tell here. The host and hostess, maybe. Not the beautiful English-looking blonde with the white-haired one in the running shoes. Looked like she wanted to dump him as soon as they walked in. And he made a beeline for the drinks.

Nothing was going to happen. It wasn't statistically possible.

Rock had been reading an old copy of *Newsweek* he found lying around the embassy. It had this piece about actuarial tables, how they showed there was little variation in longevity whether you lived healthily or not. Someone had done a study of people with healthy eating habits which showed they weren't living longer than people in the control group, but they weren't dying of heart attacks anymore. They were dying of other causes—car crashes, cancer, electric shock, bee sting, earthquake. It might be possible, therefore, that dieting made people accident-prone. But there was a suggestion also of a larger plan here. If a man tried to live longer than he was meant to, freakish forces intervened to kill him on schedule. If too many men tried to live longer than they were meant to, larger catastrophes were called for. By this reasoning, widespread dieting caused large freak accidents and earthquakes and also maybe race riots, while massive cigarette quitting caused floods and cyclones, and when enough people abstained from alcoholic beverages and caffeine in a given region, they could put the whole place at risk from annihilation by hurricane.

Actuarial tables proved there was order in the universe, and if you tried to mess with it, tried to go from, say, the lung-cancer category to the peaceful two-hundred-year-old yogurt-eating Caucasian category, you would definitely die in a plane crash.

All those people drinking and smoking in Donal McGaffney's living room formed a protective shield against the fates.

He spotted Moira at Deirdre Fanning's elbow. She was wearing the corduroy dress that covered so much of her. She was smoking one of her Marlboros. He left his post to be near her.

"Come away with me," he whispered to her. "You won't be missed for a few minutes."

She demurred, but soon she was following him down the hall to the master bedroom.

"What if something happens to the Vice President?" she asked.

"Nothing will," he said. "We're in the safest place on earth. You see, it's got the highest per capita incidence of individual self-destruction."

• • •

Dennis had one quick whiskey and felt drunk. He downed a second one and felt fine. He took a third one with him and went off in search of Caroline. She was standing beside the American Vice President. Someone had given her a glass of white wine.

"What do you do?" he heard Houlihan ask his wife.

"I type his manuscripts, raise his children, and guard his genius," she answered prettily.

"Wow!" said Houlihan. "He's a lucky man. What's in it for you?" Caroline looked dumbfounded.

"Caroline," said Dennis, nudging her with his elbow.

"I, I guess I really don't know," she said. "I mean, it's not easy to explain."

"Caroline!" said Dennis sharply. "She's going to university in the fall," he told the Vice President.

"I am?" said Caroline. "Oh, yes! That's right, I am!" she said to Houlihan. "I'm sorry, this is my husband, the great man himself, Dennis McDermott."

"Nice to meet you," said Houlihan, offering him her hand. He managed to spill his whiskey reaching forward to clasp it. "I wish I had time to read all your books. I see you're wearing Nikes. I can't wear Nikes. My feet are too square. How many miles do you do?"

"Miles?" said Dennis. "Oh, we use kilometers here now, Mrs. Houlihan. That was quite a shocker you delivered yourself of on the eve of your visit to Ireland, that bit about abortion and the wisdom teeth. Curious juxtaposition of bloody images there."

"Dennis!" said Caroline.

"I'm under strict instructions not to mention that subject while I'm in holy Ireland, Mr. McDermott. I'm going to obey my instructions for once. Good luck with your jogging."

Dermot Muldoon had been whispering in the Vice President's ear. He took her thankfully toward Aloysius Kavanagh, who had been looking about him in a neglected sort of a way.

"Dennis, you can be so bloody patronizing!" said Caroline. "I think we should go home."

"Look, there's your friend Deirdre Fanning. Why don't you go tell her she can count on our support."

He wanted to distract her so she wouldn't see him getting another drink, and he could tell she knew this. But she obliged him. On his way to the drinks table, he cadged a cigarette from Dermot Muldoon.

"What's this? Smoking again?" Leila Gebortsglück suddenly popped up in front of him.

"Hello, Leila!" he said heartily. "Just the woman I wanted to see! Congratulate me. I've won the Chair."

"Oh, Dennis! But this is great news! Come, let us tell Malachai."

She took him by the hand. He teetered.

"Dennis, you are drunk. Why is that? You are not feeling guilty enough?"

"I'm on top of the world, Leila!" he said. He took a great drag on the cigarette.

Out of the corner of his eye he saw Rupert Penrose, but why shouldn't the man be here?

"Did you know I got a letter saying, 'You must die!' yesterday?" he said to her. "That's all it said."

"It was intended for someone else, no doubt," she said. "We must find Malachai before you get too drunk."

They found him standing with Father Liam O'Mahoney and the thin, melancholy-faced Papal Nuncio Paolo Destino, who was soon introduced to Dennis and Leila. She told them all Dennis's good news.

"I, too, have good news," said Father Liam. "I am to be the Nuncio's new assistant. And he allows me to continue my teaching. I'm to become a monsignor."

"You won't know yourself for your great importance, Liam. Congratulations!" said Dennis. "Jesus, aren't we wonderful! I don't know if I can stand it. But wait now, tell me what's happened to Bishop Meany."

"Oh, he's been promoted. He's going to Rome," said Father Liam.

"God bless us all," said Dennis.

"Is it true what they say about you converting?" asked the priest.

"Aye," said Dennis. "I'm studying with the rabbi."

"Are you trying to stick your thumb in the eye of the Pope? Or do you really want it for itself?"

"Who wants to stick his thumb in the eye of the Pope?" asked the Nuncio.

Rupert Penrose was staring at Dennis. That was quite true what he had told Leila about the "You must die!" letter. He was wearing his bulletproof vest. The heat of it seemed to make him feel drunker.

"I am enjoying myself," Dennis said. "The Jews are not afraid of questions. You know, when I studied at Maynooth they were always closing off questions, trying to seal our young minds into tight, neat cells of absolute certitude. With Rabbi Quinn it is the opposite. He is not afraid of doubt."

"Quiet, everyone! Fergal Foyle is going to give us a song!" yelled Donal.

"We all know about doubt," said Father Liam.

Pete Grazos whispered to Donal that someone was backing his truck out of his garage. Was that intended? Donal nodded his head.

Fergal Foyle began to sing "How to Handle a Woman," from *Camelot*.

"The Jewish God loves to see His children using their brains," said Dennis, feeling less than sober. "Our Irish God is afraid to take too much pleasure in His creation.

"I can picture the two of them sitting up in heaven arguing it out, the Almighty Jew bearded and plump with a wise but slightly self-effacing expression and with His whole body held in conciliatory posture as if to say there could be more truths, 'but why should we argue about it? Eternity is too long for grudges.' "

"I like that picture," said the Nuncio. "Now tell us what is your version of the Christian God?"

"*Damn it, McDermott!*" Rupert Penrose yelled out suddenly.

The distraught columnist raised his gun and pointed it at Dennis from across the room. Dennis felt he was watching himself from a distance. The Secret Servicemen threw Houlihan to the ground and flung themselves on top of her. Fergal Foyle was still singing. Many people were still talking, but those near Penrose ducked.

Deirdre Fanning charged straight at the crazed man.

"Rupert Penrose, you put that gun down!" she commanded. "You'll disgrace us all! What are you thinking of? You'll make us look like the Yugoslavs!"

Penrose fired at Dennis, hitting his bulletproof vest. He fired a second shot, hitting Deirdre in the arm. She tackled him, and his third shot went out the open front door.

They all felt the next shock before they heard the sound. Down the hall, Rock and Moira felt the earth move. The entire house seemed to heave up over a swell and come down again like a boat. Everyone agreed later it was a miracle no one was killed. It was something to do with the air currents and the bulletproof glass.

Being shot at and nearly bombed to death did wonders for Dennis's mood. It was as though someone had flicked a switch inside him. He brought Caroline over to meet the Papal Nuncio. Everybody else stayed on and got drunker than ever. They had to drink by candlelight because the electrical connections had been broken. People said this made it more Christmasy. Chief Superintendent Bloom had to work all night searching the area for evidence with his men, of course. Rupert Penrose was taken away under arrest.

"You never told us what is your idea of the Christian God," the Nuncio reminded Dennis just as they were getting ready to say their goodbyes.

"I was hoping you would ask for that again," said Dennis. "He is such a familiar figure. He is a blue-eyed, close-shaven man wearing Jesuitical spectacles and a crown of thorns which He seems not to feel, despite having to wipe away the occasional drop of blood with a small linen handkerchief kept in the pocket of His white gown. He listens politely to the God of the Jews but keeps a tight hold of His facial expression, which is one of uncompromisingly cheerful, brisk holiness. Nothing gets through to Him that should not."

"And does He answer the Jew?" asked Destino. "What does He say?"

"Well, of course He cites scholarly authority," said Dennis. "He tells the Jew: 'If I may quote Father St. John Kelly, S.J., a professor at Maynooth, who puts it so much better than I: "Eternity is too long a time to be wrong." ' "

The last guests left at 2:15. Donal danced Aileen back from the front door and they tumbled onto the couch. He kissed her tenderly and said: "Sure wasn't that a great party!"

EPILOGUE

$\mathcal{R}$upert Penrose was ruled unfit to stand trial on the grounds of diminished responsibility. He spent six months in the depressives ward of St. Patrick's Hospital under the care of Dr. Roscoe Nixon and then quietly resumed his old life, finding accommodation in a neat little flat near Belgrave Square. The Dublin *Sentinel* welcomed him back, as did the Toyota Night School. His children located their mother in a Jacuzzi near the Brompton Road in London, and they returned with her to Mullingar.

The authorities could not find a trace of the truck driver. Neither could they pin anything on Donal McGaffney. They were not able to prove the Semtex had been in the truck before it was stolen out from under the noses of the Dun Laoghaire Guards. Nor were they eager to have the world know about this regrettable slipup. In any case, the amount of Semtex involved in the explosion was estimated to have been about half a pound. Whether there had ever been any more or what might have happened to it could not be determined.

The IRA could not blame Donal for what happened, either. Rupert Penrose was a deranged person acting alone. That he had been able to slip the gun past the agents at the door was a fact which intrigued the Provos, and Angus would from time to time ask Donal how this had been accomplished. But Donal had not the remotest idea. He had never noticed Penrose arriving at his party.

The Croi na hEireann Party won the largest plurality in the election. It formed a coalition with the Greens on condition that Deirdre Fanning be made Taoiseach. Kavanagh gracefully conceded to her, calling her a "great Irish heroine." She hired Moira to be her publicist but changed her mind when she learned Moira was pregnant. Moira flew to Washington for a long weekend and married Rock O'Leary. Brenda, Rock's ex-wife, gave them a little reception. It was all very confusing. Deirdre Fanning rehired Moira upon her return, and Rock began flying over once a month to attend birth classes. He insisted the explosion had proved out his theory about Ireland being the safest place on earth.

Dennis McDermott bought the house on the hill in Tuscany and went on studying with the rabbi. He continued to wear his bulletproof vest, although he received no more threatening letters. He said it made him feel relevant.

Bishop Meany was appointed archivist to the Vatican committee on canonization, a quite stress-free position. He was packing for his departure when the Virgin Mary went skittering along the wall of Christabelle's nursery and then abruptly came to rest in the Nuncio's bathroom. Patrick, the chauffeur, discovered she was connected somehow to the old bicycle which Bishop Meany had been attempting to crate up in the basement. Patrick informed Archbishop Destino.

The Nuncio's former assistant, still smarting from the business with the funds transfers, willingly yielded up the contraption. He said a friend had found it abandoned in Dalkey but that the man calling himself Redmond Dunne Danforth had told him he originally discovered it in the late Flann O'Brien's back garden on Avoca Terrace in Blackrock, which was two doors down from Danforth's mother's house. Danforth said he had learned its capabilities by accident when he dropped the bicycle down the front steps of his house. He had subsequently become quite adept at aiming the bicycle where he wanted the Virgin to appear. Her first three visitations had been calculated to disturb the lives of individuals who had each declined to hire Mr. Danforth when he sought gainful employment. But Mr. Danforth was playing a prank on a friend when he put her on the bonnet of the Mercedes, and then a thief stole the bicycle and Mr. Danforth never saw it again but of course heard about its having surfaced in Dalkey, where he surmised the thief must have taken it. He told Bishop Meany he knew it was wrong to use the Virgin as a tool for revenge, and he was very sorry. He was also sorry to have spent five thousand pounds of Church funds, and he hoped to repay the money someday if ever he could find a job.

To discover Danforth's true identity would be a fairly simple matter. All one needed to do was look up Flann O'Brien's old address and then visit the houses two doors down on either side. But the Nuncio and his new assistant kept putting off the expedition. The two friends could not agree upon the place where the Virgin ought to appear next, thus for the moment they were leaving the bicycle locked up in the basement of the Nuncio's residence.

Attracta Dorris became a first-rate advisor to the lovelorn.

Rupert Penrose saw the Virgin again up a tree in his back garden. He did not rush to tell all Dublin of this miraculous manifestation, but he wrote excitedly to Bishop Meany, who had always been sensitive to the spiritual electricity in Ireland. The bishop responded that he was delighted to hear from his good friend Penrose but was also concerned that he sounded under a strain.

"Sometimes when we have experienced a great disappointment," he wrote, "we can begin to have small wishful delusions. Perhaps you ought to find out whether others can see this Virgin in your garden."

"My dear Bishop," Penrose wrote back.

I am puzzled that you think I cannot grasp reality. I have a very clear understanding of my situation, and it is not so terrible as you seem to think. I am writing my regular column in the *Sentinel*, seeing all my old friends and embracing the new ones who flock to me at the Toyota Night School. I do not wish to tell the rest of the world about the Virgin in my back garden because I have no desire to have my house become a shrine again, thank you very much. You imply that I have imagined her there. You were with me when she first appeared to me in Rathgar. Why should you doubt me now?

As always,
Your faithful servant,
Rupert Penrose